CLEARWATER DAWN

BOOK ONE OF THE EXILE'S BLADE

A NOVEL OF THE ENDLANDS
by
Scott Fitzgerald Gray

Cover, Design, and Typography
by (studio)Effigy

Published by Insane Angel Studios
insaneangel.com

CONTENTS

For Colleen

Braern ar nay min leinn...

One owes respect to the living.

To the dead,
one owes only the truth.

— Voltaire

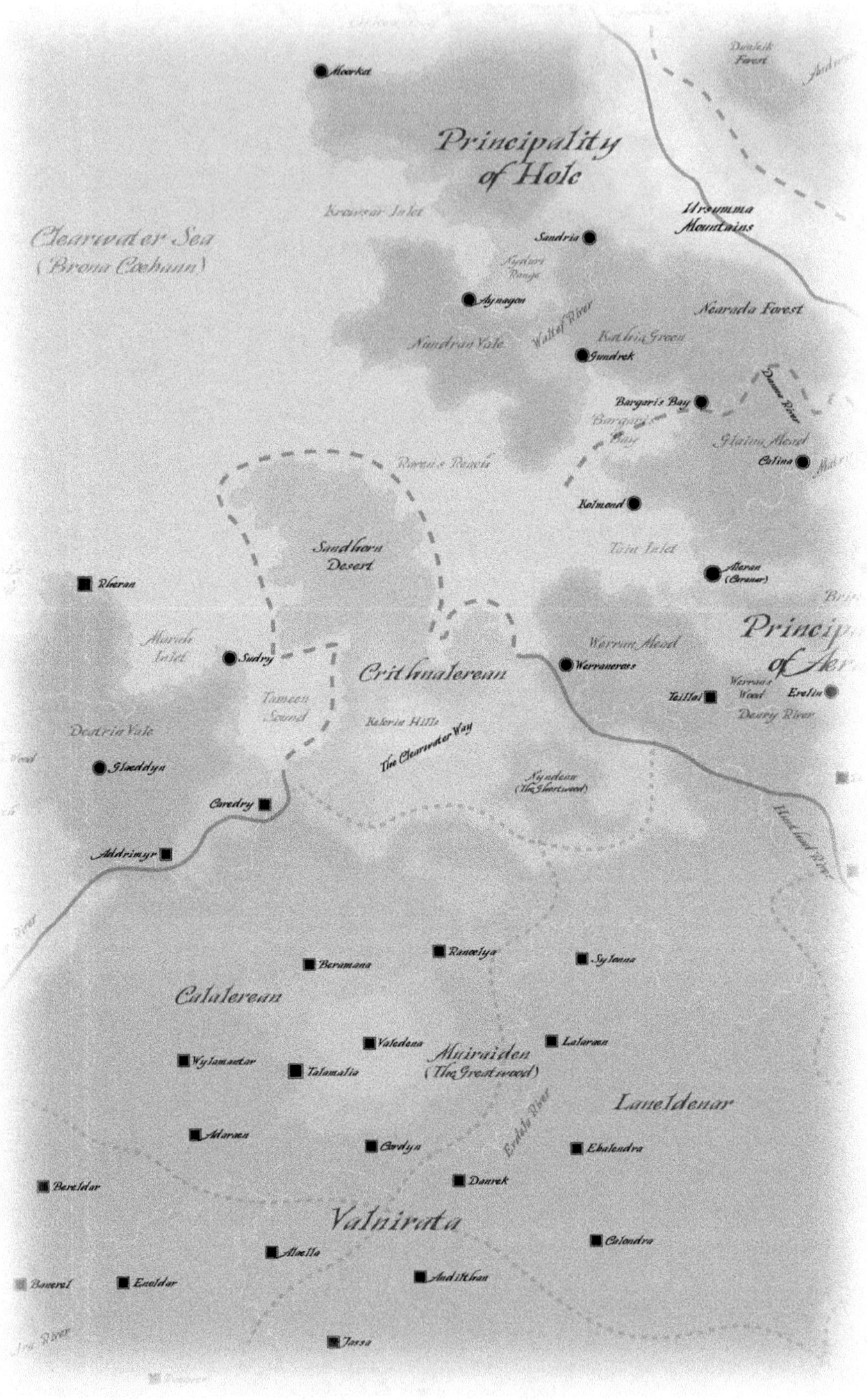

Downloadable color map available free at
http://insaneangel.com/insaneangel/Fiction/Extras.html

— CHAPTER 1 —

THE WARDEN'S DOOR

LOOK TO THE PRINCESS…

Even in the half-waking dreams of his own exhaustion, Chriani thought he could hear the command ringing in his head as he lay in his alcove in Barien's chambers. Waiting for the sleep that he knew would come if he could only quiet the ache at his chest and in his gut.

As he shifted on the thin tick, the pallet beneath it barely long enough for him, he felt the chill airflow through the narrow gap that passed for a window in the closest corner of the room. Originally an arrow slit when the Bastion was new-built a hundred generations past, it had been knocked out and roughly widened as the open fields and huts it once overlooked and defended had turned to the alleyways and flagstoned court of the outlying keep long years ago. The wind still blew in from over the southern walls, though, twisting across him now. More than half through the deep winter month of Bera, the Brandishear coast had yet to see snow, but the unseasonable warmth of the past two weeks' sun had disappeared as quickly as the day's light.

As he walked along the walls of the keep not so long before, Chriani had watched the lights of the sentry towers echo the light of the city beyond, threescore thousand strong. Like he always did, he felt the specific stillness that was the keep at night. From the southlands, from the farmsteads that spread and surrounded Aloidien and Quilimma and Cadaurwen and the fertile steppes at the mountain's feet, the trade roads ran nonstop by day with the past season's grain and cheese and salt beef bound for the docks. Destinations east and west, ports in Elalantar and Aerach and Holc. Beyond the walls of the keep that was its heart, Rheran was alive with a light and a noise and a movement that ran all night and only began to fade as the noise and movement of the next day started up all over again.

But where Chriani lay now within the Prince's Bastion, that life had never seemed more distant. As the walls of the keep marked off the heart of the city, the Bastion marked off the heart of the keep, and within that twice-isolated space, the closing of the gates marked off the end of the day with a sense of ritual formality. Whatever business carried on into the night around him now was the quieter commerce of court. Consuls and emissaries would be plying their trade in the apartments of the master-merchants and barristers and petty nobles who had long ago secured the keep's scant supply of apartments. In the prince's tower that rose just above and to the north of Barien's chambers in the garrison wing, a steady stream of servants and pages would even now be making their way along the stairs to the guest chambers where Chanist housed whatever foreign dignitaries the tide or the road had brought in that day.

The Bastion was the place of princes that Chriani had been a part of for ten years now, and it would be a part of him for two weeks more.

Two weeks until it was over, he thought from the space where sleep beckoned. Time enough.

He'd heard the words that day, found himself hoping that it might be for the last time. Ringing out across the courtyard of the keep from the stable gates, the Princess Lauresa had swept in along the city road with a half-dozen riders around her.

"Look to the princess!"

It had been Barien's voice, the deep tone of command ringing out as it always did. To the side and the customary distance behind the Princess Lauresa, Chriani saw the tall warrior rein in, dark cloak and lighter dust swirling around him as a pair of grooms took his horse, then he in turn leaped down to take Lauresa's reins in his own hands.

Chriani had been resting, slouched in the doorway of the outside armories as the twisting breeze of a bright daymark funneled through the main gates, the scent of dust and dung and roasting meat carried in from the market court beyond. The armories and the stables framed the gates like bookends, but where Chriani lingered within the doors, he was hidden by sunlight glaring off the stones of the courtyard track.

Lauresa was in white, as she usually was, draped in a shawl of ilvanweave that the Mearinn of the Tannwood made, the dust of road and trail never clinging to it. Her horse was a white palfrey mare given to her by her father to mark her nineteenth year the autumn just passed. Curls of sunflower yellow twisted as she gently returned Barien's nod of salute, blue eyes catching the light even from where Chriani stared darkly.

He was tired suddenly, watching her. He hadn't slept well the night before. Hadn't slept at all the night before that.

The Princess Lauresa is to marry in Aerach on the High Spring, the sudden proclamation had read a month before, *and all Brandishear will join in tribute for her happiness.*

Barien was warden to the princess and had been since before she was born, they said. Chriani had been at Barien's side since the day he'd been taken into the keep, ten years past now, and had been the warrior's adjutant for eight of those years. Barien had asked him to ride out with the princess's party that morning, hanging back behind the warrior for the day's ride. Chriani had begged off sick, though, just as he'd managed to work his way out of three other invitations to accompany Barien on some outing or another with Lauresa the past month.

Over breakfast in the garrison mess, Barien had appraised him coldly as Chriani did his best to look pale, but the warrior hadn't bothered speaking the disbelief that was obvious in his dark eyes.

"If you can keep from coughing up blood long enough, see what Konaugo's got for you," Barien had said, which sounded simple enough. But meetings with the prince's notorious captain and Chriani had a way of complicating themselves, and so it was that he'd found himself in the armories since just after dawn, a battalion of the prince's rangers returning from a two-month tour of Aloidien province the previous day. A full troop's worth of weapons had been left for inspection and honing, most of their blades so notched that Chriani suspected the southwest townships had been granted a reprieve from the wolves that prowled the foot of the mountains in favor of attack from an army of rocks that the troop had valiantly bashed into submission.

From the stables, the Princess Lauresa in white made her way with two escorts along the steady rise of the courtyard track for the main gates of the Bastion to the south, circling the upthrust stones on which the citadel rose. Chriani thought he saw her glance his way. He backed farther up, slipped easily into deeper shadow. Waited until she'd passed before he moved back to slam the armory doors.

Marriage of convenience, it was said in the city and among the garrison who speculated on the suddenness of the announcement. A marriage of treaty. Politics. Chriani pushed the word and the thoughts from his mind. He was far too tired to think.

It had been three years since the last time the Princess Lauresa had spoken to him. One month since the proclamation, and Barien seeming to take some great interest in having Chriani at his side while he rode out the last days of his obligation as Lauresa's warden. Two weeks more of Chriani finding excuses to keep the distance of the last three years before it was over.

He'd gone back to the stone wheel and the pile of shortspears and blades still there, another lamp lit to vanquish the shadows when he heard the doors open behind him.

"So what was it this time got you on solitary detail?"

Where Chriani looked up, Barien's hulking figure was dark against the light outside. He pulled a waterskin from within his cloak, the dust of the road falling from him as he slapped it away.

"If you've already heard, you likely already know," Chriani said coldly. He arced three spears end-first across the room, watched them slam one by one into their rack without touching the steel to either side.

"I didn't hear it, I smelled it," the wind-tanned warrior said with a grin. "Konaugo burning, all the way from the south city-gate. General insubordination? Specific insubordination?"

"I reportedly called his parentage into question," Chriani said evenly.

Barien laughed. "And how did our fine captain find that out?"

"I may have inadvertently said it to his face."

Barien laughed louder. He helped Chriani finish up, though, both of them working the wheel in silence, and what would have been a grueling day and a night became just a grueling day in the end. The short day's sun had already set as Chriani racked the last sword, bundling up a dozen that he'd spotted too-serious flaws in, readying them for the forges. But as he dumped the damaged blades at the doors, he saw a figure moving at the stable gates across the way, and in his mind, a hundred different impressions shifted and locked into place.

Through the armory, twenty different types of weapons spread across four times that many racks and shelves, but Chriani knew them all. Beneath the shock of black hair that he brushed aside, he had his father's grey eyes that would spot the faintest blemish or deviation in a single blade, or sort and catalog every shadowed rack in the room at once. He had his mother's attention to detail that would take those things in, etch them permanently and effortlessly into memory like it had long ago etched the slender figure across from him.

Where Kathlan stormed out from the stables, Chriani caught a glimpse of dark hair cut ragged above whipcord-tight shoulders. Her sun-dark arms were bare where a too-large tunic was belted with black leather, a silver-edged buckle on it that had been her father's. The trace of a limp was visible as she grabbed the reins of an exhausted horse, and the Elalantar lilt of her deceptively soft voice rang out across the courtyard where she cursed the Aerach courier who had overridden it, trying in vain to make the Bastion before last light.

"Blood, mother, and fucking moonsign!" Kathlan rattled off a subsequent string of epithets that Chriani had only heard half of before, her slight frame making her gift for profanity that much more of a shock to its generally unsuspecting victims. "By your prince's balls if you can sotting find them," she shouted, "you ever bring a horse through my gate in a lather again, you'd better have the fucking whole of the Valnirata riding up your overstuffed ass!"

Chriani watched the courier backpedaling for the courtyard track as if he expected Kathlan's tongue to suddenly lash out across the distance between them. Deep down, Chriani wanted to smile, but he knew that even if he'd searched for it, any mirth in him was long gone.

He drank thirstily from the waterskin Barien tossed, not realizing that he was staring past him until he saw the warrior turn to follow his gaze.

"Second shift at the stables tonight?" Barien said with a broad wink as Kathlan gently led the horse inside. "You'd let me know, I'd have worked faster for you."

"No," Chriani said as he turned away quickly. "I'm for bed." Off Barien's look, he added, "My own bed."

"You telling me the bloom's off that rose already? Night and daylight, boy, I'd have thought you might find someone yet you don't push to want to kill you inside six months."

"You thinking anything would be a great first," Chriani said as he handed the waterskin back. A calculated taunt, intentional. He felt the same numb pain circling in his gut now that he'd felt when Lauresa had ridden in, wanted nothing but for it to go away. Not wanting to hear the words in Barien that would reflect the words unspoken in himself.

"Seems to me the longer that mouth of yours stays open, boy, the less chance of anything worth hearing coming out of it."

"Shut yours then, old man, and show me how it's done."

The backhand blow that Barien threw was fast enough that it would have caught most people, but long experience meant that Chriani knew to watch for it. He twisted back, felt the air behind the warrior's hand as it slammed past. He missed Barien's leg where it twisted between his and dropped him, though. Too busy waiting for the other hand, not watching.

As Barien helped him up, the warrior laughed again.

"You had enough then?" Chriani said as he calmly dusted himself off.

"Yeah, on account of I can't afford to have to carry you in. I'm late for the watch."

He slapped Chriani on the shoulder, tossed him the waterskin again and headed out. But at the doors, he stopped, turned back. Stars in an endless black sky behind him cast their faint light on the weathered stone walls opposite, the gatehouse flags twisting in the chill breeze.

"Konaugo's no friend to anyone I'd want to call that, but he's captain whether you and I like it or not," Barien said. "You want to make rank before you're older than whatever captain takes over for him one day, you stay out of his way."

"I'll wait for you to take over for him."

"You'll be older still."

Chriani finished the waterskin, sprayed the last dregs across his dust-streaked face. He found an inside corner of his tunic slightly less dirty than the rest and wiped his eyes.

"I don't need the advice."

"When you stop telling me you don't need it is when I'll know you don't," Barien said. An evenness in his voice, no sign of the impatience that Chriani had often thought should have been there by now. "I know what you should be, well as you know it. Only one of us gets to decide whether it happens or not, though."

Across at the stables, Kathlan reappeared to hurl the courier's saddle unceremoniously into the frost-streaked dust of the courtyard track. She slammed the doors behind her as she disappeared inside.

"I'll work on it," Chriani said simply. In the doorway, Barien nodded and was gone.

As Chriani doused the lamps and pulled the doors shut, he felt the fatigue suddenly. A dull ache in his gut settled below the deeper pain there, reminding him he hadn't eaten yet that day, but he was too tired suddenly to want to.

The gates of the keep opened northward to the crowded city slopes that dropped to the harbor and the seawall beyond. The Bastion gate looked south, the long twist of the courtyard track sweeping east between its walls and the crowded rise of buildings pushing up against it. Chriani cut west, though, crossing the empty training grounds where the garrison practiced. He pushed himself up the narrow steps that rose along the wall that separated the grounds from the clutter of buildings to the south. Along the inside walls of the keep, the exclusive apartments and offices of the ground-level alley maze were locked up tight, lamps burning in the upper windows. In their secure island at the center of the city, the keep's residents were an elite — gem merchants and goldsmiths, scribes and sages. The offices of the silk guild and of a dozen of Brandishear's largest private trade concerns were here, as were a half-dozen merchants of spellcraft. The branded sorcerers wise enough to set up shop as close to the watchful eye of the prince's court wizards as possible.

At the prince's stables, he thought he might have caught another glimpse of Kathlan at the open window of the loft, but then he was around the Bastion wall that blocked his sight of the opposite yard. As he slipped through eddies of dust and chill wind for the steeply winding lane ahead, he didn't look back.

Tired as he was, Chriani had walked the keep walls until well past the evenmark bells, the starlight stained with red where the Darkmoon rode alone in the east. On one pass hiking above the orchard, he glanced around to make sure he was alone, swinging down easily along the rough ladder that the stones made to pluck three of the prince's last snow oranges for his pockets. From a perch above the courtyard, he let the sweetness of their slow-frozen fruit numb his tongue, watching the guard change on the stepped tiers of the staging ground that opened up before the Bastion gate. He'd expected to see Barien there but didn't, wondered absently if the warrior would be staying on for fourth watch to make up for his arriving late.

Within the sharp lines of stone and steel that rose from the rock, the Bastion's design reflected its martial origins, and the twisting of its high banners in the wind seemed almost defiant sometimes. It had been the original keep when the city was little more than a spread of sod huts around the rocky rise that overlooked the harbor, and as Rheran grew up around it, the stepped walls of the current keep had been built to wrap around the old like a salt-snail's new shell.

The rocky foundations of the bluff had been chopped away to form the near-vertical base of the outwall that ringed the Bastion now, its shattered stone giving rise to the walls of the new keep as the slope within those walls was stepped and leveled. Now, it seemed to Chriani that the place had some sense of how it had been long ago demoted to family life and court. A once-muscled sword arm turned to the lute, he thought.

Long past the point of any living memory, the Bastion had been the house of the Brandishear princes, then had been the regent's palace under the long years of the Lothelecan, the great Empire that existed now as little more than the insignia of the sun that marked the leaguestones of the roads. Then sixty years before, Chanist's grandfather had been steward when the Empire and its fifteen centuries of history had suddenly fractured, and the Bastion had had its prince once again.

It had always seemed odd to Chriani that even as Barien had let him maintain a blissful ignorance of the political structures and subtle power struggles of the present-day Ilmar nations as a youth, the warrior had maintained an almost obsessive interest in beating into him the historical highlights of the Empire that had built that power.

"The Empire's gone, though," Chriani had said, only a year into his service but already grown impatient with the impromptu history lessons with which Barien liked to fill the empty waiting of a watch. "What's the point in studying the road behind when you know you're not turning back?"

"History's use comes in using what was as a gauge for what's to come," Barien had said. "You've got to make the trip the first time to sketch the map. Second trip's easier because of it."

"What was it like?" Chriani had asked. "Living with the Empire?"

Barien laughed. "How old do I look, boy?"

Chriani shrugged. "What was it supposed to be like?"

"Peaceful," Barien had said after a moment's contemplation. "Or so they say."

"There's peace now."

"So they say."

Across from the stables, what had once been ramparts along the northwest tower was the porch of Lauresa's chambers now. A balcony extended out from a set of Ilvani-carved glass doors, Chriani watching light behind white curtains as he paced slowly past. The wind from the harbor to the south was like ice against his grime-streaked skin, but he lingered above the stables for a long while, an unused sentry post there in the shadow of the tall gates. He watched the light of the stars play out across the black expanse of sky above the Clearwater, a ripple of grey below where wind and wave caught their reflection.

As he finally felt the fatigue hit him hard enough that he decided it was safe to head inside, he nodded a salute to the guards with their dogs at the Bastion gate. He watched them check the adjutant's badge beneath the tyro's insignia at his shoulder as he passed in through the arched hall of the central court, daylight bright. Within the Bastion, the fires would burn for warmth, but evenlamps lined all the corridors of the central court and the barracks wing beyond that Chriani slipped through soundlessly. Outside the prince's citadel and the homes of the wealthier lords, the sorcerer's light was rare. Not for its expense, but for the superstitious unease with which most folk regarded it, burning always with a cold white flame that cast ghost-thin shadows.

He heard voices in the dining halls but drifted past them without looking in. As he slipped through the locked door to Barien's quarters, Chriani was surprised to see a lamp burning but the warrior absent. From the set of the oil, he'd been there and gone a while already, but Chriani was too tired to do more than simply note it.

Past the faded green cloth that marked the alcove that was his, he noisily kicked off his boots. His quarters were little more than a narrow gap running two paces deep at the corner of Barien's main chamber, and he'd never been sure whether the space had actually been intended as an antechamber or whether some mason had simply run out of stone as the walls came together.

He was fortunate at least that Barien was as he was, and though Chriani made do with the narrow space for sleeping, the warrior had long since allowed him to claim a healthy part of the chamber beyond it as his own. Chriani had known a number of tyros over the years who'd had to make do with much less.

The difference between Barien and much of the rest of the garrison was sharply marked, Chriani had realized early on. He watched the anger by which too many of the others sought to train the Bastion's tyros and their own adjutants, young apprentices graduating by virtue of a litany of scorn and scars. He'd seen it that very first day, barely a boy when he'd attempted to lift the warrior's purse, no clue as to the significance of the horse-and-axe insignia on the pouch where it hung at his belt. Not smart enough to have noticed the same standard flying from the ramparts of the keep itself, its stone walls rising across the market court behind him.

The initial curiosity in Barien's eyes as he lifted him by one frantically jerking arm was something Chriani had never forgotten.

"To the keep," the warrior had called as he tossed the boy effortlessly to a pair of guards who'd appeared as if from nowhere. But once dragged in through the enormous stone gatehouse and up the courtyard track beneath the watching eyes of what seemed an enormous number of people, Chriani had found himself not clapped in irons as expected. Instead, he'd been deposited in Barien's quarters, the same he staggered through now.

For the better part of that long day, he'd sat alone, paralyzed with fear and the expectation of the beating that was coming. But when the warrior finally appeared, he brought with him not a lash but a quarter-loaf of buttered bread, still warm from the ovens and the first thing Chriani had eaten since he'd walked to the city two days before.

He'd picked up more than enough scars of his own over the years after, but mostly from ignorance or a notorious lack of judgement on his own part. In all the years since Barien had claimed him from the street, though, the warrior had never raised a hand against him in anything but carefully measured warning, or in calculated exercises like the fall he'd taken in the armories.

Barien was cut from different cloth than so many of Chanist's guard. He could handle himself as well as any of them with sword and axe, but Chriani had seen him also hold his own in conversation with any number of lords or diplomats on morality and matters of state. Barien was a warrior, but he could think in a way that most of the warriors around him never bothered to. He knew military strategy and social graces, and he was as good a rider as anyone in the keep and a number of the rangers besides. In the deepest dead of winter, Chriani had heard the warrior pull music from the strings of a bandore that would summon up spring as surely as the scent of a fresh-mown meadow.

Above all else, though, Barien was bodyguard and warden to the Princess Lauresa. Beyond the ten years he'd trained Chriani at his side, beyond the assigned shift as sergeant of the watch, beyond the roles of courtier and rider and warrior that he switched between with no apparent effort, he was warden to the royal heir. Would be for two more weeks.

The Princess Lauresa is to marry in Aerach…

Beyond knowing that it lay beyond the Greatwood and the Valnirata war-clans to the east, Chriani had never bothered looking at a map of Aerach until the day the proclamation was made. A six-day journey by horse, longer by sea where the merchant fleets from Rheran and Sudry were forced to sail up and around the Sandhorn jutting thirty leagues into the blue expanse of the Clearwater.

Most people went by water regardless, though, the shorter overland route along the Clearwater Way cutting through the northern frontier of the Valnirata forests and the whispered threat that rode there. Last part of the old Ilvani empire to fall against the tide of war that the tribal migrations into the Ilmar had made, thirty centuries ago now. The only part of that Ilvani empire to never formally surrender, shut up in the dark heart of the Greatwood now.

As he stripped off his shirt, Chriani caught his reflection in the small steel mirror that hung between pallet and wall, the narrow table beneath it stuffed into the same space. A bone comb and a cracked enamel basin sat there. He dumped the basin's contents to the drain hole near the doorway, refilled it from the skin that hung there and made a mental note to refill that in the morning.

Lauresa would go by water, Chriani knew. *The Mealay,* Prince High Chanist's best ship, would have its decks spread with flowers like it was said they were when the princess high had been brought down from Elalantar for the prince's own wedding.

Splashing his face and his chest, he caught his reflection again, forced himself to look at the bandage covering his shoulder and chest, and all at once the ache of the day's work was eclipsed by a sharper pain. Beneath the white linen, he felt the name he'd scribed there burning next to a mark that only two people in the keep had ever seen.

The Princess Lauresa is to marry in Aerach. He'd been trying to not count the days but had failed.

Barien was bodyguard and warden to the Princess Lauresa, and that very first day, he'd waited until Chriani had eaten his fill, then tossed him a length of silken cord. It was tied with a rider's triple cinch, significantly more intricate than the hitch Chriani had slipped at the warrior's belt.

"Who taught you to work a knot like you did?"

"My ma," Chriani said. He was trying to sound defiant, but the fear in his own voice was all he could hear.

"Untie that one," the warrior had said. Chriani studied the knot only for a moment, worked it for not much longer before tossing the unfurled cord back to Barien. The warrior handed him a rusted padlock then, Chriani pulling a sliver of dark steel from its hiding place in his ruined boot. The pick was one his mother had given him to go with the instincts she'd taught him, the lock opening almost effortlessly to his touch.

"How old are you?" the gruff warrior finally asked.

"Eight full seasons this last summer. When my ma died," Chriani said.

"Father?"

"My grandfa died a month past." Chriani didn't actually answer the question, but Barien didn't seem to notice.

The warrior ordered him to fetch fuel for the brazier, gave him directions to the firepit in the courtyard where the wood cellar stood. Chriani went quickly. By the time he'd returned, staggering under an armload of kindling, the pallet in the alcove had been set up for him.

When he'd heard the wedding proclamation, Chriani had taken that steel sliver from the hidden inside pocket of his sleeve where it always rested now. He'd added another dozen picks alongside it since that first day, shaped and sharpened carefully over the years for a dozen different styles of lock. His mother's was the first he tried, though, always. His mother's pick worn smooth by the movements of his fingers across its once-honed edges. His mother's pick whose point he'd used a month before to punch carbon black into the skin of his chest, carefully scribing the lines of Lauresa's name as blood-marked glyphs along the edge of another mark that his mother had made there long ago. Another part of his life no one would ever see.

As Chriani finished washing, he felt the same anger, the same knot in his stomach that had kept him from sleep for four weeks now. But this night, for some reason, his eyes closed almost as soon as he hit the pallet. He remembered thinking drowsily that he should have turned the lamp down, saved the oil in case Barien was caught up again in some frenzied debate on reciprocal sea cargo taxes on behalf of the prince high in the dining hall. Chriani couldn't make his legs move, though. He made a mental shrug, wrote the oil off on another one of Barien's late nights that he had as little interest in as the warrior seemed to have in discussing it.

He felt the slow stretch of that last space before sleep, as he hadn't felt it in a month now. A frozen moment of time.

Look to the princess. Ringing in his head, he heard the echo of Barien's voice from earlier that day, and from all the long years before.

Two weeks, he told himself as he adjusted the bandage, tight where it wrapped across the knotted muscle of his shoulder and chest.

Time enough for this scar to finally heal.

Look to the princess…

Where it filled his head, the voice was a force that shook Chriani awake like a blow, forcing him bolt upright in the shadows. The lamp across the room was lower but still burning, his vision blurred as he forced his eyes open, staggered to his feet.

Look to the princess... Seek her in her chambers and stay with her... Keep her there...

It was Barien's voice, pounding in his head as if the hulking sergeant had been shouting face to face. In his fatigue, Chriani actually stumbled across the room, half-expecting the warrior to appear crouched behind some cupboard, issuing orders from out of sight.

Summon none else till I get there...

Sorcery, Chriani thought. He wasn't sure how, but he knew that wherever Barien was, however this was happening, the warrior knew that he was listening. He was more awake than he'd ever been before, unseen fingers twisting ice-cold along his spine.

Beneath an edge-cracked flagstone at the foot of Barien's bed, Chriani pulled a brass key wrapped in white linen. Aside from Barien and Chanist himself, Chriani was the only one who knew the key was there, was the only one who knew what door it opened.

Look to the princess...

Though Chriani had no idea where the voice had come from, he obeyed it as he always did. He obeyed it without thinking, Barien the only one besides the prince himself whose orders could do that to him. He fumbled his sword belt from the hook by the door, not stopping to make the moonsign he wanted to make with every pulse of the fear that rose in him.

He made the sign while he ran, though. His fingers touched heart to navel as they scribed the shape of the crescent, paying homage to the power of night and darkness in order to appease it. Chriani pounded into the corridor with his scabbard slapping at his leg in a way that told him he hadn't fastened it correctly, but he didn't slow. He hadn't actually been given the call to arms, knew that he could be sanctioned or worse if the urgency he heard in Barien's voice didn't warrant it, but he trusted that urgency.

He couldn't remember ever seeing the warrior afraid. Couldn't remember ever hearing the unmistakable edge in Barien's voice that he'd heard tonight.

Opposite the long hall of the Bastion armory storerooms, Barien's chambers were about as far as one could get from the heart of the barracks wing and still be in it. At the end of the silent corridor sat a nondescript storeroom, Chriani pushing through it, the light of a shrouded evenlamp bright as day to his eyes.

He locked the door behind him, though. Spent precious moments checking to make sure he was alone before he found the sliver of stone wall that slid back to reveal the keyhole beneath.

For nineteen years now, Barien had been warden to the heir of Brandishear, and proximity to the warden's door was the reason behind the relative isolation of his chambers, far from where the other officers barracked south of the dining halls. Chriani turned hard, bolts thudding faintly back as the wall sunk in and twisted away from him, then he was through, pushing the false front of stone and tile back on its well-oiled track. He heard it click into place, looking like it had never been moved at all.

A wide corridor ran north and west ahead of him, making a sudden transition from the plain stone walls of the garrison quarter to white drapes and wooden paneling. Grey-shrouded evenlamps slumbered at regular intervals into the distance, wide doors of dark wood lining the hall to both sides. No one there, but he knew there shouldn't have been that time of night.

Around the Bastion, the garrison's presence was constant, guards on the gates and walking the edge of the outwall that overlooked the grounds of the keep. The staging ground lay to the east and west, the main gate to the north, the apartments of the inner city all around. The door that only he and Barien used bypassed the great hall and the guards outside the main entrance to the throne room, though. Chriani was running now toward the prince's court — the wide hall that angled its way irregularly around the interior of the prince's quarter.

He was in the connecting hall still called the children's court, though the royal heir he raced for now was hardly a child any more. To left and right, wide doors marked off sewing and art rooms, music rooms and solaria, the chambers of the younger heirs all shut up tight as he slipped through the intersection, the hall splitting off to the north and west.

He went north, footsteps silent on pale grey marble as he heard the nightmark bells echo dimly from the tower above, announcing the slow passage toward morning. The six steady strikes of those bells made him realize there'd been no alarm, but he didn't slow. In emergency, and in the intermittent garrison drills designed to prepare for emergency, the bell rang constantly. Struck three times, then held for an equal length of silence, then struck again.

A hundred paces along the corridor, he slowed before a recessed alcove and a set of white-painted double doors, rose vines and lilac stenciled carefully around its edges. This corner of the Bastion tower marked off the last of four chambers along the corridor, the other three holding the younger heirs.

Phelan and Miani shared the connected rooms he'd just passed — the bright twins, nine years old the previous autumn. There had been celebrations then, but Chriani had been stuck on outpost duty, Barien away while Lauresa spent the High Autumn at her mother's house at Aldac, near Myrwater in the south. Between the twins and Lauresa, the Princess Peran, just turned twelve. Seven years Lauresa's junior and soon to be confirmed as Chanist's heir. Waiting for the Princess Lauresa to take her leave of Brandishear and the title she'd been born with.

To both sides, evenlamps burned. The only sound was Chriani's own breathing, slowing as he did, but against the calm he tried to force himself to feel, a sense of anxiety was quickly rising. The urgency in Barien's voice was still with him, but even in the short run, he was suddenly less sure whether that urgency was truly what he'd heard or simply what he'd felt in the unexplained unfolding of that voice in his head.

Around him, he sensed no sign of trouble. No alarm, no movement in the courtyard to which Chriani peered out through the narrow windows beyond Lauresa's doors. In the air, in the silence of the night around him, he could feel the sense of subdued order that clung to the walls like paint to plaster. A sense of security that Chanist worked hard for, Barien and the others of the garrison hand-picked for detail within the Bastion's walls.

At twenty-five, Chanist had been only seven years older than Chriani was now when he'd been made prince. All the history that Chriani had been forced to learn at Barien's side long ago. Chanist's father had been killed in the disastrous assault at Welbirk, his older brother and sister falling to Ilvani assassins' blades that same day. A coordinated assault by the Valnirata against the crown that would never be forgotten, not least by the younger princeling who should have died at his father's side.

But a shoulder injured in a skirmish across the Locanwater the week before kept Chanist from the saddle that day, saw him on the throne less than two weeks later. It was said that factions within the war-court had favored deposing the new prince even before his coronation, so great was the fear of his young and untested hand failing in the face of the increasingly uncontrollable Ilvani threat.

One year later, Chanist had slain the Valnirata exile-warlord Caradar and pushed his armies back across the Locanwater. He had forged the treaty with the other Ilmar nations that saw the Ilvani sue for peace. Few people had doubted him since.

Look to the princess, the voice had said, and Chriani tried not to think about how much of the fear he felt now might have come just from the thought of that. Having to look at Lauresa one last time.

They were Barien's orders, though. Chriani composed himself. He would check her safe in her quarters, apologize for waking her. He would wait outside for Barien's eventual arrival, or for someone else sent on the warrior's further orders with an explanation of what was going on.

He felt the sword bump his leg again, tried to adjust the belt as he listened carefully, still no sound or movement from either side. The three younger heirs had been away most of the summer, gone north with their mother. Returned just a week ago, they were preparing now to see Lauresa off, though it had already been decided that they wouldn't sail with her for Aerach. None of the family in attendance at the wedding, Barien had said. Political discretion. Lauresa was bound to some duke, marrying down because that was the importance of it all. Peran would probably lay claim to this chamber at the tower corner before Lauresa had even left the harbor, Chriani thought.

"By your leave, princess." He heard the bitter edge in his voice swallowed by the silence, carefully tapping the door with the heel of his hand. He was practically within sight of the throne room, the doors that marked the private entrance hall from the prince high's own quarters standing some thirty strides away down the northern corridor. He waited for what seemed like a long while, called again, knocked a little louder. Still no sound or movement from within.

He could call someone, he thought. It was late and she was sleeping, clearly, and to make enough noise to wake her would be enough to bring every guard within the prince's quarter down on top of him.

Summon none else till I get there.

He felt the shiver thread through him, but it was just an echo this time.

He looked around quickly, from instinct. Made sure he was alone.

As he dropped to his knees, Chriani had the picks between his fingers even before he'd pressed himself to the keyhole, feeling his way across the pins with practiced ease. Chanist's locksmiths were the best in Rheran, but they were too consistent in their construction, and Chriani had long years of practicing on the identical lock at Barien's door that gave him an easy familiarity with this one. He'd opened more than a few of the Bastion's locks in his day, sometimes at Barien's request and sometimes of his own volition, but always with the very certain understanding of what would happen to him if he were ever caught.

He'd never broken into a princess's chamber before, though. He glanced both ways down the corridor again, felt the solid click of the bolt as he twisted and pressed.

He was through the door without a sound, pushing it closed behind him. You had a better chance of being surprised outside than you did being expected inside, his mother had taught him. Figure out what you're doing before you go in if you can. Don't know what you're doing, figure it out as you go.

Inside, a small alcove opened up, Chriani's eyes alive in the faint trace of light through gauze curtains. Evenlamps burned beyond. Listening, no sound. Inside the doorway, a pair of shoes sat, soft blue leather stitched with gold. Nothing else there.

Slowly, he pushed the haze of white linen aside, found himself in a chamber twice the size of Barien's. Larger than the others along the corridor by the look of it, the bulk of the space wrapping around from the alcove, centered on the balcony whose door was directly across from him now. Through that door, light flared in the distant darkness, the steep slope that fell off to the north raising this side of the Bastion well above the walls of the keep and the fires of the distant harbor.

From the sentry post above the stables, he'd watched the princess on that balcony sometimes, standing quietly as she scanned the skies after dark, hidden in shadow from any observation from the keep below. Never suspecting that Chriani's eyes could pick her out in those shadows so that it might as well have been full day. He'd watched her movements behind the curtains, could hear her singing if the wind was right.

In the room, Chriani forced his mind clear.

The princess wasn't there.

Like the Bastion itself, Lauresa's chamber had a kind of conspicuous straightforwardness about it, the same sense of military order here that pervaded the rest of the residence. The princess too like her father, Barien had often noted, though Chriani had never seen her that way. Chanist was earth, he thought. Solid. His oldest child was air, unreadable. Invisible.

Here, two tables of dark wood, one spread with what looked like letters, two she was reading, one partly written to her stepmother, the Princess High Gwannyn. A tall shelf of wrought metal and thin marble sheets held four cases of neatly tied scrolls, a dozen bound books he didn't look closely at. A wardrobe, open. Clothes within, riding boots in buffed calfskin. Past it, three windows were shuttered against the darkness, all bolted tight like the balcony door was bolted as he slipped past.

By that door, a single chair meant that she wouldn't accept visitors here, or at least wouldn't accept visitors she didn't know well enough to sit with them on the bed. There behind white curtains, another alcove, out of sight. Across from it, a hanging filled most of one wall, painted in what he recognized was the princess high's own hand. The work of Lauresa's stepmother adorned the prince's court and the dining hall, her brushwork done in the delicate filigree style of Caella, capital of Elalantar where she was born.

He recognized the scene that the silk-cast image rendered — the view from the city, just above the harbor. Atop the slope that rose from the Rheran docks, he was looking directly into the rising dawn. The falcon that was the sign of Brandis, house of princes, soared in that first light, the Clearwater burning orange-white where the shadow of the harbor islands rose along the distant horizon. *True as a Clearwater dawn* was an expression of oath across the Ilmar, that purity caught in this wash of light and color that Chriani thought he might have fallen into if he'd had more time to linger.

A haze of evenlamp white shone through sheer lace drapes that closed off the sleeping platform. A tension threaded through Chriani even as he called, already knowing what he'd find there.

"Lauresa..."

He hadn't known he was going to say it like that. Shouldn't have said it like that. He could have found himself sweeping the stable yard for the rest of his life for addressing anyone in Chanist's family by their given names.

His voice had an edge to it that he didn't like. He was on duty, he reminded himself sharply. Barien's voice in his head. *Look to the princess...*

He'd called her Lauresa, as he used to.

As he pulled the curtain aside, he saw the bed empty, turned down but untouched. He scanned the bright shadows, felt something twist inside him, his pulse quickening now. Mechanically inspecting the bed platform, he noted the nightclothes hanging there, an ivory brush laid aside on a stool, boots standing neatly by the nightstand. The shoes had been by the door, he thought. He took all of it in, felt the impressions click into place as he slipped back to the room.

No sign of a struggle meant there likely hadn't been one. Shutters and balcony were bolted, Chriani checking them again one by one. The door was locked but it was the only way out. She'd left her shoes.

She might simply have been summoned, he forced himself to think. He slowed his racing thoughts, tried to refocus. That was the easy explanation. The princess up late, attending to correspondence, not yet to bed when the knock came at the door. Some emergency that had seen her escorted to her father or the chamberlain. Gone for a short while, back imminently. Or perhaps she was simply spending the night talking with her father. In two weeks, she'd be gone, he thought. What father wouldn't want a daughter's company by the fire in those last days?

Then even as he slipped through the curtain for the antechamber and the door, he heard the alarm ring out. Three strikes from the tower, then a silence that seemed much longer than it was before the next three strikes rang out.

Through the door, he found the corridor still thankfully empty, slowing only long enough to turn the lock back, instinctively hiding his entrance. He cursed silently as the alarm rang out again, telling himself that it should have been he who raised it the moment he found the princess gone. He'd have to move fast, head back along the prince's court and through to the armories, then around to the great hall with the rest of the garrison where they would have already been racing from the barracks. It would have been faster to have simply followed the prince's court where it turned, its five-sided perimeter marking the area of the throne room and the boundary of the prince and princess high's quarters to the south. However, the extra distance seemed more than a fair trade for not having to explain his unauthorized presence beyond the warden's door this night.

But even as he slipped the picks into their pocket within his sleeve, he stopped. Stared.

In the shadow that spread from where the evenlamp shone behind him, his eyes caught a subtle change of contrast on the corridor stones. Barely visible, even to him, so that he hadn't noticed it with the light facing him before.

Running from the door where he stood, heading southward along the route he'd been about to take, he saw a regular alternating pattern. Bare footprints, spaced at a walking pace. Smaller than his foot by a half-hand as he crouched to inspect them, low to the corridor floor. Breathing gently on the stone, he saw one outline take sharper shape, the moisture of his breath chilling just slightly on matte-finished marble, highlighting the trace marks that bare skin left behind.

The leather of the shoes she'd gone without would have been nearly silent, he thought, but leather could slip if one found the need to run on the well-soaped Bastion floors. Barefoot on stone gave the best balance of silence and speed.

As he slowly followed, he saw that she was walking, not running. Careful steps, high on the ball of the foot, trying for silence like those who didn't know how to walk silently did. No one with her, no other footprints alongside or following except his own.

Then halfway along the corridor, the tracks stopped. He marked where she'd turned to the left, stood to face the blank expanse of wall there between the doors of the younger princess and the twins. Beyond that point, nothing.

Chriani carefully fished his mother's pick from his sleeve. Along the smooth plaster of the wall, moldings of dark oak were spaced at regular intervals, the steel spike scraping carefully along the two seams to both sides of where the footprints vanished. No gap there that he could see.

Along the floor, though, he felt the slender steel point slip into a narrow depression. A space within the wall itself, accessed through the hair's-breadth gap between baseboard and floor.

It took him precious moments to find the catch, three times fishing in that narrow space with three different picks before he felt the wire, pushed it carefully to one side, then the other. He heard the faint click only because his ear was to the wall, no outward sign of what he'd done. But where he pushed with effort, a body-wide section of lath and plaster pivoted, one section of molding on the door as it swung out, the other hiding the seam on the opposite side. Something pushed back on it, a counterweight hidden, shifting silently. In the faint light of the corridor behind him, a narrow stone staircase climbed a circular shaft.

Chriani felt a chill trace through him as he saw the footprints continue up the first half-dozen steps before they twisted off into shadow above. A secret staircase, not uncommon in the Bastion, but this was the first he'd found on his own. A thing to be smugly proud of under other circumstances.

Except that the princess was missing, and Chriani knew where those stairs led. His mood was as far from smug as it had ever been.

Where the alarm had echoed from the stones, sudden silence fell, the last set of three strikes fading against the undercurrent of distant sound, rising now. Konaugo, as captain of the watch, would have arrived at the staging ground outside, would be giving orders. Chriani heard shouts from the distant great hall, listened for Barien, hoped for the familiar bark of the warrior's voice, but the echo in his mind was the only place it came.

Stay with her…

He shook his head to clear it. Behind him, the door swung shut with a faint click and a hiss of trapped air. Ahead, Chriani moved in silence, not looking back as he climbed.

— CHAPTER 2 —
WORTHY OF FEAR

WITH THE DOOR CLOSED, the gloom held no detail for even Chriani's eyes to pick out as he went, but he counted on the fact that those eyes saw better than all but a handful of the others in the Bastion. People with a secret, like him. He'd see the light of anyone above him long before they saw or heard him, he knew, but all the same, he felt the chill of fear again.

He was ascending to the prince's tower. He slowed his breathing, faster than it should have been.

He'd never been to the tower before. Had never known anyone who'd ascended to the three stories above the prince's private chambers, the secret spaces where not even Barien and the other guards went. The tower was the domain of Chanist's court wizards and healers, it was said — their laboratories and libraries and sanctums there. This much all the garrison knew, but beyond that bare fact were only rumors, of which even the least disturbing were disturbing enough.

Chriani moved carefully, feeling his way along the rough stone of the wall for a count of fifty-five steps from the bottom. He'd expected doors at any of the floors he must have passed, but he found nothing until he heard, then touched, the end of the stairwell ahead. The faint echo of his breathing came back to him as he assessed the blank wall, took a moment to find the catch from this side, the same mechanism as the hallway below.

He listened carefully before he pushed through into the middle of a silent corridor. To both sides, he saw the telltale glimmer of evenlamps, but their light was shaded by the endless ranks of shelves that distracted his eye, cost him a moment to get his bearings. He was on the uppermost level, that much was sure. No windows here from which to spy the city or the stars, but the corridor looked to be a perfect reflection of the prince's court below, running mostly north to south, hard turns west at either end. But where the corridors of the prince's court were almost unnaturally pristine in their emptiness, these tower corridors held an uncountable mass of books and scrolls. Shelves lined the walls to both sides, barely enough room for two people to pass between them in spots. Even quieter here than it was below.

No guards patrolled here, he knew. In the rumors that spilled from the tower like rain off the Bastion's slate roof, it was said that no guards needed to. They'd caught a pair of newly minted squires in the tower once, not quite two years before. The pair of them were a month past making rank, and had apparently decided that breaking into one of the secret libraries of the prince's mages would be a faster path to glory than completing the pledge of service they'd signed.

Though Prince High Chanist avoided the excess of wealth and trappings that could easily have come with the title, it was known that he did have a passion for antiquities, spell-touched and otherwise. Books and scrolls predating the history of the Ilmar filled his vaults, it was said. Volumes of lore that had come from the Imperial capital of Ulannor Mor itself before the end.

The pair were caught easily enough. And though Chriani knew as well as they how harsh a punishment Chanist could have been meted out for their treason, the prince had simply sent the two scurrying out through the gates at dawn, in full view of the garrison and the residents of the keep and the gathering crowd in the market court. The job that the sorcerous wards of the tower had done to them was deemed punishment enough, it seemed, as well as acting as the more-important deterrent for the next fools who might think to try the same game.

Their hair might have grown back by now, Chriani thought. If it ever grew back at all.

He closed his eyes, made the moonsign. Slowly, he pressed to the floor, heard no sound. But he saw the footsteps again, just beside him. Closer together where she'd stopped at the head of the stairs as he had, listening. Then she was moving again, Chriani following to the corridor's end and westward as it turned along the tower's north flank. Between the shelves on both sides, uniform ranks of blank doors were mercifully shut, Chriani glancing behind him at regular intervals, but he saw no sign that he was anything but alone.

Where the corridor turned south to again mimic the run of the prince's court below, he saw the footsteps slow. Ahead, the corner opened to a wide side-hall whose shadows cloaked a sealed set of dark iron doors. The footsteps approached, ended there.

He felt his mind pull at the image he wished he hadn't recalled, the two squires charred black from head to foot. Shocked and deafened, hairless and naked as they ran like rabbits from the courtyard, the shadows of eyebrows and scant beards seared into their skin like clown's paint.

In the light that spilled into the side-hall from behind him, his silhouette was a deeper shadow against the blank lines of the portal, unbroken except for a single keyhole. He approached especially slowly, made the moonsign again, knew that it wouldn't do any good. Without getting anywhere close to touching, he sighted through the keyhole, saw light on the other side.

He'd picked a dweomer-trapped lock once. Only once, a child's device. Barien had set him to it, a key-locked notebook sent by some Elalantar half-cousin, a gift to Lauresa that the warrior had managed to intercept and bring to his quarters one night. Just for practice, he'd said. Chriani had missed on the first attempt and felt a pulse of stinging force slam up through his arm and turn all his fingers blue. Barien's laughter had helped him find his focus to succeed on the second try, but he'd had to wear gloves for a week.

He brought the picks out, felt for calm. Like before, he made his way within the lock by touch, feeling the same mechanism as on Lauresa's door and all the others. A security oversight that he was certain the prince high wasn't aware of. Someone should mention it to him, he thought numbly.

He heard the echo of Barien's laughter in his memory again, didn't know why it chilled him suddenly.

He couldn't make the moonsign but he thought it furiously as he twisted the picks and pushed. He heard the faint click, felt the door press in just slightly under the weight of his fingers. And then, with a rush of cold insight, Chriani realized that though he'd been assuming it was Lauresa beyond the door, he had precious little real reason to think that. The princess had gone missing from her chamber, then someone had gone barefoot from that chamber to the tower in the dead of night. A hundred explanations might tie those two things together, but few of them were optimistic.

He wished for his bow as he drew the shortsword silently, clumsily, no time to adjust the scabbard that was still clubbing at him with every step. Even after as many years as he'd tried, Barien had never succeeded in making Chriani anywhere near as dangerous in close combat as he was on the archery range. Watching the grizzled veteran on the training grounds had taught Chriani how to at least look menacing, though, and he went for that as he kicked through the door. Part of him wanted the element of surprise, part of him fearing whatever power the dark iron might still have in it, hoping that the leather of his boots would at least dull the pain.

But as he stormed in, he felt nothing but the metal-echo slam of the door against the stone wall behind it, louder than he would have wanted if he ever tried that particular maneuver again. In three glances, Chriani took in the scene before him, two arms to the chamber, angled to each side around the doorway that opened up where they met. To the left, some kind of council table, black wood somehow even darker than the night outside the windows that framed it, no one there. To the right, a scriptorium of some sort, shelves stacked high with bound volumes and scrolls. No, a map room. Charts hanging from the walls to match several spread on another table, this one tall for standing, no chairs to flank it.

The Princess Lauresa was on the far side of that table, turned to him. Her too-familiar face caught the light of a single candle burning there, a flicker of fear and surprise in her expression that melted to anger in a single fleeting instant.

"How dare you?"

Chriani blinked. Nodded to her because he realized he'd forgotten to. "Highness…"

"Speak when your words are requested," she hissed. "If this brash entrance is precursor to assault in a stolen uniform of my father's guard, give me the name of your next of kin and do your very best." In her hand, a dagger flashed suddenly, Chriani not seeing it before. "Otherwise, look to that insignia you wear and remind yourself whom you take your orders from."

She didn't recognize him.

Three years since she'd last spoken to him, four years before that when they'd spent almost every day at each other's side. But in the princess's tone now, an imperiousness rang out that he didn't think he'd ever heard before. Not in her, at any rate. The stepmother's voice, he thought, but the princess seemed to have little difficulty wearing it.

"Highness, you have my apologies…"

"I do not recall asking for apology, tyro." She took two steps toward him, the dagger up in a two-handed posture, defensive, her eyes locked to his. She was in blue, he saw, a simple robe belted at the waist, dropping down to bare feet. Her hair was tied in two strands, hanging almost to the small of her back. At her throat, a pendant of lapis hung from gold chain.

"I was sent to watch you. Barien ordered…"

"Leave this chamber on the instant and I might see fit to keep this insubordination to myself."

Even against the chill in her voice, Chriani found himself locked to her gaze. Hoping to find some sense of the past in those eyes, he realized. Some hint that she still knew him, even through the anger. A thing he hadn't felt for so long now.

Instead, he saw the tip of the blade, dead steady. He felt his own anger twist deep in his gut, tried to fight it but already knew it was too late. "Highness…"

"You are testing my patience, tyro."

"Highness, the alarm is sounded."

In her look, Chriani caught a sudden uncertainty.

"What of the alarm?" Lauresa said, her voice the same but something changed in her manner as she watched him.

"The alarm is sounded," he said again because he didn't know what else to say. He felt the dark emotion in him already slamming down around his ability to think, had to focus to find the words. "The Bastion is locked down, and the Princess Lauresa is not in her chamber. I am here for you."

She hadn't recognized him. He felt the anger flare around that, spread like the hiss of flame across kindling stoked from dying embers.

"I am on orders from Barien, who is your warden," Chriani said. He took a step closer to her, made sure to keep the required five paces between them. Of all the guards of the garrison, he'd been the exception to that rule once, a long time ago now. He brought his own blade level with hers. "Highness, I am a warrior of the guard and adjutant to your warden, and on his orders, I am here to escort you to your chambers and ensure your safety there."

"You sword belt is on backward and upside down, warrior of the guard."

Chriani glanced down despite himself, felt the scabbard prod his leg again as he saw she was right. He felt an unfamiliar burning in his cheeks.

"You will accompany me, highness. I have my orders."

"You will get out…"

The princess faltered. Chriani saw the flick of her eyes, the gleam of blue catching the light as he twisted to follow her gaze. He'd left the dark door open behind him. In the faint light of the corridor, his eyes caught the ripple of shadow that meant movement in the distance. Footsteps, almost silent.

"You fool," she whispered.

Chriani wasn't listening, sheathing his sword with effort as he turned for the door, made to call out to whoever was racing toward them. No idea what he was supposed to say, but he was fairly certain that begging for mercy would be a large part of it.

Then Lauresa was moving behind him, one hand across his mouth even as the other brought the dagger up, close to his throat as she dragged him back. Chriani was startled, as much at being grabbed at all as he was at the strength in her arm. As he stumbled back, though, he felt instinct override any uncertainty. Her blade was a hand's-width from him, more than enough space to go for her wrist. No room to get a decent strike in with the other hand, but her flank was vulnerable and in easy reach, or the soft muscle of her thigh, one sharp blow that would drop her.

But even through the instinct, through all the memory of all the hand-to-hand training he'd done at Barien's side, he knew he couldn't do it.

No idea what any of this was about, but he couldn't hurt her. Not anymore.

He went for the dagger, though. No point in having his throat slit, by accident or otherwise. But even as his hand clamped around her wrist, Lauresa sang.

Close to his ear, barely a whisper, her voice unleashed a sudden pulse of blood and uncertainty that pounded in his head. A twisting cascade of sound slipped through him like wind through the bare branches of winter trees. He didn't understand the words, didn't know the melody, but it hit him hard.

It was the voice he remembered, all the imperious tone gone like swiftly shed armor. The echo of a childhood he'd been trying to not look back to anymore.

At the doorway, the first figures pushed in, but they weren't the robed stewards he'd expected, fists spouting fire and lightning like every carefully retold tale of the tower had warned. It was the regular garrison, attack dogs released first, balisters dropping in the doorway behind them. But even as they did, the gleam of the guttering candle twisted, a sudden fountain of darkness erupting. Across the room, a roiling wall of black eclipsed the light like a silent storm, Chriani frozen for the moment it took Lauresa to pull her hand from his mouth, breathe a single word into his ear.

"Move…"

Where his wrist was still around her dagger hand, she pulled him, the clamor of voice and movement loud beyond the shadow. Chriani heard the familiar shunt of crossbow fire, four bolts spraying past them, fired blindly. He heard the dogs fall back with an uncertain yelping, the sudden fall of unnatural black a thing they wouldn't enter.

Two strides beyond the table, tall windows loomed, black-framed and locked tight. The princess was still singing, Chriani realized, not noticing her start again.

Then he blinked, and the one window she dragged him toward wasn't locked after all, Lauresa kicking it open somehow as she leaped to the ledge. Chriani's momentum pulled him up behind her even as he clutched at the frame, trying to slow himself, but her hands were tight in his tunic now, no time to break her grip as she pushed off. His hold on the window not enough to support them both, his weight tipping into hers.

He felt her arms go around him. She was singing, still.

He forced himself to look down. He saw his own death beckon from dark stone below.

A frozen moment of time.

He felt the freezing wind of the sea below the city against his face, felt his feet slip from the ledge to empty air. Then they were falling, the Bastion outwall a dark blur below them.

He felt the urge to shout, not from fear but from anger at what he knew Barien would call a fool's death when they found his body. A stupid way to die, he thought. The princess he'd been charged to protect, dead beside him. All the questions that would be asked. All the answers he would have liked to have heard himself.

He felt her body against his, her hands at his neck and the small of his back. Her face was close, Lauresa shorter than him by three hands but pushed up against him as they twisted, still upright somehow. Their legs would shatter first, he knew, an endless moment of pain to herald the blood-shock that would ultimately kill them.

A frozen moment of time. He felt her breath trace his cheek, the song still spilling from her in a whisper.

Without knowing he'd even done it, Chriani found himself kissing her. His mouth pressed soft to hers as he drank in the song, felt it fade with the sharp intake of her breath.

He changed his mind suddenly. This was a good way to die.

And then, even as he recognized the timeless stretching of that last moment, he became dimly aware that the moment was somehow stretching even further than it should be. His mouth was still locked to Lauresa's, her lips impossibly soft against his, and as he hung onto that sensation, he realized that in his being able to be aware of that sensation, he was somehow still alive and kissing the princess long after they should both be dead.

He risked opening his eyes, saw the stone of the walls slipping past at what seemed like a remarkably slow pace. He felt the impact as they landed, a sharp jolt in his knees that made him stumble, but no more than he would have expected from a badly timed jump over the orchard wall. The orchard was off-limits to all but the prince's family and invited guests, so he'd done his fair share of badly timed jumps in and out of it when he was younger, generally one step ahead of the dogs that patrolled there in summer.

As he staggered back against cold stone, Lauresa was still in his arms, shorter than him now, the embrace broken as they both found their footing. She stared at him with a look that was partly surprise and partly something else he couldn't name. He could feel his heart pounding hard as he leaned down to kiss her again.

The princess hit him then, a backhand blow coming so fast that even he didn't see it. Chriani felt the imprint of knuckles and rings rising on his cheek as his head snapped back and took a moment to right itself. She flexed her fingers, didn't seem to feel it. In her look, the surprise and whatever else it had been was gone.

"Move," she said again, then she was running, racing eastward along the dark outwall above the training grounds. As Chriani followed, he could hear voices from above, didn't have to look to know that the garrison would be at the window, searching for the bodies that weren't there. Dimly, he wondered where the guards were who should already have been racing to intercept them where they stood, regular patrols walking the Bastion perimeter beneath the lights of the prince's quarter above. Then he remembered the alarm, the garrison mustered inside the Bastion, perhaps. He didn't have time to wonder why.

Lauresa slowed suddenly, dark shutters ahead that were unlocked somehow as she pulled them open. From behind them came the sound of something hitting the stones, light swelling as the guards above tossed evenlamps down to the wall, but the princess had already dragged them both back inside, running left down a corridor Chriani didn't recognize. Somewhere in the depths of the kitchens, he guessed, dark for the night.

A hundred paces down the corridor, Chriani heard movement ahead of them, tugging at Lauresa's sleeve as he pointed. She pushed a window open quickly, a narrow ledge beyond, her hand locked to Chriani's again as she hauled him out. Through darkened glass, he saw figures pounding past as she led him carefully into shadow. The only light was the Darkmoon low above the western walls, the Clearmoon vanishing to new two nights before, the stars faint beyond thin cloud.

All around, the keep was coming alive, a storm of light and voices carrying where evenlamps burned on all the outer walls now. As he recognized the light of the stables across from them, Chriani managed to orient himself, realizing where they were even as he saw Lauresa stop, peering up to the underside of the tower. Her balcony loomed above her as she clutched the corner of the Bastion wall.

"Climb," she said, and then she was gone, hands and bare feet clinging to rough stone as she ascended. Chriani kicked his boots off, stuffed them clumsily inside his jacket as he followed her. He found purchase easily in the weathered walls, but even at his best speed, Lauresa hit the balcony well ahead of him, climbing up and over with an unnatural grace. As he pulled himself after her, his scabbard scraped stone, still pushing the wrong way.

Inside the princess's chamber, he shut the balcony doors behind him, remembered that they'd been locked from the inside before. He saw Lauresa padding silently for the curtained alcove and the door to the corridor. His feet and hands were already numb, his boots fumbled on.

Slowly, Chriani approached. "Princess..."

His voice was loud in the silence, Lauresa turning back to hold a hand up in warning. He felt his heart beating fast, felt the loosening grip of an elation and a desperation that he hadn't had time to realize he was even feeling. He tried to judge the time that had passed. Only moments since they'd jumped from the tower window, the princess running from a garrison who would have answered to her orders over anyone but her father's.

There must be an explanation, he thought. It would all make sense once she explained it.

"Will you tell me why we are running?" he said, quieter now. Lauresa was pressed to the outside door. "Will you tell me how we survived?"

She glanced back to him sharply, as if she might have forgotten he was there. "No." She slipped through the main chamber and covered the glow of the evenlamps with shrouds of grey cloth, speaking softly as she went. "The hall is clear but it won't be for long. The door still standing says they haven't been here yet."

The last light was covered, the room in shadow where the glow from the bed platform filtered through its scrim of white lace. As cloud broke beyond the window behind Chriani, the faint light of the stars caught her eyes, sharp as she stepped close.

"When they come, you will challenge them. Confirm their identities. You were on guard outside when the alarm was raised. At my request and for my security, you took position within the alcove, resolved to stay here until relieved. You know nothing of what else happened tonight. You know nothing of what you saw in the tower."

As she spoke, Chriani heard the voice from the tower again, the tone of someone who was used to giving orders that would be followed without question. More expectation than command. He felt the anger wash through him again, felt it twist suddenly around the memory of the kiss, Lauresa close enough that he could catch the scent of her hair.

"I know very well what I saw tonight," he said evenly. He remembered that scent, from the fall that should have killed them, and from long before. One more thing he'd need to forget again. "I know what was done, princess, and whether you tell me why or no, I will not be directed to say otherwise by you."

He tried for Barien's voice, only half-successfully. Barien was good at giving orders and at the same time expressing how much he hated giving them, so that those who heard those orders were always very certain they didn't want to have to hear them twice.

"I am obliged to protect you," Chriani said, "not to lie for you."

Then Lauresa sang again, a quick trill of notes that spilled into the silence of the room like warm rain. With one fist, she seized the inseam of his leggings, the same strength in her that he'd felt across his cheek not a moment before. The other hand seized the lapis pendant at her neck, pulled it to within two fingers of his face. Around her fingers where they clutched the stone, a pulse of crackling energy flared white.

Chriani felt her other hand squeeze. As he forced himself to breathe, he smelled the sharply scented air that announced the advance of distant thunderstorms. He remembered the two Bastion squires and the charred shadows where their hair had been.

"I can change hands a great deal more quickly than you can stop me," Lauresa said quietly. "When the time is right, I will answer the questions that deserve answers. Until then, you will do as I command."

She broke off from him, Chriani feeling the sudden spasm of pain that rose as she released her grip. He could only nod.

"The door," she said. She had her belt undone, the robe already off her shoulders as she slipped through the curtain, disappeared within the haze of white that ringed her bed.

It would all make sense once she explained it, Chriani thought darkly. He'd barely had time to gingerly adjust the set of his leggings when he heard boots in the corridor beyond the alcove. At the door, he didn't know whether he should draw his sword or not, deciding to just put it on correctly for a start.

As he cinched the scabbard belt again, someone knocked loudly. "By your leave, princess," called a voice through the door, deferential.

"In the name of the prince, identify yourselves," Chriani said, a little too loudly. Outside, he heard the near-silent whisper of swords and daggers drawn, movement along the wall where he knew that whoever was there had flanked the door.

"In the name of the prince, identify yourself," the voice echoed back, all deference gone.

"Chriani, adjutant to Barien. Standing guard on the Princess Lauresa as ordered." A formality infused the orders and responses that passed between ranks in the garrison, and the way that words were spoken often carried as much weight as what was said. Not for the first time, Chriani wished he were better at it.

"Open this door now…"

"Identify yourself," Chriani demanded with an uncertainty he hoped they couldn't hear. *Challenge them*, the princess had said. He winced as the fading pain twisted once more through his loins.

"Ashlund with three guards, lieutenant to Konaugo, on orders from the prince high to ensure the location and safety of his children. Open this door or by Brandis's blood, tyro, I'll have your ears!"

Chriani took a breath, drew his own sword as he pulled the bolt back and stepped to the far corner of the alcove. The fact that Ashlund slammed the door open with his hand and not his boot was testament only to whose chamber this was, he suspected. The lieutenant was a close-shaven veteran, taller than Chriani and thicker from nearly any angle. Behind him, three more guards pushed in, blades still drawn. Ashlund slowed to let them pass through the curtain to the main chamber, grabbed Chriani's tunic in a fist the size and color of an uncured ham. If he noticed that Chriani held a shortsword an arm's length away, he didn't show it.

"Explain," he said, his voice a low growl.

"The Princess Lauresa is resting within, lord. I was on guard outside the chamber when the alarm was raised. At her request and for her security, I took position within the alcove."

Lauresa's lie, straight from memory. Chriani had seen what happened to tyros and squires alike who misled the garrison command about things much more mundane. He watched Ashlund's eyes, tried to slow down. "I resolved to stay here until…"

"On guard by whose orders?" Ashlund interrupted.

"By Sergeant Barien's orders, lord."

"And the sergeant is where?"

"I do not know, lord."

Chriani felt himself released, the hand that had held him pointing two massive fingers. "The next time you find yourself on the other side of a door that I ordered opened, it will open or you will go back in pieces to the gutter where Barien found you. Is that quite clear?"

"I had not heard the stand-down, lord. Should I have opened the door without even…?"

Ashlund cuffed him across the side of the head, Chriani only fast enough to roll with it. He felt the pulse of rage flare blood-red behind his eyes, fought unsuccessfully to lock his own hands at his side. As his sword wavered, he saw Ashlund smile. Waiting.

"By Barien's orders," Chriani said with effort, "I was to guard the Princess Lauresa. Am I relieved of that duty, lord?"

Ashlund's hand came up a second time, then lowered slowly when one of his guards appeared at the curtain. She whispered a word in Ashlund's ear. Chriani could hear Lauresa's voice from within, speaking to the others in hushed tones.

"Go," the lieutenant snarled. Chriani went.

Ashlund hadn't told him to return to quarters, but he sprinted in that direction anyway, past the doors of the younger heirs where silent guards were ranked two abreast, watching him as he passed. He had to slip around the corner, peering back while he waited until their attention was elsewhere, then he sprinted on straight instead of cutting east for the great hall. Down the children's court and through the warden's door, carefully locked behind him as he headed past the armories.

He didn't bother looking to Barien's quarters, knew that the warrior would be in the thick of whatever had inspired the alarm. He was breathing hard, his head still reeling with the force of Ashlund's blow that had at least erased the too-telltale marks Lauresa's rings had made.

He was nearly to the central court before he realized that his sword was still in his hands. Even with the alarm, he hadn't heard the call to arms, he remembered. He sheathed it quickly.

But when he arrived at the Bastion gate, its bars were drawn. The portcullis was dropped, as he'd never seen it dropped in the ten years he'd been there. Through the bars, the staging ground was empty, Chriani lingering for just a moment. Then he slipped carefully to the gatehouse stairs, heading up quietly to the outwall, hoping to find Barien before being ordered to duty by another officer in his stead. Because in the short run from the princess's chambers, a thought had become firmly lodged in his mind, something he might have picked up on at the time if it hadn't been for the pulsing memory of Ashlund's hand leaving little room for thought in his head.

Barien should have been one of the first at the great hall when the alarm was sounded, but Ashlund hadn't known where the warrior was.

Three times as he made his way along the outwall, Chriani passed squads of the Bastion guard racing, sidelong glances made to his scabbard as he passed. He was carrying it under his arm now, tried to make it look like he was delivering it somewhere. Not sure how believable that was in the end, but not wanting to risk Barien's wrath by abandoning it. At each tower, the garrison was out in full force now, but Chriani still saw no sign of the warrior. No officers either. Only sergeants, all of them with the same look of uniform unease.

He raced along past the spot where he and Lauresa had dropped, made it back to the top of the gatehouse when he passed another tyro racing by with a sealed message. Vanad, two years younger than Chriani and under the mentorship of Hestria, one of the Bastion's sergeants-at-arms. Chriani caught sight of what looked like the prince's seal as he called to ask if Vanad had seen Barien. She shook her head in response, not slowing.

"What's the alarm?" Chriani called, and Vanad stopped, doubled back, got close so she wouldn't have to shout. Even then, she looked twice over her shoulder before she spoke.

"Attempt on the prince's life," she whispered. Chriani stared for a long while at the younger tyro's fleeing back.

He slipped back in at the east tower then, running for the closest stairs, assuming that Vanad's account was the truth without really knowing why. He remembered the urgency in Barien's voice, needed to find him because Barien was the only one who would know what was going on. Barien was warden to the princess, had ordered him to watch her. Barien would have the answers Lauresa hadn't given.

But as he pounded down a narrow flight of stairs, a thought struck Chriani with a starkness that angered him for not having seen it before. He emerged in the archives quarter, bypassed the shadowed corridors to the side for the well-lit hall of records ahead, the central court beyond it. No sign of anyone else around him, but if the guard were searching for a would-be assassin, it was no time to be caught slipping through the shadows.

Barien hadn't known that the princess was missing when he called to Chriani. *Seek her in her chambers*, he'd said.

So then what was it, Chriani wondered, that Barien had ordered him to protect Lauresa from? What was it that had driven the princess to leap from a fourth-storey window in order to prevent being seen by her own guard?

Attempt on the prince's life…

As he'd always been able to do, Chriani played the events of those few frantic moments back in his mind as he ran. Her expression shifting as he burst in, the angry exchange, word for word.

She hadn't heard the alarm, he realized.

When he'd said it, he was doing little more than grasp for words that might staunch her anger and keep her from flinging a dagger across the table or having him demoted to the kitchens out of sheer spite. The words had caught her by surprise, though. She hadn't heard the alarm, the bells ringing through the empty night from the top of the prince's tower, almost directly above her.

When the time was right, she'd said.

He was thinking furiously as he sprinted from the side passage. Only half watching the shadows around him, so that he almost missed the blood.

As he skidded to a halt, Chriani whipped the shortsword out, the scabbard dropped behind him as he wheeled. He was in the intersection of a narrow corridor between the galleries of the archives quarter and the central court. Beyond that, the garrison wing where he'd started his long circuit was eerily silent.

It was bright in the intersection, an evenlamp blazing there. To both sides, fading in the shadows, staggered droplets of red-black ran along the wide expanse of the adjacent corridor toward the shadowed gallery halls. The archives wing was the center of Chanist's public collection of art and artifacts, a steady stream of scholars passing through it from across Brandishear and all the Ilmar by day, deserted now.

Where Chriani dropped, the telltale red marks were slightly elongated, still wet against his fingers. Someone bleeding as they moved.

He tried to judge which way the injured runner had come, had to half-guess as he took the corridor to the left, following the trace pattern where it scattered to the shadows. He was silent as he slipped through the cover of wide columns to either side of the hall, the gallery corridors lined with the busts of Chanist's father, brother, and sister. His uncles and grandfathers who had been the Imperial regents before the prince's crown had been reclaimed.

He saw Barien's body then.

A pool of blood spread past the warrior where he'd fallen, Chriani recognizing the cloak and riding gear even before he was close enough to see the pale face. As he ran to drop on the slick-wet floor at Barien's side, the sword rang out where it fell forgotten behind him. He couldn't speak, couldn't breathe. He saw Barien's chest slowly rise, heard ragged breath sounds echo wetly in the stillness.

His heart in his throat, he managed to call the warrior's name, a sudden flinch telling him that Barien had heard. But as the warrior's arm came up, Chriani saw the wound. A twisted slash across shoulder and chest, hacking through leather and muscle and bone at once. A short blade, spiked and curved from the way the flesh had been torn. Chriani had to close his eyes, tried not to think.

"You're going to be all right," Chriani whispered. "You need a healer," he said. "I have to find…"

With a speed that belied his wounds, the warrior seized Chriani's arm, held it in a grip like steel. "Princess…" As he clutched at Chriani, Barien's eyes were wide like a cat's, staring past him. "Is she safe? Princess?"

Chriani nodded, realized stupidly that Barien couldn't see him. "She is safe. I was with her, then Ashlund came."

He struggled to pry the thick fingers from his arm, but he might as well have tried to bend horseshoes with his bare hands. Barien pulled him closer, a spray of blood as he coughed catching Chriani across the cheek. "You need a healer…" Chriani whispered, but the warrior held up a bloodstained hand to silence.

"Seek the blade," he murmured. "Follow by fourteen, your only proof. Keep it safe. Keep her safe." And in his voice as he spoke, Chriani heard a sudden trace of strength. The same resolve as always, none of the fear that had threaded the words that had woken him. None of the fear Chriani felt now.

"He owns Uissa." Barien coughed wetly again. "I know not who else…"

Chriani had never heard the name before but he took it in, felt it lock into memory. As Barien shuddered, Chriani saw his eyes focus suddenly. Staring up as if he could see him, the warrior's face blurring as Chriani realized that his own eyes were wet.

"Trust him not. Lauresa. Keep her…" Barien fought to catch his breath.

"She is safe," Chriani whispered. "I kept her safe. You're going to be…"

"Chanist…" the warrior breathed, staring blindly again.

"I don't know where the prince is. I think he's safe, I don't know what happened…"

"A fool…" Barien retched again, fighting to breathe now. "A fool forgets… there are always things worthy of fear…"

Where Chriani touched it, the warrior's forehead was cold.

"Lauresa. Keep her safe…"

As if the effort of speaking the words had drained away the last of his will, Barien slumped slowly back.

Chriani stared. Shook his head, mute. He pressed a finger to the warrior's neck to feel for the life that should have been there, but Barien's blood was still.

On his arm, the thick fingers slowly loosened their cold grip.

He didn't remember standing. Didn't remember grabbing up the sword again where it had fallen. He ran, not for the healer who would have come too late now, not for the closest garrison post to raise the alarm that had already been raised, but along the trail of blood where it snaked out before him.

Through the intersection, he raced down the hall of records, the central court only forty strides away from where the trail began. Dark doors were shut fast to either side, a wider spray of blood across the floor there, the marks of large hands streaked where they'd clutched at the stones. Barien struck on this spot, falling. Rising again to run. Pursuing his attacker? Or trying to flee?

Then in the hall behind him, movement, four figures where Barien had fallen. Garrison uniforms but no faces he could remember in the fury that sent him racing toward them. He saw their lips moving but he couldn't hear the words over his scream as they stepped across the body, swords drawn. Then they were on him before he could swing, hauling him down easily in the frenzy that consumed him.

He felt something hard strike his head, the pain already there re-doubled. He felt his arms pinned, boots striking him in the stomach and back. Then he was moving across cold stone and his legs didn't work anymore.

A frozen moment of time, the ceiling sliding endlessly past above him. Then darkness took him away.

— CHAPTER 3 —

CHRIANI'S SECRET

THE SECRET CHRIANI HAD KEPT since the day he walked into Rheran through the dust of the trade way meant that he could see better than anyone else in the keep that he knew of, but that same sharpness of sight blinded him now when he finally awoke. He blinked, found himself staring up into the singular brilliance of a dozen evenlamps, a massive hanging fixture directly above him that he looked away from at once, overwhelmed by the shadow that had burned into his sight while he lay there unconscious.

As he slowly forced his eyes open, he saw an intricate pattern on the floor beneath him, blue and white tile cold against his face. An interleaving pattern of knots twisted around a blurred mosaic as he slowly looked up and across. The falcon of Brandis, ancient standard of the first princes. Its wings unfurled across the floor as it climbed, empty eyes fierce in their coldness where they seemed to watch him through a blur of movement all around.

The throne room, he thought.

He tried to focus, felt all the disparate pain from the number of times he'd been struck in the head that night twist into one solid knot. He felt rough cords at his wrists and feet, thought about trying to sit up but decided against it. The blood at his tunic was still wet, hardly any time passed. He was in the throne room but he was bound, which meant that they wanted something from him but were expecting to be able to get it without beating him in the dark holding cells behind the outwall. That was a good thing.

Barien was dead.

Where the terrible truth had circled half-remembered in his daze, it flooded him now like a plunge into ice-cold water. Against a sudden spike of anger, Chriani forced himself upright as a knife edge of pain cut through him. Across from him, he saw three guards suddenly alert, more around them, spread across the room as his vision blurred.

You will do as I command, the princess had said.

Only she hadn't commanded him on what to do in the event that his mentor was murdered and he found himself taken down and bound by the Bastion garrison. He should have run that scenario past her, Chriani thought bitterly. But then the anger wilted beneath a sudden fear, and he wondered what might happen if they used truth magic on him.

He wondered what might happen if they simply took off his shirt and the bandage beneath it.

For the mark his mother had made at his shoulder long years before, they'd kill him outright, he guessed. If the princess's name freshly tattooed along its edge was seen by anyone who could read the delicate Ilvani script, Chanist or Konaugo or the ranger captains, they'd likely torture him first.

The pain in his head flared suddenly. Chriani squeezed his eyes shut.

It had been his eleventh summer when it had started. The Princess Lauresa a year older than him but showing no signs of growing out of the breeches she still wore then and into the robes her stepmother and younger sister favored. He'd been at the keep and under Barien's hand almost three years, but even as tyro to the princess's warden, he had yet to see her at anything less than a distance. Chriani had shoveled the stables while she rode out with Barien and her father. He had watched from the wall as she walked through the gates to explore the market court with her stepmother and younger siblings.

It had been a bright spring day whose light had long-burned into permanent relief in his memory. The orchard trees were blossom-white above the walls, the training grounds wet with brief rain the night before. Images that he wished on his mother's blood he could forget.

On that day, Barien had told him to meet at the archery yard when his duties in the armory were done. Chriani was eleven then and was already outshooting Barien six times in ten, not sure why the warrior thought he needed more practice. But when he arrived on the training grounds, she'd been waiting for him. The Princess Lauresa, smiling shyly as he approached.

She'd already been shooting, a brace of arrows lying in the mud a half-dozen paces past the target and conspicuously few of them sticking in it. Like the range master who watched her, like any member of the garrison who carried arms within the Bastion, Barien was standing five paces away from the princess by Chanist's own orders. It was a rule that all who served under the prince knew as well as they knew their names, Chanist's will in this regard dating back to the days of Lauresa's mother Irdaign, the first princess high.

Chanist and she had been married just five years before the death of his father, brother, and sister marked the sixth year of the Ilvani Incursions, the war of invasion from the Valnirata Greatwood. And while most in the garrison thought the prince's caution excessive against the backdrop of peace that Chanist himself had wrought from the raw destruction of that war, it was a caution they adhered to nonetheless. The prince high had seen too many of the family he'd grown up with murdered, Barien had said. He would take no chances with the family he'd made since then.

"Don't get no ideas," the warrior had whispered with a wink as he waved Chriani in, but the boy hadn't understood what he meant. Then Barien formally announced that the Prince High Chanist had seen fit to allow Chriani leave to serve as the Princess Lauresa's personal mentor in archery, close blade combat, and riding. The warrior had somehow convinced the prince that he could allow a tyro this slight contact with his child but still keep the precepts of his orders intact. Chriani could only nod, wide-eyed.

With the warrior's prodding, Chriani approached Lauresa awkwardly, steadying her aim over the length of that first day. Close at her side, his hand wrapped around hers as he adjusted the set of her arm, told her how to breathe, how to open her eyes but focus with her whole body on the distant target.

Chanist himself had appeared across the range just before the daymark bells, Chriani only realizing it when he saw Barien and the others salute. He was at the age then when he didn't understand how clearly this new duty of his marked out the trust that ran from Chanist to Barien. He didn't understand enough of the machinations of power and politics in the Bastion to realize until much later the resentment both he and the warrior would carry because of it.

Chriani looked up now to the sound of footsteps approaching across the throne room floor, and the faint thought flitted through him that his long-ago ignorance was something he would have done well to hang onto.

Above him, a face loomed, dark-eyed. Seamed with years of hard service, a jagged scar running jaw to ear, white like the hair and the narrow beard. Konaugo, captain of the guard, was shorter than Chriani but easily twice as broad. He was in riding leathers, out of uniform, Chriani only dimly registering it as the captain motioned two guards to pull him roughly to his feet.

"Move," he said.

As they half-carried, half-dragged him toward a wide table of dark wood, Chriani's vision cleared. Ashlund was there, a look passing between him and Konaugo that he didn't like. In the press of guards around the main doors, he saw two that he remembered at Barien's body. He remembered running at them, felt the rage that had filled him then twisting away to shame now as it always did.

Though the garrison still called it the throne room, it had been untold years since it had been used as such, no throne there since the time of Chanist's father at least. This was the prince's workroom — a council chamber, a planning area, an impromptu dining hall for those occasions when guests of the court outnumbered the regular hall's ability to hold them. Before this night, those were the only times Chriani had ever been past the doors. Occasional revels Barien had dragged him to when he was younger, sitting quietly off to the side of the prince high's table where the warrior most often sat, dreamily lost in the laughter and the warm light of the central fire that burned on banquet nights.

Tonight, that fire was burning but hadn't yet cut the cold. Behind the council table, the prince high sat in quiet consultation with a figure in black robes. Chriani found himself staring at her as she worked, her hand to Chanist's bare chest where he wore a torn and bloodstained shirt of white linen, a pendant at his neck. The shirt's sleeve had been cut away where a jagged scar ran from shoulder to elbow, in the same flesh-torn pattern he'd seen on Barien's body. It took Konaugo slapping the back of his head for Chriani to remember to nod low.

The dark-clad figure was speaking softly, a monotonous incantation delivered in a tongue Chriani didn't recognize. She shifted her hand to Chanist's head, touched his shoulder, his hair. He saw the prince breathe deeply, a kind of vigor coming to him. As faint as it had been when he first saw it, the jagged scar faded still more, almost gone as Chanist nodded dismissal.

The prince stripped off the ruined shirt and accepted another from a guard standing behind him, but didn't bother to wash away the blood still streaking his arm. As the healer slipped away, Chriani fought the urge to make the moonsign, though he'd seen the healing life-magic once before. Two springs after Lauresa's training at his side had started, he and Barien had been among the company escorting the Princess High Gwannyn and the four heirs on the road to Elalantar, the princess high's mother buried there after long illness. On the road, they'd met wolves, Barien and two others left with savage wounds that Chriani had watched disappear beneath the hands of the princess high's healer.

He'd wondered then how it was that the spells of the healers could dispense with the wounds of sword and fang but not of the age that had taken the princess high's mother. He wondered now what difference it might have made to Barien had Chriani gone for help like he wanted to, brought a healer back before the warrior's blood and life had ebbed away across cold stone.

He wondered not for the first time since that long trip north what difference it might have made to his mother, her body broken when her horse had been spooked by a scrubsnake breaking from a stand of witchwillow, throwing her on the road to the trade fair at Quilimma. Chriani and his grandfather could do little more than watch, helpless around her as she died over the length of an agonizingly long blue-skied summer day.

As Chanist rose, he took whispered orders from a harried sergeant, one nod enough to send her running with two others in tow. All around was an undercurrent of tension, of movement. On the table, Chriani saw maps spread, Konaugo noting his gaze and carefully stepping across to block his view.

As his escorts stopped, Chriani staggered to a halt. Chanist glanced up, blue eyes cold beneath the blonde hair still not entirely gone to white, appraising him.

"Untie him now," the prince said.

"Lord, I would urge extreme caution…" Konaugo began.

"You think him the assassin, Konaugo? Are you mad, or do you simply wish to pretend so quickly that this is over?"

From a mostly safe distance, Chriani had heard the prince giving orders for most of his life, but that voice still held a power that could seemingly take even those used to it by surprise. Konaugo only nodded, a gesture to the two guards alongside Chriani setting them to quickly cut his bonds. He rubbed his wrists, flexed his ankles as he stepped back. Not knowing whether to nod to the prince in thanks or not, he glanced to Konaugo instead, caught the dark look there.

"My lord prince, he was detained in the act of attacking members of your own watch," the captain said evenly, speaking to Chanist, eyes never leaving Chriani's. "He carried a weapon without charge. Barien's blood was on his hands…"

"You know as well as I that no sword laid Barien down as you found him."

Konaugo said nothing. Looked away as the prince stepped to Chriani, who nodded in earnest now. Not sure which of the conflicting emotions in him would be the first to be revealed where he felt the prince's gaze reading him like a map.

But as he tried to keep from meeting Chanist's gaze, Chriani saw the tunic. Spread to a bench behind the table, the pale blue-grey worn by the prince and all his guard was stained black with blood, torn through by a single jagged slash. On the prince's cloak where it lay crumpled to one side, the same cut was visible.

"Tell me what you know." Chanist's tone was even, expectant.

All people had things to hide, Barien had often said. When Chriani had first entered the keep and the warrior's service, though, the secrets his father had given him were a great deal heavier than anyone as young as him should have been made to carry. So it was good, Barien had told him more than once, that his mother had given him the talent for keeping those secrets safely out of sight. The gifts that parents give.

The first time Chriani met the prince was when he'd taken the tyro's writ and been formally petitioned as Barien's adjutant, two years after he'd first seen the Bastion. He remembered carefully fingering the white-stitched tyro's insignia and the adjutant's badge that Chanist himself had presented, not understanding then the degree of honor implied in that. The trust that Chanist placed in Barien was repaid with a respect whose value would never be measured in rank or coin. The investiture of a tyro was normally something a junior lieutenant would take care of only if it couldn't be passed off on someone else. But there in front of the prince high, Chriani had obliviously bowed and spoken like Barien told him to, and he remembered being drawn into the warmth of Chanist's booming laughter that had seemed as wide and as bright as the sun-high sky.

"Your father died in the Incursions," Barien had coached him all the night before. "He traveled south from the village before you were old enough to remember. He was a bowyer and a militia sentry, and they say your skill on the range comes straight from his arms and eyes. You can't just speak it, you need to think it all the way through. Think of nothing else."

He remembered feeling the presence of the prince high, younger then but no less imposing. The hair and beard were just then beginning to lighten, but even now it was commonly said that Chanist would never show any sign of age but that.

Only a fool forgets there are always things worthy of fear. Barien spoke the words with his dying breath, but Chriani had heard them before. The first time was that very first day, sitting alone in the warrior's chambers.

"We learn to distrust our fear," Barien had added then, "so the things worth being frightened of, we look away from. We end up afraid of only the things we see. From all the rest, we hide."

Barien's voice in his head this night had filled him with fear he hadn't felt since that first day in the city. No way of knowing now what it meant, Chriani thought dully.

"You hide from something, you can't fight it, lad," Barien had said in response to the fear he felt then.

"Do you hide from anything?" Chriani had asked, but Barien only smiled.

Chriani felt the rough edge now that Barien's last words had torn in his memory, no way of ever asking what secret lay shrouded in that fear.

One more thing he'd never have the chance to say.

Where the prince was waiting for him, Chriani nodded even as he felt his voice choked off by the old anger, blood pounding in his head suddenly as he tried to find the strength to focus but couldn't. He heard the Princess Lauresa's directive in his memory. He felt his bile rise at the thought of it, even as the recollection of the events she'd forbidden him to speak of twisted through him.

Barien had tried to teach him to follow orders, though never as successfully as he would have wished, Chriani knew. Barien had given and taken orders his whole life.

"My lord prince, I was ordered by Sergeant Barien to stand guard at the doorway to the Princess Lauresa's chamber," Chriani said. "I did not know his reasons."

The warrior's last orders to him. *Keep her safe.*

"When the alarm was sounded, the princess came to the door, and in her uncertainty requested that I position myself within the antechamber. I remained there until Lieutenant Ashlund and his party appeared to relieve me."

It was Barien's orders he was following, he told himself. Not hers. Chanist only nodded.

"I was instructed by Lieutenant Ashlund to quit the princess's chambers but he had no orders for me. I approached the staging ground but saw the gate down and no officers. I proceeded toward the great hall and discovered…"

Even as a tightness rose in his throat, Chriani felt a faint heat on his skin. A stinging sensation, the hair on the back of his neck standing up like it might in the shifting air of a summer storm.

Truth magic. At the prince's neck, Chriani caught sight of the pendant and realized that it was the same as the one Lauresa had worn. He tried to push the thought away, mentally willed the moonsign as he wondered without wanting to whether Chanist had already had the lies sensed in the words he'd spoken.

"I found Sergeant Barien dying, my lord prince." Chriani tried to swallow but couldn't. "He died before I could leave him to seek aid. I followed the track of his bleeding to where I believe he was assaulted, in the hall of records. I returned to his body to find members of the watch there. I challenged them in my anger and fear but meant them no harm, forgive me, my lord prince."

He bowed his head, didn't want Konaugo to see the wetness in his eyes, but the captain's gloved hand clipped Chriani's chin, lifting it roughly.

"Did he speak before he died?" Konaugo said darkly. "Any words, any information?"

In the dead grey gaze of Konaugo's eyes, Chriani felt the coldness of the stone floor where he'd wept at Barien's side. He heard the warrior's voice — *Trust him not.* No idea who he'd meant, but Barien had never made much effort to hide his contempt for the captain's angry approach to leadership.

Chriani shook his head. "He asked after the safety of the Princess Lauresa and yourself, my lord prince. Then nothing."

"And when and from where did Barien summon you?" Konaugo asked. His voice was softer this time, Chriani suddenly on edge. He'd never heard Konaugo speak softly before.

He faltered. He didn't know where Barien had been. Had no idea how the mysterious summons had even come to him.

Chriani felt a sudden chill. Konaugo watched him darkly, expectant. Out of uniform.

In the hall of records, the floor had been streaked red-black, signs of a bloody struggle. Handprints clutching the stones. All the garrison around him, all the guards he'd passed as he ran the outwall had worn the uniform of the watch. All of them except the watch captain himself.

Trust him not.

"Because I am troubled," Konaugo continued, "with wondering why, if Barien's concern for the princess was so great, did he simply not stay with her himself? Why not shout to raise the alarm, any regular patrol passing by in time even if he wasn't heard at first?"

"I met him in the barracks corridor," Chriani said. "On the way from our quarters." It was first thing he could think of, trying to keep the fear he felt from his voice. "He must have been on his way to the princess's chambers himself through the warden's door. He ordered me there. I went."

"And Barien went where?"

"I do not know, lord. I saw him return through the barracks, I mean."

"You sound unsure."

"No, lord..."

"When you found him dying in the archives quarter, you said you were making for the great hall from the prince's court. Do you routinely make your way between adjacent wings by way of the opposite side of the Bastion, tyro?"

The stinging seemed to flare suddenly, faint pinpricks of fire across Chriani's shoulders and scalp. "I ran the outwall first, lord. I had no orders, I was looking for an officer but there were none..."

"The notion of finding an officer in the great hall at the service of the prince high escaped you?"

"Having been given no order, I was still under the order of Sergeant Barien, who I presumed would be in barracks or the staging ground..."

"And what were you doing out of quarters when he met you?"

Chriani felt a pressure pushing down on him, tried to focus past the chill of Konaugo's eyes. "I had returned from duty in the armories." Past Konaugo, at the far doorway, a courier rushed in, met by Ashlund. "I had been delivered a message," Chriani said instantly, grasping at that image. "For Barien. I did not find him in quarters, and so was proceeding to search for him."

"A message from who?"

"A merchant." In his mind, a randomly caught memory, the last person he'd seen pass along the courtyard track that day. A bookseller, his pushcart laden with scrolls and folios and bound volumes whose covers had been stamped with Ilvani glyphs. "A courier delivered it, no one I knew. Barien was at the armory earlier but had left. From the tone of the courier, I suspected it might be important."

"What was his mood?" It was Chanist who interrupted Konaugo before he could speak again. "Barien, I mean? When he ordered you to my daughter's protection, what was his mood?"

The prince's expression was dark, Chriani saw. Something like worry there, the bones of age showing suddenly through the strength and skin of leadership, like the ripple of an undercurrent across still water. He knew how long Barien had stood in Chanist's service. Warden to a nation's heir, the trust that had been there.

"His manner spoke of great concern, my lord prince. I had not seen him like this before." That part of it not a lie, at least. "He was afraid, my lord prince."

"And he said nothing to you before his passing?"

Chriani felt Konaugo's gaze boring into him. He slowly shook his head. "No, my lord prince."

Then from behind him, he heard movement at the side doors. The prince's private entrance hall, the northern arm of the prince's court and the residence behind it. Chriani saw something change in Chanist's expression, the shroud of age cast off to reveal the strength again. He knew who approached quickly behind him even before he heard her speak.

"Is it true?" Lauresa called. "Barien?"

Chriani felt Konaugo's hand on his shoulder, moving him back from the princess with as much force as he could get away with. Where she swept in, Lauresa wore a cloak of dark wool held tight at the shoulders, the sweep of a white nightdress visible beneath it. Her hair was down, clothes changed while Ashlund was held at the door, Chriani thought. Her father met her gaze, nodded slowly.

She looked to Konaugo, the captain's dark look softening just slightly. "I am sorry, highness," he murmured.

Chriani almost believed it.

He made a point of inclining his own head only as deep as the captain did, watched Lauresa's gaze flick across his without slowing. She held her father's hands, slipped into his tight embrace, her slight frame dwarfed by him.

"Is the rest of it true?" she said quietly. Her hand strayed to his wounded shoulder, but he held it away, gently. The business of Barien over with a word, Chriani thought. On to more important things.

"True enough," the prince high said. "Though I daresay it will take more than one of them to ever finish me." An edge of attempted humor worked its way into the prince's voice, but he didn't smile. "It is said that Barien may have attempted to come to you tonight. What do you know of that?"

"Nothing, my lord," the princess said. Chriani felt something tighten in his chest. Where it still rested on his shoulder, Konaugo's hand twitched. "Unless it concerned the matter of a message which I had asked to have delivered through him."

"What manner of message?"

"I had asked Barien a week or more ago to seek out a volume of poetry on my behalf. The *Lay of Ysabrylla*, a copy in Movyan's own hand if it could be found. A farewell gift to be sent to my mother in Aldac before my departure." As he watched her, Chriani thought he saw a trace of self-consciousness cross the mask of sadness she wore. "You had said once that it was her favorite," she said.

"And still is, I would expect." The prince managed a smile, but Chriani thought he saw an unfamiliar sadness in Chanist's eyes. An uncertainty there that he'd never seen before.

"Barien did not want me seeking it myself through the collectors' houses. Too many tongues wagging in the city in advance of the wedding as it stands, he said. He thought to not let them also wonder what secret paramour I might be sending such a work to. I had asked for confirmation from the bookseller that it had been received and sent on to my mother's house."

Chriani tried not to stare. There was no chance that she could have heard him speak the desperate fabrication only a moment before, no way she should have been able to summon up a story that tied to his so neatly.

"I have been told that Barien was coming not with a message, but to guard you. Did you see or speak with him this night?"

"No, my lord."

Chanist nodded, asked nothing more.

Chriani remembered the stinging sensation, realized it was gone now. Truth magic. His head was spinning.

As he watched the prince high and his daughter move for the side doors, they were speaking too low for him to hear. Chanist turned once, nodded to him and Konaugo in turn. Lauresa didn't look back.

Whatever had happened was over, and Chriani was aware suddenly of a sense of displacement threading through him. Voices around him, guards in constant motion. More people stood at the other end of the table, he saw, rangers with them this time. A cavalry captain bent low with the garrison commanders, her voice angry as she spoke, discussions threaded by a tension he could feel. Chriani isolated, frozen. Not a part of it.

He should have made rank at least a year before, most tyros making rank as squire and taking the arms of the guard by seventeen if not earlier. It was the anger holding him back, he knew, though Barien had never been direct enough to say so. Now Barien was dead, and Chriani was filled by a sudden void that he hadn't felt for long years.

As the side doors closed behind Chanist, Konaugo's hand on Chriani's shoulder spun him hard. He looked down at the dark eyes, the white scar.

"Take your things from Barien's chamber to the gatehouse barracks. Wait there until you receive further orders from me. Move."

"I would help in this action if you would so order me, lord."

"Barien's killer needs no more help from you." Konaugo's gaze was steel as he turned away, Chriani watching him for a long while. Then he turned, slipped past the guards at the main doors and away.

From when his mother died, Chriani remembered the feeling that was in him now as he ran through the great hall for the central court, not meeting the looks of the guards he passed. A numbness that wasn't numbness, he thought. Not like cold, not like the sweet release of dull pain that follows the sharper pain of a blow. This was the opposite of that, as if he'd been opened up to all sensation at once. Every touch, every sound, every glance, every scent, every memory all pushing in on him, overwhelming his ability to take it in so that he felt none of it in the end.

He could feel his skin separate from him, detached. He let his fingers brush along stone walls, watched them as if they belonged to someone else. As he approached the intersection of the four garrison corridors, he heard bootsteps moving ahead at speed, felt their echo push through him as if he were mist.

Chriani slowed in the intersection, stared. No one was there, the footsteps already fading to the north, running flat out but he hadn't even seen the runner pass. His sight dulled, detached like the rest of him.

The barracks were all but empty as he passed through to Barien's door for the last time, still unlocked from when he'd fled. The lamp was long-cold, Chriani filling it in the spill of light from the corridor. He lit it, quietly closed the door behind him.

Within the room, Barien's presence was already gone. Chriani had hoped even as he'd run there that some trace of the warrior, some feeling of him would linger, even for a while. Something to bid farewell to like he hadn't had a chance to bid farewell to the man himself. So afraid then, he realized. He hadn't tried to speak the sword rites, not that he would have properly remembered them. He knew that Barien probably didn't care, his roots in the northern borderlands always inspiring a discrete distance from the mainstream Brandishear customs that seemed to almost contradict his dedication to the land and the crown.

Chriani sat heavily on his pallet, dragged a battered locker from the corner where it sat. His clothes and effects were already in it, barely covering the bottom. He folded his cloak, set his spare boots in carefully on top of it before he realized that the pair he wore had long since gone significantly thinner across the sole. He swapped them, brushed the grime from the older pair as he packed them alongside a small purse of silver siolans he'd never had the chance to spend. The wooden dagger that had been the first one he practiced with was there, along with a finger guard that Barien had given him but that Chriani had only shot with twice.

The dagger Barien had carved himself, and he'd laughed when he saw Chriani secreting it away even after his tyro's writ had been handed down, allowing him to train with real steel. The finger guard interfered with his feel for the bow, Chriani had realized early on. He needed to feel the draw of the bowstring beneath his fingers to find his accuracy, ignoring the pain there as the calluses slowly built up. His mother's picks he carried with him always. He realized now how little he really cared about the rest of it.

He found a silk scarf as well. Blue-green with darker blue trim, and a ripple of white cross-stitch that marked off a flowing 'L'. Chriani pulled it slowly from where it lay neatly folded in the corner of the chest, fingered it absently. The princess had given it to him on that Elalantar trip five years before, slipping it into his hand as they'd crossed the River Daryan at Recla. She'd slowed to ride beside him along the bridge, whispered conspiratorially that it was custom in her stepmother's land that they were entering now. A lady chose a champion that way, she said.

On the other side, Barien had ridden up as she'd cantered ahead again, the scarf squirreled away within Chriani's vest but his face still flushed with an unfamiliar heat.

"Don't get no ideas," the warrior said. Chriani was only two years older than when he'd heard the words before, but he understood the second time.

In the chamber proper, he looked around, wanted to find something worth the risk of taking. Something to bring a little bit of Barien with him, but all of it was empty now. The boots and uniform, the books of lyric poetry that the warrior would read aloud on particularly dreary nights, the dress sword and the fighting blade, either of which Konaugo would have cheerfully taken back along with Chriani's head if he so much as drew them from the scabbard.

He remembered his mother's gravesite, and the stones they laid there. Taking them from the foundation of the house where they'd lived, his grandfather had built a low cairn that the moonstone capped, the carved crescent set to ward off the spirits of the night. Within the frame of stones, they placed one of her chisels, and a ring that her own mother had given her, and a bracelet that was beautiful in a way that meant it was Ilvani. From his father, Chriani guessed, but he never found out for sure.

When he'd asked his grandfather why they'd done all that, Chriani was told that the spirit of a person touches the place they live, and the things that come to represent that life. When people die, his grandfather had said, their life force passes back into the world — passes back again to the realm of life like the body that contained that life will pass to the earth in time. But the spirits of the dead lose their memory of life, and so those left behind build a place where they can look to hold some of that memory for them. A place for the living and the dead to touch again through the things their lives once touched together.

Even then, Chriani hadn't believed it. He blew out the lamp.

At the door, the locker on his shoulder, he glanced back once, slipped into the light of the corridor.

Then he stopped, turned back slowly. He stared for a long while.

Where the dress sword hung, it had shifted. Except that Chriani hadn't touched it, only glanced to it as he walked once around the chamber. He hadn't noticed the movement then as he did now, hanging in the wash of faint light from behind him at an angle just slightly differently than the angle it had always hung. Barien hadn't worn the blade in over two years, and only rarely before then. He had a great knack for somehow always managing to be on detached duty whenever official events threw the keep into formal dress, most often dukes and high lords from Aerach and Elalantar stopping by to pay respects or beg favors.

Slowly, Chriani slipped back in, set the locker down. He lit the lamp again, shut the door behind him. He paced close to the wardrobe where the scabbard hung.

With no effort, he remembered every other time he'd ever seen it, comparing the memories to where he stared now. And looking around him, he felt a sudden spike of uncertainty as he took in Barien's quarters. Pallet and footlocker, wardrobe and rough shelves, a weapons chest that held a brace of daggers and a crossbow the warrior never used. Something changed, subtle differences. Someone there, going through the room but doing their best to leave no trace of disturbance.

Things he noticed that no one else would. The gifts that parents give.

The door had been unlocked when he came back, the way he'd left it when he burst out. But if any of the garrison guards had come, they would have locked it behind them, all the barracks doors opening to the same key.

He remembered the bootsteps. Someone passing unseen, sound fading down the north garrison corridor where it led away from the barracks wing.

He was out into the corridor at a run, knowing he was far too late to do anything but wonder what he'd missed. His steps were a whisper along the dark silence of the stones, the dining halls empty of the sounds of voice and drink they'd be full of on any other night.

At the intersection of the four garrison corridors, he dropped, gazed intently across well-lit stone. He'd heard boots moving fast, mentally sketching out the distance of the stride that pace represented.

There. Two faint scuff marks, matching where they stood two arms apart. A faint crescent the thickness of his little finger, the toe of a hard-soled boot hitting the stones at a run.

As Chriani crawled to the closest mark, he inhaled carefully, tried to place the faint scent that was there. One finger touched the grey-black imprint, then was carefully tasted. His mother's lessons. The senses work in concert, she used to say, so spread your faith past only sight and sound. The creatures that will track you do so with scent, taste, touch. Don't stifle those gifts in yourself.

Steel, he thought. The faint tang that kissed his fingers when they held a blade against the whetstone or worked the picks. Steel-shod boots, passing at a run. The sound he'd heard, no one there when he passed through.

Chriani pushed along the floor, the trail picked up easily where it turned along the barracks corridor, but he still didn't understand. The boots that had made these marks were a luxury for the front lines of wars the likes of which they hadn't fought in Brandishear for a generation. As he approached the armory corridor again, Barien's chamber at the end of it, he knew which way the marks would turn.

Then behind him, footsteps. It took a moment for Chriani to realize how long he'd been hearing them already, the sound registered faintly but shunted off by the racing of his thoughts.

He got to his feet barely in time, so that he was only walking in the empty corridor instead of crawling along it when they appeared. Three guards in uniform, and Konaugo still out of it as he led them. They rounded the corner away from him, heading for the southeast tower and the armories there, opposite Barien's chamber at the other end of the hall. Chriani tried to fall back to the shadows, but he saw Konaugo glance back. He felt the steel of those eyes again as the captain raised his hand, the others halting without a word.

Slowly, Konaugo approached. "Explain." The voice came low from the barrel chest.

"I am returning to quarters as ordered, lord, then to the gatehouse barracks, again as ordered."

"Barien made it farther on hands and knees with a bloodblade wound at his chest than you've made it in the time since I gave that order."

Chriani felt something twist in his gut, saw Konaugo happily note it. He tried to fight the anger, failed under the weight of the captain's gaze. "I am sorry I have tarried, lord. May I be relieved to carry out this order?"

As Konaugo grabbed the front of his tunic, Chriani felt himself lifted to slam back against cold stone, the captain hefting him with one arm. He had to force himself to breathe.

"Get to your assigned barracks, tyro, for the sake of the memory of Barien that is all that keeps you here right now. If you are seen at liberty again in the Bastion or the keep without my leave, it will be for the very last time."

Konaugo dropped him. Chriani didn't bother with the nodded salute, just turned and ran. Down the barracks corridor, then north to the intersection, footsteps loud against the stones. Then he stopped, turned back to slip in silence along to the intersection of the armory hall again, Konaugo's voice faint to the south. The door to the tower was open, light spilling out, a weapons inventory begun from the sound of it.

Chriani headed north at speed, boots the faintest whisper of leather this time. Back in Barien's chamber, he shut the door quickly behind him, fumbled while he lit the lamp. He dropped to the floor, used the sharpness of the Ilvani senses his father had given him to listen for movement in the corridor, to scan for the traces of the steel bootprint where they filled the room.

He took the chamber apart then, piece by careful piece. He went through Barien's pallet, pulled blanket and tick to the floor and sifted through them. He went through the footlocker, the shelves, the wardrobe. He scrutinized the pristine dress uniforms and the worn grey leather that was the only uniform the warrior ever wore.

In the weapons locker, he found a locked box, lifted it carefully. Low and flat, maybe four hands to a side and one high. It was belted in brass and riveted tight, and Chriani noted the fresh pick marks along the keyhole fitting. Thin lines, untarnished as he turned them to the light.

He opened it easily, left no marks of his own. Inside was a letter in a script he didn't recognize, a ring with the prince's crest on it that any of Barien's fingers would have burst. There was a wooden dagger, a tyro's practice blade, cracked with age. Chriani felt something like a smile work its way up from the tightness in his chest.

At the bottom of the box was Barien's dress insignia. The armband of grey cloth, signature standard of the garrison, never even worn by the look of it.

Protecting the princess was his duty, Barien had told Chriani that first day he'd brought him up from the market court streets. For as long as Chriani was interested in learning at his side, the warrior said, that was the only standard he would ever be measured by. Chriani hadn't believed him at first, no way to connect the rank of a royal warden with the patchwork leggings and the jacket that looked like it had been through at least three previous owners.

"Too many folk get measured by the cut of their cloth over the cut of their spirit," Barien had said as if he could guess at the boy's thoughts. He'd watched Chriani clean himself up, the food long gone. "Too many look to the outside, afraid to look inside because they're afraid of what others would find if they looked in them."

He'd lifted Chriani's hair then, noted the sudden tension in the boy. The long locks were tied back as his mother had showed him, had told him to always wear that way. The style of courtier and ranger alike, a convenient enough disguise. Barien had touched the faint Ilvani point at the tip of Chriani's ear, let the hair fall again.

"You wouldn't be the first half-blood keeping that fact to themselves in the prince's company," he said. "You've got naught to fear from that."

In response, Chriani had slowly pulled his collar down, exposed the mark there that his mother had warned him to show to no one that he wouldn't trust with his life. Not sure why he already felt that trust in this burly warrior, sharing the secret on which his world had been anvil-struck. The mark on which his fate turned now with his mother and grandfather gone, a world around him that his mother had said would hate him for what he was if he wasn't careful.

Barien had stared. Carefully reached out to touch the war-mark of the Valnirata where Chriani's mother had set the tattoo across his left-front shoulder in its tight knot of red and black lines, as dark now as the day they'd been scribed.

The tattoos of the Valnirata clans were impressed beneath the skin with a technique only they knew. Never any fading, no sign of aging in their precise strokes. Chriani's mother had been taught by his father, he knew — no doubt one of the few Ilmari who had ever learned that ancient art. The mark was the one the father he'd never known had carried, and that his mother had told him to wear with pride in his father's name.

For a long while, the young Chriani had watched Barien deep in thought, a chill fear drifting across the warm awareness of food in his belly and the pallet in the corner that he'd hoped would be his.

"Too many judge on the outside," the warrior had said at last. "We'll show them, you and I."

Chriani crumpled to the floor now, staring at the room pulled apart around him. No idea who had been there, no idea what they'd been looking for. No idea whether they'd already found it or not, slipping past him in plain sight in an open corridor because he was too wrapped up in himself to see.

In his hand, he clutched the insignia tight, the falcon of Brandis stitched there in the gold thread of an officer of the prince's guard. Squires and rank-and-file guards wore bronze or silver stitching where they made up the bulk of the Bastion troops and the soldiers of the keep. Those who answered directly to Chanist and gave orders in his name wore the gold that he did. A thing that most would spend their lives trying to attain but never get. Barien had it, then kept it locked in a box because he believed in more important things.

We look to hold some of that memory for them, his grandfather had said, and Chriani wanted desperately to believe it now.

He clutched the insignia tight in his hand, bid farewell to it and the wooden dagger and the memory of Barien's hand on his wrist that first day, because those were the only things left.

— CHAPTER 4 —

THE NARNETH MÓIR

THEY WOULD HOLD THE FUNERAL at daymark as was the custom, the winter sun high and the silence of the keep punctuated by clear voices as the warrior's rites were sung. The body of Barien would be accorded honor in the name of the spirit it had held once, but that spirit had already slipped back within the earth.

Even before he'd finally made his way to the gatehouse barracks, Chriani knew that he wasn't going to sleep that night. He'd left Barien's chamber finally, didn't know how long he'd stayed there before he stuffed the lockbox he'd found into his own locker with the faintly dark hope that Konaugo would come looking for it.

He'd dumped all his gear unceremoniously on the first empty bunk he'd found, a dozen garrison guards in the common room sitting down to the end of a grueling night. He heard one of them mutter an oath to Barien, others drinking to the warrior's name. Chriani felt more than one of them glance to him, but he was already gone, setting off without a word to the lieutenant or the sergeants there. It wouldn't go reported, he knew. Not today.

Until well past dawn, he'd walked the walls aimlessly above the night-quiet streets of the keep, letting himself drift, doing his best not to think. However, even as hard as he tried not to, Chriani couldn't evade the sharp echo of words in his head — Captain Konaugo, Prince High Chanist both fighting to rise where he'd been pressing their voices down beneath the mud of his thoughts.

A bloodblade wound at his chest. Konaugo had seen Chriani's reaction. He might have even thought he'd known what that reaction meant.

The narneth móir, Chriani thought, the name pulled up from the distant memory of childhood stories. The bloodblade — the honor weapon of the Valnirata Ilvani who had sued for peace beneath Chanist's banner and never forgiven him.

It will take more than one of them to ever finish me…

Since he'd heard those words in the throne room, Chriani had felt an ache threading through him sharper than the knife-edge pain of Barien's loss. Sharper than the sting along the Valnirata war-mark where it touched his chest, the name of the princess still burning there.

When his mother had made that mark, she must have known what it would come to mean. Must have understood the way that fortune and the future were destined to turn. In the years of her own youth, the Valnirata had been a distant memory in Brandishear and across the Ilmar. The war-clans were legends from another time, an air of the exotic to them.

Then the Incursions had come. Chriani's father had left to fight and die against the inevitability of his being captured and killed as an enemy of the crown. Prince Goffree had been butchered alive, or so they said, his eldest heirs struck down by assassins placed within the ranks of their own attendants to leave Chanist with a nation to rule, alone. Now, the Valnirata who wore the mark Chriani did hated Chanist with a passion as strong as his reputation, the foundation on which the war-clans had been crushed and the Ilmar peace constructed.

Attempt on the prince's life.

The unseasonable warmth of the sun overhead carried a stifling closeness with it, the breeze off the harbor checked. Chriani felt a sense of stillness, uncomfortable somehow. A sense of overbearing order in the gentle sweep of the streets, the play of light and shadow across the stones. The same order seen in the movements of the keep's residents, soldiers and courtiers, merchant lords and guildmasters already filing slowly toward the courtyard ahead. At the main gate, the soldiers of the garrison were lined up six deep to either side of the single file of figures slipping in from the city. He could see Konaugo there, the keep in lockdown like it almost never was. No one coming in or out without running the gauntlet of the prince's guard.

Chriani stayed on the wall, slipping past the gatehouse as he made his way slowly along the western flank of the keep. On the staging grounds, they would burn Barien as was also the custom, like any of the half-dozen state funerals he'd watched in the ten years he'd been there. Members of the prince's guard brought down on patrol, mostly, their bodies brought back for the burning that was their right by rank. Aldis Hammeran had been the last, who was captain of the Bastion guard before Konaugo and who had finally been felled a year before by the stopping of the blood, after surviving forty years of campaigns and sorties at the prince's side.

It was said that the same life-magic that healed through the hands of the animyst casters could raise the dead. Chriani had heard the stories as often as anyone, not believing them until Barien told him once that he'd seen Hammeran himself brought back that way.

"Sotting children's story," Chriani had laughed.

"He took a Valnirata spear to the chest that was meant for Chanist in an ambush against him and the first princess high," Barien said quietly. "Last year of the Incursions. Broke his spine like kindling and pinned him to the ground. I was closest to him. I checked his blood myself, stone still."

Chriani's laughter had faded. He'd recognized the thoughtfulness in the warrior's eyes, and the long silence that followed before he spoke again. It was the province of high-ranking captains, Barien said. Merchant nobles and landed lords who returned miraculously from the dead. Deep magic, it was, and those casting it gave up some of their own life for those whose lives they restored.

"Who would do that?" Chriani asked.

"Heroes," Barien had said. "Martyrs. You want my advice, don't aspire to be neither."

On the west wall, Chriani slipped through shadow, gazed down to the tops of the fruit trees below, Barien's ashes bound there. To be scattered in the prince's orchards, as good an end as any who served the crown could expect. Far better than whatever end was likely waiting for him, Chriani thought.

In the courtyard ahead, the crowd waited. A funeral with honors, the prince high himself presiding. A thing that so many dreamed of. In his sleeve, Chriani felt Barien's insignia tucked up tight. Another thing that so many dreamed of, but Barien hadn't cared.

Below, he dimly registered Kathlan in the distant throng along the courtyard track. One face in five hundred, but she drew his eye in like a target point. He knew she would have been looking for him from the moment she got the news, knew that he should have gone to her. Too late now for any difference that would have made, he thought.

Too late now for too many things.

Outside the walls, the daytime city was quiet in a way it never was. As if it was waiting, he thought. In the market court that spread around the northwest side of the keep, there were as many of the garrison patrolling as there were merchants set up. In the weapons markets, he could see the banners of the Ilvani wains, could see the city guard patrolling conspicuously tight around them.

At the Bastion, he saw the Princess High Gwannyn and Lauresa's younger half-siblings pass through the open gates. Lauresa was behind them, walking with her father. Once Lauresa was bound for Aerach, mother and children were to have headed north, Barien set to accompany them to the princess high's residence at Tarenic Castle on the Clearwater, close to the borders of Elalantar and her kin there. As the ceremony started, she stayed at the prince's side, their hands touching in an emotionless public display.

As Chriani listened, the rites were a blur. More than once, he had to catch himself, pull himself back from a darkness that was taking root in him, seemingly growing as it fed on the empty echo of the ceremony as Chanist spoke it.

It will take more than one of them.

When Chanist had spoken it, Chriani had heard the familiar note of power in the voice, and a sense of reassurance that he knew was meant for Lauresa. But something else had lurked behind the words last night. An anger, concealed with a degree of skill that Chriani was one of the few who would have seen. *One of them...* The phrase spoken by the prince high with a contempt Chriani could feel in the remembering.

Outside the keep, along the perimeter road that flanked the wall, he saw a group of children pass. They were singing, a kind of energy to their voices and their running that seemed to have been drained from the adults around them. As they came closer, he heard the words.

Prince Goffree fought, that good old man
Ilvani from him flying
Till traitor's heart and bloody blade
Left Brandis' greatson dying
I saw his pyre before the gate
All Brandishear were mourning
I'll watch his shade lead armies east
The Valnirata burning

In every way that was important, the Ilmari and the Ilvani were one folk once, his mother had told him, so long ago now that he couldn't remember the first or last time she'd said it. One blood from long ago, separated out over time but now brought back together again. The number of mixed race half-bloods said so, as sure as an Elalantar warmblood destrier bred to an Aloidien mountain horse made a mount as strong and fast as either.

The river flows strongest that comes from two sources, she'd often said, but even along the frontier of Cresthan province where he'd been born and raised, the half-bloods that he'd known and who had warmed to him as one of them kept to themselves. They were wanderers, mostly, or they lived among the Ilvani and left that Ilmari half of their history behind.

In the market court, he could see an Ilvani merchant with the stars of the Aodarba enclave on his banner. He was arguing with an order from an irate sentry, angry movements and an energy of confrontation rising as Chriani watched, anxious for the distraction suddenly. An edge of hostility was at work in the city guard, an antagonism toward the Ilvani that he hadn't seen before. Not openly, at any rate. He saw more figures assembling on either side of the fray, two sentries managing to disengage the sergeant whose order had started the confrontation. Harsh voices echoed across the market, spilling across the walls into the silence of the funeral procession.

Without warning, one of the Ilvani turned to see Chriani watching, a kind of coldly questioning look in him that Chriani quickly turned away from. On the staging ground before him, he saw that Lauresa was gone, hadn't noticed her leave.

He hadn't seen her ascend the wall and step in to his left until he heard her voice raised in the singing of the rites.

Around her was the customary space, the two guards who'd accompanied her flanking at five paces away. The same space opened up in the crowd where she and her younger siblings had come to the wall to watch the end of the ceremony below. Her voice was crystal-pure, a faint ripple of sunlight turned to sound.

Chriani felt the familiar burning at his chest that made him look away. Standing in proximity to Lauresa and the other heirs, he realized belatedly the roughness of his own appearance. He was in the uniform of the night before, hadn't washed. His beard was in desperate need of trimming, a thing he typically put off until Barien or one of the other sergeants reminded him of the uniform code.

Where his glance strayed, a ring lay on the low riser to his right. A plain steel band that hadn't been there before, he was certain of it.

He looked to Lauresa from the corner of his eye, saw no sign that she even knew he was there. She and the ring both five paces away. But as her hand strayed at her side, he could see a steel band on her finger that matched the one before him.

He let his awareness slip out to the crowd around him, their focus on the royal heirs and on Lauresa's voice as it soared above the others around it. Chriani waited for the moment, shifted almost imperceptibly to sweep the ring up with the slightest trace of one hand, no one seeing.

Across from him, Lauresa's song trailed off with the others, silence from below now as Barien's sword and uniform were laid alongside him. Then Chanist stepped forward with the burning brand and sang alone, all the power of command in his voice turned to sorrow, it seemed.

Slowly, following an instinct he couldn't have named, Chriani slipped the ring to his finger.

Do not be alarmed.

In his head, Lauresa's voice filled him like a whisper in a close room. Her voice and not her voice, there and not there all at once. He felt a spike of cold fear, felt the echo of Barien's voice in his mind the night before as he made the moonsign, involuntary. Hand in motion before he could stop it, then realizing that all around him, others were making it as well. No one noticing him as they warded themselves against the darkness of death where Barien lay.

None around can hear the words that pass between us, Lauresa said. *You wanted answers.* Above them, the black smoke of Chanist's torch rose straight, no wind to twist it.

What sorcery is this? He tried to force the fear from his mind, not wanting it to carry across whatever link twisted its way between the princess and him.

This is the sorcery of court, Chriani. The ring you wear is dweomered and chained to this one I wear. Within the Bastion, my father and mother, my brother and sisters have access to such things. One of the privileges of rank.

The pendant, Chriani thought. He remembered the storm-scent of the energy that had pulsed in Lauresa's palm, felt an uncomfortable tightening in his groin that he tried to ignore.

The pendant, she echoed. He started, hadn't meant for her to hear him, but she had. *I am sorry for that. I was afraid, but fear is a sorry reward for the loyalty you showed me.*

It all fell into place. The shadow that had hidden them, the slow fall that had saved them. Then pushing through that memory was the memory of the endless kiss they'd shared. Chriani squeezed his eyes shut, the memory hammering at him even as he pushed it away.

You saved us last night. He shaped the words clearly, tried to focus. If she felt the other thoughts as he desperately tried to focus past them, she didn't show it.

The sorcery of the pendant saved us. It is a tool like any other. Do not fear it.

I do not fear.

You lie badly, tyro.

As his eyes opened, Chriani forced himself to stare straight ahead. He felt a faint surge of anger, familiar.

Your story to Captain Konaugo last night might have cost you your life for all the ease he would have had disproving it.

I had not intended to have to lie to Konaugo on your behalf. Chriani felt the anger kindle to something sharper, welcomed it.

I am educating you, not berating you, the princess said. *A well-told lie must be a thing that the listener wants to believe. Had you told Konaugo that you were suspicious of Barien, you could have admitted that the order to guard me came while you diced with my father's stolen crown in a Valnirata brothel. He would not have cared.*

Barien barely dead and I should have betrayed his memory to save your secrecy?

There is much more at stake here than my secrets, the princess said evenly. *When greater things are at stake, a moment's betrayal is easily forgiven, even by the dead.*

Chriani felt his heart hammering in his chest, felt a shadow twist through him. On the staging ground below them, Chanist stood alone before the flames, singing one last time. The closing lines of a lament older than Brandishear itself.

You promised an explanation, Chriani said. He saw the prince's eyes squeeze shut.

As Chanist touched the brand to the pyre, a sheet of flame erupted, fountaining out from oil-soaked wood. As much as he wanted to, Chriani couldn't look away. The tang of woodsmoke was sharp in his nose and eyes, his mind dark with a bitterness he could taste as Barien's body burned under the brilliant Clearwater sky.

I promised answers, Lauresa said. *They're not the same.*

As the prince high stepped slowly back, Chriani sensed the undercurrent of emotion in him, seeing it only because he'd seen it the night before. A sudden weariness that revealed the age beneath Chanist's straight-backed strength.

When Lauresa's voice came to him again, it carried an uncertainty that caught him off guard.

I am sorry I did not recognize you at once last night, tyro. But where you found me puts my life and future in your hands. For all my bluster then, you were right. No power or position obliges you to lie for me.

Chriani offered nothing back. Three years since she'd last spoken to him, but it felt longer now. From the platform, Chanist descended slowly. Around him was a slow shift of movement, like the ripple-spread of erratic raindrops. Through the crowd, one by one, they made the moonsign. The night-time warding, out of place somehow under the clear light of the sun.

The room you found me in was my father's war room, Lauresa said. *A place of private council and intelligence. Maps, histories, journals. Since the announcement of my marriage, I have sought and sometimes found there the unfiltered history of Allenis Andreg, Duke of Teillai and my husband-to-be. At court, knowledge is a weapon. When I arrive in Teillai, I intend to be well armed.*

As the name echoed in his mind, Chriani felt the burning at his chest again. He tried to focus past it, kept it at a level below words. *That explains your presence there but not our exit.*

For me to have been found by the Bastion guard in the prince high's war room would have created scandal. The military secrets of Brandishear are locked in my father's mind, not in any written record. But before this morning, word would have reached the markets and the taverns of my attempt to steal those secrets in order to secure my place in Andreg's court and Prince Vishod of Aerach's beyond it.

Chriani saw shadows twist within the fire, the suggestion of movement wrapping the blur of Barien's body as it was consumed. He thought he felt a great weight pulling on him, dragging him down into the heat that touched chill skin even from the distance of the courtyard below.

You offered to protect me last night, Lauresa said. *I would take that offer, freely given.*

It is, he said. No hesitation.

As the pyre collapsed in on itself, he made the moonsign again. Around them, the wall was emptying.

"You were Barien's tyro, were you not?"

It was the imperious tone more than the absurdity of the question that reminded Chriani that the princess was speaking aloud for the first time. She'd turned to face him, watched him with a look suggesting she might not have noticed she'd been standing almost beside him the whole time. The same tone of distant command from the night before, slipped into far too easily, he thought.

Yes, it is. The tone in his head was gentler. *Regardless, when you are spoken to by a member of the first family, a response is generally in order.*

Chriani cleared his mind again. "I am, highness. I was…" His voice caught on the words.

"I would have you escort me back to the Bastion."

"Yes, highness." As Chriani nodded, he saw the guards who'd escorted her up from the staging ground fall back. He ignored their looks as Lauresa turned and he fell into step beside and behind her. Following at the customary five paces as she made for the stone steps to the courtyard.

Along the ranks of private apartments that ringed the inner wall, Chriani saw more eyes on him than he would have thought possible. He felt the keep shifting back into the pace of its regular life, garrison and artisans, couriers and traders slipping quickly into the routine of high-end commerce that worked within its walls. At every intersection, he saw someone's gaze drawn to the princess, then just as steadily drawn past her to settle on him where he walked behind.

They're watching, Lauresa said through the silent link the rings made. *When they see and hear nothing, they'll conclude that this is what it appears to be. Barien was my warden. I showed a moment of compassion to his apprentice.*

And what is the point of that? Chriani asked.

Actions at court are placed under a scrutiny the likes of which you cannot imagine, she said. *If I had so much as glanced at you when I made my entrance, that fact would already have made the rounds of the keep and the markets. Living at court, one must develop more and more ingenious means of keeping plans, actions, words secret.*

How could anyone hear us?

By the same manner in which I heard you speak to my father from outside the throne room last night.

Chriani blinked. Lauresa touched the pendant at her throat, adjusted it slightly.

From the pieces you provided, I assembled something that my father wanted to hear, she said. *That book was a favorite of my mother's. A memory of a happier time for him.*

With the words, Chriani felt a sudden hint of longing — emotion and sensation he could feel through whatever link the ring made between them.

I heard Barien's voice, he thought. A connection there to the inexplicable sensation of the princess's thoughts in his head that he suddenly longed to make sense of. *When I told your father I was called to protect you, it was the truth. But it was Barien's voice in my thoughts, like yours.*

Barien had his own access to devices such as I have. He was my mother's warden originally. When she left my father's court and Barien stayed to watch over me, my mother left him more of such trinkets than I think my father knew.

Where the central court opened up to the archives quarter to the west, Lauresa slowed, Chriani matching her pace.

"I have an errand," she said as she turned back. "Accompany me."

Chriani glanced to the dim emptiness of the hall of records, a faint chill threading him suddenly. "Yes, highness," he said. He hid his uncertainty as a courier hustled past, nodding to the princess as she turned, Chriani five steps behind her.

From across Brandishear and even farther afield, students, researchers, and the occasional sage came frequently to Rheran to partake of the wealth of the knowledge Chanist's court collected. Even so, the archives quarter was rarely the busiest part of the Bastion, and less so today with the keep locked down. Along the hall of records, Chriani passed the same rows of locked doors he'd passed the night before, caught the gleam of evenlamps from the stones of the floor. Scrubbed clean, then scrubbed again most likely. No trace left of what they'd witnessed the night before except the memory he carried with him now.

At the intersection where he'd first seen Barien's body, Lauresa slowed.

Are we alone? she asked.

Chriani glanced down all four corridors, the libraries to the west, galleries north and south. No sound in the stillness surrounding them.

I believe so.

She nodded. *Show me where you found him.*

Why? Chriani's own voice in his head carried an edge it shouldn't have had.

Because whoever killed him did so in an attempt to murder my father. As Lauresa turned back, her words were just as sharp in his mind. *Because Barien was my warden and my mother's warden before that, and was no less dear to me than he was to you, and I would see the place where he fell.*

Chriani stepped past her, led her on. At the midpoint of the corridor, opposite the silent busts of Lauresa's own line, he stopped. He made the moonsign quickly, noted the look she gave him.

When you found him, she said, *what did he say?*

He said nothing, Chriani thought evenly. *You heard me tell your father and Konaugo.*

I heard what you told them, yes. I also felt the lie in your words then, as I do now.

"This errand is done, princess." Even at a whisper, his voice was a harsh echo against the stones, swallowed by his footsteps as he stalked away.

Konaugo knows it, too, she said simply. Her voice carried the same even tone in his head, unsettling somehow when she should have had to call to him from along the corridor. *Barien taught you stealth? Insight, instinct?*

My mother taught me, Chriani said sharply.

Then use those gifts. Barien was attacked within sight of the central court. He should have moved for the great hall, or the garrison quarter at least.

He was chasing whoever it was…

He was mortally wounded, tyro. Whoever had attacked him was gone or they would have finished the job.

Chriani stopped. He stared down the length of the corridor he'd followed the night before, looked south to where Lauresa stood.

He was forty strides from being able to raise the alarm, but instead, he turned east and south and died alone. Why?

Faint footsteps along the central court in the distance pushed Chriani to one side, watching as another courier ran past. He felt a trace of anger, felt Lauresa's question resonate. So obvious a point that his missing it spoke to his state of mind the night before. All the blind anger that had driven him. All the fear.

He walked back to where the princess stood, crouched beside her. Faint traces of red-black still clung to the mortar of the stones, he saw. Maybe scrubbed just once after all.

What did Barien say to you?

But even as he heard her words, Chriani's gaze slid along the stones of the floor. Something there. Faintly scratched, the outline of a dagger or knife.

"Seek the blade…"

Chriani spoke aloud as he slipped to hands and knees, ignored the look Lauresa gave him as he searched both alcoves and the corridor to north and south. He felt the instincts take over, felt his senses somehow separate from himself, spilling out into the space around him.

Along the corridor, he saw the telltale signs of others having searched, before and after the body was taken away, most likely. Konaugo and Chanist would have asked the same question Lauresa did, would have spent most of the night seeking an answer to it. But the dagger-mark was faint, barely distinguishable from the faint cracks of wear and age that veined the dark marble of the floor.

Follow by fourteen. Keep it safe… To the questioning look Lauresa gave the thought, Chriani only raised a hand to silence, following the corridor north, the direction the dagger pointed.

Fourteen paces? Not likely that Barien would have been able to make a full stride in the condition he was in. He counted fourteen flagstones instead, dropped low to the floor, the princess following. With no dagger or blade on him, he felt for the picks, took the largest out, then ran it around each stone in turn across the breadth of the passage until he found the one that shifted, just slightly.

The instincts his mother had given him. Barien had sharpened them. He let his senses fill him, tried not to think.

Beneath the stone was black sand, packed hard above the foundations below. With the picks, Chriani dug through it silently. Just as silently, he pulled up a knotted strip of blood-soaked cloth that wrapped a sheathed dagger, Ilvani glyphs across the leather.

Even as he began to work the knot free, he felt Lauresa's hand on his shoulder as she dropped to kneel beside him. *Replace the stone first,* she said. *Leave no trace.* Chriani did so, listened again when he was done to be certain that they were still alone.

In an alcove, he knelt to slip the knot easily, unfolding the strip of cloth to reveal the image stitched on its underside. The insignia of the prince's guard in gold, the same embroidery that he'd pulled from Barien's lockbox the night before. This one torn roughly along the seam that joined it, stained red-black. Chriani could only stare.

The dagger he'd never seen before, but he knew it all the same.

It was an Ilvani design, darkly malevolent where his shaking hand held it to the light. The haft was steel and bone, thin so as to lock tight to the hand that could hold it in any grip. It was set with cap and clasp of what looked like mottled silver, the same style as the narrow single guard that flared to a pair of razor-curved spikes. The twist of the blade, the perfect balance, spoke to speed and deadly fury. A scalloped blood-edge crowned its base, shaped and honed to do as much damage being pulled free as it would deal on the initial strike.

Chriani noted the double edge of the dagger etched with an intricate pattern of fine flowing scar lines. A legend engraved in an Ilvani script, unreadable to his eye. One of the older tongues of the Greatwood. Over that legend, the dull stain of dried blood clung to the well-worn steel of the blade — but in a specific and stylized pattern. The steel was acid-etched in twisted lines, creating a flattened groove whose rough surface would bind and color the blade with the blood of those it slew.

The glyph that Barien's blood made was one that Chriani had known since the day he was born.

It will take more than one of them…

The Valnirata hated Chanist. *Ilvalachna* they called him and his father alike. The Ilvani Scourge. Stories were told in the Greatwood that the rangers and the border guard would repeat in mocking tones, of how the Ilmar alliances had always been little more than gauze shrouding Brandishear's great lust for domination. Chanist plotting secretly as his father before him had plotted, seeking to one day crush all the Ilmar and the Valnirata alike beneath his foul hand.

Chriani felt a sudden chill. From a dark corner of his mind, he saw the torn edge of the wound that laid Barien down, felt the burning again where Lauresa's name was marked off on his skin. An extension of the mark his mother had made there, told him to never show but to never feel shame for. The same Valnirata war-clan mark that adorned the blue-grey steel of the blade.

When he looked to Lauresa suddenly, conscious that she had stepped away from where she'd been standing close beside him, he saw a trace of cold anger in her eyes. Looking not at the blade, but at him as he held it, stared at it with a recognition he cursed himself silently for not being smart enough to hide.

He felt the ring on his finger, forced himself to clear his thoughts again. He offered up a wordless oath on Barien's soul in the hope that she couldn't feel what was in him now.

From the hall ahead came footsteps, rising quickly. A steady guard's pace, boots loud on the stones. As he rose, he felt Lauresa's hand find his, the ring pulled from his finger. The dagger and the insignia she left with him.

"Keep it safe," she whispered, her voice as cold as her look had been. "Wait for my word. If anyone asks, you accompanied me as I attempted to obtain a selection of journals but found the archives unexpectedly closed." She was already heading up the corridor, walking slowly as she motioned for Chriani to fall in behind her.

He had only managed to slip the dagger and the insignia within his shirt when she slowed at the corner, Ashlund and two garrison guards there to greet her. Her presence requested by the prince, their message and her response a blur in Chriani's mind.

Against his chest, he felt the cold steel of the blade. He caught a withering look as Lauresa glanced back to him. "You are dismissed, tyro. We grieve with you for Barien's loss."

"Highness." Chriani nodded, caught Ashlund's dark look as he and the others escorted Lauresa away. He followed them to the central court, watched them make for the great hall and the throne room beyond as he headed for the gates.

On the walls, he walked a while longer, not remembering any details of the routes he paced or the people he passed until Vanad, the younger tyro he'd seen the previous night, came looking for him.

"Message from Konaugo," she said. "You're to the armories."

Chriani only nodded, then took his time making his way to the Bastion barracks. Through the gate to central court, a half-dozen guards were on duty where there'd been two the morning before. They returned his salute as he passed, Chriani's footsteps echoing where shadowed arches climbed into the bright light of the lamps above. The same view he'd seen through untold days, but it felt different now. An outsider's perspective. Feeling the cold in the stone as he hadn't felt it since that first day he'd been dragged here on Barien's orders. Then, he'd feared that when the gates pounded shut for the night, he'd be trapped inside them. Now, he knew that when they shut, he'd be outside.

The garrison halls were alive with movement, couriers passing in both directions alongside a steady stream of the prince's guard emerging from the armory corridors, armor and weapons bundled and slung between them as they walked two by two. He asked after Konaugo, a terse nod directing him to the southeast tower.

The armory was a great deal emptier than it had been the night before. Something happening. As Konaugo checked the edges on a brace of longswords, the ranger at his side nudged him, the captain looking up to see Chriani in the doorway.

"The prince's company rides tonight. Get two score shields and spears to the stables. Bundle three hundred broadhead shafts in quivers of twelve, as many of the officers' arrows in equal number. Be quicker about it than you were in getting here."

"Yes, lord."

Konaugo returned Chriani's salute with a detached air, but whether he'd forgotten his anger of the night before or simply had more important things on his mind, Chriani didn't know or care.

The Bastion armory had always seemed an anachronism, a legacy of a much older, much more troubled time. The larger armories of the city outfitted garrison, constabulary, and the rangers who patrolled the far southern borderlands and the Locanwater steppes along the Greatwood's edge. The Bastion armory was the prince's own, though, and as well-tested as his guard was, the long years of Chanist's peace meant that the spears he pulled from their tall black racks had rarely seen handling beyond the time it took to edge and oil them.

The air was thick with dust as Chriani worked, and over the time it took him to bundle and pack spears and shields from the armory, out of the Bastion, and across the keep to the stable gates, his lungs and eyes were heavy with it. He checked and counted out the arrows, cut himself once on a razor-sharp head. The best archers of the prince's guard cut and fletched their own shafts, a tradition that extended back to the Incursions. Each with some color, some pattern, some marking of runes along the wood that would identify them. In the time of Chanist's father, they had ranked their count of the dead that way, it was said.

Konaugo's own arrows had his K scribed on the blades, charcoal-blackened shafts and crow-feather fletching. For shooting in darkness, Chriani suspected. Invisible as they cut you down. He checked the spin and the balance as his mother had taught him, noted with annoyance that Konaugo seemed to know what he was doing.

Chriani had given up wondering by his third trip whether the captain had enlisted any other tyros to assist him, not bothering to count the subsequent trips that he spent in wondering what had happened to inspire all the sudden activity. An attack on the prince high certainly accounted for the stronger defensive presence in the keep and the Bastion itself. But in the stable, there was Chanist's own stallion being shod by Kathlan while Ashlund checked over its saddle and tack. Outside the gates, Chriani counted forty horses to match the number of quivers he unlashed the last of, watching one of Ashlund's party from the night before distribute them.

At the sight of Kathlan, Chriani faded back, a sudden reflex. From the doorway, he watched her, tried to still the pain that flared suddenly in his chest and his gut.

He drifted carefully into the shadows then, slipped behind him to the still air of the leatherworks. As anxious as he was to not let it be known he was available for further orders, he was more anxious to listen to the snatches of conversation he could overhear through the gapped wall to the stable proper. He'd had his ear to the wall for a short while, catching Ashlund mutter something about the height of the prince's stirrups and Kathlan respond indelicately that he engage in an action as disturbing as it was physically impossible.

He heard a louder voice from behind him.

"Have you lost something, tyro?"

Chriani wheeled, back flat to the boards. Across from him, the Prince High Chanist was watching from the shadows.

"Forgive me, my lord prince. I did not see you."

"Clearly," Chanist said. He was standing at a low table, carefully working an awl into what Chriani recognized was the prince high's own armor. The breastplate had the stallion and the falcon side by side in gold leaf, laid out before Chanist as he adjusted its leather fittings. "I wear this infrequently enough that either it or my shoulders seem to forget each other when they meet again. We ride tonight, as you have no doubt been told."

"Yes, my lord prince." Chriani was carefully judging the distance to the door, trying desperately to think of what excuse he'd use to try to get through it.

"Help me on with this."

As the prince hefted the breastplate, Chriani nodded, fumbling his way through dust and shadow to stand awkwardly behind him.

"Unless your arms are longer than they look, you may approach."

Chriani closed inside the customary five steps, helped Chanist lift the breastplate and settle it across his shoulders.

"What have they told you thus far, tyro? Of the events of last night?"

Chriani tried to swallow the sudden tightness in his throat. "Nothing, my lord prince."

"And what have you deduced all the same?" The blue eyes flicked back to meet his. Chanist smiled. "I ask you not to trap you, tyro. But I know how keen Barien claimed your powers of observation to be. If you tell me what you know, I can safely assume that most in the Bastion have so far deduced much less. Secrecy is of the essence for us in our action tonight. I would like an honest assessment of how much of it we have."

As he watched Chanist carefully adjust cinches and straps, Chriani considered carefully. "I know more than I should, my lord prince, and less than I would. Barien was attacked in the central court. You were attacked in the throne room before then. Whether Barien was pursuing your attacker or caught by surprise, only he can say but I know what I would believe."

"As do I." Chanist took a step away, turned at the waist so that the interlocking plates of his armor shifted and set. Chriani felt a distance in the prince suddenly, felt the weight of things going on around him as he had in the throne room that night.

"I would know the full matter of Barien's death, my lord prince."

Chriani hadn't known he was going to say it until the words were out. No idea where the will to speak them had even come from.

Chanist turned back slowly. He swung his arm through a full range of motion, adjusted something beneath his shoulder plate as he appraised Chriani. But instead of the expected anger, he saw an unaccustomed uncertainty to the prince's look as he spoke.

"To what end, master Chriani?"

"Because I have nothing else, my lord prince."

As Chanist took his bracers from the bench, he slowly pulled them on. Too late, Chriani recognized that in the prince high's using his name, there had been a subtle message sent. An invitation to choose his words equally carefully, but Chriani's thoughts were racing, too far gone for that.

Chanist was silent for a long moment before he spoke.

"Last night, Barien was waiting for me when I returned from riding late," the prince high said. "He asked for a private word. I dismissed my escort and we adjourned to my chambers, where Barien told me of intelligence of a possible assassination attempt within the court. He knew nothing more than that. I told him to find Captain Konaugo, we would meet immediately."

Chriani felt a chill thread through him. A tremor traced his hand suddenly. He squeezed it tight.

"But as I entered the throne room, I was attacked. I prevailed. The attacker apparently found his way to the war room, escaping from there with sorcery. Whatever he sought there, I doubt he had time to find it."

Chriani tried not to focus on the essential falsehood that wrapped the prince's words. Impassive as he sifted out the new truth from the truth he'd known before, then sifted again.

"Between the time the intruder escaped the throne room and gained access to the war room, he attacked Barien in the hall of records. Brandis's blood be given again, I would that he had gone straight to the tower and taken all he found there but let Barien live."

He could see Chanist watching him, tried to avoid his gaze but couldn't. A kind of power in the blue eyes that went beyond mere rank. He felt the dagger within his shirt, heard the echo of Barien's warnings, but he and the prince were alone now in a way that should never have happened and would likely never happen again.

"My lord prince, I have…"

Even then, Chriani saw movement at the doorway. He was already five steps from the prince again, backing up from some unknown instinct just as the familiar bulk of Konaugo pressed through, four others behind him.

"My lord prince," Konaugo began before the dark eyes caught Chriani in the shadows.

"A moment, please, captain." To Chriani, he nodded to continue.

Chriani felt the chill of metal at his stomach, Konaugo's gaze just as cold. *Trust him not.*

He hadn't dared reach for the dagger in the prince's presence. He was thankful for that now.

"You have what, master Chriani?"

"I have knowledge of the assassin's origins, my lord prince."

Outside, he could hear horses on the gravel of the gatehouse path, the troop saddling up. Presumably what Konaugo had come to announce.

Chanist's expression was unreadable. "Explain yourself."

"Captain Konaugo spoke to me in the barracks afterward of Barien being killed by a bloodblade," Chriani said evenly. The look that flashed from Chanist to the captain had the steely strength of a backhand blow behind it. Konaugo paled for what Chriani thought was probably the very first time. "If this is true, then one must believe that the Valnirata war-clans are behind this attempt on your life, my lord prince."

Chanist was silent a moment. "You are as astute as Barien often boasted," he said finally. In the prince's voice, Chriani heard an unfamiliar edge. A degree of respect he'd never heard before.

"My lord prince…" Konaugo began, but Chanist cut him off with a wave.

"Ignoring the fact that it was your word that would have sent the tyro to Five Hog's House tonight to swap what he knows for the thousand rumors already there, all Rheran will know where we've gone by this time tomorrow."

To Chriani, the prince high nodded. "He was Ilvani, marked of the Valnirata. He carried one of their daggers, the bloodblades. The narneth móir, they call them. An assassin's weapon the like of those driven into my brother's and sister's backs, and which cut the heart from my father before he was staked out for the crows."

Chriani was conscious of his own breathing, the silence around them absolute.

"That was the blade that slew Barien," Chanist said, and the hard anger in the prince high's voice made Chriani look away. From the corner of his eye, he saw Konaugo and both his riders do the same.

Against the prince's anger, Chriani suddenly felt his own anger fall away, and in the space it left within him, he felt the single thought rise that had churned in him for nearly a day now. The thing he'd told the prince the night before. The thing that twisted beneath the fear and the loss that battered at his instincts and his senses like the winter-driven sea.

"My daughter spoke of you at length last night," Chanist said carefully. Chriani felt himself flush, hoped the dust-streaked shadows of the stables would conceal it. "She said you stayed at her side through the alarm, waiting there to be relieved. That you didn't even open the door to see what disaster had fallen beyond."

"Yes, my lord prince."

At the High Summer celebrations two years past, he'd seen Barien not back down from the challenge of four members of an Aerach escort, their choice of weapons. Not a fight to the death, to be sure, but their blades had been as sharp as his as he'd deftly disarmed them one by one, then carved the falcon of Brandis into their captain's leather, stroke by stroke to the jeers of the festival crowd.

"An alarm raised in the Bastion," Chanist said, "and your only thought was to stay behind a locked door. I am curious as to why."

On that trip north to Elalantar, when Lauresa had pressed the handkerchief into his hands, he'd seen Barien ride down three wolves to fly straight at the brute that led them. One of the monstrous fell wolves of the Ebaradar passes to the west, the graowin as the Elalanti called them. A hulking brute, a wolf in shape only, nearly as tall as Barien's horse where the warrior cut hard past it, launching himself from the saddle and swinging into it with axe and sword.

"Barien taught me that the duty of a royal warden is to his charge, my lord prince." The strength in Chriani's voice belied the fear he felt, reflected back in Konaugo's dark look. He breathed deep, the chill of winter air coming in through the open gates.

Last night, it had been the fear in Barien's voice that had awoken him. But what could have made the warrior that afraid?

"I had been ordered to guard the princess, my lord prince, and would have done so though the Bastion fell around us both. And had you or this captain or Barien himself attempted to breach her doors last night without answering my challenge, I would have died happily in my attempt to cut you down."

Chriani waited for the blow to fall, not knowing whether it would be Konaugo or the prince himself who landed it. But instead, Chanist smiled. A weariness in his look, Chriani thought. The mask of age.

"Barien taught you to speak your mind in addition to all else," the prince said quietly. He glanced up to Konaugo and the others, a single look sending them off. Konaugo caught Chriani's eyes before he went, his malice seeming to linger in the shadows as he left them alone.

"When Barien stayed with my court after the departure of the Princess Precedent Irdaign," Chanist said, "he swore to hold my daughter's life more dear than his own..." He faltered suddenly, looked to the doorway as horses were led out, the sky already darkening in the east. "I see that dedication in you, master Chriani. It will serve you well in my court."

The prince grasped Chriani's arm then, wrist to forearm, squeezed it in a grip that Chriani had to struggle to return. A sword-hand's strength, viselike.

He should have made rank at least a year before. Barien had championed him, had given him opportunity he'd squandered to buy himself a spot in the gatehouse guard for life.

Chriani watched from behind the slatted walls as the prince's company assembled at the gates, then climbed to the top of the wall again to watch them as they took the road. The cloud of distant dust settled slowly behind them, the riders beyond it disappearing into the distant tree line, off the road and onto the secret trails the rangers used.

Beneath his shirt, Chriani felt the scabbard, thought he could feel the bloody lines that etched the blade within. The *narneth móir*, they called it.

He felt his chest and shoulder burning again. He saw in his minds' eye the pattern his mother had made there. He sensed the delicate warmark of the blade that was his own mark's perfect match.

Halobrelia forest-heart... Words from a rhyme his mother had sung to him, a long time ago now. Her songs were one of the few things from her life that he couldn't remember anymore.

It was long after dark when he forced the thoughts from his mind, later when he returned to the gatehouse barracks. Later still before he finally managed to sleep.

— CHAPTER 5 —
FIVE HOG'S HOUSE

THROUGHOUT THE NEXT DAY, Chriani heard nothing from or of the Princess Lauresa, but there were enough other things to be listened to and overheard where whispered rumors of the reasons for the late ride of the prince's guard swept across the keep and the city around it like cold rain. Despite the air of secrecy and the pall still hanging over the near-death of the king and the funeral of the boisterous sergeant who had fallen in his place, a strange and unknown energy hung in the air. Expectation, Chriani thought. Waiting.

The state of things within the Bastion he couldn't speak to, its doors closed off to him now. And for most of the day while he made himself busy with the gatehouse routine that was to become his life, he wondered what he'd do if he didn't hear from her again. In his gut, he couldn't shake the feeling like whatever part he'd had to play in the aftermath of his own life ending was over now, picked up by other people. He was a courier, relaying what he'd seen and heard, then stepping back to let other people decide the significance of those things.

He slept that night with the dagger still inside his shirt, waking to feel the welts its scabbard had raised on his skin. In a moment alone, behind the locked door of a storeroom, he tried to wipe the blood from the blade, but the glyph would not be cleansed by water or wine. The etching of the dagger's war-mark was like nothing he'd ever seen before, the steel revealing a patina of what felt like fine sand that his fingers could not rub away. The dagger holding tight to the red-black legacy of the murder it wrought.

As if he'd dreamed it, Chriani remembered the frozen tone of Lauresa's voice as she slipped away the previous day. He remembered her gaze straying from the dagger to him, but he had no clear idea what she'd heard, what she'd picked up from the secrets twisting through his frantic thoughts.

At breakfast in the gatehouse barracks, Chriani glanced up from where he ate at a table alone. From the doorway, the hulking figure of Ashlund beckoned, motioned him to follow as he turned and stomped out. Chriani felt the eyes on him as he followed, not caring. In the pale light of the courtyard, Ashlund waited with an impatient air.

"By my order, you are to report to the training grounds at daymark. In light of recent events, the Princess Lauresa has requested practice at arms, and I have no soldiers to spare." He put a particular emphasis on *soldiers*.

"Yes, lord," Chriani said, but the lieutenant was already turning away.

Chriani took his time eating, then spent as much time as he could stomach half-heartedly helping restock the gate's second-floor storerooms before informing the on-duty sergeant that he was leaving. Orders from the Bastion that would keep him for the day, he said, but the sergeant didn't seem to care.

He was there on the training grounds as the daymark bells rang out from the tower above, the winter sun at its height and already warm. He saw no sign of Lauresa, so he slipped into the armory, selected what he thought they'd need. The princess had worked only with the shortsword the last time she'd trained at his side, but he took a pair of longswords from the racks as well, plus dagger and rapier, shortbow and two quivers. He had trouble filling the latter, the stock of ammunition almost gone from when he'd been there two days before.

In the archery yard, the guards of the off-duty garrison were at practice, Chriani setting up on the small-arms field. A handful of the guard nodded to him in what he knew must have been respect for Barien's memory. Most ignored him. From a few of the older sergeants, he caught the open looks of contempt that he remembered from the days when Lauresa had trained at his side. Whatever they might have felt for Barien now wasn't masking their feelings on an unranked apprentice given training ground rights.

Behind the Bastion garrison, the city guards were within the keep this day, practicing with pikes at long rows of wooden target poles. Preparation for combat that suggested a larger mobilization than just the prince's guard riding out two nights before. Something happening, Chriani thought. The feeling of expectation hanging, heavy like the mist that wreathed the fields beyond the city at first light.

He had racked and checked the weapons twice by the time Lauresa finally appeared, Ashlund and a young tyro Chriani didn't recognize both the customary five steps away. She had on the same cloak of dark wool she'd worn in the throne room the night Barien died, but the robes were gone in favor of the well-scored leather of a training ground half-doublet, worn over a simple tunic and leggings like the princess hadn't worn in three years. Her hair was tied back in twin braids, so that it took Chriani a moment to recognize her. When he did, he found himself staring, but judging from the dark look that Ashlund directed to the garrison across the yard, he wasn't the only one.

When she saw Chriani, Lauresa slowed. She gave him an uncertain look, glanced back to Ashlund as he nodded to her.

"Are we awaiting the trainer, lieutenant?"

"You have my apologies, highness," Ashlund said, though Chriani thought he looked singularly unapologetic. "Your father's ride and the short notice of your request has left me unable to spare a trained guard."

Lauresa stepped up to Chriani with the same look she'd departed with in the hall of records. "Very well," she said.

Chriani felt the anger rise, didn't try to hide it. The princess selected a shortsword from the rack, tested its weight carefully. Chriani slipped in as she stepped away, not looking at her. And there on the rack, beside the other shortsword, she'd placed the plain steel band. He palmed it beneath Ashlund's gaze, slipped it to the finger of his left hand even as he spun the sword in his right as a distraction.

In his mind, he thought he felt Lauresa smile. Not exactly laughter because it wasn't like he was really hearing her voice. But the feel of her, the presence inside him, carried a tone of gentle reproach, no sign of the coldness her face still displayed.

A true soldier should not be so sensitive that a harsh word from a spoiled noble can change his mood.

Yes, highness. Shall we begin?

Aloud, please.

"Shall we begin, highness?" he said.

"Yes," Lauresa said. "You may approach."

Chriani nodded, crossed the five paces to stand before her. "We will practice wards and guards if it please your highness."

"Proceed."

"Thank you, highness. Follow my mark."

Ashlund left his own tyro behind but slunk away himself as Chriani took the princess through the careful training exercises that Barien had taught him long ago. The same exercises Chriani had taught her once before, Lauresa matching his movements with an ease that suggested she remembered at least some of the lessons of those four years.

You follow well, he said for lack of any other thought. He was conscious of the silence in his mind like he normally wasn't, more conscious of the stray thoughts that wanted to intrude on that silence, many of which he had no intention of allowing the princess to hear.

You taught me well, she said.

Chriani missed the last form of the set, covered it quickly by turning to face her, nodding. "Parry and riposte if it please your highness."

From the corner of his eye, as they paced themselves through fast attacks and faster blocks, he saw two sergeants of the Rheran guard watching them, sensed the gaze of the Bastion troops behind him without even needing to turn around. He felt awkward suddenly, caught up in an unfamiliar chill that her last words had set loose in him. He chose his response carefully.

I don't recall our training when we were younger ever inspiring this much attention from anyone other than your father.

When we were younger, our being here was simply a distraction, Lauresa said.

Chriani didn't ask what it was now, burying the thought within the focus on his blade as it blocked hers, darted around to strike again and again.

Now, the princess said, *they watch me because that is what they do. They watch you because they suspect you of having some connection to Barien's death that has yet to be explained.*

I'm surprised that Konaugo allowed it.

Konaugo planned it, Lauresa said, *from the moment I made my request. He thought to humiliate you at the same time he would keep you under the eye of his servants.*

Chriani had lashed the bloodblade to an extra belt that he'd cinched beneath his tunic that morning, and while it rode easily there, he felt the heat suddenly where the leather bound him. He stopped, adjusted the fitting under cover of demonstrating the form he showed her. "You are losing strength in the movement of your wrist, highness. In pulling the blade back, you fight against yourself. Let your hand direct it, but let the blade then guide your hand through. Observe me and adjust."

As he leaned in to show her the subtle shift in the placement of her fingers, he watched his hand wrap hers. Feeling her fingers beneath his as he adjusted their position on the hilt, sensation flooding him at a level below words.

Thank you for spending this time with me, Lauresa said in his mind.

"We might engage if it please your highness."

"Proceed."

Through the long day, Chriani and Lauresa faced off in the chill wind that whipped the dust of the grounds, a silence across the connection the rings made that told him she was as focused as he. They broke only when the hot lunch the princess had ordered was sent out, along with the three other royal heirs. Chriani sat alone at a discrete distance while the princess ate and laughed with her step-siblings.

There was Prince Phelan, tearing up the field with a wooden dagger, and getting as close to the weapons of the practice rack as his rather ominous nanny would allow. Where they sat and watched him with practiced impatience, the Princesses Peran and Miani were both in matching blue cloaks over shifts of white, decorated with the unmistakable beauty of their mother's own needlecraft.

All three of the younger children had their mother's fairness, and the blonde hair of both Chanist and Gwannyn in their youth. Lauresa had Chanist's golden curls as well, but also a darkness to her look that marked a sharp contrast to the younger heirs, as much so as did the clothes that she and Peran wore today.

As he watched them, Chriani couldn't remember ever seeing Lauresa in a dress at Peran's age, when they'd been already a year into their training together. From his eleventh year to his fourteenth, he'd spent almost as much time at Lauresa's side as he did at Barien's. On the training grounds where she soon came to hold her own against him in shortsword and dagger work, and on the range where Chriani's singular skill was a mark she would try to attain but never touch, and on the long rides that she loved to take, sometimes with her father, sometimes not. Barien was always with her, of course, and a clutch of garrison guards behind him. But on the days she went out without Chanist, it was Chriani alone who had been permitted to ride at her side.

As he watched her grab up Phelan in mid-run and pull him into a laughing embrace, Chriani remembered the look in Lauresa's eyes when he'd burst into the war room that night. No recognition in her then, or that recognition hidden with a degree of skill that told him equally as well that the closeness he remembered was long gone.

You taught me well, she'd said.

They moved to the longswords after lunch, Chriani walking the princess through the differences in handling to the shorter blade, though Lauresa's first attempts at the forms told him this wasn't the first time she'd held one. Her technique was sketchy, but she had a strength in her arms that belied her slenderness, and by the end of their session, they were working with rapier and dagger and Chriani was aching from neck to foot, not sure how she could still be going strong.

I would like to walk in the city this evening. Her voice in his mind after the long silence of the day distracted Chriani from the careful assessment of her darting strikes, but his dagger still caught each in turn. *I would like you to accompany me. Meet me at evenmark.*

Highness?

He followed a quick parry with a quicker thrust, the princess darting in close with her dagger as her rapier's tip danced Chriani's blade away.

Five Hog's House in the market court, she said. *I would have you accompany me.*

Princess, the keep is in lockdown.

Your powers of observation do you credit. He tried to ignore the emotion that seemed to flow through the link of shared thought, but it slipped through him anyway. The smile he'd felt before, not quite laughter.

With respect, princess, would Barien have accompanied you to Five Hog's House against your father's express orders for your safety?

No, she said. *Barien preferred the Iron Lion in the merchant's district when he went walking with me. Fewer of the garrison likely to be drinking there.*

She spun in low, hoping to take advantage of the difference in their height. Chriani had to slash down on the backhand, backpedaling at the same time as he twisted away.

I wish to hear what word has spread regarding the attempt on my father's life.

Why listen to rumor?

Because with enough time spent at court, you learn that truth is more often found in what goes unspoken than in what is said. I wish to hear the things of which my father and the guard will not speak.

This is folly, princess.

Lauresa bore down suddenly, tearing into him with a savage double strike that he wouldn't have thought her capable of making. Dust rose between them as Chriani skidded back.

I will go alone then. I am sure no harm will come to me.

In his own reaction, it wasn't anger Chriani felt, but something milder. A kind of petty annoyance that surprised him, more accustomed as he was to his emotions running ice cold or molten hot, with no middle ground between them and most often no warning when they were about to change.

Three years before, Lauresa had turned sixteen and the years of lessons on the training grounds and of long rides through the Rheran countryside had stopped. Some kind of changeover in her handling, it had seemed to Chriani in retrospect. The Prince High Chanist's young rowdy in leather and oversized tunics had given way at some point to the Princess High Gwannyn's courtier in ribbons and white robes.

Before that night in the war room, he couldn't remember when she'd last spoken to him. When he finally realized it was over, he'd tried to recall it, tried to remember the last session, the last ride. But by then, all the memories of the time they'd spent together had seemed to wither and scatter like dead leaves in his mind.

Barien was gone. His job was to look after her, he reminded himself.

I would be pleased to accompany you, highness.

She spun in low again, the same move that nearly caught him before, but Chriani was watching for it this time. A quick parry and cross-strike made as he sidestepped, her blade caught by the guard of his dagger and twisted, spinning from her hands. Lauresa stumbled back as it arced through the air, dropping behind her.

"Thank you, highness." Chriani had to fight to slow his breathing. "Be wary of repeating the same form too often in single combat. A wary opponent will recognize and prepare against it."

"Indeed. Thank you, tyro."

She stooped to pick up the fallen rapier, turned back as if she was ready to continue again. Chriani felt a twinge spike in his back to remind him he'd twisted too far for the sake of the last move. Then from behind Lauresa, he saw Ashlund approach, an unfamiliar relief felt at the lieutenant's entrance. He whispered a few words in the ear of the tyro that Chriani had forgotten about long before. Following Chriani's gaze, Lauresa glanced back.

"I think that is enough for this day," the princess said. She held blade and dagger to Chriani, who took them as he nodded, stepping back. And all at once, he felt the familiar distance slipping between them. Replacing the dying warmth of the day that had seemed much longer than he knew it was.

Evenmark. At the orchard wall.

For too long, Chriani had carried the memory of too many days like this one. Before two days ago, he would have said they were gone. Easier that way.

"Highness." Chriani nodded again.

The princess pulled her cloak from the weapons rack as she passed Ashlund, he and the tyro turning from Chriani without a word. As she paced toward the courtyard track, though, he saw the stiffness in Lauresa's movements that she finally let show. The ache at his chest was flaring now, the dagger shifting below it to dig into his side, but he waited until he'd stowed the weapons back in the armory again before he adjusted it.

Almost as an afterthought, he slipped the steel ring from his finger, slid it carefully into the sleeve pocket where his picks were hidden. He wasn't sure if Lauresa had intended that she be able to contact him, but he was determined that he didn't want to contact her without meaning to. Too many thoughts in him that he didn't want shared.

It wasn't until he returned to the gatehouse that Chriani discovered he was expected to do a full shift in the storerooms in addition to his being loaned to Ashlund for the day, and by the time evenmark finally tolled out, he'd only barely finished.

In the bunkroom, he splashed water to his face, cleared the dust of the training grounds from his eyes. Outside, he kept his cloak slung casually under one arm until the gate was lost to sight behind him, slipping it on as he climbed the courtyard track the long way around the Bastion. It would be closer to cross the training grounds, the orchard walls rising just beyond, but even from the gate, he could see the garrison practicing on horseback now, firelight and evenlamps burning brightly in the early dark.

Lauresa was waiting at the wall, lingering in shadow near the bars of the orchard door. She was changed from the day but still looking as little like herself as she had before, in leggings and tunic again, a weather-stained travel cloak tied loose at her throat.

"I was afraid you were not coming."

"My apologies, highness." Chriani had carefully scanned the wall and the grounds as he approached. Though he was sure they were alone, it seemed strange somehow to be speaking aloud.

"Which way shall we go then?"

Chriani stared. From the orchard, he heard the wind over the outside walls whistle through the topmost branches, dark fingers clutching the sky. Lauresa was watching him expectantly.

"I'm to find our way out of the keep? After gatefall, under lockdown?"

"Barien always did."

Chriani remembered Barien's late nights. He tried not to let his surprise show. "With respect, highness, what route did you take with him?"

"Out through the main gate, generally. With a promise to the guards there to bring a flagon of the Lion's own ale back."

"The guards don't know me."

"I expected so."

Her face was impassive, and Chriani thought for a moment about slipping the ring on in order to feel whether she was laughing again. He felt the annoyance flare inside him, wondered how long it would be before it became something much darker.

From around the near corner of the Bastion, he heard the horses on the training grounds, saw the stables bright with light. He deliberated for what seemed like a long while over how serious Lauresa had been when she'd threatened to go alone, then deliberated again over whether he could go through with what he suspected was his only way of keeping that from happening.

"Which way shall we go?" the princess said again.

"Come," Chriani replied.

Through the shadows of the apartments and the garrison kennels that spread beyond the low side of the courtyard track, Chriani led her on, kept her behind him as he watched for movement on the walls above. Around them, the keep was shut down for the day but Chriani didn't feel the silence yet. Something else hanging this night against the pulse and sound of the city around them, the same sense of distraction he'd been feeling since Barien's rites.

In the shelter of a narrow alley mouth that cut between a gallery and the private residences that flanked it, they lingered in shadow for a short while, Chriani watching as a pair of grooms led two horses in from the light of the distant training grounds. As they reached the stable doors, he pulled Lauresa forward, slipped in carefully behind them.

Beneath the shadowed ceiling of the loft above, Chriani quickly led the princess to the leatherworks where he'd come across her father two nights before, empty now. He told her to stay there until he returned, slipping off into the distant din of horses bedding down for the night, someone straightening nails with a faint echo of steel on steel.

In the bustle of movement that surrounded him, none of the half-dozen grooms so much as looked at him as he passed, just one more guard whose orders were best avoided. The stables were warm against the night air where it pushed in at the door, the scent of dung and hay dust heavy as Chriani slipped through shadows toward the stable gate. Even as he scanned the open edge of the loft overhead in the hopes of avoiding Kathlan, she rounded the corner from the harness room in front of him, a dozen paces away.

Her eyes were emerald-green in the light of the evenlamps across from her, the risk of fire making the stables one of the few places outside the Bastion where the sorcerer's light was found. Chriani stopped, tried to speak but could only nod. He'd been hoping against hope that she'd be gone, still in the dinner hall across the courtyard from the Bastion gate, but in the back of his mind, he'd known that with horses being ridden late, this was where she'd be. He felt her smile as much as saw it. Felt an uncertain pain trace its way around the certain pain that the name of a princess made against his skin.

He adjusted the set of the dagger belt, shifted into the shadows as she crossed the floor to meet him. She kissed him more fervently than he wanted, looked up at him as she stroked his face, his own hand straying to the fringes of her rough-cut hair.

"I looked for you at the rites," she began, Chriani pressing a finger to her lips.

"I know," he said. "I couldn't talk then. I'm…"

"I know. I understand, I mean. I'm so sorry."

But even as she kissed him again, he felt her pull back. Watching him as if she could feel the reluctance that caught at him. Words hanging, Chriani clinging to the silence like he hoped he wouldn't have to speak them. "I'm on duty," he said at last, almost the truth. "I need access out to the city, then back in later. No one else can know."

"I'll be here," she said. She squeezed his hand, cast a glance over her shoulder to see who might be watching. Then Chriani saw her freeze suddenly, looking with her to see a figure emerge from the farriers' stalls. Lauresa's face was shadowed where she'd pulled the hood of the cloak up, but Kathlan's nod told Chriani she recognized the princess all the same.

"Highness," she said quietly, but she didn't look to see the nod returned. Watching Chriani instead as she turned and limped away.

Where Kathlan led them to it, the stable gate was a wain-wide slab of steel-bound oaken beams likely stronger than the wall it was part of. The bars were chained and locked as they usually were. But with a sinking feeling, Chriani saw a Bastion guard sitting there in a way that wasn't usual at all. The keep in lockdown, he thought.

He recognized the guard. Garyan, tyro to Waltevi before he'd made rank at High Summer past. Two years Chriani's junior. As Kathlan waved him and Lauresa back to the shadows, she stomped out ahead of them. From a nearby bench, she grabbed an empty saddlebag, closed and cinched it tight.

"You!" she shouted. Garyan looked like he'd been drowsing as he started to his feet. "One of your sackless couriers dropped his horse and left whatever message he was running still on it. Deliver this to wherever it's supposed to go, now."

She threw the saddlebag, the startled youth catching it just short of his head. "I'm to watch the gate…"

"Before Ashlund decided you falling asleep in front of it would be better guard, watching the gate was my post, lack-knob. By contrast, running errands for your shite-sotted halfwit riders is most definitely not."

Garyan looked like he had something he wanted to say, but whatever it was got quickly lost under the weight of Kathlan's gaze. He half-nodded as if he'd half-forgotten he outranked her, jogging for the door.

Kathlan checked to both sides as she fit a key at her belt to the lock, Chriani and Lauresa slipping up behind her. She pulled the chain as Chriani slid the bars, a pulse of frigid air hitting them as the door cracked inward. Kathlan waved Chriani back again, put her eye to the gap to carefully check outside before she pulled one door wide enough for him and the princess to slip through.

"My thanks," he said. "We won't be long."

"I'll be here," she said again, but Chriani heard a cold edge to the voice this time. As Lauresa slipped out after him, the narrow breach of the gate slammed shut behind her. Chriani motioned her back into the darkness of the wall as he checked the road to both sides, clear. Then he motioned the princess forward, pulled the hood of his cloak up as he led her out into the intermittent light of the night markets beyond.

Outside the sheltered island of the keep's walls, the city was alive, a distant pulse of noise and movement rising like a tide against the refined silence at its heart. And in the thought of that silence, something came to Chriani's mind suddenly. Kathlan hadn't asked dismissal of the princess, hadn't nodded as she and Chriani had gone.

The air was chill, the night clear with a taste of the winter that had so far kept its distance, Chriani thought. Even with the early dark, the crowd that spilled out from the taverns of the trade quarter was heavy. Beyond the formal stalls of the night market, hawkers and merchants spilled over almost to the residential lanes, thick with the day laborers heading home from the taverns, or heading out to them. More than once as they made their way for the heart of the quarter, they passed off-duty garrison guards looking for drink or dice.

"Go slowly," Lauresa said where she leaned in close to Chriani's ear. "I wish to listen." Chriani nodded, slipped the steel ring from within his sleeve, but Lauresa stopped him with a touch. She shook her head, moved closer to him as they walked. He felt her arm brush his side.

"Two people keeping silent in a crowd such as this will raise far more suspicion than the same two speaking." Her voice was raised against the noise of that crowd, Chriani not hiding his discomfort as he gauged the reaction of the faces around them. "There are many means of concealment," Lauresa said, "including hiding in plain sight. Growing up always under the scrutiny of others, you learn them all."

Through a throng of acrobats whipping burning brands above the heads of an appreciative crowd, they drifted slowly, content to let the market's movement carry them along. The urge to slip into the adjacent shadows of a half-dozen twisting streets was sharp in Chriani, a sense of being exposed burning like a brand in his mind. But with every pair of eyes that passed across him without seeing, he realized that the princess was right. The same distance in everyone around them, he saw. Taking them in without notice, the crowd a shield that hid them in plain sight.

"Keep speaking," she said.

"What do you hope to find here?" Chriani asked. In the throng around them, he focused, a dozen intertwined conversations spilling past with every step.

"Where my father is gone."

Across from him, a dust-streaked courier talked worriedly to a thickly muscled smith. He was afraid, Chriani realized. He caught frantic words, something about fire along the frontier, getting his family north before it was too late.

"Why not ask Ashlund?"

"Because Ashlund was not told to where the prince himself and the guard were riding, as were neither I nor my stepmother."

In an alcove, he saw a young street gamin carefully present a dagger to a pair of lean farmhands. The blade was new enough that it had clearly been stolen, the boys inspecting it with a care that suggested they'd never touched one before. They had salt pork and copper to trade. The girl laughed them away.

"Even with what has happened, there are precious few things I can think of that would inspire my father to secrecy that severe."

War, someone said.

Chriani glanced around him, couldn't see who had spoken, loud enough that the voice carried across the crowd. He felt the reaction to it, though. He heard it echo back from all around him, heard the speculation.

...be at both ends of the Locanwater by tonight, someone said.

At the edge of the night market, he saw the wains and stalls of the weapons dealers doing brisker than normal business. He saw battered shortswords change hands for twice the silver they were worth.

...a message they'll understand.

At the edge of the market, two Ilvani wains were pulled to one side, the city guard inspecting them with a diligence that belied both the lateness of their watch and the innocence of the crystalware the wagons carried. As he had on the wall before Barien was burned, as he had within the keep not so long before, Chriani felt the tension hanging, the sense of expectation sharp in the voices that filled his ears and the sudden memory of Barien.

There's peace now.

So they say...

Behind him, he heard glass breaking, voices raised. He didn't look back. "We have arrived, highness."

Where Five Hog's House squatted at the corner junction of the trade road and the market court, its weathered white stones took on the blackness of the winter sky, stars impossibly bright overhead. Like anyone else who had spent a life in Rheran, Chriani had lost count of the number of times he'd passed through its doors.

By day, the tavern was packed with the merchants and laborers and guards of the market district, standing shoulder to shoulder at the bar for first call, or lined up four deep if the weather was bad and the crowds couldn't spread to the nearby lanes. By dark, the caravan traders and the dockworkers and the keep garrison would descend on the torchlit cobblestones and the constant echo of talk and laughter there.

As Chriani shouldered his way through the crowd at the door, he scanned the close shadows of the tavern's interior as he made a mental note of the half-dozen guards he recognized, grateful for the shroud where the smoke of the open kitchen vented to the chimney high overhead.

The owner of the place was a dark-eyed teller of tales that Chriani had heard called Ceiya. He did service behind the bar, filling flagons with an unnatural speed as Chriani snatched one up along with a pair of tankards. One of the siolans he'd brought with him was tossed to the tavern master, who caught it without looking.

At his neck, visible only when he wanted it seen, Ceiya bore the brand that marked its bearer as one of the mageguard, and a sorcerer with fealty to the crown. Stories circulated as freely as the steady flow of mugs to and from the taps that he'd gone by the name of Narthia when he was one of Chanist's war-mages, long years before his quiet retirement. While no one Chriani knew had ever seen the barkeep summon so much as a hint of spellcraft, the reputation of that brand kept Five Hog's House one of the more sociable establishments in the city.

As he slipped back to Lauresa's side, Chriani spotted two well-dressed traders rising on shaky legs from a corner table. But as he motioned the princess toward it, she nodded instead to a single vacant space at the open benches along the nearest wall.

Stepping past Chriani, she slapped the shoulders of the two figures sitting to either side of the empty space, dockworkers by the look of them, arms tattooed and tar-streaked where they grudgingly moved down. She pushed Chriani to the bench, slid in next to him as he sat, wrapping her cloak around them both as her body pressed close.

Chriani felt her leg alongside his as she shifted her weight along rough planking. From his first tankard, he drank more deeply than he'd planned.

Along the walls, braziers were burning against the cold, but even over the aroma of charcoal and charred meat at the kitchen fire and the close reek of a hundred laborers, Lauresa's scent filled him. Soap and lilacs, he thought, suddenly conscious of the crust of sweat and dust that the long day had left still clinging to him. A serving tray careened past them, a boy no more than twelve hefting it as if it weighed nothing. Lauresa grabbed another flagon as it passed, tossed a clutch of copper to the tray and filled the mug still in Chriani's hands. She spoke only to him, close enough that she didn't need to lean in.

"Listen," she said again.

Within earshot, Chriani reckoned he must have heard a hundred different voices. Merchants, workers, mercenaries. A clutch of half-bloods whose tattered robes marked them as monastics from the frontier lands of the south. A cross-section of laboring Rheran, a hundred different lives intersecting in a crowded tavern on a clear winter night, and one thread alone worked its way through every conversation.

Attempt on the prince's life…

All around them, word of the failed assassination was all that anyone talked of, and in that talk, one word was whispered repeatedly with the edge of a dark curse.

Valnirata.

Where a bench had been pulled close to the warmth of a brazier, a broad-shouldered Elalantar caravan chief held forth to his rapt crew on the Ilvani plot to assassinate the Ilmar's four princes, one by one. Chanist was first, he said, and even now his riders had split south and north to send warning to Holc, Aerach, and Elalantar alike. Beyond them, loud oaths against the war-clans spiked a dozen conversations, Chriani recognizing a scattering of Holc caravan guards by their habit of spitting when they spoke the Valnirata name. Closer by, he heard snippets of a heated argument between two regulars of the city watch, and though he couldn't make out where it had started, it finished with a clanking of mugs and a whispered oath.

Chanist will see all the fucking Valnirata burn…

Konaugo's slip hadn't mattered in the end, Chriani thought. The prince had been right. Word that the guard rode out against the Valnirata was on all lips, confirmation likely coming in from every courier and wagon that had passed Chanist's troop on its way. A kind of eagerness to the discussion, as if this truth had been expected somehow.

Even the Rheran Ilvani where they mingled amongst the room's Ilmari patrons said it, a little too loudly, Chriani thought. Artisans and armorers, most of them, trading with the caravans from their crafthouses that rose in tiers above the garden quarter. He remembered the scene from the wall the day before, the bare-edged anger of the Ilvani and the sentry who'd challenged him. The loyalty of crown over race suddenly seemed a thing that a great many were anxious to prove.

They sat for long enough that Chriani felt the beginning of a stiffness in his legs. The two of them listened, all the while talking of nothing against any gaze or ear that might have passed by them in the ever-shifting crowd. Chriani found himself explaining in greater detail than he ever would have wanted to what life in the gatehouse guard entailed, trying not to let his bitterness show. In the end, though, he answered more than he asked, no questions that he could think to put to Lauresa that didn't involve her leaving in ten days time.

Chriani downed three tankards in that time, hoping vainly that it would dull the sensation of Lauresa's body warm against his. She'd made more room for herself when a pair of caravan guards who'd been flashing a conspicuous amount of silver staggered for the door, but in shifting down, she'd had to slide her arm behind him, one hand resting on his shoulder beneath the cloak now. It was the appearance that the place demanded, he knew, the two of them effectively invisible as they drank and spoke low in each other's ears and took in the drifting conversation all around. All the while, though, he felt the dull burning of the princess's name at his breast, her own fingers close enough to trace it out if she'd known it was there.

Along the adjacent wall, they heard someone speak of having seen the prince's guard riding southeast, shadowing the Glaeddynfield road that ran from Rheran to Addrimyr along the northwest flank of the Greatwood. Lauresa was telling him of a time the summer before when Peran had hidden out in the throne room in order to eavesdrop on a half-day's excise negotiations, and who had been discovered when she'd burst out from behind a curtain to indignantly order the ambassador to reject the Holc delegation's offered terms.

Then, from across the room, a murmur drifted through the haze of conversation. Chriani's senses were duller than he wanted them to be, but these words were sharp, hanging as if they were meant for him somehow.

Piss-sot Bastion guard can't take out one Valnirata with a knife, don't know what Brandishear's come to…

Chriani was already heading for his feet, not even feeling the familiar surge of the rage within him until he felt Lauresa's hand on his shoulder, pushing him back. He fought to slow his breathing, glanced to the figure who had made the comment. A laborer, nearly as broad across the middle as he was tall. He had a half-dozen empty tankards before him and a wide-set emptiness to his eyes. A fool mouthing words he wouldn't remember in the morning.

His was a fool's reaction, Chriani thought.

"You know that the rumors are true," Lauresa said quietly. Not a question.

Chriani drank deeply, tried to focus. He was following two tankards of bitter with stout because that's what had come by on the tray the last time, and his tongue was already speaking the warning that he knew his head would be feeling by next morning, too late.

"When you found the blade, you knew it for what it was."

In the three days since he'd woken to Barien's voice in the dark, Chriani had become more intimately acquainted with the degree of subtlety in the princess than he'd ever dreamed he would. But though he tried to sense what insight, what interest was in her now, all he heard in her voice was a pain that seemed to match his own in a way he would have thought impossible.

Beneath the cloak, her hand found his, clutched it tight. He could feel her shaking. "I would bring Barien back in a heartbeat if I could. But failing that, I understand that he did what he did in order to keep my father safe. I would pay any price to do the same, Chriani."

War... the voices around them said.

In Barien's endless history lessons, the Empire had been a time of great advances in craft and sorcery, but the Empire's presence had given those advances direction and control. When they'd made that first transition from nations to provinces almost fifteen centuries before, the Ilmar principalities were sparsely populated, thinly defended. Today, the warrior had told him, Brandishear alone would be capable of putting an army into the field ten times greater than the combined forces of Brandis and Werran that helped turn the tide of the Migration Wars, with weapons and magic that might match the power of the Imperial Guard themselves.

In the aftermath of the Empire, Barien had said with a seriousness Chriani heard, any war that started might just never end.

Chriani squeezed his eyes shut, a numbness in his fingers where hers twined through them. *Chriani*, she'd said, and with a rush of insight that met the chill of the stout as he drank deep, he realized that she'd never called him that before. Not these last four days, not the four long years they'd trained at each other's side. Never used his name. Like he was for every other sergeant and guard in the prince's employ, he'd been 'tyro' always, interaction in the Bastion filtered through rank and station and the already-composed sets of expectations that came with it.

"Konaugo let slip that a Valnirata bloodblade took Barien's life," he said. "When I saw the blade that was hidden, I knew it for what it was."

A sudden snarling rose from the next table, the caravan chief feeding a pair of guard dogs the remains of a rack of lamb picked remarkably clean. His booming laughter drowned the current of conversation for a moment.

"Yesterday," she said, "you never answered me. What did Barien say before he died?"

With effort, Chriani pulled his hand from hers. He glanced carefully around them, not meeting anyone's gaze but confirming that no one's gaze was on them. "He said to keep you safe. He spoke of someone, I know not who."

"The killer?"

"No," Chriani said. "Someone else. Someone within the court, I think. The reason he chose to flee to the archives, to hide what he hid. He left the dagger for me to find because he feared that to reveal the blade would have put your father in even greater danger. That's the only sense I make of it."

Trust him not...

"What else did he say?"

"He said 'Uissa'. He spoke of this person owning Uissa, I don't know what it means."

Lauresa's hair touched his cheek as she shook her head. "A weapon, perhaps. Or a person in his service. Is it a Valnirata name?"

Chriani could have answered her, *No.* Almost did, in fact, catching the word only just in time to prevent his having to explain how he could possibly have known. A dull buzzing was rising in his head.

Then at the bar suddenly, he heard Lauresa's name shouted out. All the pleasant sluggishness of the drink fled from Chriani in an instant, and his hand at her head pulled her toward him, her face against his shoulder, hidden.

A toast to the royal wedding! A drunken bellow, a chorus of clanking mugs rippling out from the bar. Chriani let himself relax.

May the prince send as dowry ten thousand Valnirata heads!

Against the chorus of cheers, Lauresa whispered in his ear.

"It's time to go."

Chriani glanced to both sides, no one paying them any particular attention that he could see, but Lauresa was already rising, hood pulled further down as she slipped through the crowd for the door.

She said nothing as they made their way back toward the market court, Chriani breathing deeply of the chill winter air. He felt his head clear a little, but with that clarity came a sudden awareness that Lauresa's scent was still with him. On him now, he realized. Beneath the cushion of drink, the dull pain the tattoo made was a fading ache.

When you found the blade, you knew it, she'd said. He'd almost told her the truth then. All the truth, like only Barien and Kathlan had ever been told before. He'd felt it on the tip of his tongue, felt it burning in his throat like bile, but as words formed, they'd latched instead onto the fragment of truth that had saved him in front of her father.

Funny, he thought, how easily one small piece of truth could bury the larger lie.

They took a different route back, sticking to the lantern-lit side streets that circled the markets but would return them to the keep walls just the same. As they walked, Chriani tried to think of what he was going to say to Garyan at the door in order to get Kathlan back, but it was Kathlan herself there when he quietly knocked, Lauresa in the shadows behind him.

He saw the green eyes bright where she slid the narrow wedge of the lantern slot back to appraise him. A moment's waiting as he heard the chain and the bars undone again, then they were inside.

"Enjoy yourselves?" Kathlan asked sweetly.

Chriani nodded awkwardly. "It was important," he added, not sure why.

"An unranked adjutant escorting a princess past lockdown?" Kathlan said quietly. "Must have been." Chriani saw Lauresa glance back, caught a look between her and Kathlan that he didn't understand.

"Chriani's escort was important," the princess said. "Thank you for making it possible."

"Highness." Kathlan nodded, a little too quickly.

At the stable doors, Chriani waved Lauresa back, slipping outside by himself to carefully check the courtyard track, no one passing. Along the walls, evenlamps burned brighter than normal, he thought. The garrison still on high alert, a bad night to be walking.

Lauresa was at the door when he slipped back in, Kathlan darkly silent behind her. She waited until they were outside before she called. "Ashlund's looking for you both. Best make the story good."

Chriani glanced back to see the doors slam shut.

As far as he could tell, they made it unobserved along the narrow alley that climbed to the Bastion servants' entrance. Watching the walls as they walked, he timed their movement between the movements of the guard. Lauresa had directed him there, told him she could find her way to her rooms on her own. She wouldn't take the chance of him being caught inside, she said, a sentiment Chriani shared.

Before she went, she gave him the cover story that Kathlan had suggested they'd need, walking him through it with an ease that suggested she'd had it prepared. She'd asked him to escort her to the orchard that evening, Chriani waiting while she'd written letters in the old gardener's shed. He'd seen several of the garrison approach but the princess had made it clear that she didn't want to be disturbed.

"Personal correspondence to attend to before I leave," she said.

At the words, Chriani felt a sudden chill beyond that of the air. Something in the blur of the drink caught at him suddenly, and he was glad for the darkness. He felt her voice in the shadows like something he could have touched.

"When the cold became too much, you returned me to the courtyard. I informed you that I would make my own way from there." Lauresa returned Chriani's nod, opened the locked door with a key she slipped back within her tunic when she was done. But as she stepped inside, she turned back, Chriani still waiting.

"My father needs to know what Barien said, but wherever he might be is too far for me to send word by any court sorcery I have access to. Whether Barien knew the source of his fear, I would not trust any in the Bastion to take word to my father now. Keep your silence while I think on this, Chriani."

He only nodded, heard the bolt click as the door closed behind her.

Chriani checked the wall again before he headed back toward the gatehouse with the faint hope that he'd manage to put off Ashlund's interrogation until the morning. But along the shadows of the courtyard track, he slowed. At the stables, he saw light still burning in the loft. At his chest, the ache of the tattoo flared against the dull resolve of the evening's drink where it welled up in him.

He stood there for a long while before he turned to cross the courtyard track, made for the stable doors.

It had been more than a year since the first time he and Kathlan had found themselves together, but only a month since the news of Lauresa's impending marriage and the series of excuses that Chriani would have once thought himself incapable of making. A month in which he'd lost count of the number of times he'd come up with reasons to not make his way to the stables after curfew, up to her pallet in the loft above.

She'd come to him that first time with a fervor that had surprised him almost as much as it pleased him. Calling herself a soldier's brat, she explained that she was the product of that casual and inexorable desire that happened between soldiers out in the field. A night of unplanned passion between her parents, she'd said, with her the end result nine months on. Then she showed him that she was no stranger to unplanned passion herself.

Her father had ridden with the garrison at Uliwen, Chriani knew, and except for his death when she was barely a girl, she likely would taken up training at his side. She'd never said how he died, just like she never spoke about the accident that had taken the strength from her leg.

Her mother had been the horse master who'd ridden with her father's troop, and who had died while on patrol four years before of some sudden consumption the healers couldn't cure. Kathlan hadn't spoken of her since the one time Chriani had asked, so he didn't ask anymore. She'd ended up in Rheran some time after, made assistant to Eugen the stable master at fourteen. Kathlan was in line for Eugen's position if she ever retired, it was said, but it was said as well that Eugen was likely to work the stables till she dropped dead and a couple of days more besides.

He'd heard Kathlan set the bolt at the main doors when he and Lauresa slipped out, so he went to the side instead. It was locked as well, but he had shadow there to hide him while he picked it.

Even before she and Chriani had come together that night after the harvest fest, Barien had liked her, and that in the end was all the encouragement that Chriani had needed. She'd sung with Barien sometimes, one of the few people that the warrior would raise his careful baritone alongside of.

Where the stables' ancient stove burned bright beneath the stone chimney that twisted through the main beams above, he found her washing at a clay basin, steam still rising from the kettle close by. She had her hair tied back to a tight tail, naked to the waist. Her skin gleamed bronze in the light, edging the sharp muscles of her arms and shoulders. She glanced up when she saw him, made no move to cover herself.

"You taking all the royal heirs drinking tonight? I'll just leave the gates open for you, shall I?"

Chriani felt the anger in her but had no words to counter it. His tongue felt thick. "Where's Eugen?"

"Bringing three of Chanist's stud stallions back from Cadaurwen. She's been gone a month. Same as you."

"Kathlan…"

"It's fine," she said. She wrung the cloth out with more force than it probably needed. "I should have been smart enough to see. All's well, I forgive you, shut the door on your way out, all right?"

"It's not that way. There's been no one else. It's been busy is all."

She laughed as she wiped dust and grime from her arms. "You're a good liar, Chriani, but what you can hide, she can't."

Chriani stared, didn't understand. Then he remembered the chill he'd felt from her earlier, Kathlan not asking Lauresa's dismissal in a way that would have gotten her the back of Ashlund's hand if he'd seen.

"The princess? Care for me?" Chriani laughed, a little too loudly.

Kathlan appraised him. "Men's ignorance comes by twos, my mother used to say. Can't tell you what they mean, can't hear meaning in what you tell them."

"Kath, she's married in ten days."

A drain opened up in the floor a step away from Chriani, but when Kathlan emptied the basin, she somehow managed to land the water closer to him than it. She appraised him coldly. "She's bound for Aerach in ten days. She's not married for a month after that. Funny you getting that mixed up."

Chriani said nothing, felt a sudden heat rising in his face. Kathlan pulled a clean tunic from the back of a chair, slipped it on over her head. "Folk have been wondering who's the one she'll be leaving behind," she said, almost to herself. "She could have done better by my eye."

"That's madness, Kath."

"You can leave anytime."

"I don't want to go," he said. And not until he heard the desperate echo of the words in his own mind did Chriani realize how true they were. In all the memory of the past month, he somehow couldn't make himself recall what had kept him away. Kathlan glanced back. The look in her eye told Chriani she'd heard it, too.

Her hair was tied with a ribbon of green silk. It was one of a number of such ribbons that had been her mother's, Kathlan had said once, and Chriani had never seen her wear any others. He untied it now as he came up carefully behind her, let dark locks fall to frame her face as she half-turned away. The green eyes were cold, but an edge in her voice echoed the feeling stirring in Chriani's gut.

"I need to be up early," she said warily. "Orders from your princess."

"You're my princess," he said, cringing inwardly even as the words rose from the numb detachment of the drink. She laughed, though. The same sound he remembered from that first night two autumns before.

"If I don't have a courier's horse ready by daybreak, it's on your head," Kathlan said. She leaned back against him, found his mouth with hers before pulling away. "Her perfume's on you," she said. "Wash before Ashlund gets a whiff and lines his saddlebags with your spleen."

Kathlan moved to retrieve the basin, Chriani slipping the bloodblade out from beneath his tunic and into his boot before she'd turned back. As she peeled his tunic off, his hands found her again but his thoughts were racing suddenly. Against the thickening of his pulse, he tried to focus.

"So what sackless sot has the princess got riding out at daybreak then?"

"Didn't care enough to ask." Kathlan filled the basin again from the kettle, added cold water from an urn. "She told me while you were outside scouting the courtyard."

As she squeezed warm water against his chest from the cloth, she noted the bandage. "What's with that?"

"Got cut in practice." He carefully guided her hands away from his shoulder, flinched pleasantly as she traced her fingers across his chest.

I would not trust any in the Bastion to take word to my father now...

"I can make it better," Kathlan said quietly.

She sent him first up the ladder to the loft, followed him with the basin and another steaming kettle. But as she led him to her pallet and laid him down there, he saw the narrow windows open to the night and the courtyard. Cold air raised goosebumps on his skin as she moved against him, the light in Lauresa's window burning brightly in the darkness beyond.

— CHAPTER 6 —

THE ODE OF SEILONNA

IT WAS WELL BEFORE DAWN when Chriani pulled himself from the half-slumber in which he'd spent the short remainder of his night in Kathlan's embrace, slipping naked across the dark loft to retrieve his clothes where she'd thrown them. He pulled the bloodblade from under her pallet where he'd managed to tuck it away unseen, careful as she shifted in her slumber.

The ache beneath the bandage was fading, but the pounding in his head was as sharp as he'd expected it would be. He forced himself to focus on both the long ride that he expected lay ahead and the favor he'd have to ask Kathlan before he could make it. He wasn't sure which he was looking forward to less.

He'd hoped to be dressed before she awoke but knew it wasn't likely. Kathlan slept lightly enough to wake if one of the horses below her so much as coughed in the night. He had to light the lantern to check the bandage, was retying it when he saw her half-open eyes watching him.

"You thinking to stop trusting me with your secrets?" she said sleepily.

"I was cut," he said, kneeling to kiss her. "I told you."

"So I shouldn't worry?"

"You know all my secrets," he said.

She rose up, stretching as she glanced to the still-open window. "It's not even light. Come back to bed." She slid across, pulled the nest of blankets back invitingly, the curve of her hip in shadow where he traced it with his hand.

"I need a horse," he said.

"I know that feeling." She ran her fingers up his thigh, laughed when he didn't.

"I need a horse," he said again. "I need to ride out this morning."

Her expression changed as she rose up on one arm, wide awake suddenly.

"The courier you're readying for this morning isn't a courier,"

Chriani said awkwardly. "I think the princess means to ride out herself for the frontier. Seeking her father."

He felt her pull away even before the blankets closed around her again. She pushed back, sat up against the wall.

"This isn't about what you said last night," he said carefully. "There's nothing between the princess and I except that Barien charged me with keeping her safe. She can't be allowed to ride out alone."

"So tell Ashlund."

"I don't know if Ashlund can be trusted."

She rose, padding naked in the lamplight to find her tunic and leggings. She hit the ladder barefoot as Chriani called her name in vain. He jumped past her, hit the floor hard in the darkness. He managed to grab her up blindly as she tried to force her way past him, felt her hand come up to strike him hard. It was the same cheek Lauresa had hit. He winced as she stalked away.

"One chance. The truth," she said coldly.

From the stalls, he heard the first restless stirrings of horses. At his chest, he felt the ache that had first stirred in him a month before.

In his mind, he felt for the one small piece of truth that would hide the larger lie.

"She's a princess," he said. "I'll make gatehouse fourth watch chief when I'm sixty if I'm lucky. Use your head, Kath."

"You were close to her once," Kathlan said. With the rush of obviousness that came from an understanding he should have had long before, Chriani heard the uncertainty in her. He saw the defiance in her eyes.

"When I trained her?" In the darkness, he saw her look away. "We were children, Kath."

"I was a child the first time I fell in love," she said. She tossed kindling to the embers still glowing in the stove. "But I'm not a child anymore, and I'm not ready to wait for you to decide whether you are or not."

He came up behind her then, held her tight. He could feel her press back against him for a long moment, then she unclasped his hands slowly from her waist. As the fire caught, she tossed split fir from a neatly stacked pile, slammed the stove door closed.

"I want to ride with the rangers," she said. The defiance of her eyes was in her voice now in a way that Chriani had only rarely heard.

"Then you will."

"I can outride anyone in the keep, half the Bastion garrison."

"I know," he said, and it was true.

"I've never told anyone that. Now I'm telling you. What do you tell me in return?"

Chriani was silent a long moment. He felt the first heat from the stove, realized how cold he was.

"I don't know what you want to hear."

"That you've got ambition beyond being some noble's lapdog the rest of your life would be a good start."

She pulled on her boots, tied her hair back with her mother's ribbon.

"I can't promise you a future when I don't know yet what the future is for me," he said.

"If you don't know your own ambition, Chriani, what in nature's name do you know?"

"I know that Barien is dead for saving the prince's life, and he told me with his last breath to keep the princess safe." He was surprised to hear the anger in his voice, hadn't felt it coming. He checked it. "That's what I am right now," he said. "What I am after that's done, I don't know yet."

Kathlan's expression had softened, but her voice was cold. "Well, when you find someone to tell you, maybe you can tell me, too," she said.

She pulled tack and a saddle from a bench close by, slung it over her shoulder as if it weighed nothing. "There's a roan gelding destrier shod and ready, last stall by the gates. I trained him myself. You get him saddled and out of here before I'm done, I can tell Ashlund you stole him if he asks."

She leaned in to kiss him as she passed, though. Chriani felt the pain flare at his chest as he watched her go.

He had the roan combed out and saddled in good time, then quietly ate from the bread and cheese left at the stove bench that he was fairly certain was Kathlan's breakfast. He left her most of it but took her blanket, plus a battered shortsword and cloak he found hanging in the farriers' stalls. He had to bend the cloak to get it on, dirt caked thick enough across it to almost close over a jagged gash at one shoulder.

As he slipped past her, Kathlan was working on a lean grey palfrey farther down the stalls. She had it saddled but was still checking its shoes as Chriani quietly slipped the bars at the gate, led the roan out into darkness. He stayed close along the wall that flanked the market court before slipping off toward the trade road, less chance of being seen from the keep that way.

Crossing the square out of sight of the gates, he slipped into the shelter of a ruined archway that flanked Five Hog's House on its corner. He had good line of sight to the keep, watched for any sign of movement as he paced the horse to keep it warm. Whichever way she went, he'd be close enough to catch her, either cutting east from the gates if she was headed down the dock road, or south along the trade way to follow Chanist's troop where they headed into the sunset two nights before.

Whatever her route, though, he knew that if she'd gone so far as to plan to slip away alone before dawn, it was going to take a fight to accompany her, just as he knew he didn't want it happening within the walls of the keep when it came. He wasn't sure how she was going to arrange to slip out of the Bastion unseen, but Chriani was confident that once Lauresa's mind was made up, not much would get in her way.

Then, unexpectedly, he found himself thinking about how much explaining he'd have to do if he was wrong and it was Ashlund himself or some other garrison rider heading off that morning. Or if no one showed at all, how long would he wait before the market court filled up and he had to go back to knock at the gates with a stolen horse and an explanation he could never give?

But when he saw the stable gates open, he knew. He hadn't been waiting long enough to feel the cold yet, the sky only just edged with the copper-white of dawn. He saw the grey palfrey slip through the gate behind a figure wrapped tight in a familiar weather-stained cloak. His eyes pulled all detail from the shadow, marked the livery and saddlebags of a courier. He saw the figure carefully scan the road to both sides before she swung on to the palfrey's back.

He saw Kathlan as the gate pulled shut, dark hair framing her face as she watched him. Then the rider was moving, pushing the horse to a fast trot across the market court. Heading south, anxious to get out of sight of the keep in a hurry.

Chriani was in the saddle as she approached, breaking out from hiding as Lauresa pushed past him. She saw him, turned on him quickly. Stared with a genuine shock that Chriani found pleasing.

"Highness," he said as he pulled in beside her.

Lauresa reined to a halt, her horse skittish as the roan held steady. "Return to the keep at once," she hissed. As she tried to back away, the palfrey's hooves skittered on frosted cobbles.

"Thank you, highness, but I have a hankering to travel." Chriani circled her carefully, kept the palfrey hedged in as she turned to keep him in sight. The princess was easily his equal in the saddle, he knew, but he had the advantage of having unexpectedly scuttled what was probably a very well-laid plan. From what he'd learned these past days of Lauresa's ability to plan, he could only imagine the distress that caused her.

"This is not your affair," she said coldly.

"Not my affair? How long do you think before they realize you're gone? I was alone with you last night, you think Ashlund wouldn't have me in thumbscrews before the morning was out?"

"My absence has been accounted for. Yours has not. This is my journey."

"Yes, you said so last night. Unable to trust anyone in the Bastion, you said. I'm sorry I didn't realize I was included in that number."

Lauresa's eyes were blue steel, her breath flaring. "Go back now."

"Why did you lie to me?"

"Keeping my family's business to myself is hardly lying, tyro."

"Where it concerns an attempt on the prince's life and the royal heir riding alone into a potential war zone, this goes far beyond family business."

"Do not presume to tell me how to care for my own father!"

"I was told to watch you, and I will watch you until you pass the borders of Brandishear for the last time. With your permission or without it, I will keep you safe as Barien did."

"I trusted Barien!" Lauresa shouted, her voice an echo off the stones. Within the words, Chriani felt a cold contempt that went beyond any affectation.

"And what have I done to inspire your distrust, highness?" he said quietly.

"You knew the bloodblade when you found it…"

"As did you," Chriani said.

"I recognized that blade because one like it killed my grandfather when I was five years old and made my father prince. What of you, tyro?"

Chriani had no answer. He felt real anger from her now, not the imperious disdain she'd directed to him that first night. She looked from him to the keep, anxious. Already, there was movement along the lanes leading to the market court.

"That's what last night was about then," he said. He felt his anger twist inward, cursing himself for missing what should have been obvious. "Not just wishing to hear what word had spread, but to question me." He remembered her hand in his, the feeling of her body that shredded away suddenly to become the memory of Kathlan moving above him in the dark. He forced the images from his mind, tried to push all the memory away.

"Getting word to my father is my responsibility."

"Keeping you safe is mine."

"I order you…"

"I take my orders from Barien and none else!" It was Chriani shouting this time, but Lauresa wheeled as his words echoed, trying to break for the cover of an open lane even as he cut around her, held her to the open cobbles of the square.

Lauresa looked back one last time to the walls behind them. "Keep with me," she said. Her voice was very cold. "Fall behind and you can make your own way back."

"Highness." Chriani nodded, backed the roan up to watch her spur ahead, the palfrey off like a shot along the road, frost-steam rising behind it.

They rode hard to the city's edge, slowing only as the last trade way outposts dwindled to the first of the farm laborer's huts, smoke rising from scattered chimneys. Behind them, dawn had broken, the gleam of white from the water obscured by the rise of the headlands where the keep spread in stark silhouette.

As Lauresa trotted ahead, she made no sign that she was even aware of Chriani behind her, no signal to him when she cut hard into the woods past a small roadside cairn. A narrow patch of rocky ground there was swallowed by the woods beyond, Chriani following her to see a trail open up in the shadows, all but invisible from the sunlit road behind them. The moss-lined track had been recently torn, he saw. Chanist's troop riding through two days before.

They were alone as they rode, no sound around them but the horses' steady plodding and winter birdsong in the twisted witchwillow that rose to hem them in. Silver-grey branches scattered the light, kept them in shadow as the sun slowly climbed.

From somewhere to the right, Chriani caught the intermittent ripple of a still-flowing stream, the path following the shelter of the trees that grew in ranks alongside it, he guessed. The land was higher here, pushing steadily up from the coastal lowlands of the city, the air thick with fog that seemed to Chriani only slightly less cold than Lauresa's silence as she rode. Though they stopped twice to rest and water the horses in streamside clearings, the princess sat both times with her back to Chriani in a decidedly purposeful way.

She looked over when they stopped a third time late in the day, though, the sun beginning to burn through the haze just in time to set. He was making his way carefully through a frozen track of bog that spread ahead of where the ice-edged stream twisted back into the woods, scouring the snowberry bushes growing wild there for the frozen fruit that still clung to their branches, only ripening with the first frosts.

"What are you doing?" she called.

After the long silence of the day, her voice startled him. Chriani glanced up, saw her watching where she leaned back against an upthrust wedge of stone. Though it was heavy with moss where it jutted from the ground, it was unnatural in its placement somehow. He thought he remembered seeing others like it along the trail they were following. Ranger markers, he guessed.

"Eating, highness."

"You're out of food already?"

"I was forced to pack hurriedly, highness."

Silently, Lauresa broke half her bread, stood to toss it and a chunk of dried meat to where Chriani's saddle blanket lay, the horses tethered and grazing winter rye a short distance off.

He brought back the shirt full of berries he'd collected, set them down on the cheesecloth that served as her platter. He left her the fullest fruit, ate the rest himself as he sat. The bread took away some of the bitterness.

They made a good distance along the trail before darkness closed them in, Lauresa stopping in a small copse of alder. Green-black shadows stretched around them, cloud promising a warmer night where it pushed in, but Chriani made a fire anyway. Even so close to the farmsteads, wolves and sometimes worse ran the course of the sheltered winter waterways before the snows came.

Though she hadn't spoken since the last stop, Lauresa's mood seemed lighter somehow. Still pensive but not actively hating him, Chriani thought. Small improvements.

It was dark when she began to sing. Chriani was banking the fire up, fighting the fatigue that was reminding him how little sleeping he'd actually done the night before. Lauresa had already set her bedroll up across the clearing from him, and her voice rose from the shadows there like clear light. As with the brief fragments she'd sung the night Barien died, Chriani didn't recognize the language, but in the sustained passages she sang now, he began to make out words, sharp-edged.

Ysh nell to sull gweana caer in toryn
Tar seacla mi kaay to cirwyr saym
Al to ceimond dovya brall
Dovya nay to craym

He spoke the Ilvalantar, the language of the Ilmar Ilvani, though it had been long years since he'd done so aloud. His mother had taught him when he was a child, his proficiency making the leatherworkers of the Terever Woods laugh when they visited, trading worked belts for the delicate woodwork his mother had carved. This was different but had the same feel, somehow. A language meant to be sung, not spoken. The shape of the words seemingly tangible as they slipped through him

Nar min briev ysh craonn tau ceinn
Braern ar nay min leinn
Cal lun tau seryan ede to maynd
Lun tau seryan neld to caynd…

Chriani felt the silence of the night hanging like tapestry, surrounding them as Lauresa's voice trailed off.

"That was very beautiful." All he could think to say.

Lauresa didn't look to him, staring into the fire. "It is 'The Ode of Seilonna.' A lament of departure and leave-taking."

"I don't know the language," he said.

"Leisana. Not many do." As she set another length of deadfall on the fire, Chriani caught her face in the flare of light. She'd been crying, he saw. "The Leisanmira speak it. The wandering folk of south Elalantar and the western hill country."

"Your mother's folk."

Lauresa looked up at him. "My folk."

Though Chriani's lack of study of the histories of the Ilmar had always left him precious short on details of how Lauresa's mother had been set aside in favor of Chanist's second marriage to Gwannyn, the odes of the bards that Barien himself sometimes sang made up for it.

As a child of the wandering folk, Irdaign had been an acceptable match for the young Princeling Chanist who'd fallen in love and gotten her with child in the early days of the campaign that would quickly become the Ilvani Incursions.

The court of Chanist's father at Rheran had created a suitable pedigree for Irdaign, creating connections to a lost Leisanmira royal family that had never existed. But once Chanist had taken the throne upon the death of his father six years later, that questionable pedigree had no longer been enough.

"It sounds Ilvani," Chriani said.

"It was. Long ago."

Ilmari and Ilvani were one folk, his mother said.

"I'm sorry," Chriani said. "For my words this morning." Though he wasn't sure if it would do any good at that point, he knew it would do less good by the morning.

"It's a difficult thing having been told your whole life that you are too important to be allowed to make your own decisions," Lauresa said. "You were right. Your presence on this journey is prudent. And welcome."

A silence fell then that Chriani assumed would end the night, but Lauresa spoke once more. Her voice roused him as he stared into the embers of the fire.

" 'The Ode of Seilonna' is about the road that leads endlessly away from home. The Leisanmira have the freedom to make their home in any lands, but not the freedom to ever call those lands home. Always seeking a thing they will never find."

The darkness was full enough that even Chriani's eyes couldn't pierce it, but he thought he heard her crying again.

When Lauresa finally slept, he stayed awake for a long while. He paced around the copse a half-dozen times but saw no sign of movement, animal or otherwise, in the light of the Darkmoon or the star-studded sky. He trusted the horses to wake if they scented wolves or anything else, but he slept lightly all the same. A half-dozen times, he awoke in a dull dream-state, expecting to find the princess packed up and vanished in the night.

She was still there in the morning, though. She had the fire going, the smell of roasting pork waking him, Chriani annoyed at himself for having slept nearly until first light. The long day's ride and the even longer night before had caught up to him, he thought.

But even as he packed up, Chriani froze. Stared.

There beside his saddlebags, he saw a scrap of parchment, folded tight and bound with a ribbon of green silk. Across the top edge, *Chriani* was written in an angular hand.

"I found it in my saddlebags," Lauresa said simply. Chriani nodded, didn't look at her. He gently pulled the ribbon free, sure he was only imagining that Kathlan's scent still clung to it.

When he unfolded it, the parchment was blank.

"A message from the girl at the stables?"

"Take care of the horse or she'll line her saddlebags with my spleen," Chriani said. "She'll do it, too." He laughed, the sound wrong somehow.

They ate in silence, headed out under a red dawn that turned to a dark day, cloud still pushing in from the north as the winds across the distant Sea of Ehadne scoured the Clearwater basin and the steppes beyond. As the forest around the line of the trail they followed thinned to scrubland for a brief space just past daymark, Chriani saw what he guessed was the Glaeddynfield road to the south, a faint scar marking off green farmland beyond.

"A storm coming," Chriani said. "Evening at the latest." As she glanced to the sky, Lauresa nodded agreement. "We should take to the road. Make a village by dusk, find somewhere to shelter."

"No," she said. She cantered on, wind tugging at her cloak. Chriani glanced again to the darkening sky, wondered if she knew something he didn't.

He was about to speak again when he spotted the rider. Alone, faint against the darkening sky to the west. Chriani slowed to watch, calculated distance and trajectory along the edge of the fields where the figure bore fast toward them, perhaps a quarter-league away.

"It's all right," Lauresa said. He wheeled to see her following his gaze, spurring her horse forward. "Come."

As Chriani followed her, he slipped the battered shortsword from its scabbard, scanned the horizon to all sides but saw no sign of other movement. Ahead, the black sky had swallowed the last light of day, and he strained to pull detail from the shadow.

He'd never seen the figure before, but in the end, he knew there was only one person it could be. She rode easy as she raced toward them, features slowly coming into clear focus in the half-light. The tightly curled hair was deep bronze, the first streaks of grey only showing where it flew behind her, but Chriani recognized the blue eyes all the same. Even sharing the color of her father, Lauresa had her mother's eyes, it was said.

As Lauresa spurred toward the Princess Precedent Irdaign, Chriani slowed the roan, held back to a canter as the two came close. Irdaign was riding bareback and without reins, he saw, her black stallion slowing with just a word as Lauresa came alongside her.

Where he watched the princess embrace her mother in the dying light, Chriani saw her tears. But as she clung to her daughter, the princess precedent's gaze lifted to seek him out, and he looked quickly away. Turning the roan, he paced around them in some vain attempt at setting up a one-horse perimeter. Trying not to watch.

When she was younger, when she trained at his side, he'd felt a strength in Lauresa. Eldest child of a youngest prince, born in wartime and raised by a father who seemed convinced that every new dawn might bring the final wave of Ilvani invasion from the Greatwood's endless shadow. And though it had taken him until this moment to recognize it, Chriani realized that he'd seen that same strength in her again that fateful night in the library. Honed and shaped to a different tension, but still drawn from the same source. The strength of will and personality that marked one accustomed to having to prove herself. A strength of hand and word, like that of Barien in brawl and debate alike. The strength of the leader she'd never get a chance to be.

But in the princess precedent's arms, that strength was gone now. Lauresa was a girl who'd spent her life estranged from the mother she loved, and who had seen her father nearly struck down in her own house, and who was nine days now from the fanfare and the boat that would take her forever from the home she'd been sheltered in since the day she was born.

A sleet wind was rising, the scent of far-off thunder sharp as Chriani rubbed his eyes. He heard the low thud of hooves, turned to see Irdaign and Lauresa pacing toward him side by side, hand in hand. He sheathed the sword with what he hoped was suitable ceremony, nodded low in the saddle.

"Enough of that," the princess precedent intoned. Her face was set but he heard the smile in her voice. She wore a cloak of night-blue that he'd taken for black at first, bracelets of lapis at her wrists to match her earrings. "It's been a great number of years since anyone was compelled to defer to me, master Chriani. I don't intend to have to get used to it again."

He nodded again anyway. "Highness."

"I know a place close by," she said. "Come."

They headed back down and across the track they'd followed at the stream's edge, Chriani guardedly watching the shadows that rose around them now, the storm whispering its approach in the hissing of the wind-whipped trees. To the southeast, he saw a low rise of wooded hill that Irdaign seemed to be leading them toward, the darker stain of stone barely visible against grey-green shadow as he squinted. Ruins of some sort, almost overgrown.

"There," Irdaign said, almost as if she could sense him staring to the darkness, and where her horse turned up the hill, he saw a narrow track emerge in a twisting sea of tall grass. Single file, they advanced to the top, Chriani fighting the urge to spur ahead and check for ambush. But even as they climbed, he found himself wondering at the princess precedent's sudden arrival, Lauresa clearly expecting her.

The princess could have gotten word to her by spellcraft, he guessed. He still had the ring Lauresa had given him tucked up inside his sleeve. But even as exhausted as her horse looked, it was six days hard road riding to the Glaeddyn farmsteads from Irdaign's home near Myrwater. Even assuming that Lauresa had sent word of her leaving the night she'd given Kathlan the order to prepare a horse, the numbers didn't add up. Changing horses twice a day, it still would have been a ride to challenge the best of Chanist's rangers. Chriani felt a lingering uncertainty, didn't know where it came from, but once or twice, he almost thought he saw Irdaign's black steed casually turn its head back to watch him.

At the crest of the hill, two stone walls still stood, an ancient fir growing up around the ruined cornerstone between them, enough shelter under its boughs to hopefully deflect the weather that was coming. Across the hillside, other clumps of stone punched up from the grass like breakers on a frozen sea. More than one building here originally. A watchtower village perhaps, dating from the first wars to judge by the extent of the ruin. Too long ago to remember even dates now. The forests of the Valnirata had pushed this far once, the Ilvani dominion extending beyond them and across all the Ilmar. The Ilvani tree-cities were long gone, but the stones that the Ilmari had raised to shelter themselves through the long wars endured.

Where Chriani dismounted, he lashed the roan to a low branch, started a slow circle of the clearing to look for firewood. Behind him, Lauresa tied her horse, unhitched saddle and tack as it began to crop the tall oat grass, still full. Irdaign slipped from her own horse with the grace of someone much younger than Chriani knew she was, motioned it to follow her as she walked it to the clearing's edge.

She had no way to tie it, Chriani realized. Not even a halter hanging from it. He wondered if the beast could possibly be well tamed enough to simply stand by for the night.

But then he watched Lauresa's mother lean in close, whisper a word in the horse's ear. It seemed to nod as she stepped back. Then all at once, a light that brought Chriani's hand up to cover his eyes flared all around the animal's form, bright as any evenlamp in the falling dark. And like it had suddenly been shredded on a grate of the hottest coals, the horse collapsed in on itself as Irdaign stepped back, its skin shot through with an all-consuming white flame that raced across it like wildfire in summer grass.

Then it was gone. No flame, no ash remaining. Just Irdaign pacing slowly across the clearing toward where Lauresa had watched it all impassively, carefully setting her saddle in the shelter of the wall.

When Chriani's hand shot to his chest to make the moonsign, Irdaign hadn't seen. Lauresa did, though, watching him now as he stumbled back. Chriani saw Irdaign follow her daughter's gaze before he was able to turn away.

The rain hit early that night, the lightning not far behind it. The three of them ate in silence beneath the fir, the smoke of the fire twisting up through the canopy of branches. Chriani sat a discreet distance away, ostensibly to give mother and daughter the privacy they seemed to want. What he was watching had been a large part of Lauresa's wanting to make this journey alone, he'd realized belatedly, but the fear still twisting in his gut made him grateful for the distance.

The bardic odes also had much to say about the spellcraft of the Leisanmira, but Chriani had never paid them much mind. Watching Irdaign now, though, he felt the chill that had traced his spine when the horse had vanished, had to fight to keep himself from shivering. There was something in her manner as she whispered in Lauresa's ear, some sense of unseen power as she gazed around her, taking in the hill and the countryside below.

It was said that the old Ilvani blood flowed in Leisanmira veins. Rumors from a time before the Ilmar settlements, before the long wars that drove the Valnirata war-clans deep into the forest. One blood from long ago. Where they wandered Elalantar and the steppes of the western frontier, the Leisanmira had a reputation as hedge wizards and midwives, dabbling in charms. Darker rumors spoke of even greater power among them, somehow kept secret from the always-watchful eyes of the rangers and the local garrisons in the towns they passed through.

Until now, he'd never believed it.

When dinner was done, he banked the fire up and bid Lauresa and her mother a formal goodnight that only Irdaign answered. He heard snatches of song as he checked and stowed his gear for the morning, Irdaign's voice beautiful beyond any description as she sang quietly to Lauresa curled at her feet.

On the other side of the wall, Chriani found a space for himself that was only partly soaking, and he tried for some time to find a sitting position that would keep the tear in the cloak away from the rain. He closed his eyes once or twice, but the lightning was a constant eruption within the clouds now. The hillside pulsed daylight-bright, thunder reverberating with a fury that kept him from hearing Irdaign as she slipped up behind him, her hand on his shoulder as she kneeled.

Chriani started, fought to still his hand where it wanted to trace the crescent above his pounding heart. In the intermittent light, he might have taken Irdaign's face for Lauresa's, but she smiled in a way that he couldn't remember seeing Lauresa smile for so long now.

"One who grew up under Barien's charge should be too smart to be as afraid as you seem," she said quietly.

"Forgive me, princess precedent."

"My name is Irdaign, Chriani."

He could only nod. She was thoughtful, slowly placed her hand on his as if she knew its plan. "When one must make five days' ride in two, one needs a horse beyond what any stable in Myrwater or Rheran can hold."

"I understand, Irdaign."

"But you fear nonetheless. Barien was fond of saying that fear and understanding will make war in any mind so long as both live. You need to choose which rules you."

We end up afraid of only the things we see…

Irdaign's hand on his was warm, and in that warmth Chriani felt a shame that he hoped she couldn't see. This matron, this figure of royalty, scaring him.

In the entire garrison, Barien had been the only one to Chriani's knowledge who paid Chanist's court sorcery neither the reverence nor the superstition it seemed to demand. It had been High Winter two years previous, and the news had just come in from Quilimma in the southern marches of the rangers putting down a rogue mage. In a lost fortress high on the steep slopes of the Analatias, he'd settled himself and laid claim to the lands around him, and a half-dozen had died in the attack that finally brought him down. When the story was told in the barracks halls, all present made the moonsign but Barien.

"Folk should rightly respect what they don't know, but most folk forget that they don't know much," he'd said later that night when Chriani had asked him why. "Sorcery and life-magic are like any other craft. There's danger in the wizard's craft, to be sure. But remind folk how much danger they're in riding a badly shod horse at full gallop, they'll find as much respect for the blacksmith's craft in a grand hurry."

When Chriani glanced up, Irdaign was watching him closely. He hesitated.

"You knew Barien," he said.

He saw the smile leave her eyes for just a moment. "I did. And I am truly grieved."

Then she touched his cloak, her voice a gentle whisper of song as faint light flared beneath her fingers. Where Chriani looked to see her run them along the cloth, the cloak was whole again, the jagged tear repaired with no stitch or seam.

"It is dry on the other side of the wall," she said. "Sleep there, please. Lauresa and I must walk."

He nodded again as she rose, waited until she'd turned away to make the moonsign with a shaking fist. In the staccato shimmer of the clouds, he saw Lauresa a dozen paces off, cloak wrapped tight around her. She stepped in behind her mother, the two of them pacing off through the storm.

Chriani made sure they saw him pull his sodden bedding around to the fire, waiting until they were out of sight beyond a twisted stand of low-growing spruce before he followed. Across the mud-sodden hillside, he moved within the storm's dark spaces, stuck to the shadows as the lightning flared.

"Sorcery won't kill you any better or faster than the countless other ways to die," Barien had told him that night two years before. "Be wary of them all."

He saw Lauresa and her mother stop some dozen strides above a rocky basin, a tumbled cairn below them. For the long while that they stood there, he watched them, rain-soaked. They sang together, voices clear like crystal above the guttural rumble of the slowly fading storm.

And all the while, Chriani's hand was tight to his chest, scribing the moonsign until his arm ached as he watched Irdaign dance in the lightning. Watched her summon her own storm of fire that slammed down upon the cairn like a living wave.

In the shape of the unearthly flames that rose and twisted around the princess precedent, he thought he saw some great bird spread its wings, shrieking with a sound that drove through him like nails. Rain shadow shrouded the power she hurled with her hands, Lauresa standing to watch a short distance away, expressionless as she matched her mother's voice.

At one point, in the darkness and the blinding rain that blurred his sight, Chriani would have taken Irdaign for Lauresa. The bronze hair was lit to wet gold by the staccato pulse of lightning, all the lines of age blurred by distance and stormlight and the power that coursed through her body and struck the stone as fire again and again.

When they finally headed back, Chriani sprinted along the hillside ahead of them, pretended to be asleep as they returned to sit by the fire. He was still awake when dawn came, uncomfortably dry inside his shredded cloak made whole again.

At some point in the time that Chriani had saddled up his own horse, Irdaign's black stallion had reappeared. He said nothing, tried not to meet the gaze of the unnatural beast. But as though it could sense his fear, he thought he saw its sidelong glance seek him out as they descended the track.

Across the hillside, the cairn stood in the hollow where he'd missed it the night before, stone and grass and crusted moss charred black now. Chriani looked away.

Irdaign rode with them only a half-league or so, stopping to turn east where the road could be seen across a short stretch of open pasture and milling sheep. Along the field's edge, Chriani held back again, saw Lauresa cry once more as her mother held her. Irdaign turned back to him, though, rode up close beside him as he waited. She clasped his hand again.

"What do you mean to do?"

She might have meant one of any thousand things, but Chriani knew what she spoke of. The same answer either way, though. "I don't know."

"Barien wanted you to seek your commission."

"He had more faith in my ability to get it than I."

"Barien understood that you have the strength to walk that path. Yet you have the fear that prevents you from seeking it. Fear and understanding, Chriani." Her words had a softness to them that he remembered from his mother's voice. This woman he'd met only a day before but who seemed to know him somehow.

He nodded, Irdaign slipping her hand from his. A whispered word to the horse, then they were off. Lauresa watched for a long while, Chriani silent behind her. When the princess finally turned, her eyes were dry.

The track was mud but they made good time that day and the next, the sky bright and warm. As they rode, the tree line meandered to the south above open pasture, handfuls of farmhouses scattered like the white-faced sheep that clustered in the fields around them. As they broke from the forest track early on the second day, Chriani set them following a line of border stones along a tall trail of spectral elms. Down a steep slope beyond them, a straight-line path made toward a distant poplar bluff.

Beyond the bluff, Chriani could see the haze of the encampment they were headed for, the faint white of tents a brighter mark against a sheen of fog. And beyond it, a further day's ride in the distance, he could see the forest wall rise up to blot the land beyond. These would likely be the last farmsteads they saw, he knew. A day's ride wasn't enough distance to keep a rogue Valnirata war-band at bay.

They rode in silence through that morning, Lauresa's mood dark in a way that seemed to go far beyond this last meeting with the mother she was leaving behind. Chriani's mood was no lighter, and the silence hanging between them was welcomed for a while. In the light of day, the memory of the night before seemed distant, Chriani holding Irdaign's words close like he hoped they might shroud the memory of what he'd seen her do.

Lauresa and her mother. Exiles heading in different directions, Chriani thought. Rheran the place where both had begun, closed off to them now.

Lauresa was a problematic peerage, they'd said. Whispered voices had spread the words within the Bastion the week her marriage was announced, the same thoughts repeated more loudly in the keep and the city beyond. With her mother set aside and her younger sister's blood linked to the Elalantar line, Lauresa was half a princess in the eyes of too many. Safer then to have her relinquish any possible claim to the crown in favor of accepting title in another land. And so she would be the Princess Lauresa of Brandishear for another seven days.

Another nail in the framework of arranged marriages that bound the Ilmar principalities in treaty and blood.

"What do you know about this husband of yours?"

Chriani hadn't wanted to say it, but the words spilled too easily into the long silence of the ride. He heard Irdaign's words from the night before, *fear and understanding*. He wished he could have thought to tell her then that there was some understanding fear was meant to prevent.

Lauresa didn't look back. "A duke," she said coldly. The question was one she'd been asked enough times in past weeks that she perhaps didn't hear the bitterness beneath his version of it. Or didn't care. "Allenis Andreg, his holdings in Teillai, cousin to Prince High Vishod. He was a captain of some renown, granted title after the Incursions. *The Lion of Aerach*, they call him. Warden of the Clearwater Steppes."

It had been thirteen years since the Ilvani Incursions had ended. Chriani did the math, guessed at this former captain's age and got a number he didn't like.

"It isn't fair." He might have only meant it as a thought, but it came as words. Lauresa turned back this time.

"Many have endured a great deal more than a marriage for the land and its people to prosper," she snapped. "Your father was killed in the Incursions, Barien said. You forget him and all who made that same sacrifice so easily?"

Chriani felt his blood quicken, a trace of unfamiliar emotion twisting in him suddenly. It was no secret, certainly, this story he'd adopted on the day Barien took him in, but in all the years since he'd first spoken it, he'd gotten used to hearing it in only his own voice. He wasn't sure why it bothered him now.

He felt the pain then. Deep in his chest, spreading to the skin at the spot where her name would stay, he felt the sudden spike of frenzy that had driven him to trace those seven letters in blood in the first place. And with a rush of insight that swelled like the sudden ache that had risen behind his eyes, Chriani recognized for the first time this pain that had threaded through him for as much of his life as he could remember, but which he'd never before named.

The pain of living a lie, he thought.

He had no memory of his father in him but what his mother had told him. But even that had been buried long ago beneath the lie that had let him survive in the Ilmar village of his birth, and along the desolate road that had taken him from his mother and grandfather's graves to Rheran, and that had brought him into the Bastion at Barien's side. Now a princess's name etched on his skin over one night of anger would become a new lie that twisted in with the old like the lines of that name twisted in with the mark his mother had made. And for the very first time, Chriani recognized the ache that had twisted in his gut that long night. He recognized the pain that had echoed the searing of his skin as the needle-sharp tip of the pick punched down again and again.

This was the pain of never knowing who he was, he thought. The pain of never knowing who he might be. This was the pain that drove him to routine rage in the face of a captain's arrogance and a princess's dismissal and all the host of other missteps, confusions, and calculated conflicts that had been a part of his life within the hierarchy of the Bastion.

Fear and understanding. He felt the pulse of anger flare where its name had finally been spoken, seeking an outlet now.

Lauresa seemed to sense it, something changed in her manner. Still the anger she'd carried from when she'd seen Chriani make the moonsign against her mother, but softened somehow. "I'm sorry. I didn't mean..."

But her voice cut off as Chriani wheeled, reined in one-handed as the other hand whipped the shortsword from its scabbard with a hiss. He flipped his cloak behind him to free his arms, seized Lauresa's reins and pulled them hard, the palfrey skidding to a halt. The hand with the reins came up close to her mouth, but she'd already seen the warning in his eyes.

Behind them, beyond the shelter of the elm line, he heard hoofbeats. Muffled, running, the sound far but fading. To the south, a flight of starlings lifted from a stand of white pine, their shimmering cries cutting the silence.

"Stay low," he whispered, close to Lauresa's ear. He left his reins in her hand, slipped from the saddle and into dull grey shadow along the side of the track. Pushing straight through, he listened, no sound except the faint bleating of sheep in the distance, a dog barking farther off. He was conscious of Lauresa alone behind him, but the open expanse of fields to all sides told him they were alone. No way for anyone to get to her before he would.

He saw the tracks where the horse that followed them had stood. Pressing low to the ground, he studied the telltale marks of its wheeling to spring northward, back toward the forest and away from them.

Someone riding alone, carefully following the trail through the wind-whipped grass that the two of them had made.

At the top of the slope, footprints. Someone stepping down from the saddle to watch through the trees, a perfect view of Chriani and Lauresa as they made their way along the field's edge.

He bent low to the ground, measured out the impression with his hand. Against the scent of moss and mud, he caught a familiar tang of metal even as he recognized the heavy print of a steel-shod boot.

"What is it?" Lauresa asked when he slipped back a moment later, vaulting up to the saddle beside her.

"Nothing," he said as he spurred forward. "Farm boy thinking he can teach a draft horse to run. Making more noise than a war-band falling down a flight of stairs."

He kept close to her, though, one hand always within reach of her saddle where he rode just behind her. Lauresa didn't see him glance back at regular intervals until they finally passed the bluff. Chriani rode them up it, scanned the empty countryside around them for a long while. At the far edge of sight, he thought he saw movement to the north, but it was gone when he blinked so he pushed them on again, headed down toward the evening smoke already rising from Chanist's camp.

— CHAPTER 7 —

Lauresa's Song

CHANIST HAD HIS OUTRIDERS running a wider perimeter than Chriani expected, spotting him and the princess where they rode in almost as quickly as he saw them. One horse turned to bolt back for the camp, two more advancing. Lauresa had thought well enough ahead to have packed the Rheran standard, Chriani holding it aloft as he rode alongside and behind her.

The riders' strangled looks when they finally got close enough to recognize the princess made up for the length of time it took them to lower their bows in Chriani's mind, but just barely. By the time they passed through the perimeter, the two who flanked them were joined by four more, a regular procession riding down the ranks of troops pressing in along the sides of the muddy track that split the camp. An impromptu honor guard by the look of it, Chriani guessing at a hundred figures surrounding them, only a quarter in the grey leather of Chanist's guard. Beyond them, more astoundingly, he estimated ten times that many troops spread across a trio of low-rising hills. The troop Chanist had ridden out with had expanded fiftyfold, riders and foot soldiers coming in from Addrimyr and Glaeddyn and beyond. How many more troops might still be on their way, how far Chanist's summons had carried, Chriani didn't know.

The encampment itself was a sprawling mass of tents and platforms that he could see only part of as they turned up a rough path of gravel toward the prince's pavilion. Chriani had seen it as they'd ridden in, a clutch of five-pillar tents with a wide awning around them. Three banners were flying there — the falcon of Brandis in ascent, then the four interlocked spears of the Ilmar standard. Below that, the horse-and-axe insignia of Chanist's house, which was also the insignia of the regiment of Rheran and the Bastion — the companies of the prince's guard who served the capital and Chanist himself.

When the prince's own company of that regiment had ridden out, they'd carried nothing with them. The flags, the tents, the pavilions, the canvas canopies and walls of mess and armory and the practice range — all of it must have been summoned and commissioned from the frontier settlements. Chanist had likely ordered it all provisioned there for long years, ready to be set up on a day's notice. Just as he kept the prince's armory stocked, its weapons always honed.

In the light of the evenlamps that burned outside the prince high's tents, Chriani saw sudden movement. Chanist himself burst out past the guards stationed at the entrance, the runner who must have brought him the news trying to keep up. The prince slowed for just a moment, stared in stark disbelief as Lauresa slipped from the saddle to the ground. Her cloak pulled tight and raised above the mire, she slipped through a cordon of bodies toward him, her father stepping forward to embrace her without a word.

As he dismounted, Chriani still had the prince's standard in hand, only belatedly noticing the impatient page at his side waiting for it. Even as he handed it over, he found himself overwhelmed by a feeling of sudden exposure. As they had at the keep the day before, all eyes were shifting from the princess to him, Lauresa's bearing regal as she moved for the pavilion at her father's side. The roan and the palfrey were led away in the opposite direction, Chriani not sure in which direction he was meant to follow.

But as her free hand strayed from her cloak, Chriani saw the flash of the steel ring at Lauresa's finger. He absently scratched his arm within his sleeve, slipped his own ring on from its secret pocket.

I will need time to convince those who will be listening that my journey had no purpose but youthful indiscretion.

As the princess's voice rang clear in his head, Chriani fought to control his sudden fear, a shadow still twisting in him where the memory of Irdaign's sorcery burned.

We will need to speak to my father alone, Lauresa said.

Certainly, Chriani thought, though he was far from certain. *I'll wait.*

No, she said. *More alone than that. You will need to arrange this.*

Arrange this how? Chriani asked, a hint of anger twisting through the link.

Wait for the sun to clear the mountains. I will be ready then.

As she walked, Lauresa slowed, turning back almost as an afterthought to where Chriani waited. He nodded deeply.

"Thank you for your service, tyro. You must be hungry."

"Highness." He nodded again, turned with what he hoped was a suitable amount of indifference and headed back down the path. A hundred eyes watched him go, Chriani not glancing back until he was a good two-dozen strides into the slowly dispersing crowd. Behind him, Chanist and Lauresa slipped in through the open canvas doorway, four guards, a secretary, and the two outriders who had intercepted them all following.

Around him, Chriani felt the chill of night advancing, caught the tang of roast meat and ale on the breeze. He glanced to the mountains, the Eberedar peaks distant where the sun was dropping, a copper sky shining beyond still-breaking cloud.

But there was something else. Something in the air, he thought. Some edge of exhilaration in the movement and voices of the troops as they milled to all sides. He heard laughter and well-intentioned threats where a company worked with sword and spear on a muddy small arms field further south of the mess.

From somewhere came a snatch of song. *Prince Goffree fought, that good old man.* Across the Ilmar, from Rheran to the Greatwood frontier, they remembered a sovereign's murder in a children's rhyme.

He turned his course. He swung past the mess to slip through the barracks, small fires dotting the field of canvas shelters that stretched along the encampment's southern flank. He pulled his cloak tight around him, met no one's gaze, pulling in snatches of conversation as he surveyed the layout of the camp. They'd ridden the first sortie that morning — that much he got even before he'd passed the first ranks of tents. A dawn raid into the forest against a half-dozen Valnirata outposts that Chanist's intelligence had placed there.

Around the fires, he saw gambling and wine in abundance, and a sexual tension that was tangible. Between the guards of the prince's troop, the air of unplanned passion that Kathlan had talked of was hanging heavy. He watched partners he suspected hadn't known each other two days before slip into the deepening shadows, matching blankets and bodies against the cold.

It was a warrior's mentality, Barien had said once. Telling yourself that you were never sure whether the morning would bring your death, so you spent the night as the night was intended. No attachment, no caring. And though it had been two generations since any soldier of Brandishear had lived in the shadow of real war, old habits died hard. Or were kept alive for specific reason, Barien had often said.

Chriani passed three empty wains and the carefully piled mass of crates and supplies that flanked them, oilskin roped off and tied down against rain and wind. The two guards who walked a tight perimeter around the stores gave him suspicious looks, Chriani nodding to them. He didn't know what supplies exactly had been set there, but whatever it was had been stored in abundance. The look of a long campaign expected.

To the north, he heard horses restless in makeshift stables, a field of straw marked off by hitching posts driven deep in the mud. Beyond it, a broad tent was sealed tight, the guards around it telling him it must be the armory. Adjacent to that, a nondescript pavilion with a standard he recognized from the neck of the Five Hog's House barkeep. The quarters of the war-mages, he guessed, and he felt a shiver trace his spine.

They trained in the hills south of Cadaurwen, it was said. Some kind of arcane college there where they took the brand and gave over their lives to the crown in exchange for the right to practice their dark arts. It would have been more than a six-day ride for them. He remembered Irdaign's horse consumed by flame, made the moonsign as he turned away.

To the west, the officers' pavilion sat across from Chanist's own tents, but the urge to put off what Chriani knew was an inevitable meeting with Konaugo was strong. He slipped from the path to cut across an empty training ground, mentally tallied all the possible points of diversion he might make use of within the camp as he'd seen it. The armories were probably his safest bet, but their proximity to the war-mage's tents was a wild card. Perhaps the horses. Startle them, raise enough noise to put the camp on alert even as he avoided getting killed for his trouble.

He checked the sun again, not so long to wait. Time enough for a fast bite of real food while he tried to come up with a plan. After four days of jerky and bread on the road, the smell of roast meat again reminded him suddenly how hungry he was. He oriented on its source, stepped past a pair of couriers cantering past through the mire of the track.

But as he slipped along the edge of the archery yard, Chriani slowed. Stopped.

He felt his pulse quicken, felt the hammer of the anger strike against the dark places inside him. He pulled the steel ring from his finger, held it tight in a shaking hand. Too conscious of the thoughts rising in him that no one else could hear.

At the edge of the muddy field, a dozen target butts had been set up before a stand of young poplar. He saw the body there. A Valnirata warrior, leanly muscled. An outrider archer, Chriani guessed. Her throat had been cut, at least a dozen old wounds flagged red-black with the dried blood that smeared her naked frame. Over and around those wounds that had killed her, three dozen arrows pierced her through, chest and legs, arms and neck. She was hanging with limbs spread, lashed to the trees with rough rope where she'd been used as a target. Her mouth was open, sightless eyes long gone to the crows.

In the fading light as he slowly approached, Chriani saw the tattoo that wrapped her shoulder, a tight knot of black and green line stark against dead skin. A different coloration, a different design than the one his own shoulder wore. The one that reflected the mark on the dagger he could feel at his stomach where his breath came fast now.

A single broadhead shaft had pierced the tangle of ink at the Ilvani's shoulder, but whether because only one archer was good enough to hit it or because he'd called the hated symbol for himself alone, Chriani didn't know.

It was one of Konaugo's black-fletched shafts. Chriani stared for a long while.

When he finally turned away, he scanned the shadows, no one watching as he wrenched the black arrow free. He pulled five undamaged field-point shafts from the nearest butt, held the arrows straight along his arm as he walked, the blades of the broadhead locked between his fingers.

In the barracks, he claimed a bow from a Bastion sergeant he recognized, stole into his tent as he watched him slip into the tent adjacent with a ranger Chriani didn't know. It was a black-oak recurve, a little soft for his arm, but the balance was good. He slipped it within his cloak, wrapped tight around himself as he stepped outside.

He saw Konaugo then, storming in with three other riders through the mud of the firelit central track. His speed told Chriani that he'd been made aware of the princess's arrival. His expression suggested he'd heard who her escort was.

As Chriani faded back into shadow, he slipped past the poplar grove, skirting the muddy track for a larger stand of trees he'd passed, just inside the eastern edge of the camp. He avoided the light of the perimeter fires as he slipped into the white-bark shadows, the tangle of winter branches clawing at the darkening sky. Where two guards drifted slowly past a dozen strides away, they faced away from him, watching the open fields outside the camp.

Chriani watched the mountains to the west, waited as the disc of the sun slowly descended. He had the bow out and one field-point shaft nocked in a fluid motion, already sighting to the southwest where his eyes pulled detail from the distant shadows. From the mess tent, he heard voices raised in song, marked off an arcing line of sight to a tripod brazier near the closest wall, a hundred paces away. He let the arrow fly, watched it strike the pan dead on. As it careened over in a shower of sparks, he heard a shout go up.

He fired two more arrows after it, shooting high. As they hissed through the open side of the tent well above the heads of the troops there, he saw those troops hit the ground, both shafts shattering as their blunted ends struck the canvas wall on the opposite side.

He had a fourth arrow nocked, spinning to fire to the other side of the camp, a lantern burning there where it hung on the post outside Chanist's pavilion. One guard was close enough to it that Chriani hoped he got clear in time as his shot shattered it, gouts of oil exploding to flame. Through the officers' pavilion, he fired once more, sent a blunted shaft ricocheting off the flagstaff where a Brandishear banner flew.

He nocked Konaugo's arrow then, waiting as the alarm rose. He heard the perimeter guards behind him shouting for reinforcements, knew there'd be troops streaming past him too quickly.

Across the officers' pavilion, he saw Konaugo moving at a speed that belied his muscled bulk. Carefully, Chriani drew the arrow back, tracking the captain's movement as he shouted orders over the din. Chriani flicked his fingers, heard the bow sing. The arrow arced toward Konaugo, twisted past to catch his cloak as he ran, pulling him back by the neck as it pinned him to a hitching post behind him.

Chriani dropped the bow, slipped through the trees and out. All around him was pandemonium, no one noticing his sudden appearance in the midst of it. He ran like the rest of them, headed past the stables and across the archery yard, not looking to the body of the Valnirata rider when he passed it again.

He'd almost made it to Chanist's pavilion when his legs went out from under him, the ground slamming up as something hit him hard. He felt hands at his back, knowing whose they were even before he was hauled up, his neck cracking as he was twisted roughly around.

Where he loomed, Konaugo's face was twisted with a fury the like of which Chriani had never seen before. "You wanted my attention, boy?"

Chriani kicked, managed to catch one of Konaugo's legs with enough force to shift his balance, breaking the captain's grip as he twisted away and shot to his feet. He caught the flash of a dagger drawn, heart pounding as he pushed back to give himself room. He'd have one chance if he were lucky.

"Captain Konaugo."

The dagger was slipped away as fast as it had appeared. Konaugo wheeled to face Chanist as the prince strode through the center of the chaos, pulling his sword belt on.

"Is the perimeter secure?"

"My lord prince, the attack came from within the encampment itself..."

"Then clear the camp. Set two companies along the perimeter, instruct all others to sweep within it."

"My lord prince, a witness has placed this..."

"Now, captain."

Konaugo bit off whatever words were still waiting to be spoken. He nodded as he turned, not looking at Chriani as he motioned two sergeants to follow him. To the guards who had followed from his pavilion, the prince barked orders as he adjusted his scabbard.

"Jossel and Stevin, see to the horses. Adane, set extra watch on the stores and the armory. Tyro, attend to my daughter."

As Chanist's gaze met his for just a moment, Chriani stared. He managed to nod as the prince passed him without a word.

As he slipped past the unguarded entrance to the prince's tents, Chriani found himself in a curtained alcove, a bright space of draperies and carpeted ground beyond it. He blinked against the light of evenlamps in the first tent, saw where a council room of sorts had been set up, a makeshift table of wagon boards spread with maps he didn't slow to look at.

Beneath the central awning, the other two tents of the pavilion were closed off, Chriani looking into each in turn. To the left, a bedchamber, cut with white drapes. To the right, a study of some sort, shrouded evenlamps burning low above benches that lined the walls. In the center of the tent, a chair and a rough desk sat, a goblet on it holding down a stack of parchment. Lauresa was there, alone.

She was watching as if she expected him as Chriani pulled the canvas closed behind him. He felt a surge of warmth, braziers burning bright at each corner. He nodded to the princess but she returned it formally, distant. As he made to speak, she shook her head.

"Wait for my father," she said. "And when he comes, say nothing of what happened in the war room that night."

Chriani didn't bother to hide a questioning look. "What matter does that make now?"

"It matters to me, tyro."

In her voice, the anger of their journey that morning was back. Beyond the first tent, Chriani heard footsteps suddenly, could only nod to her as he stepped back, Chanist slipping inside. The prince pulled the canvas shut behind him, clasped the knotted ends of its lines to the tent's corner posts. As he turned to pace toward Chriani, his expression was deathly cold.

"If you'd missed and killed someone, what then, boy?"

"I shot with practice-range shafts, my lord prince." Chanist passed within a single step, Chriani fighting the urge to back up. "The Princess Lauresa requested a diversion capable of clearing your chambers."

"You have quite the arm to sink a blunted shaft into a hardwood post an arm's length behind my captain's head…"

"Father." Where she'd moved to stand behind the prince high, Lauresa's voice had a calm urgency to it.

Chanist glanced to her, back to Chriani as he circled to the desk, snatched up the goblet there. "My daughter informs me that you have some intelligence for me, master Chriani. Speak it."

At a side bench, the prince poured wine from a flagon of blue glass, a kind of dark tension in him. The age that Chriani had seen before was showing again. The prince ignored the pitcher of water alongside him, drank deeply.

"It is my belief that Barien knew of some complicity between the assassin whose attempt on your life he prevented, and one at the highest level within the court, my lord prince."

"You will forgive me, tyro, if I greet your accusations of my guard and advisors with some suspicion."

"Show him, tyro." Lauresa's voice was even in the shadows, her father glancing back to her.

From the pocket of his sleeve, Chriani carefully slipped the folded scrap of bloodstained insignia. Carefully, he pulled the dagger from its scabbard beneath his tunic. He stepped up to the desk, set both down carefully, stepped away again as the prince circled back.

As Chanist reached for the insignia, Chriani saw his hand shaking. The dagger he stared at but wouldn't touch, a tangible anger in him now.

"Tell me, master Chriani," the prince said. "Quickly."

He told Chanist then. Told him everything, from Barien's last words to the discovery of the dagger. He glanced to the princess once or twice as he spoke, saw her watching him, impassive. He told of Barien speaking the name of Uissa, saw Chanist's eyes flash cold. He told how Barien's last words had been spent in seeking word of Chanist's and the princess's safety, and as he did, Chriani saw the prince's knuckles white at the back of the chair he leaned against.

Chanist asked no questions as the story unfolded, and though Chriani had no reason to return to the events that had preceded Barien's death and the careful lie that yet wrapped them, he found himself working back to that point in his mind. No matter what the angle he chose to look upon it, Lauresa's request made no sense to him. It made no difference anymore, or should have made none at any rate.

The princess had talked about the fear of scandal had she been found in the war room that night, but how she'd planned to avoid the scandal of fleeing the Bastion in secret for a four-day ride across unmarked road alone, he didn't know. Even assuming Ashlund knew nothing about it, as master of the guard in Konaugo's absence, the fault would go to him.

My absence has been accounted for, Lauresa had said. Maybe it had been, for all that. The princess kept her secrets well, Chriani thought.

They stood in silence for what seemed a long while, Lauresa moving in beside her father. He started as her hand touched his, looked to her with something like fear in his eyes. His hands were shaking as he pulled them from the chair, let the bloodstained insignia drop to the desk again.

"To die alone is a thing we all face one day, master Chriani. To die betrayed…" The prince was breathing hard, hands to his head now. "We tell ourselves these things we do have purpose that overcomes the pain they bring. We tell ourselves that there is a reason the brave fall…"

Chriani wasn't sure who it was he spoke to.

"Barien…" Chanist's voice was hoarse, barely a whisper.

"Father…"

At the sound of Lauresa's voice, Chanist turned to embrace her tightly. And as Chriani watched, he thought he saw something break in the prince high. He saw the strength seeping from him visibly, and a shadow around him as if the relative sizes of father and child had suddenly reversed from how he'd seen them in the throne room that terrible night. Lauresa strong now against him, holding her father up like the posts that support the sprawl of an aging tree.

Chriani thought he felt Chanist's fear. He felt the memory twisting through him of kneeling at Barien's body as the warrior's life ebbed away. The same feeling of helplessness in himself that he saw reflected in a prince who stood across from him now and grieved in rare privacy.

On the desk, the bloody glyph on the dagger's blade caught the light. Chriani saw Chanist's gaze flit across it, felt the raw anger toward that mark and what it had done. He thought of Barien struck down by an arm whose skin bore the same lines that marked his own. He felt the pain shift inside him, felt the lie twist in his gut as it always had.

Chanist's voice shook him from the darkness. "Loyalty goes only as far as who it is pledged to, master Chriani. Given what you knew, you did right to keep your silence that night in the throne room. If I am guessing correctly, you did right to try to tell me that night in the stables. When you could not tell me, you did right to take my daughter's counsel. Barien taught you well."

"My lord prince." Chriani felt the first trace of the awkwardness that he realized he should have been feeling all along. As he had in the stables, he sensed the undercurrent of respect, foreign to him where it threaded the prince's words. Chanist embraced Lauresa again. Neither spoke. She would do anything to help her father, she'd said. She had been prepared to risk riding alone to bring him this news. In seven days time, the reach across which that help might come would be sundered by political expedience and a long road.

Lauresa had always been Chanist's golden girl, it was said. For long years after Irdaign had been set aside, the taverns had rung with songs telling of the number of discrete political visits Chanist continued to pay to her new home at Aldac, though less frequently on those days the Princess High Gwannyn went abroad in the city. Three lives split once by marriage, now to be split again. Lauresa, Irdaign, Chanist himself. And for the first time, Chriani wondered whether the prince saw as much of Irdaign in Lauresa as he did. He wondered at what pain the prince must feel.

To die alone is a thing we all face one day…

"The Order of Uissa," Chanist said suddenly. As he looked to Chriani, the strength in his voice returned.

"I do not know the name, my lord prince."

"Few outside the highest levels of the guard would. They are a martial order active in the west of Aerach."

"Mercenaries?" Chriani asked.

"Assassins, master Chriani. Amoral and deadly. They had holds across the Hunthad, years ago. Andreg whom my daughter is to marry was involved in action to push them back into the fringes of the Valnirata lands. A reaction to their attempting to place members of the order as spies within the Aerach court. Spies or worse."

Chriani took it in, added the new pieces of the puzzle to the old. He felt one question fall into place, but it was Lauresa who asked it.

"The assassin by whom Barien was slain was Valnirata." She was still at her father's side, holding him. "What connection is there between them?"

"The Valnirata hate the monastic orders nearly as much as they hate the peoples of the Ilmar," Chanist said. He shook his head. "If there is a connection there, it is not known to me."

Carefully, he broke from Lauresa's embrace, paced to the corner of the tent to peer out through a sealed window flap to the night beyond. Chriani was suddenly aware of movement around them, distant voices, orders shouted and received.

At the desk, Chanist fingered the bloodstained insignia once more. "Do I need to ask your suspicions in this matter, master Chriani?"

Chriani answered without hesitation. "Konaugo…"

"Captain Konaugo, tyro." Chanist's voice was even, but Chriani heard the warning.

"Of all the guard who I saw, only Captain Konaugo was not in uniform the night Barien was murdered, my lord prince. If his uniform was changed, I would be greatly interested in hearing his reasons for it."

As Chanist filled the goblet again, his gaze met Chriani's. Something there. Resignation? Chriani wasn't sure.

"To whom else have you spoken of these things?" he asked at length.

"To none but the princess and yourself, my lord prince."

Chanist nodded slowly. "You are wrong in your assessment of Captain Konaugo. That is my last and only word on that matter."

"Yes, my lord prince."

"On all other matters, I thank you. To hold allegiance to the ideals of truth even against the ideals of duty demonstrates a rare strength of heart, master Chriani."

"Yes, my lord prince."

Like Lauresa, Chanist wouldn't touch the dagger, Chriani saw. As he set the insignia down beside it, he motioned for Chriani to put both away.

"Keep it hidden," he said. "Show that blade to anyone in this troop and not even my order will be enough to save your life."

Outside, footsteps. Chanist unhooked the flap so that it could be opened from outside. Hardly any time alone, but it was all they would get.

"Speak to no one of what you know," Chanist said again. "Speak to no one of what you suspect. We will talk more on this. On your way."

Chriani nodded, pressing back at the flap as three guards pressed in, then stepping out silently behind them, no one seeing him go. He heard Chanist within, asking for word from outside, the formal give and take of report and questioning.

Across the archery yard, the mud had been churned by the passage of untold feet. As soldiers ran past him on all sides, Chriani quickly realized that he was the only one without bow or sword in hand, a conspicuousness that was drawing more sidelong glances to him than he wanted.

The armory tent he'd seen earlier had guards on all four sides now, so he headed for the officers' pavilion instead, no one there. He had to slip beneath the canvas of three tents before he found what he was looking for, helping himself to a brace of the arrows he'd packed a week before, along with the unstrung shortbow racked with them. Best to walk the perimeter, he thought as he slipped out again. If he could catch a glimpse of Konaugo at a safe distance, he could arrange to look like he was patrolling wherever the captain wasn't.

As he wandered the fringe of the barracks tents, he felt isolation wrap him even within the frantic activity of the camp, locked down on an alert that had no purpose, he knew. He heard horses circling around the perimeter, saw the lines of the forest rise like a wall against the red haze of the Darkmoon, still low in the east.

In the Ilmar, the forest was often just called the Valnirata, as if the dark wood and the Ilvani war-clans within it were one and the same. Outside of the rangers who rode the constant patrols of the Clearwater Way and the trails of the Locanwater, most folk of the Ilmar had never even seen an Ilvani of the Valnirata. Those who had called the forest the Greatwood, a rough translation of the *Muiraìden*, the Ilvani name that was older than the trees themselves. A four-hundred league expanse of towering limni — the great twisted conifers that grew only in the forest the Valnirata called home.

Chriani stared to the distant wood for a long while. Something twisted inside him that he couldn't put a name to.

The encampment was on a rise, and as he strode up toward the eastern perimeter, he saw the Darkmoon break behind thin cloud, close to full and gleaming black-red above the dark green stain of the trees. To the distant south, he saw a dull glow that he tried to imagine was the brightness of desert scrubland, the Sandhorn pushing its hooked claw of scree and wind-carved dunes into the Clearwater.

His father had died in the Sandhorn, or at least that's what his mother had told him. Into the broken desert steppes north of the Greatwood, the Valnirata exiled their criminals, their degenerates, their outcasts and insurgents. She'd told Chriani where, told him when, told him why his father had died. All the details he'd asked her for as a child but that she'd refused him until that day she lay dying herself at the side of an empty road.

She had his father's last words, held inside her for six years. Waiting, she said, until Chriani was old enough to understand.

If I make it back, his father had said, *there'll be a place for us in any part of the Ilmar that sets faith in freedom.*

He'd left the village before dawn, his mother said, only shortly before the rangers had come looking for him. He'd known it was coming, the round-up of those Valnirata Ilvani who had made the Ilmar their home. Up the roads from Welbirk and Cadaurwen, whispers of war had been drifting for a month.

If I don't make it back, tell the boy of who I was.

Like him, his father had set out to prove himself. Like him, his father had never found his chance.

Above the tree line then, Chriani saw faint black shapes flying low against the sharpness of the stars. He felt his pulse ratchet up, decided that perhaps the camp being on alert wasn't such a bad thing.

Gavaleria! Chriani heard the call go up from at least three points around him, and he moved quickly toward the light of the perimeter fires, all eyes around him on the sleek shapes of the Valnirata griffon riders as they tore past overhead. He heard a distant shriek that cut the darkness like a knife, and even as high as the griffons and their unseen masters flew, he heard the horses suddenly frantic at the stables.

But even as he skirted close to the patrol line, Chriani saw a lone figure moving slowly through the shadows of a narrow stand of poplar beyond it. Like him, like everyone, Lauresa was watching the griffons circle overhead as they scouted the position and extent of Chanist's camp. Unlike the rest of them, though, she was following their movement from the other side of the perimeter, having managed somehow to slip across it. She was alone, the night-blue cloak wrapped tight around her, just invisible enough that she was probably equally likely to get taken out by a nervous archer within the camp as by whatever might be lurking outside it.

Chriani felt a profound antipathy that he was suddenly thankful for. He judged the movements of the guards, waited for his moment even as Lauresa bore off toward a thin glade that edged a low hillock north-east of the camp. As he slipped through the line, he made no sound, left no sign as he melted into the shadows. It didn't take him long to find her trail in the frost already settled on the grass. He moved up the slope behind her, his footsteps the faintest echo of the wind that stirred the naked trees. He heard the song the princess sang, recognized a fragment of melody from the war room that night.

"Highness."

She wheeled at the sound of his voice, Chriani seeing her hand move quickly to her waist. The dagger was there that she'd turned on him that first night, but she checked herself.

"You startled me."

"As you would have startled any of the dozen patrols circulating through the area. In the interest of your not getting accidentally shot by your father's own troops, we should return."

"I am perfectly capable…"

"We have had this conversation, highness."

Above, another endless shriek split the night. Lauresa's eyes were cold as she turned from Chriani, the gavaleria patrol changing direction overhead. As one, the griffon riders arced back toward the east, hanging against mottled cloud as they slowly disappeared from sight.

As he paced around the princess, Chriani felt something twist within his chest. As she looked to him finally, a shock of hair twisted from beneath the hood of her cloak, frosted in the light of the Clearmoon where its waxing crescent broke through the cloud, falling to the west. Her eyes were the blue of the summer sky he'd screamed his heart out to on that day his mother died. In the ten years since he'd first come to Rheran, in the four years Lauresa had trained at his side, in the three years since over which he'd watched her at a distance, she had never seemed more beautiful.

From the poplar wood, he heard the call of an owl, another answering it from the distant forest, a faint echo. He felt the familiar pain again, felt the new lie twisting inside him in the deep place where all the other lies had been buried. He felt the scar her name made burning on his skin.

"What is it?" she asked.

In her look, he saw an uncertainty that he wanted to believe reflected his own. She took a step toward him.

Three words, Chriani thought. All it would take to end it, end the lie, end the pain that he only just realized had been crippling him for so long.

"Nothing, highness."

He watched indifference fall across her like a veil, the same anger, the same distance in her that he still didn't understand. She turned away, moved for downslope and the distant firelight of the camp beyond.

"I am ordered back to Rheran in the morning," she said, "under Captain Konaugo's escort. Under the assumption that you would rather not be part of his company, my father says you may remain here."

Chriani wasn't sure whether that was a choice he was supposed to decide upon or one that had been made for him. He hoped it was the latter.

At the bottom of the rise, a frozen creek bed crossed their path as it split a copse of willow, Chriani following Lauresa at the accustomed five paces. He would watch her ride out in the morning, he thought, and it would be over. No more waiting, no need to stand among the throng bidding her farewell from the Rheran docks alongside the rest of the city, because he'd be with the prince's company a hundred leagues away. Silence from him, Lauresa gone, his life back to what it should be.

Easier that way.

"Why have I angered you?" he said abruptly. He heard the words hanging in the night air even before he felt the anger spit them up. In his gut, he felt the darkness twist like a creature separate from him. The anger following its own will, its own mind.

Lauresa stopped dead. She turned back, appraised Chriani coldly. Behind her, the arms of two ancient trees twisted together to form a kind of arch at the edge of the copse, the faint Clearmoon's light through bare branches catching silver thread in her cloak that he hadn't noticed before. A faint shimmering traced the princess as her chest rose and fell for a long space of silence.

"I thought you were different," she said at last. "I was wrong."

"Different from what?"

"Different from all the rest of them. The ones who fear what they can't see, the ones who live by their superstition and their moonsigns. Regardless of the less than storied upbringing that saw her sent from my father's court, my mother is still princess precedent and a lady of

Brandishear," Lauresa said evenly. "You would do well to remember that should you meet again."

Chriani remembered the fear when he'd seen the horse vanish back to the fire it had been summoned from. He'd been feeling that fear all the time since, he realized suddenly. Feeling it feed the anger without knowing it, without knowing how to stop it.

"Superstitions are for children," Lauresa said. "I expect it in those who know no better. I did not expect it in you."

"Forgive me, princess, but I don't recall word or rumor of the princess precedent being a court wizard during her time in the Bastion." Chriani felt the words torn from the place where the darkness coiled. As she turned back, Lauresa's eyes flashed. "But that would be, perhaps, because she never was," he said.

"My mother's knowledge and gifts are her business..."

"Your mother carrying eldritch art in secrecy is a dangerous breach of law and custom."

"What do you know..."

"I know that such power must be pledged to the crown..."

"This is not about law," Lauresa snapped. "This is about you being afraid."

"The death a renegade sorcerer can deal, the people have a right to be afraid." He showed no deference now, Chriani seeking actively for the rage, feeling it spread like a warm draught through frozen limbs.

The princess was silent a long moment. Then her cold gaze shifted from Chriani's, glancing to his chest where a bandage she shouldn't have been able to see covered her own name. Chriani felt a moment's crippling uncertainty, followed her gaze to realize that she was looking instead at the bow still slung at his shoulder. He'd almost forgotten he was carrying it.

"I used to watch you at the harvest fest each year," she said quietly. Something changed in her, he thought. A sudden sadness he couldn't explain, hadn't been looking for. "I remember you winning the archery competition two seasons past, splitting the target cleanly at two hundred paces against Konaugo himself. If it had been me shooting that day, I would have just as likely killed the wardens at either edge of the range even had I spent every waking moment in practice since the last time you adjusted the set of my arm."

Chriani felt a sharp spike of uncertainty slam through him. In his chest, in his gut, the anger recoiled sharply. He heard the owl's cry again, heard the sudden beating of its wings as it took to the air, unseen.

"My mother has a power beyond you," Lauresa said. "You have ability beyond me. Should I fear you?"

The princess turned, stalking off toward the watchfires of the perimeter with a sense of purpose that told Chriani it would be foolish to follow her. It was a good thing, he thought. He felt dizzy suddenly, his thoughts racing, the echo of her voice twisting in him like a knife point.

I used to watch you at the harvest fest each year…

In the war room, he'd looked in her eyes for some sign of recognition, some sign of memory for the years they'd spent together as children, seemingly a lifetime ago now. He hadn't seen it then. Had caught only the dull reflection of the emptiness he'd felt inside himself in the month since the princess's marriage was announced.

You trained me well, she'd said on the field a week past.

All along, the princess had remembered him. Through the three years he'd pined for her, then forgotten her, then gone mad with a feeling he was still afraid to name.

Lauresa kept her secrets well, he thought.

He wanted to follow her but didn't, turning away from the encampment instead, fighting the urge to run for the star-silvered pillars of willow through which she'd disappeared. He stood there for a long while, tried to fight the ache in his head and at his chest, flaring again. Around him, the night was silent.

As the wind blew through the glade behind him, his eyes picked out the intricate play of red and white light through the leaves. The cloud had broken to reveal the moons facing each other in the sky, dark and high, bright and falling. The Clearmoon's fast-waxing crescent marked its pursuit of the slower-moving Darkmoon's full form, pushing ever closer, night by night. Chriani couldn't judge when the fullmoons conjunction would come, but he guessed it to within a day of Lauresa's departure for Aerach. An auspicious sign for great events, folk would say.

Along the scree of the creek bed behind him, he heard the faint crunch of ice and gravel beneath the sole of an armored boot.

Chriani moved fast but not fast enough. From out of nowhere, less from the shadows than seemingly from the shimmering moons'-light itself, a figure erupted in a blur of twisting limbs, and Chriani felt the boot that had warned him with its telltale sound slam into him hard. He managed to twist just enough, felt his hip take the brunt of the force that would have split his ribs had it caught him straight on, then he was spinning away, steel slashing empty air as two knives hacked through the space he'd been standing in a moment before.

He had the bow in his hands, had drawn and nocked an arrow without even realizing it. One quick shot away, firing blind, hoping for an instant's distraction, but no one was there.

Chriani fought to breathe, tried to focus. All around, the ground was a morass of frozen mud and turf, every footstep sounding out in the chill silence, but he heard nothing now. He was still turning to scan the shadows when he was struck again. A hail of blows rained down as movement erupted around him, the figure suddenly there as if he'd unfolded from the air itself.

Chriani saw a face he'd never seen before. Frozen for one long moment as he blocked one cross-hand strike, ducked back to avoid another. Older than he was, fair-skinned and placid. Ilmari, white hair cut ragged and short, cheeks marked with precise lines of ritual scars below unblinking eyes the dead black of a deep-night storm. As the figure lunged, Chriani could fairly feel his intensity, focused in silence as his foot lashed out again to drop him.

The figure wore a loose tunic of grey-white, shining like a beacon in the moons'-light, the incongruity screaming in Chriani's head, wondering how he could have gotten so close without being seen. But even as he stared, he saw the tunic and the body beneath it ripple suddenly, as if some shadow had crossed the sky. Then the white figure was gone again, a faint shimmer twisting along the edge of the trees.

Chriani fired off two shots blindly, wanted desperately to hold onto the bow, keep its familiar presence in his hand, but he was too close. Slinging it to his shoulder, he drew the battered shortsword, managed to bring it around when he heard footsteps coming in from behind.

As the figure unfolded from shadow, Chriani returned a half-dozen devastating strikes as he was pressed back, the assailant's knives ringing out against the battered steel of the borrowed blade. His eyes ached where he tried to watch the figure, the shifting light seeming to play across and through him. If he stared, if he focused, Chriani could hold the image, but the instant he faltered, blinked, let the emotionless face shift to the corner of his eye, it was gone again.

The assailant wore no other armor, carried no other weapons or gear. Where Chriani saw them completely for the first time, the razor-straight knives were nearly the length of his forearms. It was the boots he fought to avoid, though, slamming into him again and again in a kick-striking style he'd never seen before, faster than he could comprehend.

As he slashed up and around with the sword, Chriani felt it somehow hit home even as something struck the side of his head. He saw a sudden flare of white light as he stumbled, falling back across open ground. He slipped through a stand of tall shrubs and out the other side, fire burning along his back and chest, his left leg going numb where the assailant had connected with it mid-thigh.

His thoughts were unfocused, vision a blood-red blur in the twisted moons'-light. He limped for the shadows, staggered to a stop as he sheathed the sword, pulled the bow again. He fought to calm himself, pushed the rage away as he felt for the instincts, felt for his senses as his mother had taught him. Listening, feeling.

He was ready when he heard the telltale scrape of steel on stone behind him.

He loosed the arrow, then had another nocked faster than he could ever remember shooting before. Not knowing exactly where the assailant was, but knowing that he had to be on one side or the other of the first arrow — shooting not to hit but to flush him out. Unless the assassin had somehow managed to bypass the reflexes of every warrior who'd ever faced a hail of bowshot, he'd dodge just slightly away from whichever side the first shot went harmlessly past.

Chriani sensed the faint blur of movement, the first arrow flashing past harmlessly a half-stride to the right as the figure twisted and he shot again. He heard the strangled cry, caught a glimpse of the white shaft shattering that meant he'd struck bone at the shoulder.

Then the assailant was gone again, twisting away to shadow as the trees suddenly shook with the movement of his passing. No sign of him where he must have pushed through the copse, but Chriani saw blood on white bark where the Darkmoon's faint light played out.

It took him a moment to orient himself, his head still pounding as he tried to clear it.

He saw light through the trees where the figure had disappeared. Chanist's camp.

He hadn't realized how far Lauresa had led him, or perhaps he'd simply been pushed back farther under the assailant's attack than he thought. Beneath the trees, frost-streaked shadows showed the armored imprints of the assailant's footsteps pounding away ahead of him, but he heard no sound. He watched the trees, the shadows to both sides, the firelight ahead, too far. Not close enough to shout even if he'd been able to raise a voice, pain tearing at his lungs with each breath.

He could see the officers' pavilion bright in the light of a high-banked fire, the far end of his range. He could make out the distinctive figure of Konaugo pacing there, fitted a single shaft to the bowstring and fired without hesitation. Another followed it even as the first hit, and he heard frenzied shouts rise to all sides as the fire suddenly flared in a shower of ash and sparks. A third shot went long, tearing at the canvas of an adjacent awning, figures flattening to both sides.

He heard the alarm raised, the troops still vigilant after the last one, false or not. But where the assailant's tracks pounded steadily toward the light, Chriani saw them veer off suddenly. A half-dozen long strides, then the steel tread had slowed to follow a set of calfskin boots that carried on down from the wood's edge. Small footprints, slender. Spaced close together where she'd been walking slowly.

Lauresa.

Where the wood thinned ahead of the open ground below the pavilions, Chriani ran without thinking, head pounding in time with the pain that twisted across his right side. He saw no sign of the princess ahead, frantically scanned the shadows even as he silently hoped she'd made it back beyond the near line of the sentry fires.

Then from behind him, footsteps. The ambush he should have been waiting for, distracted by the sudden fear that the princess's tracks had engendered in him.

As the darkness shimmered again, he saw the knives flash out where he jumped back, too slow. He felt white-hot pain at his shoulder as cold steel cut him, but the assailant was still moving, spinning impossibly fast. When the whirlwind kick struck hard, Chriani felt it nearly take his head off, needle-sharp points of white light burning behind his eyes. Then he hit the ground with a lurch that told him he'd blacked out on the way down, something he couldn't afford to do again. He felt the knives slam down behind him as he rolled, fumbled to pull an arrow as he stood, but it was no good.

Three lightning-fast knife strikes knocked the bow from his hand, blocked the feeble jab he made with the arrow, narrowly missed his heart as he stumbled back. The kick that followed dropped him again. Still no emotion in the scarred white face as it vanished once more, but as Chriani pushed himself to his feet once more, he scooped two handfuls of freezing mud, flung them in a half-circle around him. There, the haze of light shifted, dark streaks hanging in the air for a moment before they blurred out. Chriani ran for the faint shimmer that marked the assassin's movement, no idea where the strength in him was coming from.

As he'd fallen, he felt the hidden scabbard digging into his side, but even as fast as he fumbled the Valnirata blade from its belt now, he felt it knocked from his hands, skidding unseen to the dark forest floor. Then another drop kick took him in the chest, and Chriani went down for the last time.

His heart was pounding as he tried to rise, but his arms wouldn't work. The same pinpoint flare of pain that had numbed his leg was spreading from just below his heart now. He managed to look up, saw the heavy bootprints circling slowly around him.

As Chriani focused, he brought the figure back into blurred vision, his eyes stinging where blood was running freely from his forehead. He saw the assailant bend to the ground, pick up the bloodblade where it had fallen. He looked to Chriani, smiling for the very first time.

Then a burst of light around them swallowed moons and stars and the sky at once, and the figure in white was pulled off his feet, slammed back by an explosion of white-hot flame.

Chriani saw the bird. The same twisting shape he thought he'd seen swirling in the fire that Irdaign had thrown against the stones the night before. Only it was Lauresa at the edge of the clearing this time, a rage in her that he could feel like the blast of heat that made him squeeze his eyes shut as he clumsily scrambled away.

Through the darkness, her voice rang out with the song she and her mother had made together. The white figure was up and running for her, impossibly fast, but as her voice pitched and peaked, she twisted her hands above her head and Chriani saw knives of pure light erupt around the figure, cut him down with a scream.

Where it twisted past him, Chriani saw the bloodblade, knocked free as the figure hit the ground in a haze of black and red. The assailant screamed again, Chriani feeling it. Something in the sound of that agony drove his own movement as he rose, stumbled forward six steps. He snatched the dagger from the ground, didn't slow, all his dead momentum carrying him as he drove into the figure, hit him hard from behind.

Then ropes of black shadow traced through the clearing, twisting in between Chriani and the figure even as the dagger was wrenched free of the assailant's back. Chriani watched him torn away by the force of

Lauresa's spell, holding the figure aloft even as the fire's song rose to consume him.

A searing silhouette filled Chriani's head, the outline of the figure in white caught as it burned. Then the darkness expanded to swallow all his sight, and he saw nothing more.

— CHAPTER 8 —

Things Left Unsaid

THERE HAD BEEN A DREAM when he was younger, almost forgotten now. No longer sure whether he could actually still remember it on the rare times he tried to pull it from the shadows of his mind, or whether he was just recalling the second-hand memory itself from some time in childhood.

Twice removed from the sight and sound of it, he could see himself being flung into the air, twisting between shifting fields of green grass and blue sky. He was looking down on a laughing face, grey eyes and a shock of black hair. Without knowing how, he recalled the angular lines of the eyes and mouth, the curve to the tip of the ear that marked the familiar features of his father.

He was having that same dream again now, and though he recognized it as a dream, Chriani couldn't put his finger on why it had come back to him. Because in the way it came back to him, his father's face changed to Barien's at some point, the warrior laughing like he used to. Then in a heartbeat, Chriani was at one of Chanist's throne room banquets, and he thought he could see the angular face at the prince high's own table across from Barien. He thought he saw them laughing together, but he couldn't have. His father dead long years before. Barien dead now.

Against the pounding of his heart, Chriani felt the laughter shred to silence. The face of his forgotten father was still in his head when he woke, not sure how long he'd lain unconscious in the moons'-light. He heard shouts and the crash of footsteps from the far side of the thicket, though, and the fires along the perimeter looked to be burning higher through his blurred vision. Not long enough for the watch to have reached him but enough time for Lauresa and the white figure to be gone.

He saw no sign of either of them in the empty glade as he tried to rise, the bloodblade lying in the dirt near his hand. He could barely breath as he scooped it up, could smell the charnel reek of burned flesh on the wind.

Inside him, twisting past the pain that rose with every ragged breath, he felt the fear. He felt his hand at his chest, shakily making the moonsign against the blackened expanse of turf and trees all around. He felt the memory of the cold anger in Lauresa as she'd spun fire from her hands like spider's silk. He tried to push it away, knew he never would.

He heard voices getting closer. He didn't have much time.

As he rose, he felt pain like a red-hot knife slash him from stomach to shoulder, but he forced himself to his knees, tried to clear his eyes as they sought out detail in the haze of moons'-light. He found Lauresa's footprints easily enough, swinging past the spot where he'd lain before turning for the creek bed, heading back toward the encampment. She'd lingered at his side, Chriani reading her movements in the cluster of footprints obscured by the marks his hands had made when he clawed his way upright again. She hadn't stayed with him but she'd stopped at least. That was something, he thought bitterly.

The other tracks took longer, but Chriani found them in the end. In his mind, the image of the figure in white falling beneath the hail of light and fire that had flashed from Lauresa's clenched fists had been fixed as permanently as his own name, and he would have laughed openly at the notion that anyone could have survived it.

He had, though. The one who'd almost killed him. Lurching away from the camp, Chriani saw his footsteps staggering with a drunken gait. He was favoring one leg badly, the heavy prints of the steel boots twisting to disappear across the frosted scree of the dry creek where it cut through the trees. Chriani followed for a dozen paces, expected to see the body, but there was nothing. The assassin was gone.

He felt his mind and memory flex around the word. Assassin.

He should have realized it even as they fought, he knew, but there'd been little room for thought in the near-fatal beating he'd taken. He remembered the thin smile that had played across the pale face, the Valnirata blade turning slowly in white hands.

As torchlight flared through the closest trees, he found himself wondering if Lauresa had made it back, how much longer she might need. He'd keep them busy here, he thought darkly. One last piece of obligation dispensed with.

The Princess Lauresa kept her secrets well.

At the fore of the party that came crashing up the trail with swords and bows drawn, he saw Konaugo, naturally. Chriani was still working on trying to stand when two members of the captain's guard helped him roughly to his feet, Chriani grimacing against the pain in his side. He'd broken ribs before, but this was worse. He saw shadows for a moment, then felt the cold sting of Konaugo's gloved hand across his cheek bring him back to wakefulness.

In the captain's other hand, he saw the stolen officer's arrow he'd shot, saw a lieutenant he didn't know pull the one shaft that had somehow managed to stay in his quiver where it hung haphazardly from his leg. A perfect match, Konaugo not even bothering to look.

"The prince's assassin was here," Chriani said thickly. He was overcome with retching, sent gouts of blood across Konaugo's cloak before he caught himself. "He has sorcery. He hides as he moves..."

Konaugo caught Chriani's face with his spit, gave a nod to the guards to either side, who released him even as the captain grabbed him, pulled him like he weighed nothing into the shadows.

A dozen strides away, moons'-light twisted through a copse of stunted pine, Chriani dragged there, stifling a scream as Konaugo slammed him up against the twisted bole of a deadwood snag. The captain's knife was out again, Chriani slumping to the ground, trying to rise against a blackness that rooted deep within the pain.

"Anyone lucky enough to survive trying to kill Konaugo once should be smart enough to not try again," the captain whispered. "So perhaps you're not as smart as Barien seemed to think..."

"Barien knew you too well," was all Chriani could gasp, and he felt Konaugo's thick fingers bunch his tunic as he hefted him again, hurled him a half-dozen paces to slam against the frozen ground. Chriani hit hard, head-first. He saw shadows again, felt the darkness come crashing up to meet him even as he fought to push it away.

"I spent six years riding with the rangers among Barien's Leisanmira," Konaugo whispered hoarsely. He strode slowly past Chriani where he lay prone, glanced beyond the trees to his guard, Chriani knowing that none of them would move from where they watched. "I've heard their charm-song. Seen it sap the will of the strongest soldiers. I watched the witch-princess ascend to the throne that Prince Goffree died to defend, then watched her Leisanmira lackey stay behind even after Chanist found the wisdom to finally rid himself of her reek. Whatever death found Barien in service to the prince, it was short payment for his true allegiance all these years."

As he felt the anger surge, Chriani welcomed it. He let it spike, felt it flood his limbs with a strength that wove through the pain as

Konaugo lifted him again, smashed him back against the dead trunk and held him there.

"Barien was a singularly unambitious fool," Konaugo hissed, "but what worth he saw in you defies even my ability to fathom. Your shiftlessness reminding him of the son he hadn't the sack or the wood to sire himself, no doubt. Warden to the princess so he could watch Chanist's court with her witch-mother's eyes."

Chriani caught the movement of the moonsign, Konaugo's hand moving above his chest as he leaned in close. Afraid of Irdaign, he thought.

"And does she own you, too, boy? Or was traitor a job even Barien wouldn't trust you with?"

As Chriani slammed his head forward, he felt Konaugo's nose break. The captain stifled a cry, conscious of his troops only a dozen steps away. Chriani counted on that, counted on the momentary flash of pain distracting him as he knocked the dagger from the captain's hand. He fell on it, rolled up with the blade at arm's length before Konaugo had taken his first step toward him.

The captain wiped blood from his face with his sleeve. "A chance to die quickly should not be lightly thrown away, boy."

In his voice was an anger and a venom like Chriani had never heard. And he realized suddenly that as much as he hated Konaugo, Konaugo hated him more. Had hated Barien more. Chriani feinted low, flicked the blade up to score Konaugo's cheek as he tried to grab it. The captain winced, fell back a step.

"Barien died slow," Chriani whispered. "But you'd know that, wouldn't you?"

Konaugo blinked. Surprised, Chriani thought. Good. As he lunged, the captain swore, but Chriani slashed him off, scored the leather of one bracer and felt like he caught the arm above it.

"So where did you tell the prince you were that night?" he hissed. "Hanging limp and begging for release in some half-blood brothel as usual?"

"You will die the maggot-meat you were born to be, tyro…"

"Did you make some excuse for the blood on the uniform you should have worn? Or did you bury it like the fucking cur you are?"

When Konaugo lunged again, Chriani wasn't fast enough, landing underneath the captain's full weight as they fell. The last of his strength broken by the futile display of bravado, blood streaking Konaugo's hands as they found Chriani's throat.

From the glade came the sudden drum of hoofbeats, Konaugo glancing up. Chriani's breath was gone, his heart pounding past the bursting point. But even through the roaring of blood in his ears, he heard the Prince High Chanist's voice, distant. *Where is the tyro?*

Two of Konaugo's guards raced for them through the trees, their expressions telling Chriani that they'd known what was happening there.

"Lord," one whispered, and with an effort of supreme will, Konaugo pulled his hands from Chriani's throat.

Chriani didn't remember rising, didn't feel the arms around him as he half-walked, was half-dragged from the shadows. His sight splintered once, twice more, told him he was blacking out again. When his vision cleared, Chanist and a squad of horse were there, troops running in every direction. From the haze of light to both sides, he guessed that the perimeter had been pushed out, watchfires burning every ten paces by the look of it, the camp hemmed in by flame.

He saw Chanist toss something to one of the guards whose grip was all that kept him from falling to embrace the dirt once more. Something cold was pressed to his lips, a sudden bitterness in his mouth that cleared his head in an instant. He choked, swallowed.

In his arms, he felt the pain shred and twist away. Like the warmth of fire-heated furs against chilled skin, a surge of sensation broke through a numbness Chriani hadn't been aware of. He blinked as the haze of blood lifted slowly from his eyes. Riding with Chanist, set off from the grey leather of the guard, he saw three figures in black, two cloaked against the cold, one exposed as he leaned low in the saddle, scanned the charred ground to all sides. At the figure's neck, Chriani saw the mageguard brand.

"Take him to my pavilion and keep him safe," Chanist called. "The princess Lauresa is alive this night only because of him."

Konaugo was behind the prince, Chriani saw, a darkness in his gaze that had no words to describe it, but it slipped beneath the obedient nod as Chanist wheeled past him.

"The assassin was here," the prince barked. "An attempt was made on the princess's life. Seal this camp. Anyone who crosses the perimeter in or out except by my leave dies."

Then he was gone, spurring off with the others to the fire line. Chriani watched them for a long while, tried to sort the sensations coursing through his limbs, his heart still racing. Konaugo was gone when he looked back.

He realized he could walk only when he tried it. He felt his ribs still aching, could feel the imprint of Konaugo's fingers at his throat, but the burning in his lungs was gone. As he glanced behind him, he saw contempt in the eyes of the two guards making good on Chanist's orders to escort him, but a particularly dark look stopped them. He tossed the empty flask of the prince's healing draught back, one of them catching it as they shifted off toward the fires of the outer perimeter.

As he passed the inner line and made for the light of the officers' pavilion ahead, Chriani felt the fear still with him, still circling at a distance. Like the assassin's form as he'd slipped from solid to shadow and back again, it was there, then not there. Chriani fought the urge to focus this time, suddenly desperate to not see.

He was within sight of Chanist's tents when he felt the stinging sensation rising on his skin. His senses were already on fire, something in the healing draught making his nerves jangle. He remembered the same sensation from the throne room that night, spilling his fabricated story as he'd quaked in fear of spellcraft pulling the truth from his mind.

The guards at my father's pavilion are told to expect you. Lauresa's voice in his head was the same whisper, the same close echo that it had been that first day, but Chriani felt his pulse quicken. He felt fear and anger in his heart now in equal measure, but whether the anger was directed at her for the duplicity or at himself for not seeing that duplicity, he wasn't sure.

You won't be able to come to me, she said. *I will meet you there.*

He wasn't wearing the ring, but he heard her in his mind just the same. Wondering darkly whether she'd ever even needed the rings in the first place, wondering if she could hear him now as he could hear her. A darkness in his thoughts that he wasn't bothering to hide this time.

Ahead, he saw two guards watching him from the time he appeared across the officers' pavilion, spears locked across the entrance to the prince's tents. He didn't slow down, didn't meet their gaze as he approached, the spears lifted as he passed through them, up the steps and through the curtained alcove without a word.

Inside, he found Lauresa waiting in the study where she'd waited just a short while before. She had changed from the riding clothes she'd been walking in, dressed now in a long white shift in which she seemed to float just above the floor. Her hair was tied back, her skin pale in the unnatural brightness of the evenlamps. Even more regal than normal, he thought, not sure if that should have been possible.

From her expression as she turned to see him, he realized that Chanist's draught had done nothing to affect how bad he must look. He touched his face as he nodded to her, felt still-drying blood caked there.

"Sit," she said, motioning to the low bench along the far wall. He did so without emotion, Lauresa filling a basin from the jug of water there, wetting a handkerchief she pulled from within her sleeve. She knelt as she washed Chriani's face, the water cool where she gingerly touched him. "Are you all right?"

"Well enough for you to leave me," he said evenly.

"I ran for aid," she said. "I did not know how badly hurt you were. Had I tried to move you, you might have died before any healing could save you."

"Very good of you to have it delivered thus."

She slipped the cloth into his hand, rose abruptly. Chriani ignored her, continued to scrape the crust of blood from his face and neck even as he tried to hold onto the anger that was fading suddenly.

She'd saved his life. He tried to grasp that thought, wanted to hang onto it against all others. He felt the anger rise white-hot like it always did, wanted to push it away for once. He wanted to thank her.

"You lied to me," he said instead.

"I lie to everyone, Chriani. All my life is lies. You are just unlucky enough to have seen through them."

"It was you all along," he said, not a question. "In the war room. The shadow, the sorcery that saved us in the fall. Outside the throne room, and your voice in my head. None of it was rings or pendants or any other thing. Just you."

"The rings are real," she said quietly. "Without them, I can sense your thoughts but cannot speak to you. The pendant has protective power of its own, but not the power I pretended it to have. It was me."

Chriani stood. In a mirror that hung close to the door, he caught a glimpse of himself, wiped the last of the blood from his face and hair. The faint marks of the split lips and the gash that had opened up across his cheek were still visible.

"You have no right," he said coldly.

"I have no right to what, tyro? To my life?" She matched his tone as she paced away from him, stood at her father's chair. "No right to my mother's blood? I did not choose what I am, Chriani, it chose me. The arts of my people have been handed down from mother and father to daughters and sons since before the Ilmar tribes crossed the mountains."

"What you are is your affair, princess. Choosing to hide it within the Rheran court makes it mine."

"One should have standing at court before one presumes to speak for that court..."

"You ordered me to lie to the prince high to protect your own actions against that court. Whose eyes do you watch your father with, princess? Andreg's? Your mother's? Was it on her orders that you stole into the tower that night?"

"I was in the war room as I have been many times in order to practice my art, you obtuse fool. I did not hear the alarm that night because I was in the midst of working a silence charm. In my own chambers, my father's court wizards would sense me wielding the power within me. I practice in the war room because its sorcerous wards prevent detection of the spells I study, the same wards that prevent others seeing within. No space in the Bastion is more secure."

"And your father approves?" Chriani said coldly.

In Lauresa's face, Chriani saw the sudden fragility again that he'd seen in the throne room that night. He almost believed it.

"If my skills were known, my life would be over," she said. She pushed the chair in abruptly, turned from him where she paced. "I'd have been made to become one of my father's court wizards in the tower, or sent to one of the war-mage outposts for military training."

"Many have endured more for the land and its people," he quoted back to her.

Lauresa turned on him, cold. "I love this land, but I am not of it. Not enough for my father's advisors, at any rate." A lifetime's practice had almost hidden the edge in her voice. Almost. The princess faltered for a moment. "The Leisanmira blood does not still easily. The prince high knows this."

Her Leisanmira lackey, Konaugo had said.

Chriani had circled back to the basin, watched its water swirl red as he squeezed the blood-soaked cloth out. In the captain's words, he felt another thing pressing on him suddenly, mind numb beneath the weight of one more secret to add to all the other things he should have known, should have suspected but was too blind to see.

He understood finally. Barien's voice in his head that night.

"Barien was of the Leisanmira," Lauresa said as if in echo, and as Chriani spun, he sent the basin toppling to the floor. He saw the prince's carpets stained pink at his feet where the water soaked in.

"Stay out of my head," he whispered.

"I am not in your mind, Chriani. The fear in your face can be read easily enough. Barien was my mother's warden from the moment she and Chanist were wed. They were cousins, had been friends since childhood. Sorcery and music in their blood, commingling."

Outside, sudden footsteps approached, Lauresa slipping to the gap at the corner to peer out. Slowly, the noise faded away. Chriani was conscious of the stillness around them, distant shouts echoing from the perimeter, the guards silent around the prince's tents.

"The Leisanmira summon sorcery that way, with song. The court wizards and the necromancers write their spellcraft. They need their books to study and their spell-words to utter. Ours is passed from person to person, voice to voice."

To all sides, Chriani heard the evenlamps hissing soft against the silence, had never noticed before that they made sound. He remembered Lauresa's voice in his ear at the library, remembered stealing her song away with a kiss as they'd fallen. He remembered her voice twisting in with her mother's against the storm.

"I've spent my whole life training in secret. Trips taken yearly to my mother's in Aldac, the two of us riding out alone." Chriani heard an air of confession in her now, but all it made him feel was how little the confession meant. "We would spend weeks in the wilderness, exploring. There are ruins throughout the hills and the western mountains, steeped in dweomer. Some predate the Empire and the Ilvani alike."

He felt a dull fear circling like distant shadow, visible but unformed. He tried to imagine hearing the words Lauresa spoke now, but from Barien. The warrior telling him the truth of who he was, of what he was.

"My mother knew from the moment she was set aside that I must be married off one day. For the good of the crown, for the good of the treaty. If it was known what I could do, if it was known even that I had dabbled in the Leisanmira spell-songs as a child, I would carry a cloud of suspicion with me all my days. Andreg and Vishod alike coopting the power in me even as they would wonder to my death whether that power still served my father from afar."

The witch-princess. In Chriani's mind, Konaugo's spite was as sharp as the memory of the hands at his throat, sharp as the memory of Chanist and Barien laughing together in the soft glow of firelight. All the trust that Chriani had seen run from the prince high to the warrior, and he wasn't sure now how much of it was real.

He tried to tell himself that if Barien had told him the truth, he wouldn't have been afraid.

"You are your father's child," he said numbly. He dug hard, tried to find the words he knew were hidden somewhere in the dark silence. "You had no right to take this power in secrecy. Your mother had no right to seed it in you…"

"Blood and moonsign, Chriani, think on it. I was the daughter of a princeling third in the line to a throne held by a sovereign most thought would live forever. There should have been no responsibilities placed on me, no expectations. She thought I would be free to choose my own path, and so my mother began the training with me. I began to learn the music of my people before I spoke my first words. Then everything changed."

"She had no right…"

"Once the song of the Leisanmira comes to life within you, it cannot be silenced. Not by a father's will, not by a husband's fear." The princess turned away. "Only by me," she said quietly. "For the sake of what I must become."

Chriani wiped again with the pink-stained cloth, watched it come away this time no dirtier than it already was. He dropped it where the basin still lay overturned on the floor. "How do you expect to keep this secret?"

"The war-mages will assume that the assassin used the magic that burned the glade tonight…"

"Not tonight. I mean the secret of what you are, what you've been all this time?"

Lauresa laughed quietly, almost to herself. A kind of weary acceptance in her suddenly. "While my mother was a youngest prince's wife, many knew that she carried the Leisanmira song within her," she said. "When she became princess high, those truths were quickly made to seem like rumor by the carefully placed falsehoods of my father's Rheran councilors, and those who clung to them were branded superstitious fools. Make the truth seem laughable and you give life to the lie."

He felt the urge to turn from her, run from the tent and the dull ache that was her face in the half-light where she sat now at her father's work table. He saw her hands shaking.

"None of it matters any more," she said, and Chriani heard the strength fade from her voice. And suddenly, he saw a resemblance to her father he'd never seen before. More than just the golden hair, more than just the darkness that lurked beneath the fair features.

He remembered Chanist when he'd stood in this tent before, letting Lauresa hold him against the weight of a fear that seemed ready to drag him down. He saw that same fear in her now. A kind of age in her eyes that no one as young as her should have ever shown, the expression of courtly demeanor shrouding it like fine silk might drape the bones of someone starving.

"Marriage in Aerach means the end of this life," she said. "For Brandishear's sake." Chriani felt himself pulled from the storm of thought twisting through him. From the moons-lit copse, he felt the sharp tug of memory, tried to fight it. "You have much distrust in common, you and Andreg," she said. "A shame you'll never meet."

I used to watch you at the harvest fest…

"I trust what I can see," Chriani said, but he heard the emptiness in his voice. He could feel the shape of all the things he longed to say pushing up beneath the careful mask of the words he actually spoke.

"You trusted the power that saved your life in the war room when you thought it was trinket spellcraft…"

"Because sorcery in a ring, I control. Sorcery within a living heart, hiding from the authority of crown or law, who controls it?"

"The one who attacked you tonight, the one who killed Barien, who tried to kill my father, was no sorcerer. The power that might well have killed you came from what he wore. A ring, an amulet. Do you feel better now?"

"Yes."

"And why?"

"Because I can cut the rings from his fingers and twist the chains from around his neck before I cripple him cleanly. But what's inside him, I cannot touch."

"You could kill me for what lies inside me," she said quietly. "And I would not be the first Leisanmira to die for the sake of a peasant's fear."

"Funny to hear one talking of fear who's spent her whole life in hiding."

"And what do you hide, Chriani?" she said bitterly, voice raised now. "Beneath that bandage under your tunic which somehow never needs to be changed? Some wound that never seems to heal…"

Chriani stared blankly. At his chest, he felt the pain twist through him suddenly, felt her empty eyes bore a hole through him. He slipped the steel ring from its inside pocket, tried to force the shaking from his hand as he tossed it to her feet. He felt the ache again, twisting through the words he wanted to make. But in the end, it was the anger that spoke as it so often did.

"All this talk about how badly you want not to be controlled, and yet you seem to enjoy control a fair bit. Don't you princess?"

"Goodbye, Chriani," was all she said, and he turned for the curtain and was gone.

The guards were still there when Chriani slipped back outside, not knowing whether they'd heard the heated exchange within the tent or not. With even the meager trappings of court there, it was easy to forget that the walls were only canvas. Little more than curtains, he thought, protocol alone hedging off the space and life of a prince, of a princess, officers, rangers, foot soldiers holding the most private custom of the night within sight and earshot of a thousand others doing the same.

At all the High Summer celebrations he'd attended since he came to the city, there'd been shadow plays, the market court opened up and cordoned off. He remembered backdrops of black silk that seemed to swallow the torchlight and the expectant eyes of the crowds that thronged there. He'd accompanied Lauresa and her stepmother once, long ago. The first year that they'd begun to train together, Gwannyn apparently finding more initial charm in the idea of Chriani as her stepdaughter's comrade-at-arms than she later came to.

As he walked with no goal but to keep to the empty spaces where the camp was in constant motion around him, Chriani realized that all around him now was that same feeling. The backdrop of star-pierced cloud that screened the forest and the sky, white canvas awnings tugged at by the rising wind that screened the lives that had intruded on this place. The wall of the forest so close that he felt he might touch it, might drown in its depth, caught up in that shadow like it was set out for his eyes alone.

Not afraid of that shadow. Likely the only one in all of Chanist's company who could say that.

He heard the return of the prince and his riders before he saw them, six horses pounding back through a haze of firelight along the central track. He didn't see the war-mages, still out riding the perimeter, he guessed. Setting sorcerous wards outside the sweep of the sentries.

The blur of motion that was the camp shifted toward Chanist, a bonfire burning high at the edge of the archery yard where Chriani cut past it, screening himself. He saw Konaugo emerge from the officers' pavilion and move for the prince as he dismounted.

The captain had cleaned himself, Chriani noted coldly. No blood where his uniform had been changed.

As Chanist tossed gauntlets and helmet to a waiting attendant, he stepped past Konaugo and through the shifting wall of troops that flanked him. And Chriani felt a sudden chill as a ripple of movement threaded through the mass of bodies to all sides, every face turning as it was realized that the figure the prince strode toward was him.

Chriani stopped short because he didn't know what else to do. He nodded low as Chanist slowed before him, Konaugo and a half-dozen others following at the customary five paces. Around them, all the movement of a moment before had frozen fast.

"Any soldier who stands against dark magic and an assassin's blades single-handedly is more like to end up a corpse than a hero," the prince said gravely. Beside them, the fire spit sparks to the sky. Konaugo's eyes in the haze of light were stark points of red. "I thank Brandis's blood for your sake and my daughter's that you have not, master Chriani."

Chriani felt the familiar stillness in his tongue. The subtle inflection and qualification of rank that his response demanded slowed his thoughts. "I would call myself more fortunate than heroic, my lord prince," was all he could say.

"Fortune favors those who do not fear."

"Only a fool forgets there are things worthy of fear," Chriani said. Impulsive words, pulled from memory before he had time to realize how inappropriate they were. Chanist only smiled, though. Recognition there, Chriani thought.

"Barien said so to me as well. More than once." The prince high set his hand on Chriani's shoulder, the sword-hand grip firm there, a finger's-width from the hidden war-mark and his own daughter's name. For the first time since he'd punched that name into his skin, Chriani realized that the pain was gone.

"Barien was right in that as he was in most things." Chanist was thoughtful as he continued, his voice pitched louder, Chriani realized. Carrying across the space of bodies. "As he was right about you. In his name, and in the name of my daughter whose life you saved tonight, I offer you commission in the prince's guard."

The hiss of the fire as the cold breeze fanned it was the only sound in the half-circle of five hundred figures that flanked them both. Chriani stared for what seemed like a long while.

"I am not of rank, my lord prince," he stammered at last.

"You are now, Squire Chriani."

Chanist gestured to a thickset squire at his side, motioning him to unhook the falcon's band stitched in bronze from his arm. He did so carefully, looking none too happy about it. Chriani's hand was shaking, his arm rising as if it might have been lifted by some unseen force. Chanist removed the white tyro's insignia from Chriani's arm himself, slipping on the new insignia, incongruous against the over-patched tunic, the weather-stained cloak. The prince high bound it tight across from the unseen mark of Chriani's father, his company looking on.

Chriani felt a tightness in his chest and in his throat, as all the memories that had sifted through him the past days spun suddenly through his mind at once.

I know what you should be, well as you know it, Barien had said, and without wanting to, Chriani found himself thinking that except for chance, that might have been the last time he ever saw the warrior alive. Only the broadest twist of fate had led him to his dying mentor's side that night, and to the command that in its own way had brought him here. *Keep her safe.* More time on the wall, a different corridor taken when he'd run for the central court, and he would have heard the news when all the rest did, too late.

He should have made rank at least a year before, but all the lingering darkness wrapped up that thought where it had dogged Chriani for even longer than the last year was gone suddenly. Replaced by a dark anger that this moment had finally come too late for Barien to take the pride in it that Chriani knew he would have taken. The same pride he felt now, so unfamiliar to him where it fought against the self-consciousness of five hundred pairs of eyes on him, and where it reflected the prince high's weary smile that summoned up Barien's smile that was gone now.

Chriani hadn't seen where Konaugo moved within the crowd as it slowly dispersed. He didn't want to see him, but the captain stepped in close, an anger without bound or limit crossing the darkness between them. Konaugo's shattered nose was whole again somehow. The captain with healing of his own, Chriani guessed. The privileges of rank.

"My lord prince," Konaugo said with careful detachment, "I have further questions for our newly installed Squire Chriani regarding the events of this night."

"Pass them to someone else," the prince said curtly. He stepped away, a flick of his gaze bidding Konaugo to step close, the prince's words unheard by all except the captain and Chriani. "Prepare a dozen horse and your best riders. Take a squad of rangers with you. The Princess Lauresa rides for Aerach tonight."

The look of surprise on Konaugo's face seemed as genuine as the sudden shock as Chriani stared.

"The Valnirata have argument with me," the prince high said to his captain, "and I will not return to Rheran until it has been answered. But their assassins seeking me here, and the attack that this squire prevented tonight, shows it far too dangerous for the princess to stay. She'll ride early and in secret for Teillai and the safety of her husband's house. Her goods and servants can follow from Rheran once she's there."

As Chriani stared, he felt all the anger shatter suddenly. All the betrayal, all the emptiness that he'd felt since the night of Barien's death suddenly flooded back like a winter tide.

Marriage in Aerach means the end of this life.

What true freedom the world offered almost always lay in the ability to choose, Barien had liked to say. Chriani heard the voice in his head as if the warrior might be calling to him from the other side of the fire, the memory slipping through him like the icy wind that the heat drew from behind him.

"Someone else offers you a world's worth of options, you've still got no choice of your own," Barien told him once. "Choice is you deciding that what's important is the one thing they don't offer."

Chriani had laughed then. They were riding outside the walls of Tarenic, the princess high and the children finishing a month-long stay there. The summer that Chriani and Lauresa's training was soon to be ended.

"That'd be good talk coming from anyone else," he said. "You spend your whole life taking other people's orders. What kind of choice is that you've made?"

"Prince, peasant, or in between, everyone does someone else's bidding one way or another," the warrior said. "You think the prince high sits through trade and treaty talks for the laugh it gives him? Take on a country's worth of people needing to be fed, safe, and sheltered before you get the time to think about what you need, tell me how it feels."

"Chanist still makes choices I'll never get to make. What about you?"

Barien considered for a moment. "The choice I made is to get to a place where I take the prince's orders and none other."

"Orders are orders," Chriani laughed again. "Your prince gives you an order one day you can't stand to see carried out, what'll you do?"

"Choose loyalty," the warrior said evenly. "Or choose my conscience. Still my decision either way."

As Konaugo's eyes bored into him, Chriani saw the captain nod and turn away. He heard gruff orders barked, a dozen of the guard scrambling for the stables, but he was distracted suddenly by Chanist's hand on his shoulder.

"Sit with me," the prince said.

In the mess tent, Chanist and Chriani sat alone at the officers' table, a steaming joint of beef fresh from the spit set beside them. The prince had water and wine at his side, pouring both for Chriani but only the latter for himself.

To sit alone at meat across from the prince high was an honor so singular that Chriani had never let the dream of it cross his mind. When he was younger, when he was a child, he had dreamed of other things, though he had become ever more loathe to recall those dreams the older he got and the farther from him they seemed to slip. Title and rank, a place in the prince's guard at Barien's side. Once, he'd fancied himself captain of that guard some day, back in the time of the dead Hammeran, before Konaugo had stripped the post of its honor.

But like the trappings of rank that Barien had so often ignored, Chriani felt how uncomfortably this honor fit him now. A tightness in his chest had seemingly replaced the pain that had been there, the new insignia heavy somehow on his arm. Sitting silently, he watched as the prince hacked still-dripping meat from the joint to a trencher that he pushed between them.

"I put you on edge in the yard," Chanist said as he ate. He motioned Chriani to do the same, Chriani trying to summon back some of the hunger he knew he should be feeling. "With my offer of commission. You have my apologies."

"I was simply surprised, my lord prince," Chriani said.

"As was I when Lauresa burst in to tell me you had bid her run while you fought an assassin and his sorcery to the death." Chriani could imagine that performance, but something in the prince's words caught at him. In her father's tent, Lauresa had said that the war-mages would assume that the eldritch fire had been the assassin's magic used against Chriani, sure of herself then because she'd already set that story in play.

Chanist raised his tankard, Chriani clumsily lifting his own as the prince nodded formally. "The things on which we set our sights are a pale measure of our worth when compared to the times at which fate sets its sights on us," Chanist said.

He didn't know, Chriani realized. Didn't know what his own child was, what she could do.

As he drank, he could see movement all around them, could feel movement even beyond the range of his sight. The perimeter guard still redoubled, couriers and sentries vague shapes in the half-light where the evenlamps gleamed along the distant edge of the prince's pavilion. In the center of it, he and Chanist seemed to be the fulcrum point around which all the movement turned.

Around them, the empty mess tent was thick with the scent of mud and woodsmoke, and for a moment, Chriani caught himself watching the prince as he ate with thickly callused fingers. A world away from the Bastion, Chanist seemed suddenly more at home that Chriani could remember ever having seen him before. None of the trappings of court around him now, nothing even of the white linen that marked his tents.

This was the Chanist he'd met in the stables, Chriani thought. A prince with a love of simple pleasures that reminded him suddenly of Barien in a way he couldn't express. A third-born heir, accepting of a life as soldier and father, perhaps even looking forward to that life. Then pressed to sudden service as a prince.

"You must have felt that way," he said, the words out even before the thought had fully formed.

"What do you mean, master Chriani?" Chanist spoke evenly, appraised him.

Even watered, Chriani felt the potency of the prince's wine slurring his thoughts, just as it had allowed the words just spoken to spill from those thoughts unbidden. He wondered at the stamina that allowed Chanist to drink it unmixed. "Fate setting its sights on you," he said awkwardly. "When the crown passed to you. Unlooked for." And it wasn't until he'd actually said it that Chriani recognized the subtle pressure that had forced the words to his mind.

What do you mean to do? Irdaign had asked.

Chriani didn't know where it came from, just felt it welling up inside him, born of a hundred different thoughts only half of which he could name.

Still my decision either way.

Chanist filled both their cups again, adding less water to Chriani's this time. "Yes," he said. "That part of my life is one I reflect on only rarely, master Chriani. But I was put in mind of it tonight by you."

Chriani didn't understand. "I'm sorry, my lord prince?"

"Barien was as a father to you," Chanist said simply. "I know this by how very much like a son he treated you. Barien is dead, and as an accident of that death, you have been given a chance to prove who you are. As my father's death gave me that chance. The dreams our fathers have for us that they will never see."

Chanist soaked up the juice of the trencher with bread, broke it and offered half across the table. Chriani took it, nodded thanks but couldn't meet the prince's gaze suddenly. He ate in silence, had to work to swallow as something caught at his throat. In the sharp hiss of the fire, he heard the echo of Chanist's words hanging, twisting in with the dream of the banquet that he'd woken to, and with the smoke funneling up to the steel chimney that was Barien's pyre suddenly. The burning that marked the passage of the night, or of a life.

"My grandfather once said to me that every person's station is a place worthy of respect if carried well." When Chriani forced himself to look up, he saw Chanist staring past him, the blue eyes almost black in the firelight. "He was regent to the Empire when the Lothelecan fell, but he petitioned the Imperial court and the lords to allow him to rule not by virtue of his title but of his quality. History judges too often on the basis of blood, not deed, he said. After his own example, and my father's, I hope to continue to change that."

Chanist rose suddenly, strode to the fire to toss more wood to the flames. His face was lean in the orange-white light that streaked him, eyes narrowed against the heat.

"For dying at the hands of the Valnirata, my father's name is remembered by a nation," the prince said quietly. "Your father who died likewise is remembered only by you, I would expect. But in the end, the memory that children carry means far more."

He raised his tankard again, Chriani awkwardly lifting his. The snarl of the fire as it flared twisted between them as they drank.

When he spoke again, the prince seemed distant. "I have often thought that it is some small comfort to lose those we love to the haste of death when it comes. We are given leave to lament that we had no chance to speak our love to them. But I wonder if we should know what to say to those we love if we knew that it would be the last time."

The face was impassive, but Chriani heard a weariness in the voice as the prince closed his eyes. The sense of age he'd seen in the throne room that night. Not sure who the prince was speaking of now. His own father. Barien. Lauresa, bound for Aerach on his orders. A last goodbye in the rough surroundings of a war camp not what father or daughter would have expected, he guessed.

"This sacrifice she makes…"

Chriani barely heard the words.

The prince high opened his eyes. He was silent a long moment, Chriani not daring a response. He drank again, drained his tankard and set it down. Chriani saw Chanist glance past him, over his shoulder to where the lights burned at his own pavilion.

"So many things that are left unsaid."

It was well toward dawn when they finally broke, Chriani watching from the edge of the barracks as Chanist made his way back toward the lights of his pavilion. At the distant stables, he saw Konaugo inspecting a dozen field horses, no telling how long it had been since the captain slept but no sign of fatigue in him. Chriani was surprised to feel himself as awake as he was, some side effect of the healing draught that Chanist had given him, he guessed.

At Chanist's tents, he saw three couriers slipping in and out in the space of time it took the prince to cross the open yard. The night was bright where the cloud had broken, the Darkmoon riding low in the west like a beacon calling on the oncoming dawn. Lauresa would be awake like everyone else in the camp, he knew, preparing to ride.

But as he found himself walking the firelit perimeter of the encampment, Chriani found himself coming back to the prince's words. Something was pulling at him that he'd managed to bury all the time since that terrible night, forcing him to think now on what he might have said, what he should have said to Barien if he'd known it would be the last time. Telling himself he should have known to speak his thoughts when Barien lay bleeding to death beside him. Silently cursing the silence that his fool's hope had made.

In those last terrible moments, for everything that Barien had said to him, he'd offered nothing in return. The words trapped inside him as they so often were, too late now. Quick enough with the jape or the angry insult, he thought. Slow to speak when it might mean something.

He heard horses on the move. Sprinting back across the archery yard, he kept his gaze from the Valnirata corpse still there, slowed behind the shelter of an exposed awning, canvas cracking with each gust of cold wind.

He watched a dozen riders pacing slow along the track that he and Lauresa had followed in only that day, the horses' breath twisting in with the steam that rose from the half-frozen ground beneath their feet. Konaugo's broad form was in the lead, cloak wrapped tight around him. To either side of a dozen escorts, four archers rode, outriders and vanguards already gone to sweep the perimeter. He made out two war-mages, counted four packhorses laden with tents and supplies.

In the center, Chriani saw a slender figure, the palfrey she rode the same grey as the cloaks that she and the company wore.

Chanist had made his goodbye a brief one. Easier that way.

Around the princess, Konaugo's company would ride with bows in hand until they made the bridge at Werrancross — the end of the Clearwater Way that wound across the desert scrubland between the forest and the Sandhorn. The northern steppes of Aerach lay beyond it, where Lauresa would land in a week and be married in a month to Duke Allenis Andreg who was old enough to have fought along the Hunthad when the armies of the Valnirata had poured out across the river and into the heart of Aerach like a knife.

So many things that are left unsaid…

From the pocket within his sleeve, he pulled the ribbon of green silk. He grasped for its scent, summoned up the memory of Kathlan's body against his three nights past, waiting out the dawn as she slept.

Chriani made his decision.

He slipped into the stand of poplar to the south of Chanist's tents, waited there a while. Long enough for the troop to have disappeared into the distant darkness of the track that twisted off below the rise of the encampment, but still well ahead of the coming dawn. Then he slipped back to the tents of the barracks, grabbed the first saddle blanket and pack he found there, checked to find a bedroll, a week's supply of hardtack and salt pork. He filled four flasks at the water barrels, slipped back as a pair of perimeter guards stalked wearily by.

At the makeshift stables, the roan had been tethered apart from the troop's horses, standing where he'd been woken by Lauresa's palfrey being saddled and the noise of Konaugo's force heading out. He was quiet, only glanced over to Chriani's hand on his neck when he slipped in from the muddy track behind the tents.

He would have liked to have gone for one of the faster courier's steeds, but they were stabled more dangerously close to the guards than he liked, and his own saddle and tack had been hung at the post where the roan and Lauresa's horse had been stabled alone. He bunched tack and reins into his pack and lashed the saddle blanket to it. He slung the saddle to his back, stirrups muffled as he pushed his forearm through them. Silently, he slipped the roan's tether from the twisted spike on the post, led him into the darkness beyond the fire.

He would saddle the horse later, when he was clear of the camp. He knew that Konaugo would be making good speed even by the light of stars and Darkmoon, but he wanted Lauresa's party a little distance ahead of him. They'd be on their guard, he knew. No point in being seen in pursuit and picked off by an outrider ambush. He still carried the battered sword he'd taken from the stables, but he had to steal his third bow of the night from the empty officers' pavilion, virtually the entire camp still patrolling the outlying perimeter, it seemed.

He waited within sight of that perimeter only a short while, watching for a break in the patrols as they circled, the smoke of the night's fires shrouding him as he pulled the roan through. He watched behind him as he went, seeing no sign of pursuit. When he judged himself far enough from the patrol lines, he saddled the roan as quietly as he could.

He was checking the cinches for the second time when he became aware of movement behind him. In the light from the prince's pavilion, a faint glimmer in the distance, a figure was pacing. Turning toward him, he thought.

He dropped down beside the horse, neither of them moving. Silent in the darkness. Chriani waited, watched. As quickly as it had come, the figure was gone. Nothing there but the white haze of the tents and the flags flying above as he turned quickly away, swung up to the saddle and spurred the roan forward into the night.

— CHAPTER 9 —

THE CLEARWATER WAY

WHERE KONAUGO'S TROOP rode the unmarked ranger trails within shadowing distance of the Glaeddynfield road, Chriani could read the signs of their passage with ease. As the Darkmoon dwindled west and the eastern sky dawned blue-white, he saw where their tracks had churned the frozen turf to mud, Konaugo balancing pace and stealth.

Should the speed of the road ever be needed, they could be on it in a heartbeat. Until then, however, they were effectively out of sight as they threaded the twisting contours of the bracken-choked hills. Those hills marked the boundary between the rich farmland of the Locanwater delta and the slowly rising scrubland that bordered the exile deserts and the Sandhorn, some fifty leagues north and east.

Twice before the sun rose, he heard patrols passing on the road, and he slowed the roan so as not to draw their attention. Silently, he cursed himself for not bringing anything with him from Chanist's camp that might have passed for a courier's charge, but he sifted through a dozen half-believable stories as he rode, kept them close at hand on the off chance he was stopped.

He had to take the horse off the trail and quickly into the trees at one point, the thud of hoofbeats ahead barely warning him of the approach of two rangers, moving at speed. Bound for Chanist's camp, he guessed, both riding with bows drawn and eyes to the southeast, the forest closer now, mist rising like a wall before it.

At a darkened dairy farmstead, he saw cloaked figures crouched on guard behind a low stone wall adjacent to the house. Barely boys, watching him as he passed. At another farm, he saw a rough palisade of hastily erected birch staves skirting a hilltop shed, flimsy enough that a sow might have barreled through it with little effort, but it spoke to a need for the feeling of security. Walls to hide behind.

He passed through his first real village at dawn, watched by a trio of farmhands walking the narrow track where it skirted the woods. Two had flails in hand, one with a shortsword that looked only slightly less battered than Chriani's own. The three of them made up some kind of patrol that would have been laughable but for the dead-serious challenge in their looks.

That look melted away once they saw Chriani's arm, though, and the insignia of a guard squire there. They nodded to him as he passed, Chriani nodding back as he spurred on. In their eyes, he saw the same tangible energy he'd felt in the Bastion the morning of Barien's burning. And as the sun finally rose and he spurred on against the chill of frost and the scent of woodsmoke that spread from the sparse settlements to the west, Chriani thought he could feel that same undercurrent of tension hanging across the silence. As unmistakable as the slow change in the weather promised by the freezing mist that the dawn burned away. Only days since the attempt on the prince's life, and the peace that Chanist himself had wrought thirteen years before seemed ready to unravel now. The eastern frontier already alive with the expectation of war.

All along the western flank of the road, a barrier of scrubland marked off the extent of the farmsteads as if a knife had sliced its way along the fields' edge. Beyond it, a swath of land a day's ride across was given over to willow and wolf-grass, the black loam of the delta as rich as any farmland in the Ilmar, forever left fallow for the fear that lived on both sides of the trees.

Through the fringe of the Greatwood, the scout trails cut their barely visible pathways through ever-present shadow, Chanist's rangers and local garrisons from Addrimyr patrolling there endlessly, watching for signs of movement, of any plotting from the far side of the Valnirata frontier. Like the rangers on the Brandishear side, the Valnirata had their elite *carontir* patrols, ceaselessly traversing the Greatwood as the first line of defense against the invasion that both sides seemed to have been expecting since the Ilmar treaty was signed. How much longer they'd have to wait, Chriani didn't want to guess. Old hatreds died hard, it seemed.

It was nearing dusk when he came to Caredry's walls at the mouth of the Locanwater, the river winding between low ash hills where terraced fields lay heavy with frost. The broad city-keep was the last stop and way station for those travelers and traders heading out along the Clearwater Way. It was a hard day's ride each leg of the journey to the four keeps that were the only safe stopping places along the Wayroad — Gleoran, then Durrant, Talimeth, Rhercyn, then a last day to pass through to the city of Werrancross in Aerach.

The fortified keeps existed only to protect the meager flow of riders from the perils that dogged the road. Those who walked it would have to fend for themselves on the longer journey between those isolated stops. However, those foolish enough to walk the Clearwater Way typically either had skill enough to deal with its dangers, or carried with them a wish to die that the exile lands were only too eager to answer.

Chriani guessed that Konaugo's company would have ridden past the city without stopping, not wanting to tip anyone's suspicions that his troop was anything other than a scout party on routine patrol. As close to the hostile frontier as Caredry lay, patrols would have been commonplace even before the stepped-up tensions of the past week. He pulled the roan up in front of four gatekeepers, made sure his right arm and the insignia there were in plain view.

"I seek the patrol that rides from Addrimyr," he said in what he hoped was an echo of Barien's voice. "I have a message."

"There was a troop passed just after daymark, lord," a scarred veteran said as he stepped up. "Twenty and a captain, I counted, if that was who you're looking for. They took water and headed straight out the Wayroad."

The unfamiliar tone of respect in the voice caught Chriani by surprise, and he clumsily nodded thanks and spurred off. That much time since Konaugo had passed meant that the captain was moving even faster than he'd thought. Darkness falling already meant he had no hope of even getting close to them that night.

He was just out of sight of the gates when he saw the ranger marker at the forest's edge, the tracks of a dozen horses bearing south into the wood. Konaugo would have left the road the moment its curve had masked the troop's movements from the city, a force that strong likely facing no risk of ambush or attack from within the trees.

For the most part, the exile bandits that Valnirata and Ilmari alike called the crithnala stayed clear of the wide swath of patrolled territory to either side of the Clearwater Way. The exiles called that broad territory Crithnalerean and claimed it in their own name, but the forces of Brandishear and Aerach held the Wayroad with a deadly and almost casual defiance. Their patrols swept constantly east and west, the ranger trail that Konaugo had taken marking the southernmost extents of their watch. Chriani checked behind him, no sign of anyone on the road as he made for the forest's edge ahead, but he had made only minimal headway along the trail before he was forced to stop for the night, Lauresa somewhere ahead in the frigid dark. He lit no fire himself, sleeping close to the roan when he could.

He was up before dawn the next morning and rode hard, the tracks of Konaugo's company leading him on as he watched for signs of rear-guard patrols. He was alone on the trail for the better part of the day, though, conscious of the chill silence that swallowed the horse's steady steps, wrapped him tightly.

Within that silence and the tight web that Konaugo's security would make for her, Chriani knew that Lauresa would stay as safe as she would have within the walls of Caredry or the Clearwater keeps ahead. Chanist's order had been about security in the end, and setting camp in isolation meant avoiding the eyes that would have inevitably asked as to the reasons for a twenty-strong escort and to the identity of the noble they rode for. On horseback, in the cloak of Konaugo's company, she would have passed for a ranger easily enough along the road, but within the city, it would have had to be private chambers and three guards on every door.

As dusk fell, Chriani saw the lights of the camp long before anyone in it would have spotted him approaching. In the dark that loomed within the fringe of the Greatwood, he left the roan tethered in a small copse a safe distance away, felt for the wind and circled around to keep it in front of him. He'd left his sword with the horse but slung the bow he'd liberated at the camp across his back, as much for comfort as anything else. Not much chance he'd live long enough to use it, he knew, should he come up against Konaugo one last time.

In a stand of twisted fir turned white with rime, a flock of northern dusk-thrush had settled. He came in from the south, slipped below them silently as their sharp-edged twilight song rang clear in the chill air.

Konaugo's company had set themselves atop a low rise. The mound of shale and ragged turf would come alive with green in the spring, but was a frozen expanse of wild-rose hedge and brambles now. Between him and the light lay a field of loose scree that would betray every misstep with sound. Konaugo had guards circling at regular intervals as Chriani lay low and watched.

In the gleam of the fires, he saw only one tent, standing opposite the bedrolls set up along the crest of the rise. He knew who'd be within it.

At trees staggered around the camp, the horses were tethered in twos with soft harnesses, ready to be ridden in an instant even if the need for fast escape meant no time to saddle them. It was a cavalry tactic stolen from the Incursions, Chriani knew. The Ilvani had ridden without saddle then, too many night-time ambushes claiming too many Ilmari lives in their wake. The Ilmar forces adopting the enemy's tactics like they'd adopted their weapons, the shortbow of the cavalry giving way to the more powerful Ilvani horsebow in all the years since.

He'd eaten only half of the first day's rations since the previous morning, his appetite gone as he rode. He felt a dull hunger now, though, watching Konaugo's patrols circle as he pushed slowly closer. He watched for long enough to feel the unconscious rhythm of their pacing, looked for the opening he'd need. He watched a halo of light to the west mark the setting Clearmoon pushing against the cloud, knew he'd have to move before it broke.

There, a quick gap where a narrow shelf of rock below the camp was clear. Two guards passed each other to leave a space between their movement and the passing of a third, still circling out beyond the princess's tent.

Low through the shadows, Chriani moved, the whisper of the wind and the thrush-song around him the only sound. As he slipped across the boundary of the camp, he let the instinct take him, watching the faint shifting of movement as he stood quickly, walked casually away from the firelight, his own cloak a close enough match to any of the others at the distance he meant to keep.

He was behind the princess's tent in a dozen paces, took a moment to scan to both sides, no one around. Then he was on the ground again, a shadow as he slipped up against the canvas. He had his mother's pick between his fingers, used the sharpened edge to cut his way quickly through each thick stitch along the corner seam.

From inside, he heard Lauresa sing.

At the canvas, his hand faltered as it almost never did, and twisting through him like some sleek shadow of her voice, Chriani felt a sudden rush of strength he couldn't explain. He felt himself opened up to the night, the faint shifting of movement and voices distant around him, in touch with himself in a way he couldn't remember feeling since his dogged pursuit of a missing princess that terrible night.

Though he wouldn't have recognized it at the time, the feeling of two long days' ride filled him now with the unmistakable sense of purpose whose absence had hit him hard as he'd walked Chanist's camp the night before. He was tired to his core. He felt the memory of the pain burning at his breast as if Lauresa's sweet song was brandy across the open wound her name made. He felt the tightness of the insignia that flanked that name now, remembered the fear and the uncertainty and the pride he'd felt when Chanist had bound it to him, only two nights before but somehow a world away now.

Even as it came and just as quickly flitted away, Chriani realized that he wanted that feeling again. He wanted that purpose, wanted all the unspoken faith in the salute the prince high had given him. But even as he thought it, he realized with dark humor how unlikely that all was for him now. Two nights after taking the squire's rank that every Bastion tyro coveted from the first time they set eyes on the central court, two nights after receiving the offer of commission and the singular honor of eating across from the prince high himself, he was without leave, on the run, and breaking into the Princess Lauresa's tent.

What was he thinking? More to the point, when would he start thinking? Or was this the same turbulence that had always seemed to rule his life, just taking different shape now? Fear when he was younger, growing to anger through his long adolescence at Barien's side, and now turned to something else. Some impulse of self-destructiveness, Chriani somehow obligated to tear down any bridge before he might even attempt to cross it.

Or had it always been fear all along?

Without feeling any hint of it rising, Chriani felt himself overwhelmed now with the same desperation that he remembered from the death of his mother and grandfather. The fear of the long month he'd walked the road to Rheran on the meager strength of berries and the eggs he could steal from farmhouses along the way. The fear of the mark at his shoulder and the world around him that his mother had warned him against but that she had never meant to let him face alone.

He'd been afraid of being alone until Barien took him in, and then had been afraid of failure until Barien taught him that he had the strength to succeed. Then he'd been afraid of succeeding because always in the back of his mind, he felt the weight of the secret he had carried with him since the day he was born, and that had taken on darker urgency with his mother's death.

The section of the tent wall he'd carefully split was wide enough to admit his shoulders. He tested it with his fingers to make sure there was no second layer beyond it.

He felt the pride falter. Twisting cold in him suddenly, he felt the memory of Chanist's smile, and of Barien's faith in him that had never been repaid.

Like Barien, Chriani knew what he should be. He could feel it, could see it some days like a waking dream. And even as he felt it, he felt the fear that told him the person he should be would never be as strong as the person he was.

He heard Lauresa's song again, sharp in the silence, and without his even looking, her voice told him that she was on the opposite side of the tent and that she was alone. The two things he most needed to know as he slipped his cloak off, pulling it behind him as he twisted through the narrow gap of shadow he'd made. All the long years he'd watched her, all the time spent atop the walls across from her balcony, he'd never once heard her sing in anyone else's presence.

When he had carefully pressed the gap closed again, Chriani found himself within the princess's own bed, the near half of the tent given over to thick layers of sheepskin piled on a narrow palette. A pale scrim of gauze hung against the other half, a shrouded evenlamp burning close to where the flap at the opposite wall was sealed tight.

Beyond the gauze, he saw her. Four steps away, she stood turned from him, naked except for the plain steel band at her finger and the chain of the lapis pendant where it gleamed at her neck. She was washing at a steaming enamel basin, her voice a delicate echo of glass as she half whispered, half sung the same song he'd heard on the road. 'The Ode of Seilonna.' The song of leaving.

Where a thin shift of ilvanweave hung at the tent pole, she slipped it on, draping herself in white as her voice slowly trailed off, and Chriani crouched there for a long while, expecting her to turn in surprise at some point, then needing to correct for the silence of his entrance when she didn't.

"That was very beautiful," he whispered.

Across from him, Lauresa flinched. She didn't look back.

Chriani had half-expected her to wheel on him in fright or anger, some echo of what he'd seen in her that night in the war room. Knowing that it had all been artifice. Some part of the elaborate strata of lies that had always made up Lauresa's life. Expecting it to be real now, real for once and the last time. But when she finally spoke, all that he heard in her was a kind of expectation he didn't understand.

"How did you get here?" she said quietly.

Outside, Chriani heard voices rise above the thrushes' song, someone laughing at an unheard joke. In his mind, he picked through a half-dozen different explanations that would likely have made a better impression than the truth, but there was no point anymore.

"Stole a horse and rode after you," he said. "Broke across Konaugo's perimeter. Cut my way in through your tent."

Chriani heard her laugh, but there was no mirth in the sound. "You came to prove how easy it will be for the assassin to undo all my father's intent to protect me?"

"I came to tell you I love you."

He saw her start, look back to meet his gaze, just for a moment. She was in shadow, the white of the shift that draped her seeming to flow and merge with the pale throat, darkness clinging to it where it tented gently across her breast. Chriani saw that breast rise and fall with her breathing, loud in the stillness. In her eyes, in the brief instant before she'd turned away once more, he saw a look that he'd never expected to see again beyond the dreams that he'd always known would haunt him.

"I'm sorry," Lauresa said.

Chriani heard an edge in her voice that he could almost place. "You have nothing to be sorry for." All he could think to say.

"I have my deceit to be sorry for," the princess said. And through the clear tone, he heard the girl's voice he remembered from all those days together. All the rides that had taken them out across the Rheran farmsteads and beyond. "I have my anger from that night in the war room, when all I could think was that you were working for my father. That my own lack of care had seen you discover my secret."

"I would never betray you," Chriani said.

"You are a member of the prince's guard," Lauresa said coldly. "You serve my father and his court. Betraying me is your duty now."

Chriani hadn't seen her react to the bronze insignia in her quick glance, wondered if she'd noticed.

Choice is you deciding what's important, Barien had said.

As he pulled the armband from his sleeve, Chriani was certain she heard it tear. He tossed it to the floor in front of her, saw her glance down.

"I know my duty, princess…"

She was silent a long while, Chriani still watching her back, the slight tremor that threaded the rise and fall of her shoulders.

"Please go," she said at last. It was the voice from the war room again.

"Look at me first…"

He had no idea why he said it. No idea why it was suddenly as important as it seemed, the need to see the blue of her eyes one last time. The need to seek what he thought he'd seen there a moment before.

"No rank that you will ever have gives you the right to order me, tyro. Get out."

"Squire," Chriani corrected her, knowing how little difference it made. "Look at me."

Lauresa laughed. "Do you not understand? Two day's ride with nothing else to think about, and not even now is this clear to you? I saw this moment coming, Chriani, since the day our training ended. This laughable obsession. Love me? You are a fool."

Chriani felt a measured anger in her now, and as she paced away from him, he followed, trying to circle around her but she was quicker, her face always shifting away.

"Every knight who serves a princess falls to this same pathetic sickness of the heart," she said. "Barien himself said as much to me before the princess high ordered my training ceased, but I had no idea until now how right he was."

Chriani felt something twist inside him, Barien's name like a knife in his gut. "Look at me."

"In the midst of what looks like it may be war between the Ilmar and the Valnirata, I am married in a month. Do you imagine that I have the time for your puerile fantasies?"

"Look at me then, and it'll be the last time."

"Get out, Chriani." He heard the coldness in her, feared for a moment that someone outside the tent would hear them.

"I've loved you since we were children," he said. He felt the rush of words within him open up like some long-drawn sluice gate had been suddenly and finally freed. "I would have done anything for you. Anything to win you. Anything to make you happy."

For most of the past month, he'd tried to remember the last time he'd seen that look, tried to remember when the feeling that had wrapped itself up in that shared childhood had finally broken, but he couldn't. He could remember the times it had been there, could remember a time when it was incontrovertibly gone, but the transition had slipped past him somehow. Unseen.

"Please go," she whispered. The anger still there, but something else twisted in with it now. Something familiar.

Outside, Chriani heard footsteps approach but he didn't care, the ragged cadence of his pulse seeming to twist in with the regular rhythm of those footfalls as they passed away again.

"Look at me."

"Leave…"

"From the moment I stood behind you and guided your hand on the range that day, I loved you, Lauresa. Every moment I spent with you. Look at me."

"We were children…"

"Children younger than we were then have known war. Children can know madness, children can know deceit, can know fear. Tell me they can't know love."

Beneath each word, Chriani thought he saw her flinch. Some trick of the light, Lauresa suddenly frail as she twisted from him, held her hand to the tent's central pole as if she was steadying herself.

"And children can know friendship," she whispered hoarsely. "Children can know devotion that crosses lines of rank and class, but these things aren't love."

"I was there, Lauresa. I know what it was. Look at me…"

She turned then.

Chriani saw the tears where they tracked her cheeks, saw the eyes in the glow of evenlamps burning the blue of a High Summer sky.

He saw the look he remembered, felt it flood through him like warm rain.

"I loved you, too, Chriani…"

And then she was against him, her hands in his, her mouth at his, and there was no sound, no movement, no time.

He understood. He understood it in the taste of her, and in her hands at his head now, holding him tightly, and in her tears where the blue eyes squeezed them free. All the distance in her, he thought. All the arrogance, all the false pride designed to push him away because she'd spoken the truth.

She had known this day was coming. Her obligation to marry in the name of the state, and the pain of them losing each other like she knew they would some day. Easier to turn away before it ever had a chance to happen.

Lauresa hid her secrets well.

That night in the war room, he'd looked for recognition but there'd been none, but in the blue eyes as they opened now, he saw a familiarity that seemed to burn with its own clear light. He thought he saw himself reflected in those eyes, knew that was impossible.

I remember you…

Outside, the bird-sound shifted with the wind, a trace of woodsmoke drifting where the chill breeze must have turned. The thin shift bunched in his hands as Lauresa's own hands found his neck and pulled him close, and her breath in his ear was a music as sweet as any song she'd ever made.

As she held his face in her hands, she gently closed his eyes with her lips, kissed him again to the salt taste of her own tears. She was in his lap and his cheek was wet as they both wept now, Chriani not remembering how they'd slipped to the floor. And over and over, she whispered words that he had to focus to finally understand.

"I'm sorry…"

He found the strength to place his hand to her mouth. He felt her breath trace chill fingers as she kissed them, not sure how long they held each other until he became suddenly aware of laughter at the distant fire, punctuating the silence of the night and the sound of his own heart in his chest.

Chriani froze.

As his hand came up, it seized Lauresa's where she stroked his cheek. Outside, he could hear the ripple of wind as it plucked at the canvas, but the plaintive song of the dusk-thrushes had faded in a way it shouldn't have. He hadn't heard it go.

Then came a distant hiss that Chriani recognized with an awareness rooted deeper than memory, and he pulled Lauresa under him as he rolled, the sheepskin up and over them both as a volley of ash-grey arrows shredded the tent.

From the camp, the shouts of alarm and the screams of the dying came with no measured space between them. Chriani didn't remember pulling Lauresa out through the gap he'd cut in the tent wall, didn't feel the freezing night against the wetness of his eyes where he frantically wiped them. He had his hand locked to hers, taking in the scene in a single glance. A frozen moment of time.

From the downwind side of the camp, a rain of dark bowshot cut through the frantically running troop and the screaming horses. He saw archers returning fire, but they were pushing back toward the remains of Lauresa's tent, trying to protect her rather than take the cover that the hollow of the hill would have given them.

He saw the Valnirata then. Some twenty strong, they raced in on horseback behind the hail of their own missiles, rolling across the perimeter guards as they fell. Chriani recognized the lean horses they rode, woven reins clutched tightly as they hurtled up the low rise of the hill. In the light of the near-half Clearmoon just descending toward the trees, he recognized the knotted lines of the war-marks on their cloaks.

In the center of it all, one rider swept through on a coal-black charger. Chriani saw sharpened steel at the stallion's hooves, heard it screaming in rage as it reared and slashed at the troops that tried desperately to circle around Lauresa's tent. He saw the two war-mages already down, bodies riddled with arrows as they were crushed beneath a flurry of hooves. As he pulled the princess with him, Chriani instinctively wrapped his own cloak around her to cover the white shift, slipping through the shadows as he sought a point of safety in the chaos.

He saw Konaugo.

On the opposite side of the encampment, the captain was a blur of motion where he whirled with an axe in each hand, dropping two Valnirata on foot even as he spun to take the legs out from under a horse as it tore past him, its rider screaming as he fell. Chriani didn't know how he managed it, but Konaugo saw him somehow. From across the encampment, through the haze of flying hooves and the frantic shouting of his troops, he turned. The rage in his eyes was one Chriani recognized.

He pulled Lauresa behind him as Konaugo charged, but the time it took him to fumble the bow from his back was all the captain needed to cross half the horse-churned ground between them, moving at a speed that belied his thickly muscled bulk. Even as he notched an arrow, Chriani knew it was too late, Konaugo screaming as both axes left his hands in a single fluid motion. Then Chriani saw the scything steel arc past him to the left, and he instinctively shot his arm around Lauresa, dragging her down as the two Valnirata stealing up on foot behind them were cut down.

As he rolled up again, Chriani managed two shots, a horse bearing down on Konaugo from behind narrowly twisting past him when its rider took both shafts to the chest. Konaugo had somehow pulled the sword from the dead rider's saddle scabbard even as the horse careened away, already running again, and Chriani realized that it was the princess his eyes were locked to, hacking through two more faltering horses as they tried in vain to scramble back.

Chriani watched the first rider fall from his stumbling horse, more slowly than seemed possible. He saw the Ilvani's hands grasping blindly for the arrows that had been in his own hand only moments before.

He had shot by instinct. No thought to it except protecting the princess and Konaugo. He saw the Valnirata slam to the ground and lie unmoving. He had never killed anyone before.

He was distracted. Didn't see the black stallion.

Konaugo was still running, didn't have time to check himself as the steel-shod horse slammed into him. Chriani watched him fall as the sword was torn from his hand, close enough that he heard the sharp crack of bone. Close enough that he could lurch for him, grabbing without thinking, trying to pull the bulky body out of the horse's path but catching only his cloak.

Konaugo was there, then he was gone. Chriani felt a stabbing pain lance through both arms where his fingers felt like they'd been torn free of his hands, and the force of even that secondary impact knocked him from his feet as the screaming stallion's hooves drove Konaugo to the ground.

Chriani saw the stallion bear off, hooves striking sparks from the shale rise at the crest of the hill. As he crawled close, he had time to watch his captain die. Konaugo's left arm was shattered, the hand of his right clutching frantically at the air as Chriani forced himself up, tried to clear his head.

"Princess…" the captain whispered, and Chriani realized that he was speaking to Lauresa as she scrambled through the mud, helped Chriani rise.

Konaugo said nothing else after that.

Where the black stallion skidded and wheeled, it churned the frozen hillside to mud again. Chriani recognized the rider then — the scars across the pale cheeks visible to his eyes where the hood of the cloak had shifted. No sound from the assassin as he slammed the steel boots hard into the screaming horse's side, bearing straight for them.

"Move," Chriani said.

He grabbed Lauresa's hand in his, slick with blood. Where it lay in the open mud before him, he snatched up one of Konaugo's handaxes as he headed for the woods, cutting by instinct for the frosted shadows of the rose hedge that edged the steeper slope of the hill. Behind him, he heard the stallion pounding closer. Then at the last moment, he pulled to the left, leading Lauresa in a leap from a plunging bluff of shale and sand that the rider would have to circle around in order to descend. He heard the horse skid to a frenzied halt, didn't look back.

They skidded along a narrow cleft where loose scree skittered underfoot, then hit the grass at a run, a horse and rider suddenly looming up. One of the outrider archers, bow dropped as a handaxe whirled in the moons'-light. Chriani broke from Lauresa to dive beneath the startled horse, swinging himself up the other side. He had even less aptitude for the axe than he had for the swordplay Barien had taught him, so he let the rage carry him, let it drive his arm as he slipped beneath the rider's slashing attack and hit hard. With Konaugo's weapon, he smashed down relentlessly to the sound of breaking bone and the warm spray of blood and the Valnirata rider's strangled scream.

As he fell back to the ground, Chriani ran for Lauresa. The horses that Konaugo's troop had ridden were dead or scattered, but the Valnirata steeds were an unknown he didn't want to contend with. Not sure whether the aggressive Ilvani horses would take a rider other than their own. But even as he grabbed the princess's hand, an image fixed in Chriani's racing mind. The quickest glimpse of the fallen archer, twisting from one stirrup as the frantic horse tried to shake the dead weight that pulled it to one side. Only it wasn't an Ilvani whose slack features slipped from the bloody cloak as it tore free.

It was no face Chriani had ever seen before, but the one who wore it was unmistakably Ilmari. Her dark hair was cut rough and short. Across her face, he saw the same ritual scars that lined the cheeks of the assassin play out, the skin pale as if it had never seen the sun.

Chriani felt a chill he didn't understand, but he had no time to think. He sensed the shape and movement of the battle around him as he set a straight line course for the copse, hoping the roan was still tethered there more then he'd hoped for anything in his life. He could separate out at least six horses in the storm of hoofbeats that followed them, tried not to judge the distance that remained to the trees against how fast the sound was moving.

At the forest's edge, he saw a faint shimmer of shadow. Movement played out across the endless wall of green-black, a rustling sound rising above the hiss of the wind.

He pulled Lauresa to the ground again without knowing why. Even later, even thinking about it in the exacting detail with which his mind remembered that moment like it remembered all moments, he could never put a name to the instinct he'd answered when it spoke to him at a level beyond words. Like some voice calling to him from the edge of the Greatwood that was the place his father had been born.

From the tree line to the south, a wall of shadow erupted like the one that he'd seen in the war room that night, and from within the shadow, a hail of arrows shredded the moons-lit night. He heard the screams of the riders behind them as they were cut down, heard their Ilmari voices shout out in strangled cries, but he couldn't look back as another Valnirata war-band emerged at full gallop from the trees.

The livery and the arms and the cloak that the dead rider wore were all the same as those the new troop of Valnirata that bore down on them, but they seemed to have as little trouble picking out the original band that the imposter had been a part of as Chriani did now. No comparison in their tactics or their movement as the two forces smashed against each other. He saw the tight lines of the war-mark on the half-dozen of them who rode bare-chested, including one who bore down on them with a longspear and a fury in her eyes that cut Chriani to the core.

At his ear, he heard Lauresa sing. In her hand where she tore it from his grasp, he saw the twisting bird-shape flare, a bolt of eldritch fire fanning out. The panicked horse cut hard left even as Chriani cut right, swinging up to hit hard with Konaugo's handaxe, feeling it break through leather and bone and stick there fast as he rolled away.

From the chaos around them, Chriani heard a clear voice utter words in a tongue he'd never heard before. It was Lauresa who pulled him to the ground this time, rolling with him as the night around them was split by a flash of spell-lightning that blinded him. He heard more screams from behind as he stumbled up, didn't know whether it was the last of Konaugo's troop or the false Valnirata who were dying now. He pushed Lauresa ahead of him, running hard again as they slipped into the trees.

Barien had spoken of having seen even hardened combat horses panic at the signs of spellcraft, but the roan was waiting where Chriani had left him, clearly on edge but mercifully making no sound. He hefted Lauresa to the saddle like she weighed nothing, her arms seeming just as strong as she grabbed him by the jacket and hauled him up, not giving him the time to decide whether to send her off on her own.

"I cannot ride and work my spellcraft at once." As she whispered in his ear, Chriani realized the princess was fighting for breath, and for the first time, he noticed the burn along her exposed arm where the lightning she'd saved him from must have caught her. He shifted forward, felt Lauresa wrap herself tight around him as he pulled hard to turn the roan for the clearing ahead.

In his hand, wet against the reins, he felt something. He glanced down, saw Konaugo's blood-soaked insignia held tight there. Pulled free from his cloak when the horse had overrun him, Chriani guessed. He must have carried it the whole time and never known.

In the haze of moons'-light, the real Valnirata were sweeping the hillside with a precision that made the lightning-fast attack of the first group of riders seem clumsy by comparison. Lauresa's tent was burning now, Chriani frantically scanning for an escape route along the shadows of the tree line even as Lauresa whispered in his ear.

"Straight on…"

Ahead of them, he saw Valnirata archers ranking themselves to both sides, Lauresa presumably not seeing them where the moons'-light shone as brightly to Chriani as it did to them. He pulled to the left as the horse ran, thought he spied what looked like a trailhead, but she reached forward to pull the reins back.

"Straight," she said again. "All speed. Hold on."

Chriani heard the conviction in her voice. He spurred the roan.

Ahead, the column lined up, Lauresa singing again even as she pulled both of them low against the horse's neck. Chriani heard the order to fire barked over the sweetness of her voice in his ear, saw the hissing wall of ash-grey shafts erupt in front of them.

As Lauresa's song peaked, Chriani had to force himself to keep his eyes open, had to fight the urge to leap from the horse in the expectation of it being cut down. And as a score of arrows arced in against them, a faint haze of eldritch light flared where they shattered like glass, deflected harmlessly off the horse's flanks. The roan didn't so much as flinch. *I trained him myself*, Kathlan had said.

They'd fired as one against the charge Lauresa had ordered him to make, shooting head-on in rank. Now, they'd have to waste the precious time in which they might have managed side-on shots, Lauresa understanding the Valnirata tactics far better than he ever would have. The sound of intermittent bowshot rose behind them, but the roan was already hurtling around the far edge of the hill, running at a speed that belied how little it could actually see of the ground ahead.

As Chriani cut hard against the sight of two outriders closing from the right, he felt something heavy slam into him. He clutched the horse's neck against a wave of sudden darkness, a razor-tipped Valnirata shaft protruding from his right shoulder. He reached behind with one hand, screamed ahead of the pain as he snapped the end of the arrow off, pushing into the forest and under cover. But before he could wrench the head free, he felt Lauresa's grip across his chest suddenly weaken, his free hand clutching at her.

She was still singing, fighting to force the eldritch melody from her. As Chriani felt her collapse against him, a shroud of sudden darkness boiled out from the air around them, even as an unnatural silence fell. Chriani couldn't hear the shouts of the Valnirata behind them, couldn't hear his breathing or the pounding of the horse's hoofs or his voice as he called Lauresa's name.

With his good hand, he clutched both the princess's hands as they started to slip from his chest, pulled her tight against him. With his other and his knees, he banked the roan hard left, fighting the searing pain of the arrow as it lanced like fire down his arm. More arrows whipped past behind them, fired blindly at the point where they'd been a moment ago. Ahead, he could make out the narrow cleft through the hills that marked the path back to the road, and he bore straight for it along a well-used rocky track, wanted to make it an easy guess where they'd gone.

Just short of the road, he saw the scout trail open up where he knew it would, the stone marker there that he recognized now but that anyone not looking for it would miss in the darkness. Though the Ilvani of the exile tribes harried the Clearwater Way whenever possible, Chriani already knew that these were no exiles behind them. No idea why one of the carontir, the elite Valnirata ranger patrols, would push so far into the unclaimed northern forest, but the hope that they wouldn't know to look for the track straightaway was the only hope he had of escape now. Chriani turned the horse hard, Lauresa's sorcery still in effect as they plunged into the shadow of the trees without a sound. He risked a glance back to see pursuit pass by behind them, the Valnirata riders heading for the road where they thought he'd gone.

Along the side of the trail, a fast-moving stream still flowed between shoals of ice hanging along its banks. Chriani took the roan in, raced him silently through the water for a short while, wanting to obscure their trail even if the Valnirata doubled back.

Lauresa was still slumped against him, both arms aching now where he held tight to the reins and her. Then ahead, he saw another ranger-trail marker, nudged the horse up across icy gravel and into the trees again, and they were gone.

— CHAPTER 10 —

THE CRITHNALA

THEY RODE HARD for the rest of the night and long into morning, Chriani watching the roan for signs of exhaustion even as he watched behind them for the pursuit he knew would end the chase the moment it came. The horse ran without effort, though, and the forest behind them stayed silent even as a stain of blood-red light spread in the east.

Lauresa had regained consciousness almost as soon as they left the stream, but even after the dweomer of silence around them had faded to the steady pounding of the horse's hooves, she'd stayed mostly silent as she clung to Chriani. More than once, he'd wanted to break north for the road but she'd directed him to stay on the trail where it pushed northeast along the forest's edge. A marsh spread there, a wide expanse of bog that the stream they'd followed earlier must have emptied into, and the air was thick with fog that Chriani hoped would obscure any pursuit as effectively as it obscured the trail before him.

He knew they should have been safe enough, no traffic or settlement to speak of within the narrow strip of forest and scrubland they traversed. The Ilvani of both the Valnirata and the exile lands stayed back to avoid the well-armed Clearwater Patrols, even as the patrols stayed back to avoid the Ilvani. But in Chriani's mind, in the aftermath of the attack, too many questions still turned.

The subterfuge of an assassin's troop posing as a Valnirata warband. The real Valnirata hunting far closer to the exile lands and the Clearwater Way than they should have been. The idea of Lauresa being followed in the first place. He didn't understand any of it, not yet. Pieces of a puzzle whose edges he couldn't make out, couldn't set into place.

But even as he allowed himself a moment's acceptance that they seemed to have evaded pursuit for a time, Chriani had to force himself to focus on the fact that it would be a long road back to Caredry. The unseen final outcome of the battle the night before was still very much in his mind, and in particular, the fact that he hadn't seen the black stallion's rider on the field in the end. No idea whether the assassin had escaped or been brought down with the rest of his troop. No idea what might be waiting for them as they made the journey back, alone.

At some point, he became conscious that he didn't feel the cold he should have felt with his cloak wrapping Lauresa behind him. More of her spellcraft, he guessed. It was nearing dawn when they finally stopped in the shelter of a fir grove, a dark island in a brighter sea of snow-streaked rock and sand. The roan was spent, Chriani likewise, but it wasn't until he dismounted that he felt the pain at his right shoulder, the arrow wound he'd somehow forgotten spiking in sudden agony that drove him to his knees.

Where Lauresa dropped to Chriani's side, she pulled his cloak from her own shoulders, draped it across him as she knelt to examine the splintered shaft.

"On your side," she said, and Chriani lay down without arguing. She looked shaken, he thought, mouth set as she carefully flooded the wound with frigid water from the skins in the roan's saddlebags. The Valnirata dagger still concealed at his stomach was the only blade Chriani carried, and he saw her hand shaking as she pulled it from its sheath.

He nearly blacked out when she used it to carefully cut the flannel of his tunic out from where it had been punched in through his skin. Then he did black out when she pulled the shaft free, the pain a flash of white light in his head that suddenly shifted through to shadow as his eyes flickered open. The sweat that had beaded his face was frozen. Where he lay, he'd been covered by the bedroll from his pack. The pain at his shoulder had spread down his side and his spine, but it had faded slightly. Slowly, Chriani raised himself up on his good arm.

Across from him, the roan was sleeping. The wind in the trees was a faint rustling, and he had to groggily look around him to see Lauresa on the far side of the grove, knees folded where she sat against the bole of a single towering tree. On her face, in the set of her body, he saw a distance he'd never known in her before. Her eyes were closed but she hadn't bothered to wipe the frozen tracks of her tears away.

As he tried to stand, Chriani felt the blanket rub the bare skin of his chest where she'd stripped his shirt off. She'd taken the grimy bandage from his left shoulder and used it to bind the wound on his right. Exposed to the sun as it never was, below the princess's own name where it had been gently etched, the tight lines of the Valnirata war-mark swallowed the light.

"It appears that we both had our secrets," Lauresa said quietly.

When Chriani looked up again, she was watching him, but the words he wanted to say were lost somewhere in the tightness that had seized his chest and throat. An oblique realization struck him, twisted through the fear and the nausea that flared with the pain.

He remembered her words in her father's tent. He'd wondered then if she'd known what the bandage hid, whether she'd seen it with sorcery, or read the secret in his or Kathlan's thoughts. She hadn't. All of it bluster, all of it part of the delicate game of deception the princess played.

Chriani winced as he reached for his tunic, saw that the bloodstains and the jagged gash through front and back were gone. He remembered Irdaign fixing the torn cloak under the subtle shifting of her fingers, had to fight not to make the moonsign as he carefully slipped it on.

Where he'd set its delicate lines into his own flesh, Lauresa's name had healed, Chriani saw. Some kind of side effect of Chanist's draught, not even noticed. The black lines he'd scribed had meshed in with the older mark now, indistinguishable. And he realized as he glanced to where the princess sat that it would have been the warmark alone that she wept for. Her own name was scribed along that mark's edge in plain sight, but she wouldn't have been able to read the delicate Ilvani glyphs.

Chanist's captains and rangers all spoke and read the Ilvalantar tongue of the common Ilvani, close enough to the Valnirata dialect to allow for interrogating prisoners and understanding the rarely intercepted intelligence of the carontir patrols. Outside the military, though, an understandable distance from Ilvani culture was maintained within the prince high's court.

"I've cleaned the wound as best I can, but the arrow nicked bone." Lauresa wasn't looking at him. "You'll need a healer within two days at best or the blood-fever will finish you."

Chriani only nodded. He could see his breath in the chill air but couldn't feel the cold, still comfortable despite the wind that twisted through the trees, sent a faint shimmer of frost between him and the princess where she sat.

Should I fear you? Lauresa had said to him three days before.

Between them, Chriani felt a sudden emptiness that had swallowed all the emotion of that brief moment the night before. The memory of her against him was a waking dream, a coldness in her now as she stared out to the wastes before them. The same distance in her that he'd felt in the mock anger of the war room, but the emotion that wound tightly through that distance was very real now.

Fear and understanding, Irdaign had said.

"I must sleep," she said. "If I'm to regain my strength." Sorcerous or otherwise, she didn't say, but Chriani shook his head.

"We must ride now if we're to make Caredry before dark. We've tarried too long."

"We won't be taking the road," she said. "We ride for Aerach, and we will not make it unless I rest."

Chriani stared. Lauresa still wasn't looking at him as she shifted to softer ground, but she seemed to sense it anyway.

"It was the assassin's force that struck the camp last night. The Valnirata saved us in their own way."

"I saw it as well as you did," Chriani said. "The one who attacked us, when she fell."

"You should have known long before that," the princess said. "The Valnirata do not attack with any moon behind them. Their elite carontir patrols use only the sword, never axes."

In her tone, Chriani thought he heard a measured condescension. The same dismissiveness he'd heard the night before, more than artifice now.

"Brandishear patrols the Clearwater Way east of Rhercyn." Her voice was even but Chriani felt all the emotion held in check there. "Whoever is behind this plot, the insignia that Barien hid proves that they reach to the highest levels. I don't know how deep within the guard this treachery goes. I cannot go back."

"Your father the prince high can better protect you than any greybeard duke…"

"I ride for Aerach with or without you, squire." Lauresa pulled his cloak around her as she turned away.

Chriani managed to make himself stand, walked once around the outskirts of the grove to confirm that they were still alone as far as he could see. To the south, the forest loomed. To the north, he thought he could see the haze of white that marked the Sandhorn, and the darker line that must have been the Clearwater Way in the distance.

By the time he'd circled around again, Lauresa was sleeping where she lay. He set the blanket over her as well, kept walking because he knew it was the only way he'd be able to force himself to stay awake while he watched her.

The sun had climbed to a cloud-streaked zenith and crossed over when she awoke, the roan already up and eating. Chriani had the meager remainder of biscuits and pork from the saddlebags out, set them down before the princess as she stretched.

"I've already eaten," he said.

She didn't bother showing her disbelief as she took half of the half-day's ration remaining. Chriani quietly bundled the rest away.

"You can eat while we ride," he said. He hefted the saddle to where the roan greedily cropped silver-grey stalks of winter grass along the edge of the clearing.

"We must reach Aerach before word of what's happened can reach my father," Lauresa called from behind him. "As long as I'm missing, he'll search for me. He'll burn the Valnirata to the ground if that's what it takes."

Chriani heard a subtle shift in the tone of her voice. As he looked back, he thought he saw her looking to his shoulder before she quickly glanced away. But she circled slowly around him as he finished saddling the roan, looking up to her approaching footsteps as he picked stones from the horse's shoes. She looked past him, Chriani following her gaze to the wall of shadow where the forest loomed behind them.

"You're not afraid of this place," she said. Not a question.

"No."

"You've been here before?"

"No. My father…"

"I don't want to know." A sudden chill in her voice as she turned away.

Considering the ride they'd made, the white shift was still unnaturally clean in the manner of the ilvanweave, but she must have used the Valnirata blade to cut it off roughly at the knees, fashioning and tying a twisted belt from what was left of the hem once the burn at her arm had been wrapped. Her feet were still bare, but it didn't seem to bother her.

"The Valnirata will be seeking us," Chriani said. In the time that she slept, his resolve to see her back to Caredry and into the protection of a Brandishear garrison had hardened, even as he suspected the argument he'd spent all that time preparing was already fated to fail.

"The carontir don't patrol into the exile lands unless their need is great," Lauresa said as she stowed the bedroll and the waterskins.

"Their need was great enough to bring them to the camp…"

"Because my father's sortie forces brought them to the borders." Chriani found himself rankling at the impatience in her voice again, wondered whether that was her goal. "Likewise, those forces will keep them along the Brandishear frontier. Both they and the exiles will be that much fewer along the Aerach side."

"If there were survivors, they might have talked. The knowledge that Chanist's daughter is at large in the exile lands would suit the carontir or the crithnala just as well."

"Konaugo hand-picked his company. They would die first."

Chriani said nothing as he cinched the saddlebags on. He felt a sudden darkness twisting in him that he realized he'd been working hard to avoid since the bloody chaos of the attack. All the anger he'd always felt from Konaugo to him, all the certainty he'd had that the captain had been the one that Barien's last words had warned him of.

Konaugo had died, like Barien, saving the life of the one he was sworn to protect.

"We ride for Rheran," he said darkly. "The risk is too great."

Lauresa swung on him with the same backhand that had tagged him that first night he kissed her, but even with the pain that twisted through him, Chriani was faster this time. He had her down in a moment, both hands locked tight in one of his as he dropped to the ground behind her. Lauresa's rage was tangible as she tried to break away, but he had his other hand across her mouth, wary of the havoc her voice could wreak.

"I am sworn to protect you," he whispered to her ear, "in your father's name. He sent you on this journey with a full company and his best captain, and you know as well as I that he would not have you attempt to complete it with me as your only escort. I will protect you by returning you to him."

Lauresa did nothing. Made no move, waiting. Slowly, Chriani took his hand from her mouth.

"My father is the one who I protect, Chriani." Her voice was barely a whisper. "I am the one this assassin seeks."

He let her up, slowly. Her hands slipped from his as she turned to face him, brushing herself off and not bothering to hide a contempt that reflected the uncertainty Chriani knew she saw in him. Something twisted in his mind, impressions that had previously locked into place suddenly shifting. New patterns emerging that he realized had been hidden by the patterns he'd made before.

"Think," Lauresa said coldly. "At the camp, it was more than chance that found he and I both outside the perimeter. He sought me there but saw your dogged pursuit of me as a barrier to be overcome first. At the Bastion, Barien told you to keep me safe, my father an afterthought."

"On the road to the camp…" Chriani remembered the tracks of the steel-shod boots following them. Following her. He cursed himself silently.

"Whether the assassin meant to kill me and was thwarted by Barien, or whether he sought Barien as a first step to getting to me but was forced to take flight, I don't know," Lauresa said. "But my presence in Brandishear puts my father, my family, the entire court at risk."

Around them, the wind picked up, whipping the branches above. Chriani tried to make sense of it, too much anger in him suddenly. Too many things he should have seen.

"Why?" he said simply. All he could think to ask, not caring that he was admitting he didn't know.

"Someone wanting to prevent this marriage. The Valnirata hoping to undercut the treaty, I don't know."

"The Order of Uissa," Chriani said. He remembered suddenly what Chanist had said. "Andreg fought them…"

"And having fought them, who better to protect me now than him? Who better than my father to deal with the Valnirata that they serve? But my father does not realize the extent of this plot because he does not know that I am its target, and he will not know until we reach Aerach and can send safe word back from one of Andreg's seers to his. And we are wasting time."

As she stalked toward the roan, Chriani stood where he was, a familiar tightness in his chest. Something dark had passed across his vision suddenly, grey shadow blotting out the faint warmth of the sun.

He was the one who led the assassin to Konaugo's camp.

There it was, the thought finally freed from the darkness of his mind in which it had circled unseen all the while since the attack. Locking into place now with all the other understanding, no other explanation he could think of. His own arrogance, his own need driving his actions, clouding his mind. So concerned with the road ahead that he hadn't bothered to think on the road behind, or on who might be taking it.

He looked up to see Lauresa watching him, silent for a long while. Something had softened in her expression, he saw. Hesitant.

"When I was eleven," she said quietly, "I was summering at my mother's house in Aldac. While riding one day, a band of disgruntled Elalantar mercenaries with ransom on their minds struck my escort down. I hit their leader with a force ward. The white knives you saw, but from as close as I am to you."

Chriani paced slowly toward her, fumbled the horse's reins from the tree he'd lashed them to.

"I lost control," she said. "I let the fear and the anger in me decide my actions. One moment his face was there, the next it was gone. I can still hear his scream."

"Princess…"

"All the years I've known you, I've seen that anger and that fear in you, Chriani. I've seen you fail because of it, seen it cripple you. Last night, you would have killed Konaugo without a thought if you'd been able to, just as you butchered a rider we could have evaded with ease. I look at you and I see what I felt that day I was attacked," she said. "At the mercy of a madness you delude yourself into thinking you control."

She stepped back to let Chriani climb to the saddle, pulled herself up behind him without taking the hand he offered. "You judge by anger and by fear, Chriani. You judge by the instinct of emotions that have their own will, and you never understand that will until too late. You never learn to think except by your rage. The soldiers' fields are full of those like you."

In his mind, Chriani heard echoes of that anger, unleashed at Lauresa in her father's tent. He was more tired than he thought possible, and he focused on his still-throbbing shoulder and side as a means to clear his head. And in that clarity, he was forced to admit that far beyond all concerns for the princess's security, escorting her to Aerach even on a safe road was suddenly the last thing in the world he wanted to do.

"Princess…"

"Ride, Chriani."

He felt her arms wrap around him again, but the distance in her touch was far wider than the space that separated them. Silently, he spurred the horse, slipping back along the line that marked off the forest's edge from the sand hills ahead.

For the better part of the day, they rode easy, Chriani conscious of a lingering weariness in the roan's step, still not completely rested from their frenzied flight of the night before. Along the least-traveled side trails, he kept them to the rocky ground when he could, balancing the noise of their passage against the increased difficulty of their being tracked.

As they pushed ever eastward, the wind was against them, and he was increasingly grateful for it the three times he felt the horse suddenly shy at some scent carried on the breeze. Where they pulled back to the deeper woods each time, they managed to slip past whatever the horse had sensed without seeing it, Chriani alert to a degree that belied his fatigue. Desert wolves and white lions were common across the desert and the wasted badlands beyond, and the scorpions that the patrols of the Clearwater Way called the sandreapers. Some were as large as dogs, they said, laying silent for days as they sought for the footsteps of those passing too close to their shrouds of wind-driven dust.

They made camp of a sort before dark fell, the last fingers of light streaking the underside of the clouds that had rolled steadily in above them for the balance of the day. From a thinly wooded spur of the forest to the south, a bluff extended out to great height above open ground below. Across rough scree and sand, Chriani saw the land thrust upward in the distance, a league away perhaps. Like twisted shadows, the sandstone pillars of the exile badlands rose to the south and east, the relative safety promised by the Clearwater Way lost beyond them.

On the bluff, a kind of thicket rose, a stand of twisted shrubs Chriani didn't recognize screening the top of the rise while still allowing anyone on it a clear view of the forest behind and the desert below. On rocky ground, he set the bedroll out for the princess, the saddle blanket for himself. They risked no fire but had Lauresa's spellcraft to keep the cold at bay again, and they sat in silence as the sun set and the moons kindled their light against the darkening sky. The only movement in all that long waiting was the wind-whipped trees behind them and the black shadows of a flight of griffon riders, crossing the haze of starlight far to the south.

They had refilled the water skins at the icy stream they crossed earlier in the day, but Chriani had found nothing edible on a short foray through the nearby woods. The roan had found winter rye in plenty, though, eating heartily before collapsing into a soundless sleep Chriani envied.

Where she sat across from him, Lauresa was as quiet as she had been most of the day, but the anger and the fear that had prefaced that silence were replaced by a kind of distant thoughtfulness now. She was staring out to the northern skyline, the haze of starlit white there that marked the desert of the exile lands, her own eyes shining bright where Chriani's gaze pushed the shadows back.

"You should sleep," he said. "I'll keep a watch."

"Aside from your short stint unconscious, when is the last time you slept?"

"I'll be fine…"

"You'll be dead, as will I, the first low-hanging branch we meet with you fallen asleep on the horse." She motioned toward the bedroll laid out a safe distance between them. "I'll wake you."

But even as Chriani tried to find the argument he felt lurking in him somewhere, he knew she was right. He nodded, lay down on the bedroll, and felt a wave of fatigue drop across him like a black veil. The ache in his shoulder was just enough to counter it, though, and he was still shifting, trying to ease it into a more comfortable position, when Lauresa spoke.

"Last night," she said quietly.

Lying with his back to her, Chriani felt his heart quicken.

"Last night," Lauresa said, "you told me you loved me. The night before that, you told me you couldn't trust me. How do those things reconcile, do you think?"

Slowly, he turned to face her where she sat with legs drawn up. She had his cloak wrapped tight around her, a faint sliver of the white shift showing at her chest.

"How do they reconcile in me?" he asked.

"In general. It seems a foolish thing to profess to love someone you can't even trust."

"You're set to love a man you've barely met," Chriani said. He felt the words tumble out through the weariness. He didn't care. "What's the greater foolishness?"

Lauresa looked away. Inside, Chriani felt a shard of spite rise from nowhere. He tried to seize it, tried to break it. His felt his mind slow like it always did when the anger took him, all the words he should have spoken twisting away somehow, just out of reach.

Along the edge of the bluff wall below them, something moved.

Chriani was over and across the ground toward the princess in an instant, motioning her down as he slid in behind her. He glanced to the still-sleeping horse, weighed whether to leave it that way and hope for silence, or to wake it in case of the need for fast escape.

"What is it?" Lauresa whispered, but he only shook his head, senses as suddenly sharp as if he had slept a month. As the half-full Clearmoon broke behind the scudding face of cloud drifting fast above them, he saw a single figure shifting carefully across the sands, silent in the shadows that Chriani's eyes stripped away. A cold wind hissed, the figure not looking up where it moved low to the ground.

"Even coming across the sands, the Valnirata would have killed us long before we saw them." Lauresa's voice was in Chriani's ear, her breath warm against his neck as he nodded.

Some thirty strides across the scree field, a jutting spine of wind-etched stone rose like an island from the sand. The figure was making its careful way there, just enough shelter for someone to hide behind.

"With or without me, be ready to ride," Chriani whispered as he pulled the bloodblade from within his shirt. But as he slipped forward, Lauresa reached for his hand, squeezed it hard. Chriani glanced back, surprised. He squeezed back, uncertain. Tried to read the emotion in her eyes, but there was no time. He felt her fingers slip from his, then he was through the encircling wall of shrubs and into the shadows beyond.

Where an ancient rain gulley dropped from a narrow cut at the head of the rise, Chriani slipped down the edge of the bluff, feeling his way along a soft chute of sandstone without a sound. The Clearmoon slipped behind cloud again as he hit the bottom, but when he emerged, the figure was gone.

He checked the light, tested the wind as he scanned the shifting darkness. He saw the single set of tracks running in from the northwest, already obscured by drifting sand where they swung around behind the low rise of stone and disappeared. At best guess, it was a lone exile wanderer seeking shelter in the wrong place at the wrong time. A bad reason to have to kill someone, he thought, but attempting to fight a Valnirata exile to submission on his own ground presented odds that Chriani didn't like.

He tested the weight of the blade in his hand as he circled the low rise. In his head, he heard Lauresa's words from that morning. *A madness you delude yourself into thinking you control…*

As he circled around across the silent sand, Chriani slipped toward the low rise of stone from behind. He felt the pain in his shoulder only as a distant distraction, felt the bitter surge of strength that had long since pushed all the fatigue away. He felt for the anger, let it push him to what he knew he had to do.

He didn't see the shape erupting from the sand at his feet until it was too late. His first thought was he'd stepped into a scorpion field, but even as he twisted out of the way, he saw the figure rise to almost his height, shrouded in a sand-grey cloak that seemed to absorb the shrouded moons'-light. Then four other figures were rising from where they'd been buried all around him, as silent as the soft hiss of sand as it flowed from them like water.

The one closest to him had a handaxe, a wicked curve to the overlong blade that he'd never seen before, the rest wielding the curved backswords and long-knives that the Ilvani of the Greatwood favored. Chriani spun with the dagger in hand, shifting side to side to prevent a quick strike from behind. The one with the axe feinted as Chriani dropped back, swinging around to kick the legs out from under another behind him. Then he was rolling past, through to the other side of the circle so that he stood between them and the bluff where he knew Lauresa would be watching.

Chriani dropped to a crouch, shifting back as they spread out across from him. No hope of standing against them, he knew, but he could slow them. Give Lauresa enough time to get onto the horse and away.

Then the figure with the axe held up a hand, some complex flash of finger-signals making the others freeze.

Chriani could see his breath, white on the chill air. Beneath the hooded cloak as it was slowly pulled back, he saw an Ilvani standing before him, canvas tunic and patched leather the same black as her hair and eyes. She was lean like some bird of prey as she stepped back slowly from an attack stance, muscles knotted along her arms and stomach where the armor had been cut away for speed.

From an unseen scabbard at her back, she drew a blade that Chriani recognized. He saw her hand lock tight to a haft of steel and bone, saw the razor edge of the spiked guard catch the Clearmoon's light as cloud was shredded away on the wind. A bloodblade of the Valnirata, its red-black glyph a twin to the one held steady in his own hand.

He saw her face, the sweep of brow and ear that marked the Ilvani. He watched her pull the loose tunic down to reveal her breast and shoulder, and the red and black war-clan mark there that was the same as the one scribed on her blade. The same mark as that etched on his blade. The same tattoo that had marked his own shoulder since the day he was born.

Halobrelia forest-heart, his mother had sung to him.

Awkwardly, he pulled his tunic down at the shoulder, showed as much of the mark as he could without revealing Lauresa's name there. The Ilvani stared for what seemed a long while. When she spoke at last, it was in a tongue Chriani recognized at a level below memory, but which he didn't understand. He caught her glance to the bluff behind him and *'How many'* before he lost the thread of her words.

"Only one," he replied in the common Ilvalantar he knew. He spoke carefully, too long since he'd had any practice with the complex tongue. "Decide which two of you die before you reach her."

The Ilvani's eyes narrowed as she appraised Chriani. Then with a flourish, she spun the axe to a scabbard at her hip, slipped the blood-blade to her belt. All around her, the others lowered their blades, Chriani slowly following suit.

"You had best retrieve her yourself then." She'd switched to the Ilvalantar with no apparent effort. "You don't have much time."

As Chriani raced back up the bluff, the Ilvani followed close on his heels, her band scattering to points unseen at another flurry of hand signals. Chriani stayed low as he approached the cut but climbed with as much noise as he could risk. He wanted to make sure Lauresa heard them coming, didn't like the idea of being caught at the wrong end of the power he'd seen her wield.

As Chriani pulled himself up to the rocky summit, Lauresa and the roan stood back in the shadows of the forest's edge, already packed and saddled. Her relief when she met his gaze told him she'd watched it all, but then Chriani faltered as he saw that relief suddenly melt to a stark fear he recognized.

He glanced behind him, saw that Lauresa was watching the Ilvani where she'd clambered up effortlessly. He recognized the look on the princess's face, but not from any time she'd been afraid before. It was the pose, he realized. The affectation that came so easily to her, and that had fooled him too many times.

The Ilvani gave Lauresa a quick appraisal, her gaze lingering longer than Chriani liked on the Ilvanweave shift, pale in the moons'-light. A noble's garb, Chriani thought, recognized now.

"Any more in hiding? Any other horses?" she said to Lauresa, but the princess said nothing, glancing to Chriani with exaggerated uncertainty.

"She doesn't speak any of the Ilvani tongues," Chriani said. "No," he added. "There's no one else."

"Dargana." The Ilvani offered her name up to Chriani and Lauresa in turn. She slapped right hand to left shoulder, some kind of salute.

"Leisana," the princess replied, barely a whisper. She nodded in a clumsy rendition of Brandishear custom.

As Dargana looked to him, Chriani thought about returning the salute but simply nodded in return. Something in her eyes as she watched him that he didn't like.

"Chriani."

"Move quickly," Dargana said.

As they ran for the short edge of the bluff and a low bank that the horse could negotiate, Dargana pointed out a high outcrop of sandstone a hundred paces distant, a narrow spit of winter grass sheltered beneath it. "There," she said.

The sand was firm where Chriani led the horse across, Lauresa running quietly alongside him. Behind them, he saw Dargana back slowly down the trail they'd followed, casting handfuls of sand in what seemed a random pattern. On the flat, she moved more quickly, her cloak trailing behind her as she twisted it side to side. Beneath it, their footprints and the horse's heavy tracks disappeared, no trace of their passage that Chriani could see.

He felt Lauresa's hand in his suddenly, couldn't understand why until he felt the chill touch of the steel ring there.

Within the grass, Dargana's troop lay waiting, eight in all now. Along the wall of rock behind them, Chriani had to blink to see four horses standing motionless, the long cloaks covering them somehow blending into the mottled darkness of the stone. He slipped the ring on as he dropped, Lauresa close to him, Dargana on the other side of her. The princess was trembling in a way he knew was meant to demonstrate the fear she was feigning, but she was silent in his mind.

They waited only a short while in silence before they saw movement along the edge of the wood ahead. A party of four on horseback, moving at speed despite the darkness. As the leader leaped from the saddle of the black stallion, Chriani saw the scarred cheeks as lines of shadow, the dark eyes scanning the bluff.

"You know who they are?" Dargana whispered.

"No," Chriani said.

"Monastics of the Hunthad Wood. The order of Uissa. They attacked a camp off the Wayroad last night."

In his mind, Chriani felt the faint sensation of contact, like fingertips across his skin. Lauresa was listening, he realized. The Ilvani that Dargana spoke was somehow translated across the bond the rings made. He tried to look surprised as he glanced across to meet her gaze, hoping to read what he saw there. "You saw them?"

"Afterward. What was left of them at any rate. They were dressed as Valnirata, and the Valnirata don't take kindly to their livery being worn by the *laóith.*" The Valnirata epithet for the Ilmari had no translation. Dargana spat it with a venom Chriani could feel.

"Why would they take on the uniform of the Valnirata?" Chriani asked carefully. Like with every exchange he'd ever had within the rigid formality of Bastion military protocol, he felt the importance of how he spoke, felt Dargana seeking for the meaning beneath the words themselves.

"I don't know. Not yet."

On the bluff, he saw the assassin on hands and knees, following their tracks down to the bank where they'd descended. But when he came up against the screen Dargana had laid across their trail, he slowly pushed past it, continuing on into the trees.

"We owe you our thanks," Chriani said evenly.

"More than you know. We shadowed them for two days where they rode north from across the Hunthad. They'd set themselves up on both sides of the Wayroad the night of the ambush."

In his chest, Chriani felt something twist. A single facet of understanding, of knowing, suddenly shunted into place where it had been set wrong, all the pieces adjoining it cascading into new alignment.

"It's a long way from Uissa to the Brandishear borderlands," Dargana said, "especially at such urgent speed."

He hadn't led the attack to Konaugo's camp. The assassin's forces had lain in wait for them there, in wait for Lauresa, Chriani thought. Knowing somehow that she would be taking the road, some sorcery at work to get word from the camp to Uissa's forces. The unknown traitor who he thought was Konaugo, still there.

Dargana was watching him. Chriani shook his head, tried to show an ignorance that was only partly feigned. "Who was it they attacked?"

"A company of the Brandishear guard. Or so it appeared from what was left of them."

Chriani felt the pain at his shoulder flare, felt something sharper in his heart. He did his best to shape it as a questioning look. "Off the road? Why?"

"War, half-blood."

Chriani heard the implicit coldness in the epithet, felt something twist in his gut. He wasn't sure how Dargana would even have been able to tell who he was, what he was, but as he felt her gaze appraise him, he glanced away. "War in the Ilmar would be news to me."

"News travels a great deal faster within the Muiraìden than beyond it. The Prince Chanist has already ridden out against positions beyond the Locanwater. They'll be fighting as we speak."

Chriani laughed. "Brandishear break the treaty…?"

Dargana laughed louder. Chriani played his uncertainty to the hilt, glancing from her to the other exiles watching him darkly. His expression one of hoping to get in on the joke they shared.

"Chanist's mission in forging the Ilmar alliance was in the hope that the Valnirata would fight the two-front war he challenged," Dargana said. "Domination over the Muiraìden as a first step to controlling all the Ilmar. Caught between Aerach and Brandishear, their destruction at his hands would be assured. It's said that when the Valnirata sued for peace was Chanist's darkest day."

"News to me if Brandishear's moving against the Valnirata," Chriani murmured. A hint of indifferent pride, not too strong.

"No doubt." Dargana smirked, still watching him darkly. "But what interests me more strongly is why…"

Then from above, a steel shriek suddenly cut the night. Against the moons-lit clouds, a flight of six griffon riders passed into view, soaring fast along the forest's edge.

"Move," Dargana hissed.

Through shadow, the exiles fell back, slipping to where the horses waited, skittish suddenly at the griffons' cries, loud on the wind. As the crithnala jumped to their mounts, Chriani saw Dargana take the reins of the roan.

"You won't keep the trail on your own. Ride with Abrindra. You, with me." She pointed to Lauresa, swung herself up to the saddle and extended her hand. Lauresa waited for Chriani to gently push her forward, the same carefully crafted dread on her face as Dargana dragged her up. Playing the part of the frightened girl, Chriani thought. He caught her brief glance as he swung up onto a desert-lean grey stallion, the tall exile who rode it holding out a rough hand for him.

The griffon riders had split, three following the assassin and his escort where they disappeared into the forest, the other three circling over the bluff, searching. Dargana's company was spotted almost as soon as they broke from cover, the griffons' shrieks loud above them. Chriani had never heard anything like it before, a chill dread filling him as they raced across open sand. All the crithnala riders except Dargana and the one who carried him had bows out, firing freely above them as their horses ran seemingly of their own accord.

Even as the griffon riders closed in, Chriani felt a sudden lurch, and then they were descending into a narrow channel he hadn't seen before, a hidden cleft cutting hard into the tortured canyons ahead. Walls flashed past so close he could have touched them, and then they were through and into a narrow maze of scree and sculpted rock that cut the faint light of the sky. Above them, Chriani heard the shrieks of the griffons slowly fall away.

They rode for what seemed the whole night through the tortured badlands grottos, the Ilvani horses moving faster than they had any right to along a twisting maze of rough trails that even Chriani could barely see. Three times, he sighted scorpions scuttling across the ledges above them, archers driving off the first two, the third destroyed with spellpower cast by one of the crithnala riding behind him. Against the thundering echo of hoofbeats, wolf-song sounded out more than once, filtered down through the twisted canyons in ghostly echo. At no time did they slow.

The sky was still dark as they hit open sand bearing southeast, and he followed Dargana's gaze up and back as she rode ahead of him. He saw griffons beneath the moons' diffuse light, shining from the height of the cloud-streaked sky, but they were low in the distance, circling the scrubland at the forest's edge to the south.

They rested twice that day, sighting griffons three times in the sky above them. They rode on throughout the night again, their route a blur of shadow in Chriani's mind. When they stopped, Lauresa would rest with eyes closed, drinking sparsely when water was offered. Saying nothing through the ring, not meeting Chriani's gaze. None of the crithnala spoke to them, though he picked out a handful of words in the whispers that passed between Dargana and the others. Chanist's name was spoken more than once, along with the oath name the Ilvani game him. Ilvalachna.

Lauresa clung to Dargana as they rode, Chriani trying to make eye contact with her whenever the horse he was carried on pulled up alongside the crithnala leader. The princess's eyes were always squeezed shut, though, as he tried to send his thoughts to her. A stark fear visible in her expression and the tightness of her body, but Chriani knew it was for the exiles' benefit. All of them watching Lauresa in a way he didn't like as the troop rode on.

— CHAPTER 11 —

A Good Way to Die

THEY SPENT TWO FULL DAYS in the end riding the trails of the exile lands, the second night nearly done when they reached the forest. As their horses swung east along the chute of a rubble-strewn canyon, the twisting pillars of the badlands fell away, and in the distance, perhaps a league off, a wall of trees rose dead black against the lightening eastern sky. To the south, Chriani could make out a white scar of sand hills that cut an island of forest off from the Greatwood, towering limni spreading their twisted branches to form dark archways into deeper shadow.

Along an unseen trail, the horses plunged into that shadow without breaking stride, and almost before they'd even passed within its walls, Chriani felt the scent and the sense of the forest threading through him like something alive.

The day was fading, light swallowed by the shadow of the towering trees when Chriani saw the ruins.

Across a massive clearing, a dim light shone. Moss glowed where it clung to the boles and high-spreading branches of the great limni that rose around them, but whether some natural effect or the result of sorcery, Chriani didn't know. He saw what looked like enormous flagstones set into the ground as the troop slowed, half-hidden beneath a carpet of the broad, scaled leaves that were falling from the great evergreens like a slow rain.

The clearing was some kind of settlement long gone to decay and the encroaching wood. Like an extension of that wood, tiered terraces of mottled green and brown radiated out from the surrounding trees, whose massive branches were slung with spires and trusses that might have supported dwellings once. All of it was rotted now, long loops of mossy rope trailing down like cobwebs in the shadows.

Chriani realized he was staring as his horse slowed, and he slipped down from behind its rider to stretch life into his cramped legs. In his heart, in his head, was a sensation he'd never felt before. An ache he couldn't name. He remembered when he'd looked on the Greatwood from the edge of Chanist's camp, the awe he'd felt then eclipsed now by the weight and the fear of a window into a past that he could remember without knowing how.

Something was moving deep in the shadow inside him, deeper even than the lost feelings of his mother. Memory or longing, he didn't know. When she'd dismounted from behind Dargana, Lauresa ran to him, slipped shaking into his arms.

Snaking through the maze of trunks that surrounded them, Chriani saw ruined walls of mosaic stone rise up from the tangle of vines. Some kind of courtyard, he guessed. Scattered through the ruins, he saw a dozen encampments, archers posted in the ruined platforms above the trail along which they'd passed. He counted at least sixty crithnala, all watching Lauresa and him as the riders of Dargana's troop stood close by. He felt Dargana's gaze on him even before she circled around to face him. For once, he didn't try to hide the uncertainty he felt.

"What is this place?"

"Nyndenu," Dargana said. "The Ghostwood."

As Lauresa stared around her, Chriani saw a wonder in her eyes that the mock fear couldn't hide. Even in the dankness of decay, he felt a beauty there that cut him, but Dargana's dark gaze as she paced past him sent it away.

"You see before you the seat of the exile kingdoms," she said. "Abandoned by the Valnirata even before Muiraìden fell. The gavaleria won't follow us here."

"Why?" Chriani asked.

"Because they fear this place. And because they don't know you're here."

As Dargana raised her hand, the two crithnala at Chriani's side were on him before he could move, Lauresa grabbed up as quickly. One of the Ilvani had to stifle the scream she tried to make, Chriani catching the song hidden within it, not fast enough. He watched them gag her, saw her bound even as his own hands were tied before him. Even still, he managed to slip the ring carefully to his first finger, kept it hidden beneath his thumb. He tried to catch Lauresa's gaze, but she was playing the fear to the hilt, eyes shut tight to squeeze out tears.

Dargana sat down on a shadowed stone block that Chriani realized was a cistern. From a bucket, she drew water with a wooden dipper, drank deep.

"Who hunts you?"

"I don't know," Chriani said, that much true at least of everything going on around him. "The Valnirata patrols…"

"If the carontir wanted you dead, you would be. Even assuming you escaped them, they would have simply flushed you north. In the scorpion wastes between the forest and the road, you'd be nothing but bones by morning."

The sense of amusement in her tone set Chriani on edge more than any antagonism would have. A game had been set in play that he and Lauresa had little chance of winning, and he had to fight to punch the rage down where it flared in him, seeking for the appearance of helplessness beneath the crithnala leader's cold gaze.

"What lives here that the Valnirata fear?"

Dargana laughed. "The past, half-blood. Remembering the greatness they once came from. They fear to remember the great capitals they built across the Ilmar, their glory turned to war camps and hidden cities deep inside Muiraìden in a hundred generations since then. The Valnirata need to cast themselves as vengeful victims so as to starve their hunger to fight."

In her words, Chriani tried to seek some sense of whether these were things he should know, should agree with, should violently deny. He needed to sketch out some sense of who he should pretend to be in order to get past her scrutiny.

"You have walked the Muiraìden, half-blood?"

Lauresa was still silent in his thoughts, no advice there. He didn't understand why.

"No," he said. "My family turned its back on the weakness there before I was born." Around him, he heard a ripple of sound, whispered voices twisting through the silence of the night.

As his tunic suddenly shredded across his stomach, Chriani saw the dark lines of Dargana's bloodblade in her hand. He flinched in spite of himself as it flashed twice more in the faint light. On his stomach, two razor-thin lines bled faintly where she'd cut the hidden scabbard from him, her look dark as she unsheathed his blade that matched her own.

"Carrying a narneth móir of House Halobrelia is to invite slow torture before the merciful death that your lineage warrants in the first place," she said. "Had you not borne the war-mark, I would have slain you on the sands."

"I wear that mark by right," Chriani said quietly. "My father was a Halobrelia exile. Like you."

Dargana struck him with a backhand blow that darkened his vision for a moment with the force of it. Even sharper was the touch of Lauresa's mind, and the sudden spike of fear he felt there that made Chriani understand suddenly what had driven her silence all this time. All the fear in her that she didn't want him to feel. All the truth in him she didn't want to hear.

"No half-blood compares its fallen father to what I am," Dargana said coldly. "Do not make that mistake again." But before Chriani could respond, the crithnala leader had turned to Lauresa where she was held. "And then this one."

As the princess shrunk back, Dargana had to lift her head, glanced back once to Chriani. "Even without that mark, you're no closer to Brandishear nobility than I am. But this one's never been more than a week away from a featherbed and a suite of servants. You make for strange traveling companions."

What did you tell them of me last night? Lauresa's voice in his head for the first time was a cool breeze against the heat that had risen in him. No trace in it of the fear she feigned for the crithnala's benefit. Dargana's words were being translated for her again, clear through the ring as they echoed in his own mind.

I told them I would die for you, Chriani said. No hesitation. And even as they formed in his mind, he knew the words had never been more true. In the emotional undercurrent that slipped beneath his thoughts, he felt her reaction. She closed her eyes again, something more than fear there this time.

I am Leisana, daughter to the master merchant Keithan at Glaeddyn. You are a young bravo of the thieves' guild, hired to intimidate the father but desiring the daughter instead.

"She's from Glaeddyn," he said. "Her father's Keithan, a merchant lord there. She's with me now."

"With you how?"

"I was sent by my guild to encourage the father in a commercial alliance of sorts," he said with what he hoped was suitable evasiveness. "I decided to take an additional commission on the job."

Dargana smirked. Good, Chriani thought.

"Where did you ride from?" she asked, still watching Lauresa as the princess tried her best to look away.

We hid out at Caredry for a day and a night, hoping to find a caravan across the Clearwater Way. Even as Lauresa thought it, Chriani echoed the words, feeling them spill from her mind to his voice in a continuous stream. *When the Glaeddyn garrison came first, we stole the horse and fled. We couldn't take the Wayroad, we didn't know where else to go.*

"Kidnapping then? How did you plan to collect a ransom in the crithnala lands?"

They're after me, not her. She came of her own will, but her father is having trouble adjusting to that. We were making for Aerach. Get far enough from the Brandishear guard to make a life.

"You're scaring her," Chriani added to Lauresa's words. "There's no need." The necessary illusion, the subtle undercurrent that Lauresa's story wove, was of uselessness, he realized. Anything that Dargana thought she might get from the pair of them, she had more than enough power to take it.

Dargana turned to him, held the bloodblade that had slain Barien up before him. "What of this then?"

No voice came to his head this time, Lauresa and Dargana both waiting.

As he almost never had in all the years since his mother died, Chriani found himself thinking of her cairn again. The separation between life and the things that life touches, that his grandfather had talked about.

"My father left the blade to me," he said. It was the only answer he had in him, the connection between the narneth móir and the mark at his shoulder requiring an explanation he didn't have.

Dargana nodded thoughtfully, spun the blade in her hand. Then she punched down in a fluid motion. And where Chriani's bound arms were held in front of him, she hacked the steel ring and its finger cleanly off. No mark at all on the thumb that had hidden the ring. No mark on the other finger beside it.

Chriani fell to his knees, fought back the scream that welled up in him. He tried to fight the wave of nausea and the dull echo of Lauresa's fear, very real now, that had shunted itself into his mind as the connection between them had broken, a pain in that break almost as great as the one shooting up his arm now.

As Dargana stooped to pull the ring from Chriani's severed finger, she glanced darkly to the rider who'd searched him, directed him to Lauresa with a nod. The princess didn't struggle as her own ring was pulled roughly from her hand, but the fear was gone from her look now, replaced with cold rage.

Dargana met that look and sent it back in kind, but it was Chriani she turned to.

"That dagger belonged to the greatest of my people, half-blood." In her voice, in her eyes, her movement as she stepped slowly toward him, Chriani felt a menace that told him he was already dead. "I am Halobrelia," she whispered. "I can read the cipher of that blade's engraving as easily as I read my own name. Something you should be able to do if you had any claim to that name yourself."

"My father was Halobrelia…" Chriani said through clenched teeth, but Dargana kicked him hard, doubled him over where he fell.

"Your father was a race-traitor and a laóith-whore's mate. My father was Halobrelia, as was the clan-brother he followed. The warlord Caradar, the exile king whose weapon this was. The simplest Valnirata child knows how your Prince Chanist dropped Caradar with an arrow to the back, then slit his throat with this blade as he pulled it from his dying hands."

"So you thought to revenge him by slaying Chanist and his heirs with that same blade?" Chriani shouted. "The assassins of Uissa doing the work you fear to do yourself?"

She kicked him again, pulled him up by his bound and bleeding hands and slammed him against the courtyard wall. Chriani felt what was left of his tunic shred as she seized it to spin him, one hand snapping his head back by the hair, the dagger held to his throat with the other.

"Your lies are as weak as your traitor's heart, half-blood. The blade of the exile king has been in Chanist's hands since the day he claimed it in his dead father's name. For the sake of my family's memory, tell me where and how you obtained it that I might slay every laóith and half-blood hand to have touched it since, and I may let you die quickly."

But Chriani wasn't looking at her as the razor tip of the dagger hovered a hair's-breadth above his throat. He was staring past her, watching Lauresa where she watched him.

She hadn't heard what Dargana had said. Hadn't understood the Ilvani, the link of translation gone with the ring.

He forced himself to look away. Not wanting Lauresa to see the realization in his eyes that he knew he couldn't hide. He felt memories, images, impressions pushing through him in a flood even as he fought to push them back, tried to deny the sudden understanding that had rooted in him.

"So what was it?" Dargana's voice as she circled around him brought him back, forced him to focus. "You stole the dagger from some museum of Chanist's, then set your eyes on bounty more fair? Some prize rich enough that a company of Ilmar riders and a force of

Aerach assassins would venture off the Clearwater Way and into the crithnala lands in search of it?"

Then she faltered. Stared.

Shakily, Chriani followed her gaze down to his own chest. Where his tunic had been torn almost to the navel, the edge of the war-mark was exposed. He saw her read the name scribed there, saw her look up to meet the fury in his gaze.

As Dargana looked slowly back to Lauresa, he saw a smile of dark understanding form at the hard edges of the crithnala leader's mouth.

"Chanist's greatest riches are his children, they say…"

Chriani tried to mask his reaction, but the crithnala leader saw it all the same. Her laughter chilled him, set the anger flaring like an oil-fed fire. He sought for it, called to strength that he needed now, one exile behind him, another that he'd have to get through in order to reach Dargana herself. He felt the pain in his hand flare white-hot, let it stoke the rage.

"Kill the thief and save his head," Dargana called to the exiles around her. "Give the Ilmari princess water, then drug her. We ride for Brandishear at dawn."

Chriani was set to spring, had already run the mechanics of every possible last effort at escape through his mind. Having deduced Lauresa's identity was a good thing, he realized suddenly, as it meant they couldn't kill her now. More value to the crithnala as a hostage than a corpse. Whatever happened, she'd make it back to her father. She'd be safe.

He could hold onto that, he thought. That duty fulfilled, at least, before the end that was coming.

Dargana would die with him, though. He would let the anger take that as a last gift before the end.

But even as Dargana turned, a flare of light came from above. The ruins blazed with white fire suddenly, as if the slow-rising sun had come on all at once. Above, the raw shriek of griffons split the night, sudden chaos twisting through the crithnala as they scattered for the shadows, and where Chriani watched, he saw Dargana's attention taken for the moment he needed.

He slammed his head back into the face of the crithnala behind him, felt him stagger back as he came up under the arm of the guard before him and swung into Dargana with a roundhouse kick. Like he'd hoped, she dropped the bloodblade she'd taken from him, and because he'd been hoping, he was already falling on it as it spun to the ground.

He sliced skin from his wrists as he slit the ropes that bound him, rolling out of the way as Dargana's axe slashed against the stones where he'd lain a moment before. He kicked out at her hand, dislodging her grip as she cried out, but where they both jumped for the dagger, Dargana got there first. Chriani backpedaled, snatched her axe from the ground as he ran.

From the air, a rain of arrows fell, the griffon riders' eldritch light still burning bright in the tallest trees above them, illuminating the crithnala below even as it screened their own aerial movement. Behind him, Dargana screamed orders in no language Chriani recognized, some kind of exile cant. But as the rest of the troop melted back, she sprinted after Chriani, already moving for Lauresa where her crithnala guards were dragging her into the trees. She was watching him, brought her foot up hard into the groin of her closest captor. As he staggered, she twisted away, circling behind the other so that his attention was distracted for the moment Chriani needed to drop him.

He didn't kill him. Couldn't kill him. Just swung hard with the flat of the axe as he wheeled in, a blunted blow that dropped the crithnala more effectively than Chriani's lack of skill with the weapon would have normally allowed. He felt the rage peak, felt it stoke a sense of control he couldn't remember feeling before. He grabbed the fallen warrior's bow, gambled precious time as he tore his quiver and cloak free.

Dargana was circling along the edge of the ruins, Chriani pulling Lauresa with him as he ran for the opposite side of the clearing, fumbling the princess's bonds and gag free as they ran. All around was chaos, sorcery and bowshot ripping the air as a storm of light and fire erupted in the forest around them. Dargana's look said that she'd been truthful when she talked of Nyndenu as a place the Valnirata would never come, Chriani wondering as he pushed for the dark of the forest what would make them change their minds.

When Lauresa sang, he got his answer. From her hands, he saw the knives of white light flare, saw them flash past Dargana and into the trees as the crithnala threw herself to the ground. From behind her came a scream, two archers in white staggering from the shadows where Lauresa's sorcery had struck them, pale skin and scarred cheeks. The bloodblade flashed as Dargana wheeled. They both died quickly.

The assassins had followed them there. The Valnirata griffon riders had followed the assassins in turn, likely still not knowing what prize the Order of Uissa sought but hoping to gain it for themselves.

Dargana shouted another coded command to the unseen troop

shifting through the dark forest around her, and all across the clearing, a boiling wall of shadow rose. In Chriani's head, in his heart, Lauresa's song was exquisite agony, twisting with the pain still lancing through his arm as his hand bled freely. She sent the white knives of force out against two more archers as they ran, sent a pulse of yellow fire skyward against a griffon as it dove for them, dropping from the darkness with a shriek. Chriani saw its rider veer away, screaming as its armor burned.

He saw Dargana then, moving fast through the trees ahead of them. He pulled Lauresa back, changed direction sharply, but the princess caught sight of the crithnala leader, held her ground for the moment it took to change the pulse of the song that flowed from her. As the princess twisted her hands, Chriani saw Dargana suddenly spin as the bloodblade was pulled from her fingers, grabbing at it, too late. She watched as it sailed through the shadows and into Lauresa's grasp.

The princess slipped the dagger into Chriani's good hand but he swapped it to his left, fought the agony and the slickness of his bloody grip as he held it tight.

That blade has been in Chanist's hands…

He pushed the thought away, didn't want to face it. Didn't want to believe.

He held Lauresa's hand tighter, kept her fingers locked to his as they ran.

Within the shelter of the towering limni, no light fell from the stars, the Clearmoon and Darkmoon masked as they climbed beyond the forest wall. Behind them as they ran, Chriani could see the twisting flare of the sorcerous light that the griffon riders threw down, but where he and Lauresa made their way along a barely visible pathway, a shadow settled around them that told him they weren't pursued. Not by the Valnirata at any rate.

He ran on instinct, drinking in the distant sounds of battle against the closer silence, eyes open to the maze of trails that surrounded them. No way to tell where they led, he and princess following dead ends twice, doubling back at speed. All around, he could feel the ruins even beyond the range of his sight, as if the voices of the unknown past were calling to him through the shadows. He tried to block them out, focused on his footsteps and Lauresa's beside him as the forest swallowed all sound.

He slowed. Ahead, a shadowed space opened up, starlight faint through the trees.

Against the faint light of stars above a roof of gnarled branches, the remains of an Ilvani forest-tower rose. Between living pillars some ten strides across at the base, semicircular platforms climbed within a tangled web of ropes and rotted gantries. Curved beams of blackened wood marked their edges, dark arches pushing out from the trunks of the trees themselves to buttress them. They twisted past each other where they hung suspended, most at dangerously oblique angles where some of the rope-supports that lashed them into place had given way.

Faint behind them, Chriani heard voices, too far away to make out. Ahead, rising like the terraces of some Elalantar garden, broadly stepped platforms swept up from the ground to the tower, gaping holes marking where their wood had long-rotted through. He looked up, saw the level edge of one high platform, moss-crusted ropes still lashed tight from its edge to the bole of the ancient limni that anchored it. As tall as any Bastion tower, he guessed. A perfect vantage point from which to try to spy the escape route they desperately needed to find.

"Come on," he said.

Carefully, he and Lauresa climbed the twisting tiers of rotting steps, making their slow way up within the space of shadows the limni made. Twice, they had to edge their way along the narrow span of a single beam, Chriani reaching back to help Lauresa across. She had spellcraft that could have made it easy, he knew, but she was weak, stumbling. The power she'd unleashed in the ruins below had seemingly drained her to a degree that alarmed him, some part of the casting rituals drawing strength from her and the meager sleep she'd had the day before not enough to recover it.

Where the stairs ended, the platform was a moss-green field of twisted planks, thick spars visible beneath them where arched beams radiated out from the limni's weathered trunk. Above them, the canopy of green-grey ropes that had once held the terrace in place was mostly gone, thick vines hanging in its place. The half-dozen stanchion lines that had survived this long spoke to the skill that had crafted them in the first place, Chriani stepping out carefully to gauge their strength. Only when he was sure the platform would hold did he motion Lauresa to follow.

In the shelter of a shredded thatch canopy, she took Chriani's mangled hand without a word. She tore an edge from the rough-cut hem of the shift, used half to clean and half to bind the wound as best she could. The pain when she touched it was like being cut all over again, but Chriani focused past it, staring into the stillness around them. As high as they were, he could see the stars now where the cloud had all but gone. More importantly, he could see the flare of eldritch light to the south, the griffon riders pushing farther away, he hoped.

When Lauresa was done, he had her lash the quiver to his leg, his hand not strong enough to do it. He tested the draw of the bow with shaking hands, checked the supply of arrows. Lauresa was tight against him, her head on his shoulder. For a long while, neither spoke.

"Why did you save her?" he asked at length. "The leader, Dargana?"

"The Uissa archers were targeting you," she said. "My power is spent, Chriani."

She rubbed his wrist gently, wouldn't meet his gaze. With his good hand, Chriani raised her face to his.

"I don't want it to end this way," she said.

He kissed her then. Felt the familiar surge of blood and the quickening of his pulse beneath which the pain faded, just for a moment. He held her tight, felt her body press into his as it had in the tent, felt her breath on his cheek, her lips at his neck.

That blade has been in Chanist's hands...

With all the strength that his anger had ever made, he tried to force Dargana's words away. He didn't want to think it, didn't want to understand like he understood now with a certainty he would have given anything to deny.

As she'd died on that day of quiet summer so long ago now, Chriani's mother had spoken haltingly of people she said she saw in those final moments. Her own mother, dead since before Chriani was born. His father. *I know now,* she'd said, over and over with a laugh that seemed to suggest she was only ever just a moment away from standing up, from sweeping Chriani into her arms as she always had.

In the shadow that loomed in the back of his mind, Chriani saw the dagger in Chanist's hands, Barien clutching at the blade as he fell at the prince's feet. He squeezed his eyes shut tight.

With her last movements, his mother had traced the mark she'd set at Chriani's shoulder. *You are the crossroads,* she'd said. *You are the place where two worlds meet...*

"I'm sorry," Lauresa whispered. Chriani was trembling. "Does that hurt?"

Seek always to see, his mother had said.

Chriani saw the blood in the hall of records where Barien fell. The archives quarter deserted, no witnesses. No guards patrolling there, no servants passing like there would have been in every other quarter of the Bastion on any given night.

"You need to get away," he said with effort. "Ride for Aerach. Stay off the road, avoid anyone you see until you get to your husband's house."

As Lauresa raised his eyes to hers, she watched him, uncertain.

"It's two days to the frontier," Chriani said. "Whatever horse you're on, ride it hard, don't stop."

"I won't go without you."

"There's no other way…"

She didn't speak any of the Ilvani tongues. The languages of the forest and of the ancient arts and of the history of the Ilmar that predated the migrant tribes. The speech of those who had cut her grandfather's heart out with the blade Chriani clutched in his hand now. The finger missing, the ring hacked away so that Lauresa hadn't heard.

"What is it?" she whispered, and Chriani felt his vision blur, a fear he couldn't name twisting inside him as the shadows shifted at the stairs.

He felt the sudden surge of instinct, had Lauresa behind him even as the bow came out, an arrow nocked and shot. He saw the blur shift to one side, got a second shot off even as a dizzying kick slammed him back. He was ready this time, though. The cloak he'd taken from the crithnala he'd dropped whipped out across the blur even as it faded back. Sand-grey cloth seemed to suddenly twist in the air as the assassin tried to disentangle himself, Chriani fighting the pain and the tremor in his hand to sink two arrows into him from four strides away.

Where a flash of steel shredded the cloak, it fell to the ground, Chriani catching a glimpse of two hooked blades in the assassin's hands as he staggered back. The loose tunic was a grey stain against the darkness, the shimmering blur gone where it had concealed him, but for how long Chriani didn't know.

One arrow had taken the assassin through the side, the other sticking through his thigh, but as the cold eyes burned into him, Chriani watched as the hooked blades hacked both shafts off short, front and back. No sign that he even felt it. No words, no sound as the dark gaze flicked past to the princess behind him.

As one, he and the assassin moved. Chriani was faster, barely. He saw the figure shift again, slipping into shadow as he ran, but whether the injuries done him had affected the sorcerous power he wielded, or whether Chriani had simply learned to focus past it, he got in front of him, firing once more, point-blank through the shoulder before he swung the bow hard across the pale figure's throat.

The assassin cried out this time, Chriani pulling the dagger as the pale figured blurred into view, staggering back, shimmering as he faded from sight again. Chriani cursed, scanned the vine-strewn spaces around him, but he was gone. Behind him, Lauresa was sticking to the shadows, skirting a decaying field of planking where it flanked a narrow riser along the platform's edge.

"There," Chriani whispered. "Climb, quickly."

Lauresa was hesitant, stepping back carefully between gaps in the weathered planks, Chriani following. He kept her behind him as he pressed back. He waited, watched the silent shadows all around. To the south, he heard a griffon scream, the distant hiss of arrows through the canopy of leaves. In his mind, he felt all the pieces of this puzzle shuffle into place, new layers on top of the layers he'd seen before, never realizing how deep they went in the end.

Lauresa had been right in noting that when they'd met outside Chanist's camp, the assassin had gone for Chriani first. Not as a means of clearing a path to the princess, though. For the dagger. The Valnirata bloodblade that had struck Barien down and been hidden, and which was the only thing now that might halt the relentless wheels of a plot that had taken a lifetime to bring to fruition.

Across from him, Chriani saw marks punch down into the rotting floor. Footprints, the assassin moving serpentine as he ran for them, the steel boots that seemed to give him his incredible speed breaking through the soft rot of the wood that surrounded them. Chriani was ready, two arrows unleashed quickly as he tried to focus, one flying wide, the other hitting the mark. With a muffled cry, the assassin blinked into view with a shaft in his chest, but he snapped it off with a grimace as he leaped for Chriani, both hooked blades flashing as he swung.

Chriani dodged, too slow. He felt searing pain on his injured side, and a red haze filled his eyes as he drove the bow into the assassin's throat again, knocked him back. Too close to shoot again, he dropped the bow as he pulled the bloodblade from his belt.

Across the decaying floor, they shifted back in a frenzied series of attacks and feints, Chriani stumbling, trying to keep Lauresa behind him, but he'd lost her suddenly in the shadows. He was conscious of the riser's crumbling edge behind him, conscious of his left arm going numb as he tried to balance his dagger strikes, catching empty air again and again as the assassin wheeled, just out of reach.

He felt one of the curved blades tag him at the hip, but it was the splintering wood underfoot that took him down, slipping as he tried to roll with the blow. But even as the assassin loomed over him, a single arrow suddenly slammed through his chest, spinning him as Chriani rolled and rose. Behind them, Lauresa had the bow, was trying to nock another shaft with shaking hands. Too late.

As the assassin leaped past Chriani, he raced for the princess, astonishingly fast. The pale figure had time to grab her arm, one blade shredding the white shift but missing her side as she pulled back, and then Chriani was on him, tearing him from Lauresa as the dagger sought for his throat but found his shoulder as he twisted away. The three of them fell together, hit the platform as one, Chriani twisting the bloodblade, feeling it shred bone as he pulled it free.

The assassin screamed. Chriani rolled back to grab Lauresa's hand, the two of them stumbling to their feet as the figure in grey rose behind them. One arm was limp, blood pouring from the shoulder where Chriani had hit deep, the other clutching the hooked blade as he staggered forward.

All around them, the platform shuddered.

As the assassin backpedaled, four of the ropes stretching from the edge of the terrace to the trunk of the massive limni twisted and sheared away. As the weight of the platform pressed down on it, one rotted spar snapped, the rope attached to it unraveling in a blur of grey and green.

The terrace lurched, then fell.

Chriani pulled Lauresa to him as the floor tilted beneath them. In the twisting field of his vision, he saw the forest dark below, his good arm grabbing at the tail end of a rotted line where it snaked past them, a fall of rotting timber sliding past to precede them to the ground.

When the rope snapped taut, the force of the impact slammed through his arm and shoulder, and he screamed against the pain that threatened to tear him in two as he locked his other arm to Lauresa, held her tight.

A frozen moment of time.

He felt Lauresa's body against his, felt the pain smash through him in slow waves as he fought to keep from blacking out. Below, the forest floor twisted through the haze of his sight where the collapsed edge of the platform crashed down, maybe four stories if they dropped, too far.

Above, he could see two hands on the rope, had to focus to realize that Lauresa had grabbed on with him, was holding him up as much as he was holding her. He could hear her breathing hard in his ear, could feel her other hand fumbling between them where she'd locked her legs around him.

She was silent, hadn't cried out as they'd fallen or when the assassin struck at her. No power left in her that her voice might have made.

Without her weight, he might have been able to climb. Without his weight, she might have been able to, but at the edge of what was left of the platform above, he saw the assassin stagger into view. Nowhere to go.

At her throat, beneath the torn shift, he saw Lauresa pull the lapis pendant free.

Above, he saw a hint of triumph break the impassiveness of the dark gaze as the assassin appraised the rope, angling back to the exposed beam it was lashed to.

Chriani felt Lauresa's hands in his, something cold against his skin.

The assassin swung back with the hooked blade, struck hard at the rope where it stretched taut. Chriani felt a lurch, and then the pain in his arm was muted as the rope's pull on him suddenly failed.

In his ear, he heard Lauresa sing. And all at once, he felt a joy so unexpected that it had no name.

She was staring upward, seemingly watching the assassin as he smiled coldly, watching them fall. But she had power left, Chriani thought as the song filled his mind, filled his heart. Something held back in reserve.

She would make it to Aerach in the end. She'd be safe there, would never have to know what he knew now, the thing that would have killed her as sure as the fall would smash his battered body like glass.

Everyone has secrets, Barien had said.

The pendant has power of its own. Lauresa would save herself, was strong enough to make it to her new home.

Keep her safe, Barien had said, and Chriani had done his best, he swore he'd done his best.

This was a good way to die.

The ground was spinning toward them. Then he felt the princess slip the lapis pendant around his wrist, one finger touching it as she pushed herself away from him into the timeless dark of their descent. He heard the song fade away, and then she was gone.

But no. Lauresa was there, but farther below him now. The scene around him had changed suddenly, the ground a more distant blur as he plunged toward it through green shadow.

At his wrist, the pendant was flaring with pale blue light. Below him, he saw the platform and the figure of the assassin, and he realized that he'd moved upward somehow — shifting through the air to a place above where they'd fallen even as he continued to fall, picking up speed.

He had the bloodblade in his hand. Instinctively, he twisted, lining up along the path of his descent.

He saw the assassin suddenly falter, staring around him as he spun, trying to see where the suddenly vanished Chriani had gone. Too late, he looked up.

Chriani saw fear in the dark eyes as he hit.

As he slammed down with all the speed of the fall, the force of his impact punched up through his arm as the blade drove into and through the assassin's chest. Chriani felt something hit him hard, and then darkness rose around him.

When the darkness cleared, he was at the edge of the ruined terrace, the lifeless body beside him. He felt a sharp flare of pain as he tried to breathe, felt broken ribs and his injured arm hanging lifeless at his side. The lapis pendant was ash-black now, its stone cracked.

As he dragged himself to the edge, he saw a figure in white, lying unmoving on the forest floor below.

How he managed to descend the stairs without blacking out, he didn't know, but he was conscious all the while of the distant sounds of battle over the pounding of blood in his head. He fell the last half-dozen steps, slamming through rotting timbers to hit the soft loam of the forest floor below, but he was beyond pain now. Driven by some instinct, some energy that ignored the white-hot fire in his chest.

But as he stumbled toward Lauresa where she'd fallen, he froze. In his good hand, he squeezed the bloodblade tight.

Ahead, the princess lay face up, arms splayed, skin pale like the ilvanweave that draped her. Over her, Dargana crouched, dark eyes watching him. A broken arrow through her arm seemed to bleed the same black as her leather in the half-light.

As she watched him approach, she pulled the shaft free without so much as a grimace, emptied the contents of a crystal flask into her mouth. Chriani watched her shudder, saw the haze of pain clear from her eyes, the bleeding suddenly slowing as the wound at her arm scarred white. She tore a chunk of cloth from Lauresa's shredded hem, wiped the grime from her face.

"Get away from her." Chriani's voice was hoarse, throat raw as he staggered closer.

"You're not looking like a person in much of a position to give orders."

"Touch her again and you'll join her just the same," he whispered.

"What, dead?" Dargana said mildly. "Not this one. Not yet." She flexed her arm carefully, touched her finger to Lauresa's throat. "Not like you."

As she stood, the crithnala pulled the long-bladed handaxe from her belt, spun it easily. "You, I'll kill for touching that blade with your half-blood hands. You, I'll make suffer for every time you've thought yourself worthy of my family's name."

Chriani felt the anger twist in his heart, felt the pain fuel it with every ragged breath even as he fought it. "Listen to me…"

"For the lives of my company that are lost today, this one will go back to her father in pieces. When I've done with you, you'll have nothing to do but watch."

"This is the Princess Lauresa of Brandishear…"

"And for her, half my troop are dead," Dargana shouted. "Twenty of the Uissa have hunted the Crithnalerean for a week and more, twice that number of gavaleria after them. Chanist's guard push farther into the Greatwood than any army since his father's. The carontir are concentrating their offense across the entire northern frontier. Tell me what it is that makes her worth all that, half-blood?"

"The war that starts if she dies today…"

Dargana laughed. The rage in her as strong as it was in his own heart, Chriani realized.

"The narneth móir was to be used to slay her," he said. "The assassins of Uissa were commissioned to do it, to take the part of a Valnirata war-band ambushing the princess and her escort on the way to her wedding in Aerach." He spoke quickly, erratic, words tumbling from him because he knew that if he thought on them for any length of time, the anger would freeze them in his mouth. "The bloodblade that Chanist would give them was to be the proof that would start total war."

"You talk madness, half-blood…"

"The madness of a prince who hates the Valnirata enough to have his own daughter killed as a means to destroy them…"

Trust him not...

A wave of pain hit him, made him stagger where he stood. He felt faint, heard his heart hammering in his head. Barien's dying voice was in his ear again. *The prince...*

The truth in front of him the whole time, but some truths are too terrible to know. Easier to think only with the rage, with the fear.

He was a fool.

"If she dies today, you'll follow her." He felt himself hanging desperately on the edge of consciousness, one blow from Dargana likely enough to kill him.

"You talk bravely for one half-dead."

"By my hand or not, and not just you. Your people, the exile tribes, the war-clans, all of it. If the Princess Lauresa dies, all the Valnirata will burn..."

We tell ourselves these things we do have purpose that overcomes the pain they bring, Chanist had said. Speaking of Barien who was dead, or of Lauresa who was meant to die, Chriani didn't know. The martyrs in whose name the Valnirata plague would be extinguished at last.

The dreams our fathers have for us that they will never see...

Over the length of that meal, the prince high had played him with the grace of a Caella troubadour bent to the bandore's strings. Sending him off on a fool's mission to unleash his feelings for a princess, those feelings as obvious to Chanist as they had been to Kathlan, to Lauresa herself. Ensuring that the earnest young squire could be blamed for leading a Valnirata patrol straight to the company's camp. There would have had to be survivors, ready to tell the tale. Chriani knew he wasn't meant to have been among them.

Make the truth seem laughable and you give life to the lie.

"Chanist wants war," Chriani whispered. "An excuse to raze the Greatwood as a first step to controlling all the Ilmar. You said it yourself." All the stories from across the Greatwood borders, repeated and laughed at in the barracks and the alehouses as proof of the paranoid race-madness that lived in the Valnirata blood. Rumors that Barien himself had shaken his head at.

Old hatreds died hard.

I wonder if we should know what to say to those we love if we knew that it would be the last time. Chanist had said it to him, a father's unspoken words to a child he loved and knew he would never see again. *This sacrifice she makes...* Chriani's stomach turned.

Above them, he heard the shriek of griffons again, the battle swinging closer. But as he tried to move for Lauresa, Dargana dropped to her knees, snapped the unconscious princess's head up by the hair as she raised her axe.

"Think on it," Chriani shouted, desperate now. "A score of the Uissa within Valnirata lands. What kind of wealth could have commissioned that number for so dangerous a raid? Who could have obtained the livery and weapons of a full Valnirata carontir patrol except for one who had captured it over a decade of border skirmishes? Chanist pays for Uissa's loyalty, but their own hatred for Aerach and the Valnirata distances him from this deed should that loyalty ever break."

"Chanist could make war on the Valnirata in a heartbeat..."

"And he'd never win that war. Not alone." Chriani saw the anger weaken in Dargana's expression. Something else now in the black eyes where they watched him. "Think on it," he said again. "A Brandishear princess betrothed to Vishod's cousin in Aerach. A noble of two nations, tied by blood and marriage to two princes. Murdered by a Valnirata war-band while traveling to her wedding day. War on both fronts of the forest, east and west. And once the Valnirata is purged, what then? Brandishear's borders pushed by Chanist to Aerach, then beyond. Holc and Elalantar have no hope of standing against him."

"What kind of madness would murder its own issue for the sake of blind ambition?"

Trust him not...

Chriani remembered the prince being treated by the healers, the blood-streaked tunic there. The insignia of the prince's guard missing from it, but no one would have thought to look for it. He felt the sickening sensation overwhelm him again, felt his thoughts slipping into shadow.

"But for providence, the princess would already be dead and the Valnirata would be watching the armies of two nations amassing on their borders. But if she dies now while you stand and watch, all that will pass. On your decision, all Chanist's plans will come complete."

Dargana looked once to Lauresa, back again. Slowly, she lowered the axe.

From within her tunic, she pulled another crystal flask, the same healing draught she'd taken herself. She set it carefully to Lauresa's lips as her fingers touched the princess's throat again.

Where Chriani stumbled to kneel beside her, he waited for an impossibly long moment. Then he saw Lauresa shiver, a spasm shaking her as her breath started up again. Like the wash of warmth across chilled skin, color flooded her face.

As Chriani looked up, Dargana was watching him. There was nothing to say.

She slipped a third flask into his hand, and the blood-spattered steel rings with it. "Take the draught before you drop," she said coldly, and then she was sprinting for the close edge of the wood. Chriani made sure that the flask was stopped tight, kept it clutched in his good hand.

"What will you do?"

In the shadow of the trees where she'd stopped, Dargana called to him, watching where he cradled Lauresa in his arms. He knew what it was she asked. "I don't know."

Her gaze carried a familiar contempt, but it took him a moment to recognize Konaugo's look. The same dismissive assessment that the captain had always made of him. The sense of failure that Chriani had always carried.

"If Chanist were the father of one I loved, I would cut his living heart from his body," she said. "No Halobrelia blood flows in your veins, laóith."

As she slipped into the darkness, Chriani felt the words twist inside him that he'd only ever spoken to two people before. Barien, who had taken him in and showed him a strength that Chriani had never known was in him. Kathlan, who had showed him that he had the will to use that strength, and who had been the only person besides Barien to have ever seen the mark at his shoulder.

"My father was exiled before the Incursions," Chriani called, not sure if Dargana could even hear him. "For arguing against the move to war. He traveled to the Ilmar, lived with my mother's folk. When the conflict started, he came back to the crithnala lands. He joined the factions here allying themselves with the Ilmar."

He saw movement in the trees. Dargana slipped back through the shadows.

"They feared a war that would destroy the Ilvani and the Ilmari alike," Chriani said. "They fought hit-and-run skirmishes against the Valnirata from the south. He was killed."

"My father and kin were exiled for daring to dream that the Valnirata might reclaim some of the glory that Chanist's fathers stole from us," Dargana said coldly.

"My father believed the Valnirata's march to war would extinguish that glory in a way that even Chanist's fathers never could."

Chriani said nothing more. Dargana was silent for a while.

"We have a fallback point on the northern flank of the forest," she said at last. "My troop will be regrouping there, riding west. The gavaleria will likely presume we have the princess and follow from the air. Come in after us, your horse will be there."

Chriani only nodded. His heart was hammering in his chest, pain scouring his lungs like embers each time he breathed.

As his numb hands clutched her, he thought he felt Lauresa stir.

"There have been scout reports of Ilmari forces scouring the Wayroad," Dargana said. "Looking for Chanist's lost treasure, I expect."

"We can't trust the road."

Dargana nodded, thoughtful. "Follow the forest edge north and around. Bear east along the stream you'll cross, then make for the northernmost point of the Greatwood, west of the Hunthad. Cross the water and you'll be in Aerach."

Lauresa stirred again, Chriani holding her with what felt like the last of his strength. As her eyes slowly opened, he tried to smile, fought the pain that wracked his body like the crippling fear that wracked his mind.

He wasn't watching as Dargana slipped away.

— CHAPTER 12 —

THE ROAD HOME

IT WAS RAINING COLD, almost turning to snow as he passed alone through the last of the crossroads villages marking the southern extents of the Rheran hills. The escort he'd traveled with along the Clearwater Way from Werrancross had been left behind in Caredry four days before. The high cloud that pushed south across the Sea of Ehadne had finally brought the winter with it, but the true cold was likely still a week or two away. To the south as Chriani rode, mist had shrouded the Greatwood, silent and dark where it spread unseen.

For the five-day ride back along the Wayroad, he'd hooked up with an Aerach ranger unit for safety, passing himself off as a messenger. With his dagger, he had shaved himself clean for whatever disguise it might offer. He stayed cloaked and hooded when he could. When they stopped each night, he kept to himself. He watched the faces in the barracks of each of the Clearwater keeps in turn, not yet sure how safe he was. Not sure if he ever would be.

He made sure to show his maimed hand as often as he could. The unknown healing power of the Ilvani draught had darkened the flesh of his missing finger, making it look as though it was lost years before. If scouts from Brandishear were looking for him, that would be one more detail to confuse them. The pain had ebbed after the first few days, but Chriani still suffered spasms if he gripped anything too tightly.

He hadn't tried his hand at the bow yet, not sure how it might affect him. Not sure if it mattered anymore.

It was pushing to evening already as Chriani and the chestnut mare he was riding now came in along the well-traveled road through the coastal farmsteads. He was weary, fighting to stay awake against the rhythm of the horse's light steps beneath him. Dark was descending quickly enough that he should have stopped for the night. He meant to arrive in Rheran late, though. Easier that way.

The roan had been found saddled and ready where Dargana said it would be, field rations and water left beside it. They'd hidden in the trees after Lauresa awoke, waiting for the forest to fall silent again before they moved. Even still, Chriani led the horse out along a roundabout route on the least-trodden paths threading the wood, not completely trusting that silence even after it was clear that the crithnala and the griffon patrol pursuing them had gone.

Even with the Ilvani draught, Lauresa was still shaky, had come closer to death than Chriani wanted to dwell on. He'd hoped to save the second draught Dargana had given him in the event the princess needed it later. She saw him try to slip the flask away inside his sleeve, though, next to the picks and the two bloody insignias hidden there. The one that Barien had torn away from the prince's own cloak. The other, Konaugo's, who that same prince had sent to his death with a word. She forced him to take the draught himself, Chriani adamant that he could ride with a broken arm until she told him she'd walk out alone unless he relented.

The taste of the draught was wholly different than the one Chriani had been given after Konaugo's beating in the woods outside Chanist's camp. He felt no surge of warmth, but instead a faint chill that washed through him slowly and took the pain with it. Some difference in the Ilvani magic, the draught taking its time to work as they waited.

Not until the sky was darkening did they make their way carefully past the Ghostwood's edge. As they followed the tree line south and east, they saw no sign of pursuit, but they rode hard until nightfall nonetheless, pushing on more slowly until dawn when they finally stopped to rest.

As they rode, Chriani told the princess what had happened as she fell, filled in the missing pieces. He told her of Dargana's role in saving both their lives, but in response to the princess asking how it had happened, he said only that his being of her own blood had changed the crithnala leader's heart in the end.

They made camp at the edge of a small horn of forest that pushed out from the unbroken green of the Greatwood. They were close enough to see the muddy brown line of the Hunthad where it wound its way north, the scrub turning to terraced farmland across its opposite bank.

The crystal-clear air carried a warmth that hinted of the spring still a long way off, and they stayed close all that long day and into the next night. Always one sleeping while the other kept watch, but never leaving each other's arms. And while he watched Lauresa rest, Chriani almost managed to convince himself that he could do what he wanted to do. Almost convinced himself that he could deliver Lauresa to her new life in Aerach without telling her what he knew.

If Chanist were the father of one I loved, Dargana had said. Chriani hadn't even wondered at the time how she could have known his feelings with the certainty her voice displayed. And in the end, in a way he hadn't expected, it was her contempt that forced his hand, made him find the words that he knew would cut deeper than any blade.

If he was to kill her father, Chriani thought, Lauresa deserved to know why.

The princess wept that next morning as though she'd somehow known the truth even before Chriani spoke it, her father's betrayal absolute beyond any imagining. And as he had when he'd told Dargana of his own father — as he had when he'd first made that same confession to Kathlan — Chriani found himself thinking about that absent father in a way he almost never did. Thinking about how much of his own life had been defined by his belief in who his father was, of what he had done. The secrets his mother had told him to never forget.

As he held the princess who had been a bright pain in his heart since he was eleven years old, he wondered what would happen if all that was taken from him now. How would it feel if all that he'd believed in — all he thought he was, all he'd ever loved — were suddenly to be revealed as lies?

For most of the next day, Lauresa sat alone while Chriani gathered snowberries to supplant the dark bread and jerky Dargana left them, and though he sat close to her beneath the canopy of sun-touched boughs, he knew there were no words he could make that would take away the pain behind her tightly closed eyes.

Sunset was streaking the sky when he finally spoke. "Come away with me."

She was silent a long while. "To where?"

"To anywhere. We can go to Cresthan province, find my mother's kin. Elalantar, sail to the islands. Somewhere far from everything."

The sky was darker when she finally spoke again.

"How far will we need to go to escape the war that begins when we disappear?"

Chriani said nothing after that, but she moved to settle herself against him. Despite her spellcraft that pushed the winter chill away, she was shivering, and he pulled the bedroll around them, held her tight against him as all the words he'd said that night in the encampment twisted through his mind. All the words he'd waited his whole life to say, that he wanted desperately to say again, but even as he opened his mouth to speak, she put a finger to his lips, kissed him gently.

"Don't speak anymore," was all she said.

Even beneath the steady drizzle that filled the gutters to overflowing, Rheran was loud as it always was across the market court, and Chriani felt the familiar sense of movement around him as he led the mare through the late-night emptiness of the trade road. He didn't know whether the city guard would be watching for him like the keep garrison almost certainly were, but he kept to the well-lit spaces and the huddled crowds, hiding in plain sight. Lauresa's words coming back to him from when they'd walked that night.

He slipped into shadows only in the last stretch along the wall, carefully watching movement at the distant guard posts above him as he knocked at the stable gates. He'd sent the message on that morning with a city-bound rider under cover of a merchant's bill, but he didn't know whether Kathlan would be inclined to answer it until he heard the bars slide back, her face in shadow as one door cracked slowly open.

He saw an expression in her eyes that he couldn't read as he pushed the hood back. Her gaze took in the strangeness of his shaved face, the beard just starting to grow back. Then she looked to the mare.

"What the sotting fuck have you done with my horse?"

Chriani led the mare in as the gate was shut behind them, the stables deserted. Kathlan seemed more interested in the horse's state than in his at any rate, only glancing his way once to level a dark look at the well-run swelling in the chestnut flanks as she unsaddled her. He splashed water to his face at a basin near the stove, sat resting in the shadows for a long while as the mare was carefully groomed and shod. When the horse was fed and stalled, Kathlan hefted the saddle, stalked past Chriani where he sat. She slowed, though, turned back to appraise him.

"You find what you went for after all that?"

"I have now," he said.

Kathlan said nothing, carried the saddle to a workbench across the room. The limp was more pronounced, he saw. Her leg bothered her sometimes when the weather changed.

"They said you were dead." Her voice was even but Chriani felt a faint pain twist through it. "Along with her and her escort."

"Don't believe all you hear."

Kathlan inspected the overly ornate riding saddle, pulled out needle and cord to cinch a loose fitting that probably only her eyes could see. Her hand was shaking, just a little.

"What else do they say?" Chriani asked.

"I expect you know more than I do."

"Tell me what you know just the same. Who attacked them?"

Kathlan gave him an odd look. "Bandits from some monastery north of Aerach. Some axe to grind against the lord she's marrying down there, so they thought to make him a widow before the wedding."

"How many survived the attack?"

"None's what they said. Konaugo and two score others gone. Ashlund's captain now. They said you…" She broke the cord, tied it tight. Chriani heard her fighting to slow her breathing. "They said just the princess escaped, but she took her sweet time doing it."

"That's what they say?"

"That's what I say." Kathlan inspected the stirrup straps, saw something she didn't like as she bent low with an awl. "It looked like war for a while. Word from the frontier that it was the Valnirata ambushed the escort. Then word came through one of the prince's seers that she was safe, that it had been the monastics who did it. Got that same word in from traders coming in on the Clearwater."

Chriani nodded, thoughtful. The story that Lauresa had crafted, that she had told upon her arrival, had made it to where she knew it needed to. Her own lie given life in the streets and the markets and the taverns in order to counter the lie that her father had needed to make it all work.

"Wedding's over and done a month early, word out of Five Hog's House says. Duchess Lauresa Andreg now. The Bastion had to scramble to have Peran declared heir, quick ceremony four days past. Prince came back from the frontier in a hurry."

"He's still here?"

"Last anyone told me," Kathlan said, but Chriani heard an uncertainty in her tone now. As if she'd felt the sudden chill that threaded him where he sat in shadow. "Are you all right?" she said at length.

"You remember what you asked me before?"

"I remember asking you a lot of things over time, Chriani."

He nodded. As he stood, he stretched the ache from his back that the long ride had given him, crossed to where Kathlan worked. He kept a watchful eye on the awl still in her hands as he slipped close, kissed her gently.

"And what was that for?" she said as he broke off, but her voice had abandoned the anger.

Chriani slipped the green ribbon into her hand. "I know what I'm meant to do," he said.

Two days' ride from the forest horn, the two of them had crossed the frontier at sunset, making their way over broad wild meadows turned to dun and silver by frost. They rode slowly, waiting out the cover of darkness they'd need to steal a horse from one of the outlying farmsteads. In the stables of a vineyard estate, Lauresa used her dweomercraft to enchant the stablehands there to a sleep they didn't wake from in the time it took Chriani to get the chestnut mare saddled and ready. Lauresa rode the roan as they headed out along the low lines of stone fence that marked the western acreages. Chriani would take the stolen horse north with him. One less question to be asked.

The night was as clear as any he'd ever seen as they made their slow way east and north, intermittent light in the windows of distant farmhouses the only witness as they passed.

The Darkmoon was up, the full-waning Clearmoon just rising when he saw the faint spread of light and shadow that marked the city in the distance. As they slowed, his hand found Lauresa's, riding close beside him.

There were no words.

Chriani slipped out through the stable doors to the shadows of the courtyard track. He'd told Kathlan to stay back, but he saw her in the faint light of the loft window, watching him as he nodded to her, then was swallowed suddenly by shifting shadow, gone from sight.

On his right hand, he wore the ring of plain steel. On his left, he'd slipped on the black iron band taken from the assassin once Lauresa had awoken and he'd been healed. Both of them had made their careful way up to the fractured terrace then. Chriani searched the body carefully without telling her why, hoping for some token or sign that would connect the assassins to Chanist, but at the level of the bargain they'd struck, he knew he'd come up empty. He took the assassin's ring, though, feeling its power as he slipped it to his finger and watched his hand shimmer and fade like the dawn-faint shadow it cast.

Though he'd felt their power in the speed they gave the assassin's relentless attacks, he left the steel-shod boots behind. Their echo along the corridors of the barracks that night was a memory he wanted to forget but knew he never would. The assassin's eyes had stared sightlessly up the whole time, the emotionless set of the face taken to the grave.

He'd never even learned the killer's name, Chriani thought now as he slipped south across the staging ground. Never heard him speak. The last one to die in the name of Chanist's ambition? Or simply one of many who would die if that ambition came to pass?

What kind of madness? Dargana had asked, and not for the first time since that terrible moment of realization, Chriani hoped he'd never find out.

From the steps of a narrow alley, he watched the guards and the dogs at the Bastion gate for just a moment, slipping silently between them as he sent a scattering of pebbles and horse dung across the courtyard where Barien's body had been burned. A moment's distraction of sound and scent, but it was all he needed to send him silent and unseen along the bright marble of the central court. There would be no way in past the guards in the great hall, he knew, so he went the old way, through the barracks to the warden's door. The familiar corridors to Barien's quarters, walked ten thousand times.

The dining halls were alive with raucous laughter as Chriani slipped through the garrison quarter, twice flattening against the wall as he was passed by guards he recognized, but it seemed as though their features had changed somehow. Faces from a dream he might have had once. Less than three weeks since he'd passed through these corridors for the last time. Less than three weeks since Barien had fallen to save five nations from war without knowing it.

Or had he known? The thought came from nowhere, circling in Chriani as he slipped past what had been Barien's door, what would have become the new warden's quarters, whoever had inherited the title and the responsibility for Peran now. That night, had whatever intelligence Barien stumbled upon laid all of Chanist's dark plans out and unconcealed? Or had it been simple instinct, protecting the princess without ever knowing why? Just trusting that it would make a difference in the end?

As dusk fell along the edge of the farmsteads surrounding Teillai, seat of Allenis, Duke Andreg, Warden of the Clearwater Steppes, Chriani and Lauresa parted. They had sought out and found a place to ford the Hunthad just before dawn that day, its winter waters running low and cold. The rest of the day's ride had been slow and silent. They embraced one last time. Then Lauresa spurred the roan ahead, and it seemed to Chriani that continuing on for the road north and west was the hardest thing he'd ever had to do.

So he didn't. Not at first. He slipped the steel ring to his finger as Lauresa rode away, the mate to the one she said she'd put on if ever she needed him again. *Wear yours always*, she'd said, and he knew he would. Then he followed her for a time.

He rode slow behind, stayed close enough to see when she reached the city walls. A squad of riders barreled out from the gates shortly thereafter, presumably expecting the whole of the Valnirata to be seen sweeping eastward when the missing princess told them who she was, where she had come from. Chriani waited, turned his mind to listening in desperate hope for one last word from her, but there was only the silence of his own dark thoughts.

He saw one of the riders pointing westward like they might have seen him lingering there, the grassland shimmering silver around him in the Clearmoon's light. Chriani turned quickly, spurring the mare toward the long road ahead.

The lock in the storeroom wall looked like it had been rekeyed, but it didn't slow Chriani as he opened and closed the warden's door behind him one last time. In the children's court, the evenlamps were burning bright but he was less than a shadow as the ring's dweomer wrapped him, no sound coming from any of the dark doorways he passed. At Peran's chamber, which had been Lauresa's chamber, he saw light beneath the door. She was twelve, the same age Lauresa had been that first day on the training grounds. Princess High Peran someday.

Though he tried to hold it back, he felt the dark anger flooding him now. He felt the chill in the shadowed stones, felt an oppressive weight in the night-time Bastion silence. A place he loved once. A place he dreamed of spending all his life, but its pristine stillness carried an emptiness that galled him now.

Once, he'd dreamed there was greatness here.

Four days before, Irdaign had been waiting for him on the road just outside Caredry. She was wrapped tight in a cloak of black wool, but Chriani caught the flash of bronze hair even at a distance. As he approached, the same horse she'd ridden before watched him with its unnatural gaze.

Chriani was as surprised to see her as he was relieved, an anger he could sense in her telling him that she already knew of the things he didn't think he could have brought himself to speak of. Lauresa had gotten word to her somehow, Chriani thinking he might have caught a glimpse of a steel ring at the princess precedent's finger.

"I'm sorry," was all he could think to say as he slowed next to her.

"You have nothing to be forgiven for, Chriani. And much to be thanked for in the end."

"Thank me when the end comes."

Her look told Chriani that she would have known what he was thinking without him ever speaking it. Would have known just as Lauresa had known it. The thing she'd begged him to not do, an unearthly echo of her mother's words now.

"Spare him," Irdaign said.

In that last morning together, Chriani had met the princess's plea with silence, but Irdaign reigned in close to him, held his gaze in a way that forced his voice.

"Why?"

"Because whether you are successful or not, you will most certainly die. And because there remains good that he can do."

Chriani laughed, cold. "You can forgive him?"

But he felt the laugh cut off, the bitterness in him buried beneath a sadness in her eyes that took his breath away. Lauresa had her mother's eyes, it was said.

"I will never forgive him," the princess precedent said softly, "and he will know that from me. But there are forebodings in my heart which I have learned to trust, and those tell me that without him, the land will suffer. Young Peran has the seed of statecraft in her but not the years that will let that seed bloom. For her sake, for the sake of the land that Lauresa has given her love and freedom to strengthen, let him live, Chriani."

Along the shadowed north hall of the prince's court, he moved with no sound, like Barien had made him practice, day in and out. Sending him to the kitchens some mornings before dawn to fetch a loaf of the prince's own bread, hot from the ovens. Or to the servants' quarters more than once. Delivering invitations to Marjir, the princess high's tailor, long after the Bastion had been locked down for the night.

Barien had always done his best to confine those requests to the warmer nights of spring and summer, and it was on those evenings spent alone outside his rooms that Chriani had first settled himself in the old sentry post. Watching Lauresa's windows from the shadows of the wall, hearing her voice as song spilled out from her balcony to the darkness.

At the smaller entrance hall to the throne room, the doors were open like they shouldn't have been.

Chriani slowed, pressed flat to the wall. He felt the power of the ring thread through him, saw no shadow behind him that the evenlamps should have cast, but he knew his concealment likely wouldn't last for long. The throne room was alive with sorcerous wards, it was said.

He'd left the sword behind at the stables, the idea of what he was going to do to get past the guards a thing he told himself he'd work out when he got there. The throne room or the prince high's quarters alike, there should have been guards. Now, though, their absence seemed even more of a threat. As he approached, Chriani slipped the assassin's ring off, his shadow suddenly flaring to either side of the corridor.

At the end of the short hall, another set of double doors stood closed. Chriani felt a quick twinge of apprehension at the thought of an ambush waiting beyond, or coming up on him unseen from the prince's court behind him, or of what power his attempts to pick the lock might unleash.

In the end, he simply pushed at the plain brass ring that marked the center of the left-hand portal. At his touch, the door swung wide with the faintest creak.

Within the throne room, the fire was burning high, just as Chriani remembered it from any of the long nights of celebration he'd seen there. The countless times he'd sat by the hearth to watch Barien and Chanist together at the head table, laughing like brothers.

Chanist was beyond that table now as Chriani slipped silently inside. The prince high was in a plain tunic of grey flannel, a jacket of the guard draped across a chair close by. He was standing with arms folded behind him where he watched the fire, not looking back at the sound of the door in a way that told Chriani he was expected. He felt a knife edge of fear push through him, buried it quickly beneath the anger that he welcomed this time as he never had before.

What kind of madness?

Save for the two of them, the chamber was empty, and somehow even larger than it usually seemed. Chriani's voice echoed sharply from distant walls as he spoke.

"I'm afraid I could not stay for your daughter's wedding after my escort duties had been fulfilled, my lord prince. But I bring two messages from the bride."

Chanist turned back to give him a withering look, Chriani feeling the weight of all the power in that gaze. All the history, all the strength that had been purchased with deed and bravery and a will that had made Brandishear great. A lifetime spent dedicated to keeping a nation safe. He had to feel for the anger as it flagged, had to force his mind to the thoughts he would have given anything to forget.

"If I might be so forthright, my lord prince, your security measures need improvement."

"My security followed your progress from the moment you entered the city and passed within the keep by way of the stables, master Chriani. You are here are at my indulgence. You are alive at my whim. Do not forget that."

"My life will be spent as I wish it, my lord prince."

The prince high laughed. "Do you come to kill me, boy?"

In the booming voice, Chriani heard the same warmth that he had lost himself in as a child. It sent a chill up his spine now. "No, my lord prince."

Chanist shook his head, a trace of weariness in him suddenly. "So what keeps me from killing you, then?"

"The same thing that stopped you from having me killed anywhere along the road from Aerach. The person who knows the truth the Duchess Lauresa and I know, and her instructions to make that truth known to all should either Lauresa or I come to harm."

Chanist paced around the table slowly. He had wine there, Chriani saw. He filled two goblets of black glass, beckoned closer. Chriani approached, balled his fist before seizing his drink so as to quell the trembling in his hand.

The prince high drank, thoughtful. No doubt in Chriani's mind that Chanist knew of whom he spoke. "A man might die many ways, squire."

"Then for the sake of your rule and your name, you should hope that none of those ways find me for some time."

Close as he was, Chriani saw a flash of blue at the prince's neck, a lapis pendant there to match the one Lauresa wore. The court sorcery that had saved Chanist and him both in the end.

"You escaped that way," Chriani said. There it was, a thought given voice, summoned up from the long contemplation of the road. "Barien fell but not before taking you down. It was your blood and his in the hall of records that night. You used the pendant to escape to the throne room." All the way back, nine days ridden in silence, he'd tried to put the last pieces of the puzzle together. Questions still hanging around the events of that night when everything had changed.

"You are to be complimented on your intuition, master Chriani. Perhaps Barien did teach you something after all."

"Speak the name of Barien in my presence again for any reason, my lord prince, and despite my vows to the contrary, you will die."

In his voice was a deadly earnestness that Chanist heard. Chriani locked his gaze to the prince's, didn't look away. He had to set his jaw against the trembling that traced its way up from his shaking fists, squeezed tight again. The prince's blue eyes were colder than he'd ever seen them.

"I would give anything to have avoided what happened that night, master Chriani. You can take that truth for what it's worth."

"The truth of one who would kill his child for ambition's sake is worth very little, my lord prince."

Where the prince turned away to refill his goblet, Chriani caught the tremor in his hand.

To die alone is a thing we all face one day…

When Chanist had said it in his pavilion, Chriani had heard the pain. He wished now to be able to seize that pain, drive it like a slaughterhouse spike into the prince high's heart.

To die betrayed…

It had been the fear in Barien's voice that had awoken him. He understood now.

"Barien uncovered your plot," he said quietly. "He intercepted the dagger where it had been left for the Uissa assassin to procure that night. You would have used spellcraft to conceal it. To code a message, perhaps. You never guessed that Barien had sorcery of his own that would reveal it."

Chanist turned away, paced back toward the fire, but Chriani followed. "When he confronted you with the dagger, you attacked him, but you weren't good enough. Not young enough anymore. A struggle. Barien recovered the dagger and struck. He would have killed you with a second stroke, but you used the pendant's power to escape. Court sorcery. It took you back to the throne room."

In the end, it was still all supposition on his part, but the expression on Chanist's face when he finally looked up told Chriani he was close enough to the mark. The pieces complete, finally. A Valnirata revenge scheme unfolding over two generations, but no one would ever suspect which side it was taking that revenge.

"Your apparent astuteness would have served you better in seeing through how completely and effectively you have been used in this unfortunate matter, my lord squire." Chanist's tone was mocking.

"Even for all that, I survived, my lord prince."

"Apology accepted, master Chriani."

"How is it possible to hate as much as you do, my lord prince?"

Chanist laughed again, but as he turned, he hurled the goblet to the fire, black shards shattering with an explosive crash. "I order soldiers to battle knowing full well that they may die before the end of it. Do I hate them, my late-anointed squire?"

Chriani hurled his own glass straight at Chanist's head. The prince high grabbed it from the air almost without looking, the wine it had carried spraying out to the tile behind him.

"Your own blood…" Chriani whispered.

He thought he caught the shadow in the prince's gaze, the weariness of age and rule clouding the bright blue eyes, but Chanist turned away.

"Blackmail is a sport for harder folk than you, master Chriani. State your demands and be on your way."

"I have no demands, my lord prince. But I will take what has been offered by you, in public and before witnesses."

Chanist looked back as he refilled the goblet and drank again. "Commission." He managed a thin smile. "You would serve me after all this? To what end, master Chriani?"

"To watch you, my lord prince."

The smile faltered just slightly.

"To remind you," Chriani said, "of the price of your ambition. And to give you the chance to redeem your name in the name of a daughter and her mother who both beseeched me spare your life."

At the mention of Irdaign, Chriani saw a crack in the facade of strength the prince high wore. There again, the weariness he'd seen that night in the throne room, the same uncertainty when Lauresa had used the mention of her mother to distract Chanist from the truth in front of him. *A memory of a happier time.*

"I'll need an adjutant," Chriani said, "as I was to Barien. Kathlan, the stable master's assistant."

"The two of you will make fine company."

"Kathlan can outride most of your company as it stands now. She'll do better once your healers have made her leg whole again."

"No healer will ever mend the essential weakness of your own heart, master Chriani."

"I was told once that everyone's station is a place worthy of respect if carried well."

"This meeting is over, squire."

The prince high paced slowly back to the fire, footsteps hard across the tiles where the falcon of Brandis dived. Chriani felt himself summarily dismissed, fought the urge to run for the door. So much that had happened, so much that would never be the same. All of it swept away with a prince's word.

Chriani called from where he stood. "If you had been successful then, when you first crafted the treaty, would you still be fighting your war to this day? The Valnirata purged and all the Ilmar under siege while you crafted the kingdom your father never made?"

"Get out." Chanist spoke to the air, stared ahead as if he were already alone.

Chriani stepped closer, tried to pace around the prince high. "You would sacrifice your name, your history for this? You would bring war to the Ilmar again regardless of what its people want?"

"Get out, boy." The voice was colder. Chanist still wasn't looking at him, shifting to keep Chriani behind him.

"Regardless of what the Valnirata want…"

"I ceased to care what the Valnirata want on the day they cut my father's living heart from his body!" The prince's voice was a terrible sound, filling the empty room with a fury that echoed from cold stone. And where Chriani watched Chanist spin back, he saw the prince high finally break. His voice trailed off to dark silence, choked off with age and an anger that Chriani recognized because he'd seen it every day for ten years. A dead numbness in the prince's eyes that he recognized from the small steel mirror that hung between pallet and wall in Barien's chambers.

On that terrible day that his father, brother, and sister had fallen, Chanist had been spared.

Where he stood now, the face of the prince was gone, melted to the shadows of the firelight. In its place, Chriani saw the son who should have been there to stand at his father's side at the end. He saw the young princeling whose heart had burned for fifteen long years with the question of whether his being in the ranks of his father's forces at Welbirk might have made some difference. He saw the warrior who had woken each night from the empty dream that his sword, his strength, his will might have single-handedly turned back the Ilvani tide that washed over Goffree's forces that day like a bloody storm.

He saw the king who had never wanted the crown, and who had wished every day since it was set upon his head that he had died in his father, his brother, his sister's place.

This was hating what you were.

Slowly, Chriani unclasped his cloak, let it fall to the floor. He pulled his tunic over his head with one hand, stood naked to the waist so that the red and black lines of the war-mark could be seen, stark in the fire-light. No bandage covered it. Lauresa's name was still a seamless extension of the intricate web of black line, but three more joined it now, just as seamless by virtue of the healing draught he'd stolen from a sergeant's saddlebags in Caredry that morning. Chriani had watched the days-old web of scabbing skin slough off, the dark glyphs beneath it that he'd carefully etched in by night on the long road back. Lauresa, Barien, Irdaign, Kathlan, who had all taught him what he needed to understand.

The prince high could read the Ilvani lettering. Chriani saw the anger in Chanist turn to cold shock for a moment, then twist back to a greater anger that showed red in the prince high's face. His lip was trembling, as were his hands.

"My father was Halobrelia," Chriani said, "and for standing against the same warlord Caradar who you stood against, he died in exile for his pains. Does that make any difference to your madness, my lord prince?"

In Chanist's hand, Chriani's goblet shattered. The prince stared down in apparent surprise, blood and wine spilling freely from his fingers.

All that endless day, Lauresa and Chriani had lain together in the shadowed glade, Lauresa's magic keeping them warm. She would have a daughter, she'd whispered to him in the end, Chriani not asking how she could possibly know. Thinking that he could feel that different sorcery where it shifted just beneath her skin, his hand on her belly as she slept beside him.

He was awake at dawn to watch the full moons pass, the Clearmoon circling close around the Darkmoon against the brightening sky. An auspicious sign for great events.

All that day, there were no tears, but Lauresa cried when Chriani gave her the dagger. *Give this to her when she's old enough,* was all he'd said. *Tell her I cannot take back the evil it has done to her line. Warn her of the hate and love that is her birthright.*

"I have, my lord prince, brought two messages."

Tell her she is the crossroads, he'd said to Lauresa. *Tell her she is the place where two worlds meet…*

From within the pocket in his sleeve, Chriani pulled the slip of parchment Lauresa had stolen from the stable master's quarters in the vineyard estate that night. She'd had no quill or wax in the glade, had used spellcraft to write and seal it. He read it from memory.

"To the Prince High Chanist, I bring word by her own voice and hand that Lauresa Andreg, Duchess Teillai of Aerach, hereby relinquishes all power vested in her as Princess Lauresa of Brandishear, daughter to Prince High Chanist Brandis and Princess Precedent Irdaign Leisana, and in such act abandons all claim to title, throne, and family."

Chriani did his best to twist the last word as he tossed the sealed packet to the floor. He thought he saw Chanist flinch.

"To the father who would have had her murdered, I bring Lauresa's second message, my lord prince."

From within his sleeve, Chriani pulled two scraps of grey cloth. One pristine, the other blackened with blood. Barien and Konaugo. The eagle of Brandis in gold thread gleamed in the firelight as he dropped two insignias of the prince's guard on top of the packet at Chanist's feet.

When Chriani spoke, he felt the same pain thread his voice that had worked through Lauresa's that day. Her final question to her father, given to Chriani to carry.

"How many more will you watch die in order to further your ambition?"

"As many as it takes ere I see the Greatwood burned to ash and spread on the Ehadne winds…"

Where Chanist turned to him, the strength had returned. A prince's might in the great voice, straight-backed as he spoke. "Do you think to stop me, master Chriani?"

Chriani slipped his tunic on again, pulled the cloak around himself. "Good night, my lord prince." He didn't nod as he turned away.

His footsteps were a faint whisper on the stones as he made his way to the doors of the great hall. The guards beyond were shocked in a way that told him they had no idea how he'd gotten there. Wary in a way that told him they weren't ever going to ask.

He walked the Bastion outwall once, then scaled down the rough stone of the tower beneath Peran's window to the courtyard below. For a long while, he hiked the walls of the keep, the guards he passed recognizing him, letting him pass without challenge. Chanist's word had reached them already, Chriani didn't know how.

The first hint of light was in the east when he finally slipped back to the stable, found his way up the ladder and to Kathlan's bed. She'd been waiting for him, was asleep almost the moment he slipped into the nest of blankets beside her. He'd thought throughout the whole night's walk about what he'd say, what he'd vow to her, but in the end, there were no words. He felt the change in himself, felt the truth and all it promised.

At the window, the Clearwater sky was brightening, the east free of the cloud that had blown off in the night. Chriani watched for a long while, felt the chill breeze twist against the heat of the stove below the loft and Kathlan's body against his.

It was later, the morning blue-white outside, when he finally slept.

Fiction by Scott Fitzgerald Gray

SIDNYE (QUEEN OF THE UNIVERSE)

THE EXILE'S BLADE TRILOGY
Clearwater Dawn • Three Coins for Confession
The Timeless King *(Coming 2016)*

WE CAN BE HEROES

A PRAYER FOR DEAD KINGS and Other Tales

BLACKHEATH (with Quinn Hamilton)

THE VOICES OF THE DEAD — Dark Tales & Lost Souls

TALES OF THE ENDLANDS
The Twilight Child • Shadow to Shadow • The Moonsign Scar
Daeralf's Rune • The Game of Heart and Light • The Voice
Black Run • A Space Between • Stories

ONE SIZE FITS ALL (as Gary Scott)

Scott Fitzgerald Gray is a writer, fiction editor, story editor, RPG editor and designer, and man about town. He shares his life in the Canadian hinterland with a schoolteacher, two itinerant daughters, and a large number of animal companions.

More info on Scott and his work (some of it even occasionally truthful) can be found by reading between the lines at **insaneangel.com**.

Colophon

Acknowledgements and gratitude are owed to
the following, for those things they do.

Special Thanks and Honors of the Prince's Guard
Jennifer Landels
(The spare keys to the Ilmar are always under the mat.)

The Bastion
Colleen, Shvaugn, and Caitlin

The Court Scribes of Rheran
Colleen Craig, Jennifer Landels, Gabriel Duclair

The Couriers of the Clearwater Way
Diana Cox, François Bertrand

Artistic Acolytes of the Princess High
(studio)Effigy, Pawel Lyczkowski, Ben Goode, Peter Polak,
Dragi Stankovic, Veronika Vasilyuk

Tales Told in Five Hog's House
Luka Bloom, Jeff Buckley, Elaine Cunningham, John Debney,
Evanescence, Lisa Gerrard, Ed Greenwood,
James Newton Howard, Guy Gavriel Kay, Howard Shore,
Mary Stewart, Margaret Weis, Gene Wolfe

CLEARWATER DAWN

BOOK ONE OF THE EXILE'S BLADE

Published by Insane Angel Studios
insaneangel.com

Cover, Design, and Typography
by (studio)Effigy

ISBN 978-0-9868288-7-4

v1.4
April 2013

We try to make sure that no errors creep into our work, but publishing is a chaotic enterprise at the best of times. If you spot a typo or a formatting glitch in an Insane Angel Studios book, email insaneangel@insaneangel.com with details (including which e-book version you're reading, if applicable). If any errors you spot are ones we haven't yet caught and are in the process of fixing, you'll receive one of our e-books of your choice for free.

www.ingramcontent.com/pod-product-compliance
Lightning Source LLC
LaVergne TN
LVHW020710110826
845149LV00012B/2192

* 9 7 8 0 9 8 6 8 2 8 8 7 4 *